MW01144632

The Shadowy Third

Farrago

By

HUW EVANS

1663 Liberty Drive, Suite 200
Bloomington, Indiana 47403
(800) 839-8640
www.AuthorHouse.com

This book is a work of fiction. People, places, events, and situations are the product of the author's imagination. Any resemblence to actual persons, living or dead, or historical events, is purely coincidental.

First published by AuthorHouse 06/20/05

ISBN: 1-4208-1033-2 (sc)

Printed in the United States of America
Bloomington, Indiana

This book is printed on acid-free paper.

DEDICATION:

To Alison

This Faerie grows not old
she lives within my mind,
and youthful laughter echoes
a sound with joy defined.
In soft, sad, haunting vision
she turns and smiles to me,
for she, my sweet, fond shadow
lives on in memory.

ACKNOWLEDGEMENT:

To my children and grandchildren, whose existence has made my life a wonderful and worthwhile adventure.

To Harvey M Anderson whose encouragement and enthusiasm made this book possible.

To Sally Evans for reading the manuscript and making many helpful suggestions.

OUTLINE OF 'THE SHADOWY THIRD'

Suddenly you are struggling to keep your nose above water. Your leg feels numb. Your mind is throbbing as water keeps splashing over your head. Grappling for a small boat, a hand reaches out. Amid the terror of that moment your mind flashes back to London.

So begins a narrative of a wartime story of real love. Working alongside each other in the office of the Southern Oceanic Line, Trina and Alan instantly become inseparable friends. Every available moment is spent together and their friendship soon accelerates into a vigorous romance. Driven by their total commitment to each other an unwritten bond develops. That allegiance is tested often by the wavering demands of a wartime schedule and the uncertainty of the times.

Can the power of true love overcome the expectations of such a treaty? Or are the pressures of the surrounding battles enough to distract and crush the most solid promise? You will be fascinated by the many trials Alan and Trina face and a most unexpected ending.+

PROLOGUE - AUGUST 1949

Love goes toward love, as schoolboys from their books;
But love from love, toward school with heavy looks.

Shakespeare - Romeo and Juliet

The salt water splashed against Alan's face, stinging him back from oblivion. When he tried to open his eyes he found their swollen lids reluctant to obey and, giving up the attempt, relaxed. There was nothing to look at, only a few square feet of restless sea. The pain in his chest and leg had eased, and he was free to think of other things.

What was it Trina had said in her letter?

`Imagine my surprise when I found your name on the list of travel agents attending the conference. I am looking forward to seeing you, and perhaps we'll be able to have a drink, or a meal, together. Is Marcia coming with you? There are many tours available, and you may want to take her to see the various beauty spots and places of interest.'

The envelope, marked "Personal", had been lying on his desk unopened. When he picked it up, Alan felt time stand still as he recognized Trina's handwriting, and fought to keep the shock of excitement under control. He tried to be casual as he reached for the letter opener, but saw his secretary watching him and wondered if she had noticed anything unusual in his reaction.

The careful phrasing was so unlike the Trina he remembered that it might have been sent by a casual acquaintance, yet the meaning behind the words was not casual; Alan was sure of that.

Her letter had continued.

`... Naturally, you know all about Southern Oceanic's travel agency. Well, after I called off my engagement to Keith, I was given the opportunity to manage its Bermuda office. I jumped at the chance and have been here ever since...'

The words "I called off my engagement" left Alan shocked and bewildered.

It was three years since he had seen Trina, and then she had expected to be married within a few days.

`Why didn't she tell me?' was his first thought, followed immediately by the knowledge that she could not, would not, have told him.

The past had dissolved into the present and the fact that he would be in Bermuda within twenty-four hours was all that mattered. Excitement grew. It was a warm anticipation that scattered all other thoughts, all other plans, and nothing else was important. Alan knew that Trina was saying, `Maybe it's not possible, but if it is, I'd like to see you again. If you think not, then so be it; and if your wife is with you I'll be on my best behavior.'

Alan had put the letter down, hesitating before speaking to his secretary.

`Leave the mail for a minute Sally; I want to think about this letter. I'll give you a call when I'm ready.'

Alone, Alan adjusted his thoughts to accept the words he had just read. For nearly eight turbulent years he and Trina had flirted with love and laughter, tenderness and tears, parting in friendship and folly. Memories filled his mind, and more than five minutes passed before he was ready to trip the switch on his intercom.

`I want to send a cable right away,' he told Sally. `Would you come in now?' When she returned he said;

`It's to Trina Grant, and it's a cable address.' He picked up Trina's letter and checked the heading. `Oceantrav, Bermuda,' he said, and continued. `The message reads: "Will see you tomorrow, wifeless", message ends.'

Alan then leaned back in his chair and enjoyed the sudden sense of well being.

Sally looked up from her notebook with ill-concealed curiosity.

`How do you want it signed?' she asked.

`Alan,' he had said, smiling, `Just Alan.'

* * *

What would Trina be thinking now?

Alan shook his head and tried to focus his thoughts. How long had he been in the water, and how long since the explosion? Two hours... ten hours? There had been too many spans of oblivion for him to keep track of time.

At the airport there had been a morning fog, and it was a few minutes after eight before the plane rumbled away from the terminal.

They had been flying for just over an hour, and the cabin crew was serving coffee when the explosion came. Afterwards there was surprisingly little panic: most passengers seemed stunned rather than afraid. There was even time to fasten life jackets as the plane lost height, and Alan caught glimpses of the sea as the pilot fought to keep control. Then came the jarring shock of impact, and in the same instant he lost consciousness.

Water splattering against his face brought Alan back to reality. Vaguely he was aware of people struggling and crying out; while beside his head the fuselage was torn and gaping. Water cascading over him roused Alan to action.

By the time he managed to unfasten his seat belt the water was up to his chest, then, as he tried to stand, the plane tilted, throwing him off balance. Something hard and heavy struck his back, and Alan just had time to take a deep breath before the water closed over his head. The light began to fade and Alan fought to free himself.

With a despairing effort he thrust towards the opening, only to be held back as another crushing weight slammed into his legs, pinning him against the seat.

Alan was sure that this was the end, and had ceased to fight, when another movement of the plane released his legs. As he pulled himself clear, his jacket caught on torn metal and he clawed frantically at the material, not even noticing when he cut his hands on the broken metal edges of the fuselage. Then, suddenly, he was free. It seemed an age before he burst into sunlight, and with his first gasp for breath there came a wave of pain. His last act before losing consciousness was to pull the tags and inflate his life-jacket.

When Alan came to, he was alone in the ocean, and there was no sign of wreckage or of any other survivors. With his head barely clear of the water there was little to see. He called out several times, but heard no answer and shouting was painful.

Later, too late for there to be much hope of a reply, he remembered the whistle tied to his life jacket. The shrill sound dissipated into the wind with no response, except the swirl and hiss of curling wavelets that danced over the longer swell. His left leg was dangling, useless and broken, and when he tried to raise his arms pain exploded in his chest.

Now there was nothing. Even the pain had gone, and Alan knew himself to be no more than a speck in an immensity of water. Trina must know by now that he was not coming.

Poor Trina, poor eyes, bruised from weeping yet again.

His mind began to drift while a need for water, fresh water, nagged at his fading consciousness.

`The sea's got me after all and I thought I'd cheated you. That was six years ago... Why now?

`I was thirsty then... We were all thirsty, and there were twelve of us in the boat...'

CHAPTER ONE

. . . when youth and pleasures meet
to chase the glowing hours with flying feet
George Gordon, Lord Byron

June 1943

With no moon the night was dark, yet there was enough starlight to be able to make out eleven shadowy figures.

`Hell,' Alan muttered to himself as he eased his sore body into a slightly different position.

He was lying curled in the bottom of the boat, trying to sleep and not succeeding too well. The hard edges of the boat's ribs and sheathing planks saw to that. His white shorts were torn, the pocket ripped as he had scrambled into the boat, and his sweatshirt was stained and grubby. Like the others, he had a week's growth of stubble on his face, a minor irritant to add to the boredom and discomfort of an open boat.

Already the survivors' tempers were fraying. Seven days since their ship had been sunk, time enough for mannerisms to irritate and for a clash of personalities. Their isolation on the vast expanse of empty sea was echoed by the space within the lifeboat itself; meant to seat sixty, its size emphasised how few they were and how forlorn their state.

Mostly, Alan sat in the stern with Jim Bristow, the stockily built Fourth Mate, who was technically in command. Jim's slightly arrogant manner had sparked several heated exchanges during the previous few days, particularly with the abrasive Huskins. Jim had been on watch when the torpedo struck and was still in uniform, with jacket and gold braid. His shoes he had kicked off while in the water.

A little further for'ard, on the starb'd side, Joe Hayter sat with Con Mahoney: the one as large and fat as the other was small and skinny. Both wore blue and white check pattern trousers, part of their uniform as Baker and Chef. Joe had saved his white coat. Mahoney had discarded his and had only a white singlet for protection.

The next group, five in all, was sprawled amidships on the port side where they were trying to rest These five, the two Allward brothers, Queenie Pellew, Rapley and Higgins wore stewards' working clothes of open-necked white shirts with black serge trousers. John Allward, Chief Barman, was the centre of this group, dark and burly, a formidable looking man who had recently started to show signs of flabbiness. In contrast, Basil, his brother, was small and dapper. Next, sitting slightly apart, came Higgins, somehow seeming to be inconspicuously neat, even though his clothes were stained and crumpled from immersion in seawater. He, too, had curly black hair, and looked more like Basil's brother than did John.

The remaining two were Rapley and Queenie. Rapley with his few wisps of grey hair and lined, well-worn face was by far the oldest in the boat, and looked frail. Queenie, in contrast, appeared calm and accepting, despite the haunted look in his chubby face. Though well muscled, and neat in his movements, there was gentleness in his manner, and when he spoke his voice was low and soft.

Separated from the others by several feet and sitting well for'ard, Len Huskins, 3rd Engineer, wore oil-stained white overalls. An unmistakable Scot, he was tall, lean and angular, with sandy hair and piercing pale blue eyes. Len's nature was to look for trouble and he was quick to find an insult, real or imagined. Tense and short tempered, he, more than anyone, showed signs of breaking under the strain. Blacklock lay in the bottom of the boat, cushioned as much as possible with life jackets. There was little evidence now of the raw boned strength, controlled yet latently explosive, that had been the hallmark of his character. He did not complain, but beneath the stubble of his beard and deep tan, there was a foreboding pallor that accentuated the dark shadows around his eyes.

`Alan, wake up.'

For a few moments Alan was confused, then realized that Jim was shaking him.

`It's time for you to take over the watch.'

`Oh damn!' Alan groaned inwardly. `I must have dropped off to sleep. Why couldn't Jim leave me to cheat a few more minutes out of their passing? Wonder how long I was asleep?'

Slowly, Alan eased his cramped limbs. Already Jim was moving away from the stern seat, making room for him to take over.

At last Alan stood, swaying unsteadily as he tried to stretch the stiffness from his muscles, and mentally cursed Jim.

`Why the hell doesn't he unship the rudder? I suppose he feels more "in command" with his arm resting on the tiller. We're just drifting. The only sail left is the jib, and with no mast or even an oar there's not much we can do with it. Even if we could hoist a sail there's no breeze tonight. All we're doing is riding the roller coaster of a long slow swell, a rocking lullaby of frustration, and we see a horizon that expands and contracts with rhythmic monotony.

`Jim can't find any way to get comfortable either. He may as well give up and wait till exhaustion dulls his senses.'

Time became their enemy, an infinity of dreary seconds stretched beyond endurance, and Alan invented small chores as a defense. These he rationed, jealously spreading them through the night watch to punctuate its passing.

Now, he reached down to unfasten the lid of the flare locker, lifted out the box and placed it beside him. He then allowed a space of time to drift away before methodically checking the flares, taking them out and slowly, almost caressingly handling them, finally replacing each flare in its exact, established position. If asked, he would have said he was making sure he knew exactly where to put his hand if he should need a flare in a hurry. He had rehearsed the sequence so often that his movements had become automatic, and he also knew that a delay of one or two seconds would be unlikely to make any difference.

`God! Let me see a ship,' he thought. `They'd never see us, not at night, but they'd see a flare. They couldn't miss that.'

He sat with one flare still in his hand, lost in thought. `Even so they wouldn't investigate ... Can't blame them. We'd have done the same; afraid of an enemy ruse to lure us into torpedo range. They wouldn't even break radio silence, and it might be days before the sighting of a flare was reported.

`A convoy now, that would be different. One of the escorts would check it out ... 'Imagine being able to stretch out on a mattress again, or even a hammock ...

'Suppose a Liberator on patrol spotted us, they'd call up a support group ...

`We're so small, so insignificant. Is it right to hope? Better, perhaps, to make our peace, each with himself as best he can. Accept the dissolution of self as inevitable, for there's no ship, no Destroyer, no aircraft, just our floating timber coffin and the uncaring sea. All that disturbs the night is the occasional grunt or restless movement, except when Blacklock starts coughing. He's getting worse ...

`Rough and tough damn your eyes Blacklock, the ship's Storekeeper. He can't last much longer, poor devil. He must have broken ribs and probably a punctured lung.'

Just on dusk Alan had gone to Blacklock and asked him how he was feeling. Blacklock had looked dreadful; his face more like a caricature in clay, and it had been painful listening when he tried to speak.

`I'd ... feel a bloody sight better ... if some of the bastards ... who got us into ... this mess had to risk their necks ... out here, instead of sitting ... comfortably at home.'

Blacklock was gasping and in pain, but ignored Alan's urging to rest quietly.

`Baldwin ... Chamberlain ... the lot of them ...bloody useless demagogues.'

`Why the hell does he have to talk?'

Blood bubbled from Blacklock's lips and Con Mahoney leaned over to wipe them.

`Shut up and lie still. You stupid bugger.' Yes, though Mahoney's words were rough, his friend's suffering distressed him and his true feeling showed in the gentleness of his actions.

Alan tried to speak lightly.

`You'd better do as the little man says or he'll bash you.'

Blacklock looked from Alan to Con Mahoney and made an effort to smile. Alan could take no more. He shook his head sadly, then clambered back to the stern.

`Demagogues!' How that word took him back, back to Tower Hill and the lunch time orators and crusaders, each with his own small group of devotees, and each grinding the axe of his own particular fancy.

`Tower Hill, and Trina,' he thought, and felt the swift ache of memory.

`How young we were.'

* * *

Alan stepped off the bus and pulled up his raincoat collar. It was no more than a shower, and as he looked at the sky he felt the pang of a prisoner about to return to his cell. The wet streets, the toneless sky and the blank windowed offices promised no more than hours of incarceration.

The footpaths were not crowded. The morning tide of humanity, the rush hour surge, was still half an hour or more away.

Already Alan had come to dread the days spent with musty ledgers, journals and cashbooks in the accounts department of the Southern Oceanic Line. It felt much longer than a week since he had started this, his first job, working at a high desk in the gloomy, Victorian office of a respected shipping company. Those late autumn days in that year of 1938 called to him. He shuddered at the prospect of a life spent indoors huddled over endless figures, but jobs were not easy to find.

At the head of the wide stone steps that led to the ornate entrance, Alan paused before entering. Inside, no more than a quarter of the light bulbs in their old fashioned fittings were switched on, and the large main office was a patchwork of dark shadows and pools of glowing yellow. Antique racks held heavy books bound in red leather, where every passenger's payment was recorded. Separate books for each ship's voyage, and these, together with manifest binders, demy folio journals and account books, looked more like the records of Judgment Day than those of a commercial operation. The passenger counter of polished oak ran the full length of the floor. Three and a half feet high and three feet deep, it gave the impression of a barricade to protect harassed clerks from irate passengers.

On the other side, the freight department had a far less imposing counter; a mere twelve feet long, and although it, too, was of polished oak, its panels were plain compared with the elaborate carving of the passenger counter. However, the freight department desks compensated for the inferior counter. No low, flat desks here. The freight department desks were long and high with slanted tops, and a wooden rail on which a row of freight clerks, seated on high stools, could rest their feet.

Even when all the lights were switched on, the ground floor office created a somber mood, as if laughter were sacrilegious, and dull, staid industry the rule. The floor was deserted, and Alan's footsteps echoed on the bare tiles as the tap of each heel echoed into the high ceiling space. To reach the far stairway, he had to walk the full length of the floor along a passageway wide enough to cope with inquiring passengers, as well as scurrying messengers carrying freight notes and flimsy bills of lading.

Behind him he left forty or more empty desks waiting for their slaves, and giving promise of no more than another day's monotonous toil. In three-quarters of an hour the desks would be occupied, and the cavernous floor filled with the hum of sedate bustle. At the head of the stairs Alan could hear a woman's voice coming from the room on his right. Beside him was a lectern on which the big attendance book lay open. He entered the time, signed his name, and then made his way towards the sound of voices.

One week in six each junior, both male and female, was rostered to come in early to open the mail, and this was Alan's first experience of the duty. His partner at the sorting table was a young woman and they began a conversation while opening the letters. She spoke first.

`Hello, I'm Trina. What's your name?'

Her voice was crisp and matter of fact, yet oddly intense, as if every detail of what went on around her must be understood.

`Alan,' he answered, slightly disconcerted by her directness and self-assurance.

`Been here long?' she asked.

`This is my second week.'

Trina looked at him and smiled, and with that smile a quite different character appeared.

At first sight she had seemed aloof, unapproachable. Her neat black hair was cut into soft waves, but it was her grey eyes that gave the distant, untouchable air. Her eyebrows tended to confirm this impression. They were plucked and penciled into immaculate arches of cool efficiency, and her lipstick looked to have been applied with scientific precision.

The moment she smiled, the carefully schooled facade crumbled. The smooth, controlled face dimpled into warm friendliness, and the grey eyes danced with teasing laughter. Suddenly, she was no longer a young lady, but a girl of Alan's own age.

`I can beat you,' she announced, putting on an air of triumph and tilting her head. `I worked all last week, and most of the week before.'

Alan stood and made a sweeping flourish with the letter opener.

`I bow to your seniority and vast experience.'

`Stop chattering you two, and hurry up with that mail.'

The letter opening ceremony was presided over by an elderly spinster of formidable tongue who, during the day, ruled the typists' pool with cold efficiency and a complete lack of humor. Trina raised her eyebrows as she and Alan exchanged looks before returning to their task.

At midday Alan thankfully abandoned his desk as one hour of lunchtime freedom beckoned.

`Where do you have your lunch?' Alan was running down the main steps outside the office, but recognizing the voice he stopped, and spun around in almost the same movement. Trina stood, smiling, at the top of the steps, framed by the massive bronze doors and for the first time Alan had a clear view of her figure.

That morning, while they worked together, there had been a table between them, then, when the mail had been sorted, the elderly spinster told him to put the letter openers on her desk at the far end of the room. When Alan turned around Trina had gone.

He looked at her now, and Trina paused, conscious of his survey, confident of herself, and with good reason. She was dressed in a mid grey suit, with the line of a cream blouse showing at her throat. The jacket hugged her waist and the skirt had just enough fullness to add grace to her movements. It was a neat elegance that emphasised her figure, and Alan studied her admiringly. No hour glass model, her outline was lithe and supple, and Alan very definitely approved.

Trina was perhaps a little taller than average, and if there were the slightest blemish it was in the suspicion of bandiness in well-shaped legs. So slight that Alan did not notice at this, his first inspection. Later, when their friendship had grown, he would tease Trina about her fondness for horse riding.

What Alan did not know was that Trina had become aware of him many days earlier, due to his inability to walk sedately up or down stairs. His job often took him down to the cashier's desk on the ground floor where Trina worked. From her desk, she had a clear view of the main stairway and first noticed Alan because of his headlong descents, and for the way he would run back up, taking the stairs two or even three at a time. He gave the impression of caged energy, and Trina sympathized as she, too, felt confined within the office routine.

She had determined to meet him, and the lucky chance of them both being rostered for the mail gave her the opportunity she wanted. When Alan came downstairs on his way to lunch, Trina had been ready for several minutes and moved to intercept him.

She had made her bid, and now had to suffer his inspection. Although his deliberately blatant appraisal made her want to laugh, Trina could not avoid a slight tremor of nervousness while waiting for the answer.

'The same place you're going to.' His eyes returned to her face as he spoke.

'I've never seen ...' Trina checked her words and her smile broadened.

`Past or present do you mean?' she queried.

`Quite definitely present.'

Trina laughed, then ran down the steps and reached for his outstretched hand.

`Well, where do we go?' she asked.

`Where do you usually go?'

`The ABC cafe down the street, but only because I haven't found anywhere else. Where've you been going?'

`I doubt if you'd like the place I go to.'

`Why not?' The words were crisp, almost curt, as though Alan had been guilty of some improper suggestion.

`You look much too elegant for the bar of a very ordinary back street pub,' he suggested.

`Try me,' she insisted. `Which way do we go and … er ... do we eat? Or do we just drink?'

`Bread, cheese, pickles,' Alan stated firmly. `And one glass of beer.'

`If the bread's crusty, the cheese tasty and the pickles whatever it is pickles should be, I'll be happy with that.'

Trina held Alan's arm as he guided the way through the lunchtime crowds and traffic. Alan found that the touch of her hand was as decisive as her nature; it was light and sure, yet in no way possessive. They made their way down the steady slope towards the Thames, past Mark Lane and on in the direction of the Tower.

While walking, they discussed Trina's dilemma. Were pickles supposed to be `spicy' or `picklely', `tantalizing' or `stimulating'? Trina plumped for `spicy' while Alan held out for `appetizing', and they were still wrangling when they reached their destination. It was the first of the nonsense arguments that became such a part of their relationship. No quarter was given, and the insults that crept into their repartee did not hurt because there were seeds of laughter in each one.

The pub was just around the corner from Tower Hill, and Alan led the way to a small table jammed beside a pinball machine in the far corner of the room. Leaving Trina to squeeze into one of the chairs, he went over to the counter. The regulars at the bar had turned their heads in curiosity when Alan and Trina entered, and there had been a pause in the buzz of conversation. As he approached the bar, Alan made the conventional remark.

`Good day, gentlemen.'

Normally, there were a few audible responses, but on this occasion he was conscious only of a disapproving mumble. He grinned to himself. `More fun talking to her than to you lot,' he thought.

After paying for his order, it took two journeys for him to carry the food and drinks across to the table. He then sat down and looked at Trina. She seemed quite composed, and not at all disconcerted by the fact that she was the only woman in the bar.

`What do you think?' he asked, pointing to the food on the table.

`Spicy,' Trina insisted.

`Appetizing! And, even with the beer, about half the price you'd pay for a soggy meal in the ABC.'

Alan picked up his glass of bitter. `Cheers,' he said.

Trina responded, and as they drank he watched her face. Alan's experience of drinking with girls was, admittedly, limited, but Trina was the first he had seen who drank draught bitter as though she enjoyed it.

Alan soon forgot what they talked about over that meal, but forever remembered Trina and the way she had looked. The dialogue did not matter; they were discovering each other, allowing their senses to seek and find as they probed in exploration, their words punctuated by the clackety clack of the pin-ball machine beside them; and they were both very aware of their knees pressed together beneath the tiny table.

Trina's wit and vivacity delighted Alan and as they sparred and sniped playfully at each other, he found pleasure in her voice as well as in her comments. When speaking, Trina bubbled with enthusiasm. There were odd little pauses for consideration and then the question, quip or answer would come with a rush of words. Her quick, intense manner emphasised the laughter that sparkled in her eyes.

`Demagogues.' Yes, Alan had used that word. When they finished their meal there was still nearly half an hour left of their lunch break.

`Would you like to go and listen to the demagogues on Tower Hill? It's what I usually do.'

`Sounds interesting.'

Trina started to writhe her way from behind the table, still talking.

`I've listened to the soap box orators in Hyde Park but I've never been down here before.'

Including the mail sorting, they had spent little more than an hour together; yet already there was an affinity, an unspoken acknowledgment of a beginning. The first slender threads were being stretched between them.

Trina and Alan walked the few yards to where Tower Hill slanted down to the Thames. On turning the corner they saw half a dozen clusters of people, and Alan pointed towards one group.

`That's Donald Soper, dispensing his philosophy and brand of religion.'

Trina's eyes followed the direction of his finger.

`Do you want to go over there and listen to him?' she asked.

`Not really, I pointed him out because he's the best known of the regulars here, and I thought you'd have heard of him.'

Trina nodded and stood for a few moments taking in her surroundings. `Who's the one with the impressive growth of hair?'

There could be no doubt which one she meant.

Alan shrugged. `Don't know his name,' he said, as they moved closer to the speaker.

They could hear the raucous voice and see that, though clean-shaven, the orator's hair was an uncontrolled, bushy mass of fiery red.

`I've seen him here often,' Alan told her. `But I've never heard his name, and as far as I know he's never made the headlines. Communism's his theme. He makes the excesses of the French Revolution sound quite mild. He substitutes "Capitalists" for "Aristos", and is convinced it's only necessary to slaughter a few millions for the world to achieve the desired millennium. Correction, I don't think "millennium" is the right word. It tends to have a religious implication, and religion he's definitely against.'

`I see,' Trina laughed. `The communist caricature even down, or up, to his hair. I must get a closer look at it. Do you think it's real? It's quite unbelievable.'

`That's why it suits him.'

Trina looked up at Alan, smiling, and they moved away from the harsh fanatic voice that urged revolution and promised rivers of blood. As they walked back up the hill, Alan felt Trina's hand slip beneath his elbow and rest upon his arm.

* * *

`Well, he was right about rivers of blood,' Alan thought. `They've flowed, even if not in the way he intended. Yet, who knows? Society may be quite different by the time this war ends.'

Blacklock was coughing again, and it was this that had brought Alan back to reality. He looked at his watch; surprised it was still working.

`My God! How the hell can Jim sleep like that? He'll have a bloody stiff neck when he wakes up.

`Stop coughing Blacklock. I feel sick just hearing him and there's nothing I can do to help ... can only try to shut my mind to it ... think of something else.'

* * *

It was through John Marsden, son of Sir Harold Marsden, Chairman of Southern Oceanic, that Alan discovered Trina's family connections.

One morning, a week or two after that first meeting, Alan walked into the office a few minutes early and saw Trina already at her desk. He stopped to say hello and John Marsden came over to join them. Alan and John played Rugby for different London clubs, and knew each other by sight.

`Hi Trina!' John said, then looked at Alan.

`Things didn't go too well for you last Saturday I gather.' He grinned and Alan smiled back ruefully. `I'd rather forget about it thanks,' he replied.

Because of injuries Alan had been moved from his usual position on the wing. His team had lost by a large margin, and he had not been happy with his own performance. John turned back to Trina.

'Dad tells me Aunt Katherine's coming to London for a few days.'

'Yes, Mum's arriving next Thursday, she thinks.'

Until that moment Alan had known little of Trina's family, and was stunned by this revelation. For the moment he said nothing, but looked at the clock.

'I'd better go!' he exclaimed. 'I must get upstairs and sign in before the deadline.'

'See you later,' Trina called as he ran up the stairway.

Over lunch that day he said, accusingly; 'You didn't tell me you were tied up with the ruling family.'

'Oh, I'm only the country cousin,' she laughed. 'Anyway, why should I tell you?'

'No reason at all,' Alan said a little huffily; but there was no resisting Trina's laughter, and he found himself grinning back at her.

'Still,' he said. 'It comes as a shock to find that the simple girl I've been meeting is a member of the hated capitalist class and is, therefore, in danger of being strung up to the nearest lamp post by our violently red headed mentor.'

Trina considered. Then protested; 'I'd prefer you to say "unpretentious" rather than "simple".'

'What makes you so sure I meant unpretentious?'

It gave them something to squabble about over lunch.

The following Saturday Trina went to watch Alan playing. Her whole family were Rugby fans, so she was happy to go with him each weekend. This time, though, she would be going with her mother. They were to meet after the match, and Alan, a little nervously, wondered what Mrs Grant would be like and what her attitude would be to him.

At half time, he was able to pick out Trina in the stand. She had arrived after he went in to change, and her mother was sitting beside her, but in the shade of the stand he could see little detail. He thought back to what Trina had said the previous day. They had been outside the Tower leaning on the wall that overlooked the moat.

`I've been telling my mother about you,' Trina said. Alan knew that her mother had just arrived in London.

`What does that mean?' he asked.

`She's coming to the match tomorrow. I told her your team would be playing against John's, but she wasn't all that keen on coming.' As she said this, Trina looked at him with mischief dancing in her eyes.

`So?' he queried.

`I guessed that mother was planning to take me out Saturday night, but she hadn't actually said anything. She was taking my agreement for granted. When she said she wasn't interested in watching the match I told her I was going anyway. Then I said you and I were going out after the game.'

`What did she say?'

`Mum was quite indignant; "I was going to take you out on Saturday" she said.'

`Look, if you feel you should ... ' Alan started to say, but Trina interrupted.

`No, listen. I said to her; "How was I to know? You didn't tell me. Alan and I go out every Saturday after the game, and most Sundays as well." That was when she decided to come and watch the game.'

`So now you've provoked your mother into checking out this threat to her daughter's virtue.'

Trina opened her eyes wide. `Is that what you are? How intriguing. You must tell me about it sometime.'

`I'd love to,' Alan answered, and made his voice as serious as she had made hers innocent. `But I'm not very good at explaining things. I'll probably have to demonstrate.'

Alan was looking directly at Trina, and for the first time ever she failed to match his gaze. Instead she quickly looked away.

After the match, Alan showered, changed and went out to the back of the stand where Trina and her mother were waiting. He had just been introduced when John arrived and the conversation turned to family matters. However, John was in a hurry to get away, and as soon as he left Mrs Grant turned to Alan.

`Alan, I've booked seats for a show tonight and I hope you'll both join me. Trina said she was sure you wouldn't mind, and we could have a meal together afterwards.'

`I'd love to, thank you. That's very kind of you,' he replied.

Mrs Grant had come up to town by train, and had borrowed a car from her brother, Sir Harold Marsden. She had driven Trina to the match and now offered Alan a lift home. He would have to change from his casual clothes, and they arranged to meet later at the theatre.

Trina's mother could, perhaps, be best described as a slightly daunting lady of great dignity. She accepted Alan as Trina's friend, yet he felt that she was reserving her judgment. He was left wondering whether "tolerated", rather than "accepted", might better express her true reaction to him.

Like Trina, she was reasonably tall, and her figure, though mature, was upright and trim. Her hair, dark and well tended, retained its color except for two streaks of grey, and her dress was elegantly expensive. Mrs Grant was hardly the typical wife of a country clergyman, but then she was a Marsden with money in her own right. Though not an overbearing person by intent she tended to be autocratic, but as Alan came to know her he found Mrs Grant considerate, though unbending. Probably it was a natural reserve on her part, and he later discovered that she could be refreshingly tolerant.

`You must tell me about yourself.'

Her first words once they were seated in the restaurant were typically direct, and she followed them with:

`What are your interests?'

Alan was tempted to say `Trina!' but stayed on safer ground, fearing that Mrs Grant might not share her daughter's sense of humor.

Throughout the meal he was cross-examined, pleasantly and tactfully; but there would have been little chance of concealing anything, even if he had so wished. Trina did not help Alan. Whenever he caught her eye he saw that she was bubbling with suppressed glee; and when her mother's attention was diverted to the waiter, Trina took the opportunity to whisper;

'The Importance of Being Ernest.'

The thought of the eligibility scene in Wilde's play was, in the circumstances, almost too much for Alan's gravity, yet he managed to survive the evening without doing anything to arouse Mrs Grant's active disapproval.

During that winter of 1938 the slender threads multiplied, bonding Trina and Alan into a fastness of exclusion sufficient to themselves. They became one unit, conscious of what was happening in the outside world, yet careless of anything beyond their mutual boundary.

Cold, rain, snow, slush and sleet were all the same as they roamed the frenetic London scene during the fading twilight of peace. A London redolent of Noel Coward, Ivor Novello, the Ben Travers's farces and a Palladium indivisible from the Crazy Gang; a London of art and variety with the grace of ballet, the richness of opera and the sleaziness of Soho. They enjoyed the fantasies of escape from reality as they queued for the cheapest theatre seats; their evening meal a hot dog and a milk-shake. With light hearts they battled the weather and public transport, accepting as inevitable, but ignoring, the menace of violence.

These were days when mental and physical violence eroded the fabric of tolerance throughout much of the world. Though Blackshirts and Communists clashed in London's side streets and political expediency gambled away the future, Trina and Alan looked only to each other and were happy with what they found.

Together they joined post-match Rugby parties, and visited the mushroom clubs of London's West End. Through Rugby friends they gained entry to the sanctum of the amazing Rosa Lewis, whose youthful beauty and vivacity had so captivated her noble lovers, a beauty that still showed through the white hair and aging features. These parties at Rosa's were evenings of pink champagne and bawdy song, while the inevitable Guards officer leaned against the mantelpiece, his uniform trousers too tight to allow him to sit in comfort.

Boredom was something they never knew. It was not until May, when they had known each other for over six months, that they became lovers.

It might have happened earlier, one Sunday in April when Alan borrowed his brother's car. They had hoped for a bright Spring day; instead, they found themselves driving in a soft misting rain. The car was a Morris Ten two-seater with dickey, and was at least eight years old. The rain penetrated through every crack between the canvas hood and the side screens. In spite of the rain they were excited and happy. They were alone with some measure of privacy. This had always been a problem. Throughout the winter so much of their weekends had been taken up with football and, with no car, their activities were restricted. They could not afford hotel rooms in which to experiment, and it was hard to find anywhere else where they could be alone without fear of interruption. Apart from a few snatched moments, this was the first time they had been securely free from unwanted eyes.

They decided to explore the by-ways of the Weald of Kent, hoping to find a secluded spot, even though the rain would interfere with their plans for a picnic.

`The rain's coming in on me.'

Trina had been fiddling with the yellowing celluloid screens for several minutes.

`You can always move over to my side,' Alan suggested.

`This car isn't big enough to have sides,' she retorted. `It only has a middle.'

Nevertheless she moved closer, sliding an arm over the back of the seat so that her hand rested on Alan's shoulder.

Trina had never driven through the Weald before. She exclaimed over picture villages, and was fascinated by the narrow lanes, and the high hedges that allowed occasional glimpses of stately homes and manicured gardens. In spite of the weather there was luminosity in the sky, for the rain, though persistent, was light enough not to hide distant views, giving them instead a translucent magic.

Soon after midday they stopped, but stayed in the car to eat their lunch. It was too wet to picnic, and when they finished eating they were in no hurry to drive on. Alan reached for Trina, drawing her to him. She was soft, warm and pliant, and their world shrank to a small oasis of canvas and leather-cloth.

The car was parked off a narrow lane beside a farm gate. They kissed and fondled, knowing they wanted each other, but it was not the right moment; not there, awkwardly struggling, cramped and confined. Cars and trucks passed within a few feet and a tractor was working in the field beyond the gate. It was sufficient to savor the promise of pleasure. They now knew the moment would come, and all that remained was to find the right time and the right setting.

It was April, the month sacred to Venus, and the sensuous goddess smiled on them bringing a solution to their problem. They had often yearned for a car of their own and the freedom it would provide, but their pay, as junior clerks, did not permit such luxuries. More than once Trina had said;

`It wouldn't hurt Mum to buy me a car. I've even suggested that the running expenses would make me find new ways to economise.' Trina laughed; `I don't know why, but I just can't make her see it my way.'

`A most ingenious argument,' Alan agreed.

All the same he was grateful that Trina was kept short of cash. She was paid the same as all the other female juniors and her salary was even less than his. If she had been given a generous allowance he would have felt like an impoverished suitor, and his pride might have spoiled their relationship.

Venus truly guided them that rainy day. On their way home, they were passing through a small cluster of houses when Alan saw a battered Austin Seven, standing next to a petrol pump outside the village store. It stood, downcast and shamefaced, with its price - `Sixty-nine shillings' - painted on the windscreen in uneven letters.

He swung to the side of the road and stopped.

`Why are we stopping?'

Alan had already jumped out and was hurrying around to open the passenger door.

`Come on,' he said. `There's something I want to look at.'

Trina peered out at the rain that was now falling more heavily.

`It's wet,' she complained.

`And you're made of sugar and spice I suppose.'

She slithered out of the car and looked at the sky while Alan rummaged in the dickey.

`It's all very well for you. Frogs and snails like rain.'

`Here, cover your sweetness with this.'

Alan handed her a torn, disreputable raincoat that his brother kept in the back of the car, and Trina hung it around her shoulders.

`Well?' she asked.

He led her to the Austin.

`My finances might stretch to buying this.'

`Who,' she said, emphasizing the word heavily, 'is going to push it?'

Alan very deliberately ignored such pessimism.

Admittedly the outward appearance was not encouraging. The canvas hood was in shreds, the paintwork bare in places, and there were plenty of scratches and dents. Alan went over and over the car trying to make up his mind.

He soon found that the radiator leaked, but the tires were passable, and when he started the engine it ran – just. Alan was no expert, but he thought that new plugs and points might make a big difference. As far as he could tell the engine was making no disastrous noises. Finally he took it for a drive down the road, then regretted his folly when the brake pedal went straight to the floorboards. Luckily the hand brake held.

Alan decided to gamble. `I'll take it,' he said.

The sullen youth who had come out to make the sale disappeared for a few minutes, and returned with a length of oil-soaked rope. This he handed over so that Alan and Trina could tow the car away. Probably the owners of the store were anxious to see their bargain removed as soon as possible.

Trina refused to drive the Morris, saying that she had never towed another vehicle.

`I'll take the Austin,' she insisted. `As long as you go slowly I think I'll be all right.'

`If that's what you want, but, remember, grab the hand brake each time I signal to slow down.'

The sixty-nine shillings had stretched Alan's resources to the limit. Penniless he might be, but he felt the pride of ownership even while towing his purchase home. Peering into the rear vision mirror, he could see the concentration on Trina's face as she held the steering wheel with one hand and the hand brake with the other. The towrope was none too long, and within minutes Trina was none too dry. Soon she was sodden and bedraggled, but stubbornly refused to change places.

For the next few weeks Alan spent every spare hour working on that car. Trina helped at weekends, keeping him company, passing spanners and making sympathetic noises when he skinned his knuckles.

A radiator from the wrecker's yard cost half a crown, and did not leak. The brakes would have been better with new linings, but when adjusted they were adequate. Alan took the engine apart and found that, as he had hoped, most of its troubles lay in the plugs and points. With these replaced, the carburetor cleaned and the engine tuned, it was a different car.

Their first drive was to Tilbury. Alan had spoken to one of the Company's sail-makers and, in return for a couple of bottles of beer, the sail-maker had promised to cut and stitch a new hood. The materials cost nothing. In the dockside store there were many remnants of canvas and carpet discarded from the ships. The sail maker used these to make the hood, new covers for the seats and carpet the floor.

On the way to Tilbury Alan claimed that the car was running sweetly, even though it still looked a wreck.

`What's that noise though?' Trina demanded.

It seemed to be coming from the bodywork behind them, and was a harsh sound rather like a rusty gate.

`You tell me. I don't know.' Alan, too, had been wondering what it was.

Trina leaned over into the back seat, prodding and listening.

`It sounds like a Corncrake,' she said after a couple of minutes of futile search.

Alan never did get rid of that noise, but the car had found a name. From that moment they knew it as `Corncrake'. Late in May their means to freedom was complete. The dents had been beaten out and, although not expertly done, the improvement was dramatic. Freshly painted and more or less mechanically sound it awaited their pleasure. It was time for adventure.

The sun shone as they left London. The day was warm, with a touch of freshness in the breeze that sent the blood tingling through their veins and ruffled Trina's hair. They drove out into the Surrey countryside, and after passing through Epsom headed towards Guildford. At Ashtead they turned left, taking a side road to Headley.

`How about stopping here?' Alan suggested when they had driven for another a mile or so.

Without waiting for an answer he swung to the side of the road, parking near a stile set in a wire fence. Trina did not speak, nor did she look at him, but just opened her door and started to get out.

Alan was first to the stile. He jumped it, then turned to help Trina over. He could feel the adrenaline pulsing through his body and his heart was pounding. As Trina stepped down her face was pale and tense, the pupils of her eyes dilated. She smiled nervously and Alan took her in his arms holding her tightly. They stood like this for several seconds saying nothing, a physical contact electric with anticipation. Then, `Shall we go?' Alan asked.

Trina nodded, then slid her hand into his, clutching fiercely.

From the stile, a path led to the woods about one hundred yards away. Both knew what was going to happen and the walk across the field was dreamlike and unreal. It seemed to take forever until they reached the shelter of the trees.

Later they lay side by side, relaxed, and Alan propped on one elbow, looked down into Trina's face. She was smiling and calm; unbelievably different from the way she had been a few minutes earlier. Then her eyes had been wild and unseeing, her breathing fast and shallow, her throat choked with words she could scarcely utter.

`I knew you were going to be a threat to my virtue almost as soon as I met you.' She reached out as she spoke and ran her fingers lightly down the side of his neck, and Alan dipped his head to brush her lips with his own.

`Well, it'll never be threatened again,' he said.

Trina pouted at him, then laughed. `In that case, do you think I should tell my mother there's no reason to worry any more?'

`If you did tell her, I wonder how she'd react?'

`That's easy.' Trina reflected for a few seconds, then continued. `She'd show no emotion at all. She'd look at me for a while before saying anything, then she'd say rather frigidly: "I trust you had enough sense to take precautions".'

`Is that all?'

`Well probably not quite all,' Trina laughed. 'But, yes, she's like that. Once something's done she'll accept the fact and won't waste time in useless recriminations.'

Trina dimpled at him.

`Shall I ask the traditional question?'

`Which one?' Alan queried.

`Oh, Is there more than one? I'd only thought of - Do you love me? What's the other?'

`Was I any good?' Alan grinned back at her.

With great deliberation Trina rolled over towards him, and with no warning bit him on the arm.

It was quite painful.

CHAPTER TWO

Carpe diem, quam minimum redula postero
(Grasp the day, but expect little from the future.)
Horace – Odes

Alan's fingers probed his arm as if seeking the bruise marks made by Trina's teeth, but they had long since faded and now there was only the bruise in his heart. That day, that moment, was too far away, and distant in more than time.

Memories had become painful, and Alan dragged himself back to the present.

'It's eerie,' he thought. 'I've never felt more alone, and it doesn't matter that there are ten others in the boat.'

There was so much of nothing, an empty sea and an empty sky, nothing except the cold glitter of distant stars. Although the sullen sea was bare he knew there was life within, and that it was empty only to surface vision. In the depths of his mind Alan could hear the echo of a splashing, and looked out to starb'd as if expecting to see Peter. Yet he knew it was no more than a haunting imagination, and remembered how they had all watched, silent and helpless, as Peter raised his arms and sank out of sight.

Peter Redpath was Purser of Ocean Monarch. When Alan joined the ship in 1941 and met Peter he was given a stiff, cool welcome. Later, he realized this was not unusual and was caused by a self-conscious shyness. Among people he knew Peter could relax and be entertaining and witty, but his temperament did not make the social side of his job easy. This handicap was offset by an engaging, nervous smile and a natural charm that most people found irresistible.

Alan soon found that he and Peter shared a sense of the ridiculous that helped their association. Peter made few strong friendships, but when he did they were firm and lasting.

There were mornings when Peter failed to appear on deck, and Alan soon learned that Peter suffered from fits of depression. At first Alan suspected him of being an alcoholic, but later found that Peter suffered from bouts of insecurity and a fear of the world. He would lock himself into his cabin, answering only after repeated knocking on his door.

`Who is it? I can't see anyone.'

`It's Alan here, Peter.'

`Alan, take my place on Captain's rounds? Say I've got the shits and can't make it.'

`Can I get you anything Peter? Are you all right?'

`Just bugger off and leave me alone.'

Alan found that arguing with Peter was a waste of time, and it only made matters worse. With the help of the Ship's Surgeon it was always possible to cover for him.

Although Peter was not a heavy drinker there were times, in port or ashore, when they all drank too much. Wild parties relieved the tension they knew while at sea. Stress was a constant companion realized only by its absence when in port. At sea they did not drink as, with thousands of lives in their care, the ever-present threat of submarine attack made a clear head essential.

Alan brought his mind back to the present and made a search of the horizon, but his movements were mechanical and directed by habit alone.

`What was it Peter had said about seamen and their women?' he mused.

* * *

The ship had been anchored in the Clyde, and it was late evening when Peter and Alan returned on board after spending several hours of tramping the countryside. When not at sea, they invariably had a few drinks before dinner and they went first to Alan's cabin. There they relaxed over one or two pink gins before moving to Peter's cabin where a cold meal had been served. Later, while the steward cleared the table and tidied the cabin, Alan and Peter went up to the boat deck where the breeze was drifting in from the sea, stinging their faces with a chill freshness. No lights were showing either from the blacked out ships or from the shore, and there was a haunting quality to the night. The moving water held a soft, dark sheen, and the distant hills only hinted at their presence. The wailing notes from a distant piper floated through the air, faint, but distinct and in tune with the setting.

Peter had been moody all afternoon, one moment talking freely and the next lapsing into a brooding silence. As they paced the deck he seemed to have no desire to talk. Alan, lost to the magic of the night, was happy to drift along, allowing his imagination to weave around the lament of the pipes and the putt-putt of the duty boat as it ferried between the shore and the anchored ships.

After half an hour they returned to Peter's cabin, where he poured two drinks of Scotch. Peter handed one to Alan before slumping into his favorite chair.

Alan tried to get a conversation started.

`You remember the last time we were here, just before we sailed, I sent off a box of kippers to my parents?'

Peter turned his head to look at Alan, but gave no other sign that he had heard the question.

`Well, all that reached them was the board that had the address written on it.'

A slight lift of his chin was Peter's only response.

`With rationing, I suppose it was too much to hope that it'd get all the way from Gourock to London without being pinched.'

Again there was no response apart from a slight head movement.

`All right, don't talk then,' Alan thought. He leaned back in his chair and gazed at the deck head, conscious of the faint thrum from the generators far below in the engine room. `Maybe I should shoot through and leave him to himself. I might even get some letters written.'

`Drink up.'

Peter had picked up the bottle and was waiting for Alan to pass his glass.

`I ought to be writing to Trina,' Alan protested as he allowed the glass to be refilled.

Again there was no reply, and with a fresh drink Alan tried again to get Peter talking.

`You haven't said much about your leave. Did you get up to town at all or did you just stay at Faversham?'

An odd, drained expression came into Peter's eyes, and it was some thirty seconds before he spoke. As the silence hung about them Alan regretted asking the question. In these moods Peter could take almost anything as an invasion of his privacy. All the same, it had seemed a fairly harmless question.

`I've never told you about my fiancée.'

The bald statement took Alan completely by surprise, and his face showed his astonishment.

`I didn't even know you were engaged,' he said.

`I've been engaged ten years.'

This was even more startling, and Alan found it hard to believe. Peter rarely mentioned his private life, other than an occasional bitter remark about the advantage of having no family, and Alan knew that Peter gave `None' as next of kin when signing Ship's Articles. Now he claimed that he had been engaged for ten years. Why so long an engagement? And why not give his fiancée as next of kin?

Alan had time to puzzle over these questions, as Peter did not elaborate. Instead he pulled out a handkerchief, dabbed it against his lips, then toyed with it as if embarrassed by his own disclosure. Alan remained silent: if Peter wished to say more he would, meanwhile it was better not to probe.

When Peter did speak, he seemed as if he were trying to change the subject, but without being too abrupt. `You and Trina have known each other for quite a while, haven't you?'

`Almost four years,' Alan confirmed.

`That's longer than most seamen stay with the one girl, or that she remains faithful to him.'

`D'you think so? Of course for the first two years we were working together in the shore office.'

Then to keep the conversation going, Alan asked:

`What makes you think four years is a long time?'

Again Peter did not answer immediately; instead he refilled their glasses. He took one sip and then sat leaning forward holding his drink in both hands, forearms resting on his knees and staring into the whisky glass.

Once more there was silence between them, and Alan wondered what Peter had been like at twenty-three, the age he would have been when he became engaged. Physically, probably very little difference. In height Peter was shorter than average, but stocky and well muscled, and at that age he might have had some hair on the top of his head. Possibly his eyes would have been brighter, without that worn look that made him seem older than thirty-three. Alan felt sure that the years would have made little difference to that plump, cherubic face.

Still lost in thought Peter took out his handkerchief again, but this time used it to mop the top of his head. It was not warm in the cabin, but when Peter had more than a few drinks his bald head would always become moist.

The action caused him to look up and see Alan watching him.

`I talk too much,' he said with a wry smile.

`Not surprising the amount we've drunk.'

Peter shrugged. `It's not that. I've never told anyone about my engagement before, not on board ship that is.'

`That's all right. I won't mention it around, if that's what's worrying you.'

`I don't mean that. I didn't think you would, but there's more to it than just the engagement. I should have married her as soon as possible.' He took a long sip of his Scotch before adding; `Then it might never have happened.'

`I'm sorry Peter, you're losing me.'

With a quick movement Peter tossed down the drink he had been studying so intensely, then looked at Alan.

`What's the matter with you?' He pointed accusingly. `You're dragging your feet.'

Obediently Alan gulped, then passed his glass for a refill.

'I suppose I may as well tell you the rest of it now.'

Though not exactly sober himself, Alan could see that Peter was showing emotional stress, and wondered if he might tell things he would regret in the cold light of a morning hangover.

'Are you sure you want to tell me?' he asked.

Peter did not answer, but his eyes became vacant as he retreated into thought. Then, as if making a decision, he reached into a desk drawer and took out a leather folder, handing it over without comment. Alan put down his glass and opened the folder. Inside was the photograph of a young woman, head and shoulders, enlarged from a snapshot. The girl was attractive, though she could not truthfully be called beautiful. She had not smiled for the camera and looked a little solemn, but the slender features were delicate and thoughtful.

'That's Elizabeth.'

'Your fiancée?' Alan returned the photo.

Peter glanced at it, nodded, then closed the folder and put it back in the desk. He picked up his drink and looked steadily at Alan.

'For over a year, after we became engaged, I was happy. My mother died while I was still a child. I was never close to my father, and he died when I was eighteen, soon after I went to sea. When I met Elizabeth I felt that at last there was someone who really cared. It gave me something to look forward to, knowing she was waiting when I went on leave.'

'I see.'

Alan took refuge in this innocuous remark. He had a bad feeling about the turn of the conversation, and was worried by Peter's manner.

'If we'd married I'm sure we could have managed, but we decided to wait until I was promoted and my pay went up. Meantime, with both of us working, we'd save as much as we could.'

There was another lengthy silence with Peter clearly affected by his own words.

'It's not as though we'd nowhere to live,' he continued. 'My father had left me the cottage at Faversham, and we planned to modernize it with the money we'd saved. Yes, we could've managed, and, if we had, it would never have happened.' In spite of his misgivings, Alan was becoming intrigued by these oblique references. Peter hesitated, as if choosing his words, then sipped at his drink a couple of times before resuming his story.

`Elizabeth lived with her mother, in Rochester. She worked in a bank, and while I was away she rarely went out, except, perhaps, on a Saturday night when she might go to the cinema.'

There was another long pause, and Alan wondered whether Peter was already regretting his impulse to tell what was on his mind. He had clamped his hands together, fingers interlocked, and his knuckles showed white from the strain.

`It was one Saturday night ... her home was on the outskirts of town, and as Elizabeth walked from the bus stop she was attacked by three men. They dragged her to a vacant piece of land and raped her, all of them.'

There was nothing he could say, and Alan waited for Peter to continue.

`She never recovered, mentally that is. The shock affected her mind and she became childlike, helpless in many ways. Her mother died six months later. Elizabeth's not violent, not uncontrollable; nothing like that. She just needs constant looking after.'

For the first time since he started speaking, Peter looked directly at Alan, who nodded his head, as he could find nothing suitable to say.

Peter did not seem to expect any comment.

`There's not much I can do,' he explained. `I can't bear to look at her. I go to see her each day when I'm on leave, and I'm ashamed: ashamed each time when I say goodbye because I'm glad to go. It hurts me to see her and be with her. I remember Elizabeth as she was and I love her ... and I hate her because she won't come back. I hate myself because of it. Do you think I'm mad too?'

There was a defiant aggressiveness about the way Peter asked this last question, and Alan had to be careful.

`I think it's the affliction you hate, not Elizabeth. It wouldn't be natural if you didn't react strongly.'

Peter stood up and seemed a little more relaxed now that he had told the story.

`I couldn't let her go into some asylum,' he said. `She's been in a nursing home for the last seven years.'

They had finished the iced water, and Peter leaned across Alan to press the bell. He waited in the doorway for the night watchman, then handed him the thermos jug to refill. He went back to his chair and sat, then said, softly, yet bitterly; `It's expensive, but what else have I got to do with my money...'

* * *

`Well, Peter's dead. Eleven of us in the boat now, and if we aren't rescued soon it'll only be ten.'

Alan stretched and then stood up.

`Hell!' he exclaimed softly and thought, `I've been sitting still for too long. I've got a numb bum, as well as pins and needles in my right leg.'

For perhaps two minutes Alan remained standing, massaging his buttocks until the circulation was restored. When he sat down his thoughts were still of Peter.

`Strange, I'm sitting here because Peter couldn't sleep and woke me early to play quoit tennis. But for that I'd still have been in my bunk when the torpedo struck.'

* * *

Amazing how swiftly the end came. At the speed Ocean Monarch was making, and with a long, heavy swell, no submarine could have expected to hit her. She was plunging into a head sea, groaning in protest as she buried her stem into each oncoming wave.

It must have been a fluke shot, and the torpedo struck within a few feet of her bows, blowing them wide open. The heavy sea combined with her own momentum to kill her. The force of twenty-eight thousand tons deadweight drove her on, and the collision bulkhead collapsed under the lethal pressure of water that jetted into the forepeak. Ocean Monarch recovered, staggered, and plunged ahead. Three times she smashed into the oncoming sea then, as if in despair began to swing broadside to the waves, listing to port before she finally capsized.

When they started the game of deck quoits, Alan and Peter draped their life jackets over one of the lifeboat hoists. They had played a few points of their second game when the explosion came, and they felt a shudder in the deck beneath their feet. The sound seemed remote and there was no damage to be seen. Alan made for the port rail closely followed by Peter, and they leaned out over the ship's side trying to see what had happened. There seemed to be no immediate danger and Alan climbed over the rail, ducking under the boat so that he could lean out further.

`Must be right up for'ard,' he told Peter. `But I can't see far enough to be sure.'

As he spoke, Ocean Monarch's opened bow hit the first of the oncoming waves. It was as if a giant hand were holding her back. Her stem could no longer cut through the water, and Alan saw a foaming mass of water boil its way along the ship's side. The unexpected lurch almost threw him off balance, and he pulled back to a safer position.

`That's it Peter,' he shouted. `I reckon it's a torpedo right up in the bows.'

`Better there than in the engine room.'

Peter was leaning over the rail as he answered, and before he finished speaking the ship hit the second wave. This time Ocean Monarch staggered under the blow and was noticeably slower in recovering. Her bow hung down buried deep in the water, her stern unnaturally high, and from within the hull Alan and Peter could hear strange sounds and feel vibrations. Her bow tried to rise, but by now the wave had passed her length and was holding up the stern. With her stem still buried she made her first heeling lurch to port, and then the third wave hit.

That was all the warning they had. Ocean Monarch, down by the head and still not recovered from the previous wave, rolled even further until she had more than a sixty degree list, and there she hung.

`She's going over!'

Even as he shouted, Peter was scrambling over the rail and Alan did not stop to argue. They dropped into the water almost together and the ship hung over them, immense and threatening as the next wave swung her around. Then she was sliding away, her momentum carrying her well clear before she went right over.

Swimming was not too difficult in the light clothes Alan and Peter were wearing, and once or twice in the first minutes they saw the heads of other swimmers. They also caught glimpses of the upturned hull heaving sluggishly in the heavy swell, but finally that too disappeared, leaving them isolated and abandoned.

After half an hour they had given up looking for other survivors, and with no life jackets were beginning to tire. It was then they heard a shout and there, appearing and disappearing with the movement of the waves, was a lifeboat. Alan and Peter swam towards it, but the boat was drifting and for two or three minutes they seemed to be making no headway. Then the boat veered, seeming to change direction, and suddenly was almost on top of them.

The boat was swamped, its gunnels barely above the surface, and Alan and Peter had little difficulty in climbing on board. To find a boat was a miracle. A raft, yes, that could be expected, but it was incredible that one of the boats should have got away. As it turned out they never saw a raft, although many must have floated to the surface as the ship sank. Still, in that broken sea they could have been within a few yards of a low-lying raft and never have seen it.

Later, when they had time to think about it, they decided that in those last frantic moments someone had knocked out the boat's securing pin, allowing it to swing free on its davits. It must have come unhooked from the falls when the ship sank, then worked itself free and floated to the surface. The mast, mainsail and oars had gone, and all that was left was the jib trapped beneath one of the thwarts. As well, there were three watertight ration boxes and a drum of fresh water secure in their lashings. The signal flares were safely in their locker in the stern.

The urgent need was to bale, and they found the baler hanging over the side at the end of its rope. The bung had not been screwed into place but was there, fastened to the keel with a short length of chain.

Jim Bristow was rescued about three minutes after Alan and Peter had climbed on board, and he immediately took charge. They took turns at baling while the rest kept a look-out for anyone still swimming. When they saw someone they could only shout, for there was no way of moving the waterlogged boat to help. Some swimmers did not hear them or see the boat: others hampered by clothes and exhaustion failed to reach it. A very few succeeded. When night fell, twelve had been saved. That first night they slept little. Fatigue could not overcome the discomfort and apprehension they felt, and the night was spent in talk and speculation. The ship had been sailing for New York unescorted and with no passengers. Ocean Monarch's speed, and constant course changes, should have made it almost impossible for a submarine to get into a position from which a torpedo could be fired with any hope of success.

`It had to be a fluke.'

Jim Bristow broke into a conversation between Mahoney, John Allward and Rapley.

`We weren't on a normal convoy route,' he explained. `So it's not as though they'd have had a pack of U-boats strung out in a line. It must have been on its way to or from a patrol area. The bloody thing just happened to be in the right place to get off a torpedo.'

`It was so quick.' Blacklock grunted the words out. During the long afternoon he had tried to do his share of the baling and had lost consciousness two or three times. Finally he had given in and was now stretched out on a thwart, moving a little every so often, trying to ease the pain in his chest.

`If we'd had troops on board it would've been more of a shambles.'

Peter's voice was toneless and sullen as he made this comment and Jim immediately disagreed.

`If we'd had troops on board it wouldn't have happened so quickly. In convoy we'd be making no more than thirteen knots, and the ship wouldn't have ripped open the way she did. We'd have had more time, and some of the escorts would have stood by while survivors were picked up.'

Peter Redpath had behaved strangely, muttering to himself and saying that there was no hope of rescue. Alan and Jim tried to shut him up as he was making everyone depressed, but he kept insisting that there was no hope: they would just have to sit and watch each other die. By the evening of the second day he was rejecting anyone who spoke to him, and moved to sit apart from everyone else. At dusk on the third day he had said, quite calmly and in the most matter of fact manner:

`I'm not going to wait. I can't stand it. Better to have done with it.'

Before anyone could grasp the meaning of his words he had stepped over the side. For an instant they were too shocked to react, and when Jim and Alan tried to catch him they were too late.

`Don't be a fool Peter!' Alan shouted. `Come back.'

They watched as the gap widened. Alan made a move as if to go after Peter but Jim caught hold of his arm.

`It's no use Alan. Even if you catch him you'll never get back to the boat.'

All they could do was stand and watch, and Alan found himself thinking; `What a clumsy swimmer.'

He had seen a man swim to his death, arms flailing, and been unable to rid himself of that irrelevant thought. Later, in the quiet hours of the night the full horror came to him, and he remembered how Peter had thrown his arms in the air as if in a bizarre gesture of farewell.

`Yes,' he thought. `Peter has gone and in some nursing home a poor bewildered girl has lost her protector. What will happen to her when the fees are no longer paid?'

* * *

Alan first heard Peter's name in August 1939, when he saw the statement for a recently completed voyage by Ocean Monarch. The statement was headed; "Purser Redpath in Account with Southern Oceanic Steam Navigation Company" and this recollection brought with it a flood of poignant memory;

`That was the last account I worked on before going on holiday.'

He looked at the restless figures in the boat and was suddenly bitter, bitter with the impossible desire to return to those last few carefree days before Germany attacked Poland. So much had happened since, and Peter Redpath was no longer `In Account' with the Southern Oceanic Line.

* * *

Old fashioned light fittings hung from the ceiling over the desks, and in the area where Alan sat they were switched on permanently. His desk was some sixty feet from the nearest window and he could not even see daylight, not unless he leaned far back in his chair to look behind a stationery cabinet. Whenever he left his desk, Alan would look out of the nearest window and see the sunlight reflected from the windows of the offices across the road.

He would return to work with a feeling of depression; and the smell of ink, and dust, and leather bound journals would be more distasteful than ever.

The weather had been magnificent for most of that summer and Alan thought; `Please let the sun shine next week, and the week after.'

Trina and Alan had made up their minds to go away together, and when Alan was given the dates for his holiday she soon arranged for her own to coincide. The manager of the freight department was only too pleased to grant a request from the Chairman's niece, but there were other problems to be overcome.

In London, Trina lived with her father's sister, who had to be told that Trina was planning to go away. It was not in Trina's nature to make up an elaborate cover story, and she simply told her aunt that she was going away with a friend. When pressed, Trina admitted that Alan was the friend and a shocked Aunt Margaret rang Mrs Grant.

Next day Trina told Alan.

`My mother phoned last night and we had a row.'

`What about?'

`Us.'

`What do you mean? Doesn't she want you to see me, or has she found out about the holiday?'

`That's it. Aunt Margaret told her we were going away together, and when Mum rang she wanted to know if it was true.'

`What did you tell her?'

`The truth, what else?'

`And now what happens?'

They were in their favorite spot overlooking the Tower moat, and a party of excited school children was being herded past them towards the Tower entrance. Trina waited until the noisy crocodile had gone.

`We go ahead with the holiday.'

`What did your mother say? Surely she didn't agree. You said you'd had a row.'

Trina smiled as if remembering something faintly amusing and did not reply immediately. Alan prompted her.

`I don't expect she was pleased.'

Trina's smile faded, to be replaced with her more usual eager manner.

`She wasn't. She started off by saying she was shocked that I'd even considered it, that she would never have thought it of me and that she wouldn't tolerate it. Then she said I was to go home for my holiday, and when I said I wouldn't, Mum laid down the law. "You'll do as you're told," she insisted. It was then I told her that we'd been lovers for quite some time. You should have heard her.'

`I can imagine. But didn't she still insist that you go home, instead of going away with me?'

Trina nodded vigorously.

`Not only that, she said I was to give up my job and go back home to live.'

`But you said we were still going away together. What else happened? What have you done? Cut yourself off with a shilling or something?'

`Oh nothing as dramatic as that. When Mum simmered down a bit, I asked her just what she thought she'd achieve if she made me go home. I said it'd make me miserable and I'd see to it that I made her life miserable too. I warned her she'd be only too glad to get me out of the house again.'

`Surely she didn't accept an ultimatum just like that?'

`Not quite, but she knows how stubborn I can be. I'm very like her in many ways you know, and I've told you how she faces up to facts. After I'd had my say she stopped being merely angry and became analytical instead. She asked if I were really serious, and I said I was. Then she asked, "Do you want to marry Alan?", and I said; "Yes!"'

`Is she sending your father down, armed with a shotgun?'

Trina giggled. `No, before she got around to that, I told her we'd agreed not to get married for a long time yet.'

`That must have been a relief to her.'

`I think it was. Seriously though, I explained that we'd talked it over, and knew we were far too young to think of marriage, but that didn't stop us from being old enough to be in love. I think that appealed to her sense of logic. Do you know what she did?'

`Sang the Hallelujah Chorus?'

Trina looked at Alan mischievously.

`No, better than that. You'll never guess.'

`Tell me then.'

`She's made an appointment for me with her doctor, to be fitted up so I don't get pregnant.'

`Good God! What does Aunt Margaret have to say about all this?'

Trina's eyes were alight with amusement.

`She's going around the house muttering phrases that start with words such as; "In my day...," and "I can't understand young people..." as well as "not knowing what the world is coming to..." at frequent intervals.'

Partly to save fronting up to landladies, but more for reasons of economy, they decided on a camping holiday. Alan was able to get hold of a small tent and a spirit stove. These, with a ground sheet, airbed, a few cooking utensils and cutlery were all they needed. Even so, by the time they added their own suitcases, Corncrake's back seat was piled high.

That Saturday morning, the first day of their holiday, they kept turning to each other as they drove out of London. Each time their eyes met they laughed with excitement and anticipation. The sun was shining and that was wonderful, but they would not have cared if it had been snowing a blizzard. They were eighteen and had a fortnight's freedom, and they were going to spend all of that time together.

Corncrake must have been happy. He behaved beautifully, and even his rasping voice was almost silent, overawed, perhaps, by the unaccustomed load of baggage.

There are some moments that remain in memory, forever vivid as on the day they occurred. For Alan, one such moment was his awakening the next morning. For the first time ever, he woke to find Trina asleep beside him and he lay quietly examining her face in detail. How odd that even with a face he knew so well there could be so much that he had never noticed before. With Trina asleep, he was not distracted by her teasing manner, and for the first time saw the minute scar at the corner of her right eye. He was able to study the curl of her eyelashes and found that those of her right eye were slightly longer than those of the left. He was content to lie beside her and just look.

The flimsy canvas cut them off from the rest of the world. They were secreted in a small space, now strangely luminescent as the rising sun brought a filtered brightness through the stained, green material that enclosed them. The curtained light grew stronger and Trina turned restlessly before opening her eyes to stare directly at Alan. In that first moment of awakening there was a startled look of "Where am I?", then, in almost the same instant her eyes became alive and she was smiling and aware. They kissed and knew the freedom of their nakedness.

The sun was high in the sky by the time they packed up and left.

They went to many places during that short holiday, but now, sitting in the stern of the boat; the tiller wedged beneath his arm, all Alan could remember was Trina. Trina in the foreground of his memories with a series of changing backgrounds.

A rocky headland battered by Atlantic gales and Trina's slim figure buffeted by wind gusts as she looked out over the edge of a precipitous rock battlement, her soft dress molded to the curves and hollows of her body. A streamlined body that challenged the elements and was in ecstatic harmony with the wildness of her surroundings. A laughing, teasing Trina dancing her way upwards as they climbed Brown Willy; and the headlong scamper when they raced back down, hand in hand, singing the saga of Jack and Jill. A pensive figure kneeling at the edge of Dozmary pool, her imagination alive with the legend of King Arthur and Excalibur's farewell flourish before being taken into the unknown depths by the solitary hand thrust from the water.

A sprite of wicked innocence who held him tethered by a band of gossamer, a band that might stretch or fray yet seemed unlikely to break.

A Trina generous in the joy of love, her sleep drugged lips holding a sensuous smile of satisfaction. Dark hair spread against a white pillow; high cheekbones; the smooth, youthful contours of nakedness responsive to his touch, and above all the joy of giving and receiving.

These were the snapshots of memory printed on the emulsion of his mind. For two weeks they ignored the war clouds, and created a closeness of understanding they never completely lost.

Too soon the careless days were gone and they spent the last Sunday of their holiday driving back to London. It was not until they reached Trina's home that they heard the news. A tearful, apprehensive Aunt Margaret told them that war had been declared that morning.

CHAPTER THREE

'Tis with our judgment as our watches, none
Go just alike, yet each believes his own.
Alexander Pope

Queenie stood, then moved across the boat to where Blacklock was lying. He reached out to touch the Storekeeper's head, and bent down as if listening. From the stern, Alan could see Queenie moving, but it was too dark to make out what he was doing. He watched as Mahoney got up and stood next to Queenie, who was now kneeling beside Blacklock.

'What's the matter?'

Alan spoke quietly. Apart from the occasional soft slap of water against the boat's side they were drifting within a circle of silence. The night was still, with no breath of air to stir noisy wavelets or carry their words over the sea, and the darkness seemed to demand a hushed voice.

Queenie turned to face Alan.

'Blackie's in a bad way. He's not breathing too well. Seems more like he's unconscious than asleep.'

'Try propping him up a bit. See if that helps.' Alan hesitated, wondering whether he should go over and look for himself, then decided against. It was a job for two people and a third would only get in the way. He watched the indistinct shapes, guessing, rather than seeing what they were doing. Queenie had lifted Blacklock slightly, and was holding him while Mahoney rearranged the life jackets.

`Can't be any more comfortable than lying on the bare planks,' Alan thought. Except for one kapok life-jacket they were all of the old type, just blocks of cork sewn into canvas and not much use as cushions. He waited until Queenie straightened up.

`Do you think that's helped?' he asked.

`Yeah, we've raised his head quite a bit, and he might be a bit easier, poor sod.'

`I suppose there's nothing else we can do?'

In reply Queenie shrugged and spread his arms in a gesture of helplessness, then stooped over Blacklock and listened for half a minute before turning back to Alan.

`Still doesn't sound too good.'

Alan nodded, though it was doubtful whether Queenie could see the movement. But what could he say? He knew only too well that there was nothing to be said or done, nothing except a mounting feeling of helplessness. He stared for'ard seeing their shapes only as a solid blackness against the darkness of the night.

`It's a weird tableau,' he thought, `Shadows in the night: the reclining Blacklock and his attendants.'

He had begun another routine check of the horizon when his attention was distracted by angry voices.

`Watch it poofter! What the hell do you think you're doing?'

Queenie had stumbled and perhaps trodden on Len Huskins.

`Get stuffed.'

Queenie's reply was brief. He turned away from Len and went back to sit in his usual place.

Alan grinned to himself. `If it came to a fight, I'd back her any day.'

He continued his search but his mind was still on the recent scene. `Queenie looks much older without her toupee,' he thought, then found himself checking his unspoken words. `Funny how we think, and even talk about some homosexuals as "she" and "her". That's the way they talk among themselves, and the rest of us tend to fall into the same habit.'

Alan knew that every ship's company had its quota of homosexuals, and that shipboard life was a natural refuge for them. Generally, other seamen accepted them with tolerance and good-humored banter. Such problems as did arise were nearly always among themselves; jealousies, love triangles and the like. Queenie was in his mid forties with an aura of soft womanly plumpness. This impression was misleading, as more than one over-confident bully boy had discovered, emerging from the subsequent contest with a bruised ego and a battered body. Queenie was sensitive about his hair, which was thinning noticeably, and had sulked for days when his boy friend called him `A bald headed old bastard'.

Blackie was dying. Queenie was sure of that. He had been tending him from the time Blacklock first collapsed, and sensed that the end could not be far off. These last long days in the boat had left too much time to think, and caring for a sick man helped take his mind off his own sorrow.

Now he sat, head on hands, and felt the ache in his heart mingle with a foreboding of doom. It was a feeling that took him back to his boyhood and to the moment when he had stood, naked and shivering, in a cold unfriendly room. The picture was vivid in his mind and Gordon Pellew forgot Blacklock, forgot the boat and his companions, forgot everything except that naked, terrified boy...

* * *

Partly, it was the chill that made him shiver but mostly it was apprehension, fear of the unknown as well as loneliness. From the instant the gates of Borstal shut behind him he had known the terror of a trapped animal. So much had happened during the previous few days, and he had lived through a nightmare that unfolded, mercilessly, leaving him powerless to influence its course.

It had started some months earlier when one of the masters at his school had shown an interest in him. Whenever there was a suitable occasion, Mr Carmichael would take the opportunity to talk, often placing his hand on Gordon's shoulder as they walked, and Gordon did not find it strange when the first invitation was given. He was just leaving the classroom when Mr Carmichael called him back.

`Gordon.'

`Yes, Mr Carmichael.'

`Yesterday, you were saying that you're fond of music.'

`Yes, Sir.'

`Well, I think you might like some of my records. Would you care to hear them sometime?'

`Oh yes, Sir, I'd like that.'

`Good. Now let's see: tomorrow's Saturday. Would you like to come over in the afternoon, say about two o'clock?'

`Yes Sir, Thank you Sir.'

That was how it had begun.

The first time Mr Carmichael kissed him, Gordon was startled, but discovered that he liked it. He also enjoyed the warmth that flooded him when he was undressed and fondled.

Now, as Gordon stood on that bare stone floor, waiting for a doctor to examine him, it seemed a distant memory. In fact, it was only a few days since the thunderous banging on the door of the cottage, when Mr Carmichael had opened the door only to be flung aside as wrath, in the person of the Headmaster, Mr Christmas, strode into the house.

Gordon was terrified, huddling into the bedclothes as Mr Christmas stood in the doorway, his eyes shifting from the shrinking boy to Gordon's clothes draped over a chair. Then came humiliation as he was dragged naked from the bed and ordered to dress. Afterwards, he had to face the torture of being led home and made to stand in silent agony, as his father was regaled with the details of his son's behavior.

`For the boy's sake,' the Headmaster had announced, `I will take no legal action against the scoundrel who led him astray. However, he shall resign his position immediately, and I shall see to it that he finds no further employment as a schoolmaster.'

After Mr Christmas left, Gordon faced his father alone. Mr Pellew was very conscious of his status as accountant at one of the local banks. His anger was made worse by the fact that he felt some guilt towards his son. To tell the truth, he had never held much love for Gordon. Love was an emotion that Mr Pellew found difficult to handle, and even with his wife his manner was stiff and formal. This lack of warmth and interest caused him to leave Gordon's upbringing very much to Mrs Pellew, confining his own share in the process to one of sniping criticism.

Gordon worshipped his mother and he and she would find comfort together, shutting out, as far as possible, the withdrawn, pompous man who shared the house with them.

Mr Pellew's rage now boiled over against this boy he had never tried to understand, and with whom he felt no bond. He went for his walking stick.

`It's time I knocked some sense into you.'

This was the moment Gordon's mother tried to intervene, only to be thrust aside roughly by her furious husband. As his mother stumbled and fell to the floor, Gordon attacked, fingers and nails tearing at his father's face.

`By God! He even fights like a woman.'

The heavy stick came into action, with Gordon stubbornly gritting his teeth and refusing to cry out. Apart from the blows, the only sound was the hysterical screaming of his mother, and his father shouting; `Get out! Get out!'

When Mr Pellew threw down the stick Gordon struggled to his feet, with his father's words running through his mind.

`Get out! Get out!'

His mother was still screaming, and his father shouting at her to shut up as Gordon let himself out of the front door. Half shuffling, half running, his only thought was to get as far away as he could. The despair of that night was something Gordon would never forget. Much of it he spent in the back yard of a service station crouched inside a derelict car. Next day he wandered aimlessly, alternating between the desire to go home to the comfort of his mother, and fear of another confrontation with his father. Mingled with these emotions was the shame of his exposure, and a sense of outrage at what had been done to him.

In the morning he continued his wandering and found a park where he could sit and think. For the first few hours the novelty of being alone in a strange area helped pass the time, but he had not eaten since lunch the previous day and by mid-afternoon hunger had become pressingly urgent. In a playground area Gordon drank from the water fountain, but the cold thinness of the water lay uncomfortably inside him and did nothing to ease his hunger. When darkness fell he gave in, and started on the long walk home. Then a final spark of rebellion flared, and for the second night Gordon sought shelter in the derelict car. It could have been no later than eight-thirty when Gordon crawled into the car, and no matter how tightly he coiled himself he could not stop the ache of hunger. He checked the rubbish bin in the yard, hoping for some scraps of food, but it held only paper and an oily rag. The temptation was a window in an alcove beside the rubbish bin, and inside the car Gordon moved restlessly. If he could lever that window open he might find some loose change in the garage; enough, perhaps, to buy something to eat. For half an hour Gordon resisted the temptation but in the end hunger won.

Leaving the car, he picked up a length of scrap metal that was lying on the ground and climbed on to the dustbin. The lid buckled beneath him, and he had to grab at the windowsill to save himself from falling. For nearly half a minute Gordon stood there, his heart pounding heavily and too frightened to move. Then, tentatively, he slid the end of the metal strip under the window and pressed. When the catch broke, the sound was like a pistol shot and left Gordon sick with terror. Time seemed to stand still, but gradually his heartbeat slowed and he was able to control his shaking limbs. It was now a simple matter to raise the window. One inch, two inches before the silence was broken by a clamorous alarm. For what felt like an eternity Gordon remained frozen, chained by the tumult he had released and then he ran, ran in blind panic until brought to a standstill by a stern voice.

'You there! Come here!'

A police car had pulled into the kerb just ahead of him, and as Gordon was bundled into the car he burst into tears.

There were questions, questions and still more questions. Next day, in a room starkly furnished, and with a bare wooden floor, he was taken before a magistrate. His father was present but not his mother. Mr Pellew's manner was cold and cruel, embarrassed and blaming Gordon for that embarrassment. He gave no support, being more intent on condemning, than on defending or excusing his son.

Gordon sensed more compassion in the magistrate than in his father, who described Gordon as willful and uncontrollable. Mr Christmas was called to give evidence; and his anger, at what he obviously felt to be a slur on his school and himself, led to a harsh assessment of Gordon's character.

In the end though, it was the magistrate, with his father's approval, who recommended Borstal, the correctional school for young offenders. Borstal, where he now stood naked and vulnerable, and so, so, frightened. .

* * *

Queenie raised his head from his hands and looked about the boat. Blackie seemed quieter, and the others, too, were still. It was obvious that Mr Anderson was awake, but only because he was sitting upright and swaying slightly to counter the movement of the boat . . .

* * *

Yes, that first day in Borstal had been one of the worst of his life, but there had been other bad times and the worst had been his homecoming.

`I suppose you'd better come in.'

Gordon looked at his father, and hesitated before accepting the begrudged invitation. His father's hair was thinner than he remembered, with more grey in it and his face more deeply lined. The only thing that had not changed was the permanent look of dissatisfaction.

`Where's Mum?'

During the years in Borstal, Gordon had received only one letter from his mother. In it, she told him his father had forbidden her to write or to visit Gordon. Knowing his mother's fear of her husband, Gordon knew how scared she must have been just to write that one letter.

Gordon walked through to the kitchen, the one room in the house where his mother had some measure of independence. His father entered behind him.

`She's dead,' he said coldly.

`Dead?' Gordon echoed that unbelievable word.

`Yes dead, and it's you and your unnatural ways that killed her.'

Tears stung Gordon's eyes, and he felt the blind rage of sorrow clutch at his heart and explode in his mind.

`It's you! You! You've been killing her for years,' he shouted. `You treated her as a slave, a skivvy to wait on you and do as she was told. You never let her have any life of her own. She hated you! Do you hear? If she hadn't been so frightened she'd have left you years ago. She hated you. Do you know that? She hated you!'

Again, as on that day so long ago, his father was raging and Gordon brushed past, heading for the front door. He heard his father follow, spluttering and choked with anger and shouting;

`It wasn't me. It was you. You!'

In the hallway Gordon stopped, and turned to face his father.

`I was going to take her away. Somehow she and I would have managed, but she's dead and you've denied me even that.'

With a sense of detachment Gordon watched as his father reached for the walking stick.

Mr Pellew was no longer dealing with a child. The years in Borstal had hardened Gordon. The son was now more than a match physically for his father. As the stick swung, Gordon caught it, twisting it from his father's hands. Impelled by hate and sorrow, Gordon used the weapon to strike his father.

The blow left Gordon feeling empty, and he flung the stick aside. For an instant he paused to look at the once awesome ruler of his life, then quickly turned and stepped outside into the fresh air.

Three hours later he was standing beside his mother's grave when the police found him.

Again he returned to a life of doors and gates slamming behind him, the sound echoing from walls of glazed brick. In Court, Gordon listened to his father's self-righteous voice telling how he had been the victim of a vicious, unprovoked attack. He had listened, impassively, while a heavy-jowled magistrate denounced him as a vile, unnatural son, subject to uncontrolled outbursts of passion. Gordon refused to speak in defense. What was the use? Nothing he could say would make any difference. Instead he was expected to be grateful for what the magistrate called leniency, and to consider himself lucky.

Nine months with hard labor.

Serving that sentence was something Queenie had no wish to remember, and even in his thoughts he skipped over the horrors of those months. He left them blank, and picked up his memories from the time of his release from jail.

Less than twelve hours had passed since Gordon stepped through the prison gates. Some instinct drew him to the bright lights of London's West End, a reaction, perhaps, from the colorless monotony of a prisoner's life. He felt himself a stranger, a being from another existence who now stood on the outside looking in. Soon he tired of the glitter, the artificial gaiety of flashing billboards and floodlit shop windows.

The noisy, crowded pavements frightened him. He remained nervously alert, dreading physical contact with the jostling theatergoers. Soon, he could stand it no longer and headed for the darker side streets. So it was that he found his way to the Thames, and leaning on the Embankment wall gained some measure of peace. Later he would need to find shelter for the night, but for the moment Gordon was content to gaze at the slow moving, wrinkled surface of the dark river. There were few conscious thoughts in his mind. The water was alive with dancing pinpoints of light casting an hypnotic spell, and Gordon was happy to let it weave a blanket of oblivion around his senses.

For half an hour he lingered before deciding to make a move. There was a coffee stall further along the Embankment, and there he would ask for directions to the nearest hostel. Gordon jingled the few coins in his pocket; a cup of tea perhaps.

After making his inquiry, Gordon stood at one end of the counter where the rays from the lamp were dim. His fingers curled around the mug of tea in a double-handed embrace, cherishing its warmth. There were two other customers, and the one next to Gordon was a taxi driver, sipping hurriedly at the scalding liquid, anxious to get back to his cab.

If clothes were any guide, the customer at the far end of the stall was a gentleman of means. He was wearing an opera hat and overcoat with a loosely draped white silk scarf; beneath this a black bow tie could be seen. Gordon could not help wondering why the man was drinking coffee on the Embankment, instead of being at dinner or a theatre.

Then their eyes met, and Gordon looked away, embarrassed at being caught in his scrutiny.

The cabby finished the last dregs from his cup, and with a murmured `G'night' to the stallholder, hurried away. Only the length of the counter now separated Gordon and the gentleman. Gordon drained his mug, put it down and turned to leave.

`Excuse me, are you in a hurry?' Gordon hesitated and looked at the speaker. He shrugged his shoulders, and the gesture was accepted as an answer.

`I'd be obliged if you'd join me in another cup of coffee, or is it tea?'

The man had walked over to Gordon and stood close behind him, speaking quietly.

`I like someone to talk to. I hate being by myself. I thought you looked as though you might be lonely too.'

He placed his hand on Gordon's arm, gently pressing him to turn back to the counter. There was almost a caress in the touch and Gordon knew what was happening. The years spent in Borstal and later in prison had taught him many things. Men and youths had disputed for his favors, and at times he had been forced to submit to sex play and rape. Gordon had learned that "unnatural" tendencies were not peculiar to him alone, and that there was a hidden world of sex, strange and more exciting to him than heterosexual love.

Edward, as the gentleman insisted on being called, questioned Gordon discreetly, and soon discovered that Gordon had just come out of jail. When they had finished their tea and coffee he suggested a stroll along the Embankment, and while they walked he encouraged Gordon to tell his story.

`You haven't had an easy life,' he said when Gordon finished. Edward stopped and turned towards the river, resting his hands on the Embankment wall. They now stood midway between lampposts, two shadowy figures silhouetted from the waist up against the lights on the far side of the Thames.

`And now we have to decide about your future,' Edward said softly, then asked;

`Would you like to come back to my flat? You have to spend the night somewhere.'

Gordon accepted the invitation, knowing the unstated reason for the offer. That night a relationship started that was to last for five years. At first, Edward supported Gordon, providing money for clothes and encouraging him in his ambition to become a dancer. Their association was comforting and satisfying to them both, and it was not until Gordon's career showed signs of prospering that their happiness began to falter. Perhaps it started when Edward realized that Gordon no longer depended on him, resenting the fact that Gordon relished his financial independence and had new-found self respect.

A source of friction was Gordon's taste in clothing. He delighted in ostentatious styles that were anathema to Edward, whose one desire was to remain inconspicuous. Gordon was making a new circle of friends and acquaintances from among his fellow dancers, and Edward was becoming jealous. Gordon had just been given a small solo part in a musical, and was so elated that he did not pay much attention to Edward's moods. It came as a shock when he returned to the flat one night to find his wardrobe and chest of drawers emptied and his clothes in a pile on the bedroom floor. Edward stood beside them, his face flushed and his manner petulant.

`You can pack your things and move out!'

His voice was shrill and the corner of his mouth twitched. Gordon looked from Edward to the mound of clothes and started to protest, but Edward refused to listen.

`I've been watching you. I saw you tonight when you were leaving the theatre. If you prefer that... that thing to me you're welcome I'm sure, but don't think you're going to stay with me.'

`It didn't mean anything.'

Gordon's own voice was taut with anger. He had guessed what was causing the trouble, even before Edward finished speaking. Ronald, one of the other male dancers had been making approaches to Gordon; but there had never been anything more between them than a few friendly words. That night he had paused outside the stage door and spent a few minutes talking to Ronald about the show.

Gordon tried pleading, but there was no changing Edward's mind. Reluctantly Gordon packed; deciding it would be best not to make a scene that could only make matters worse. He felt sure that, in time, Edward would relent.

During the next few days Gordon tried to contact Edward, but either the phone was hung up as soon as he spoke or it was left unanswered. When Gordon called at the flat Edward refused to let him in, and when Gordon tried to talk to him through the closed door Edward made it clear he that would not listen.

`You can go on talking if you like,' he called out. `But I'm going into the bedroom where I won't be able to hear you.' Seconds later Gordon heard the bedroom door being slammed shut.

About a week after leaving the flat, Gordon again tried to phone, but an unknown voice answered, and when he asked to speak to Edward there was no reply. He was able to hear some muffled whispering, and then the line went dead.

A few evenings later, Gordon was on his way to the theatre when he saw Edward walking towards him. Edward did not see Gordon until they were almost face to face, and when he did his startled look of recognition held an element of panic.

`Edward, please! Can't we go somewhere quiet where we can talk? I've got a few minutes to spare before I have to be at the theatre.'

`There's nothing to say.'

`How do you know? You've never listened to me. You've jumped to conclusions.'

`I don't want to talk about it.'

`Please Edward, you can't treat me like this, not after all this time.'

Gordon caught at Edward's sleeve in his anxiety to convince him. With an angry gesture Edward snatched his arm away.

`Edward, it's not fair. Don't be like this.' Edward had taken a pace or two backward and Gordon followed him tenaciously, determined not to lose this opportunity to make him relent. He reached for Edward's hand.

'Please don't go. I've been so unhappy.'

`Is this person annoying you?'

Gordon dropped Edward's hand and turned to see who had spoken.

The owner of the voice was a policeman, who had approached unnoticed. His bulk seemed to loom over Gordon as he questioned Edward.

`Yes... yes, he is.'

Edward's words were quick and jerky, and the constable looked at the flamboyantly dressed Gordon with obvious distaste.

`I know his sort, Sir. We can deal with him all right.' This could not be happening. In bewilderment Gordon looked from the policeman to Edward, and then back again. Suddenly he saw it all. Edward was terrified. Terrified that his aberration might become public knowledge. Terrified that he would be forced to resign from his position as a senior public servant.

There was pleading in Edward's eyes, and Gordon felt pity for him. He did not protest, nor claim close friendship with Edward, but allowed himself to be led away.

Again Gordon tasted the bitterness of imprisonment. In Court, his past was made known, and during his time in jail Gordon determined to find a new life. If he entered into the shadowy world of London's deviate nightclubs he would, inevitably, find himself in trouble with the law. He was now a known homosexual, and could expect persecution from those who considered him to be abnormal. He had been told that there was more tolerance for his kind among seamen, and this was where he decided to look for refuge.

Happiness had been a fickle companion for Gordon, but during the next sixteen years he established a working compromise with life. Friends had come and gone, but within the iron womb of the ship he felt safe. The pains of his youth were still bitter, but no longer caused sharp distress. Still fresh was the memory of his mother. He had no photograph but did not need one; when he closed his eyes it was easy to see her face.

He did so now. Whenever he wanted comfort he turned to her image, and if ever he had needed comfort it was during these last days. Freddie was dead. He was sure of that. Freddie would still have been in his bunk when the ship was hit. He, Gordon, had been up early, working with the two barkeepers reorganizing the storeroom in readiness for the stores they would be taking on board in New York. They had finished and were enjoying a breath of fresh air on deck, before getting ready for the rest of the day's duties...

* * *

A sound brought Queenie back to the present moment. Blacklock was trying to stand up and Queenie moved quickly to restrain him.

`Hang on Terry, it's all right. I've got you.'

From the stern Alan saw the struggle and moved to help. Then, seeing that Mahoney had gone to Queenie's assistance he sat down again. He could hear Con Mahoney organizing. `Careful Queenie, don't touch the poor bugger's ribs.'

Slowly the fit passed and Blacklock seemed to drift back into unconsciousness. Queenie and Mahoney lowered him back onto the pile of life jackets.

`It's a bastard!' Con Mahoney was muttering to anyone who cared to listen, and then repeated.

`It's a bastard, there's bugger all we can do for him.' Queenie patted Mahoney on the shoulder, then turned and went back to his seat...

* * *

So it happened. He had lived and Freddie had been trapped, drowned in the rush of water. For more than four years they had been together, and never quarreled seriously. Again he must embrace his grief. Another compartment of his life must be sealed off, and emotions shut away until he could trust himself to look at them dispassionately. Only by concentrating on the here and now could he hope to allay the pain. The act of caring for Blacklock helped. Terry's need could almost make him forget his own hurt.

* * *

`It's a bastard!' The comment echoed in Alan's ears. Once, a long time ago, he had heard Con Mahoney use those same words, but then they had been at Southern Oceanic's wartime office outside London, near St Albans.

When planning the emergency office, the Company had realized that distance and transport disruptions might make it difficult for some of their staff to travel to and from their homes each day. Therefore, they rented a building that had previously been a private school, and this was ideal for their purpose. The classrooms converted to offices, while the dormitories, together with the teachers' and domestic staff' quarters, provided sleeping accommodation. The school had been called "Barringdale", and crew from the ships were sent there to look after the catering and cleaning. At first this staff came from ships laid up for conversion from passenger liners to troopships. Later they came from crews who had been torpedoed, and were waiting for new ships.

`It's a bastard!'

Con Mahoney was the first chef to be sent to Barringdale and this was how Trina and Alan heard him express his opinion of the place, the job, and the fact that he had been sent there. Soon after Trina and Alan returned from their holiday, he had been told that he was to be one of an advance party going to St Albans. Trina promptly arranged to be included in the team, and for two weeks the group at Barringdale slept on mattresses on the floor while preparing the temporary offices. Day after day consignments of desks and furniture arrived, and at the end of the fortnight the transfer of files and office equipment began.

During the second week, Mahoney and his staff arrived. Trina and Alan were in the kitchen while he inspected his future domain. The inspection was thorough, stove, lockers and working surfaces.

`It's a bastard!'

Trina and Alan looked at him enquiringly as they waited for an explanation of the outburst

`I should be on paid leave, like the rest of the crew. Instead the bastards send me here to run a kitchen that's not even fit to boil water in.'

He turned on his grinning assistants.

`What the hell are you standing there for? Go and get into working gear, and come back here - quick!'

He soon settled in and found compensations. Most evenings Con Mahoney held court in the kitchen for any of the office girls who were interested. He would give them hints on cooking, but mainly he held them there by his outrageous tales of life at sea. His Irish imagination, given free rein, was never at a loss.

When the transfer was complete, the Company asked for volunteers to stay at Barringdale over the weekends. Trina heard about it first, and suggested to Alan that he offer his services.

`Have you heard they want someone to stay here over the weekends?' she asked him.

`Why's that?'

`It's in case of fire, or some such emergency,' Trina explained.

`They particularly want someone from the accounts department who'd know the most important records to save.'

`How many do they want?'

`Two or three, and I think you should volunteer,' Trina smiled and raised an eyebrow.

`And what about you?' he asked.

`Of course!' Trina grinned and added; `Aunt Margaret's being very self-sacrificing. She told me the other day that she feels she has a duty to provide me with a home, otherwise she'd go and live with her sister in Scotland until the war's over.'

`Did she now?'

`Yes, so I thought I'd make my own sacrifice - for her sake, of course.'

'Of course.'

They were sitting on a bench at the edge of the school playing fields. There was no moon, but it was a cold, cloudless night with a star filled sky. Trina's head was resting against Alan's shoulder and he had his arm around her waist.

`You know Miss Fitzwilliam, I suppose?' The question came quite suddenly after a few moments of silence.

`Miss Fitz?' Alan checked. `That large, rather puddeny girl who works with you?'

`That's unkind, but yes, that's the one.'

`What about her?'

`She lives on her own in a bed-sitter somewhere in the Earl's Court area. I know she'd like to move in here permanently and she'd make an excellent chaperone.'

`You reckon you need one?'

As Alan spoke, Trina twisted her head so that she could look into his face and see the familiar quizzical expression.

`No, but yes! For appearances as you might say,' she explained. `My family has hardly got over the shock of our holiday. Miss Fitzwilliam would be a salve for their sense of fitness, especially as our being here would be known to all the staff. I don't think Uncle Harry would agree to just the two of us living here. I can handle Mum, but if Uncle Harry says "No!" then that's the end of it.'

`Doesn't Uncle Harry know about us and the holiday?'

`He's never said anything, but then he wouldn't, would he? But of course he knows. Mum would be bound to tell him.'

`In that case, don't you think he'll object, even with Miss Fitz?'

`I don't think so,' Trina paused thoughtfully. `No, Uncle Harry's pragmatic. If he thought it'd reflect on the family then he'd stop it, but this way appearances are kept up. People may know, or guess, that we're having an "affair" but they'd never dream that my family knew all about it, and certainly wouldn't suspect them of condoning it.'

`Sounds like a great arrangement to me - if it comes off.'

Trina snuggled closer for warmth, and sneaked her hand inside Alan's jacket.

`I don't expect any difficulty. Uncle Harry's not the type to interfere in anyone's personal life if he can avoid it.'

As she had expected, Trina's family did their best to ignore the situation, and Alan organized himself into a convenient room just at the head of the stairs. Although there were two beds in the room, Jim, the other occupant, was never there at weekends. Jim was engaged, and would often make the long trip home in mid-week to see his fiancée. The female staff slept on the floor below, and when Jim was away Trina could easily creep up the short flight of stairs without being seen. Alan and Trina settled in to make the most of these new conditions.

During the weekends they saw little of Miss Fitzwilliam. She had a voracious appetite for romantic fiction, and spent her time reading. In warm weather she would sit out on the terrace, and when the weather turned cold would move to a comfortable chair in front of the fire.

The school was well equipped with tennis and squash courts, a swimming pool and even a gymnasium. Later, Southern Oceanic installed billiards and table tennis tables. Trina and Alan had no trouble filling their days with activity.

In sunshine and in rain they explored the countryside, walking many miles through the Vale of St Albans, or over towards the Chilterns, whose rounded silhouette beckoned against the skyline. When Alan had spare petrol they would drive out and climb the hills to enjoy the carpeted view spread below. They came to know and love this countryside, with its echoes of the continuity of life. There were constant reminders of Roman, Saxon, Elizabethan and other influences. They discovered that the Chilterns, with their surrounding vales, had drawn many poets and writers to live and work in their shelter.

Deliberately, they thought only of themselves, their own pleasures and their love. They tried to ignore the relentless pressure of the war. Alan was below call-up age and conscription was not a threat, but constantly in the background of his mind was the moral pressure to volunteer. All the same, during the winter of 1939, that winter of the phony war, he managed to ignore these twinges of conscience. There was only one incident that, for a few moments, seemed to threaten their relationship.

It happened when Alan mentioned that he had met a girl called Ann on the nights when he went ice-skating. This was the only activity he and Trina did not share and her reaction was immediate, interrupting him in mid sentence.

`So that's it, that's why you go ice-skating. I might have known. All right, if you want to go out with another girl that's fine, but don't expect me to be one of many.'

Trina was furious, and Alan, indignant at the accusation, snapped back.

`If that's what you think, suit yourself.'

`Oh!' Trina was seething with anger and Alan grabbed her hands fearing she would try to slap his face. The action, and the touch, brought him to a slightly calmer view.

`We've practised figure skating together,' he said bluntly.

`Oh!' This time the exclamation was slightly less violent, as Trina realized that she may have been a little hasty in her judgment.

`I only skate with Ann, but I make love with you.' Alan had recovered his balance and was smiling.

`Oh?' However, now the tone was mollified, and the familiar flick of humor had returned to her eyes.

`Is she attractive?' A suspicion of jealousy still showed in Trina's question, and Alan could not resist teasing her.

`Well,' he drawled the word as though considering, and then gave his judgment. `She hasn't got jockey's legs.'

`Pig!'

Trina tried to act huffily, but the situation was back to normal.

CHAPTER FOUR

The centipede was happy quite,
Until the toad in fun
Said `Pray which leg goes after which?'
And worked her mind to such a pitch
She lay distracted in a ditch,
Considering how to run
Mrs Edmund Craster

On the third Monday in October the 'Penguins' arrived. Southern Oceanic had arranged for coaches to bring most of their staff on this first occasion. The men, especially the 'Penguins', looked out of place as they walked up the gravel drive. In this setting of contoured lawns, trimmed hedges and ash trees, they intruded on the landscape, advancing in a phalanx of bowler hats, umbrellas and striped pants, self conscious and awkward with unaccustomed suitcases in hand. A rare individualist sported a black homburg.

On the periphery of each busload a flutter of the younger office girls chattered excitedly, but the older ladies formed a tight, disapproving band, their expressions showing that they expected, and were determined to find, the worst.

Apart from those who arrived in the coaches, there were some who traveled independently, using public transport and walking the final hundred yards from the bus stop. Among the last to arrive were a few 'King Penguins' driving their cars.

In those early war months there was a fair spread of age groups, but conscription and volunteering soon took their toll and the twenties group began to thin out. Not surprisingly, the younger people were able to cope with the change in their lives better than their elders. With a few exceptions, the senior ladies were spinsters of set habits who found it very hard to adapt, and appeared to find satisfaction in an attitude of martyrdom.

Late one evening, some two weeks after this influx, Trina and Alan were playing billiards. `Barton, Stephens and all that crowd are funny, aren't they?' Trina demanded Alan's corroboration.

`Define funny.'

`Don't be silly, you know what I mean. They try to go on behaving as though nothing has changed, as though they're still catching the 8.15 each morning.'

`Mentally I expect they are. They've been doing it for ever, most of them.'

Trina stood up and chalked the tip of her cue as she continued her theme.

`They come down to breakfast, dressed in their striped pants, and they're obviously embarrassed to meet each other over fried eggs and bangers. When they've finished breakfast, their conditioning tells them to put on their bowlers and set off to work. I think they'd feel better if they did. They could walk around the house and come back in through the front door. Perhaps they'd then feel the day had started in a right and proper manner.'

Alan, who had been laughing at Trina's vehemence, now took up her theme.

`Have you noticed they try to stick, rigidly, to the routine they've followed for years in London? Take Barton, for instance. At exactly quarter to five he leaves his desk to go to the washroom, just as he did in town. In London, when the clock hand moved to five, he'd reach over to lift his hat and umbrella off the hook. Now, his conditioned reflex looks for the familiar routine, but there's no hat, no umbrella and nowhere to go. He's not going home, so there's no train to catch, no stream of fellow commuters or rush hour scurry. All that's ahead is an evening of empty hours, and he's no idea of how to fill them.'

Trina finished her break and stood aside as Alan moved to the table.

`I've watched him too,' she said. `Have you noticed the remark he always makes?'

Alan postponed his next shot and imitated Barton's pursed-lips voice.

`I think I'll take a constitutional.'

Trina listened to the performance critically, and gave her judgment as Alan returned to the billiard table.

`He always fidgets first and gives a little cough before making that speech.'

She paused while Alan potted the red, then said, `Beast! That takes you over the hundred.'

`Another game?'

Trina shook her head. `Let's go for a walk.'

They left the gymnasium, holding hands as they strolled along the gravel path that led to the pavilion and the playing fields.

`That speech of Barton's,' Alan returned to the topic they had been discussing. `At least it gets him out of the office.'

Trina did not answer, and he thought she must have lost interest in the matter, then, after a short silence, she asked:

`I wonder why they persist in dressing the way they do, especially here in the country? I'd have thought most people would hate wearing look-alike clothes.'

Trina seemed genuinely puzzled and Alan agreed with her.

`Yes, I know. I'd hate it, but then I'd look ridiculous in a bowler hat, let alone the pants and jacket.'

`You look ridiculous in that stupid pork pie thing you wear.'

Trina was still pondering the merits of business dress, and her retort was an automatic reaction. Alan protested, but his indignation carried little conviction.

`What's wrong with it? It's a very fine hat.' And with scarcely a pause he continued;

`Anyway, there are lots of reasons why the Penguins dress the way they do.'

`Give me one good reason.'

`Well, first they can lose themselves in the anonymity of the multitude, and if I thought I was like most of them I'm sure I'd want to lose myself too.'

`That may be a reason, but I don't think it's a good one.'

`You're probably right. I can only give reasons, not good reasons.

Here's another. They've been brainwashed into believing it's the done thing. Just like the "white man's burden", the done thing is; well - the done thing.'

Trina laughed. `I might almost pass that one as a good reason.'

`Finally, by being look-alikes, no one can tell exactly what they do. They go off to work in the morning and return at night. Provided no one looks too closely at the shiny seat of his pants, Mrs Penguin can say, if anyone ever asks, "My husband? Oh, he's something in the City".'

They agreed that the most confirmed 'Penguin' was Barton, Mr Garrick Barton. The 'Penguins" lives had been disrupted and for some it would never be quite the same again. In particular, Garrick Barton could never have foreseen what the future held for him.

* * *

Alan came out of the past and back into the boat. A noise, or movement, had disturbed his thoughts. Perhaps it was John Allward who was snoring and obviously asleep, but it was difficult to be sure about the others. Every so often there was a soft scraping as someone shifted position, or it might be a cough. Generally all was quiet and even Blacklock had settled down.

Few clouds drifted across the sky, seen as occasional dark shadows that hid the distant stars as they passed overhead. Alan watched them for a few minutes then turned his attention from the sky and began the monotonous routine of scanning the horizon. The search was automatic, and allowed memories to creep back into his mind.

`What was I thinking about? Oh yes, Garrick Barton and the strange events at Barringdale in 1940.' He smiled into the darkness. `Sounds like the dust jacket of a mystery novel.'

* * *

But Garrick was not really a mystery: the motives behind his drama were old as life itself.

Garrick Barton was in his mid fifties when war broke out and Southern Oceanic asked him to take charge of the Freight Department at Barringdale. He took the appointment with a sense of satisfaction that his worth had been recognized. All the same, it was not really a promotion. For fifteen years he had been head clerk under the department's manager, Mr Grimsby, who had decided to continue working in the City, at least for the time being.

In London, Garrick Barton had been responsible for the day to day running of the freight office, and the new arrangement made no real change in his status. The only difference was one of distance. Mr Grimsby was now at the end of a telephone line, instead of at the end of a corridor. Garrick considered this a distinct improvement, as Mr Grimsby had an acid tongue and an uncertain temper.

`Besides,' he thought. `It shows confidence in me. They must think I can manage without someone to direct me all the time.'

When he arrived home that night he told Jean, his daughter, and her husband Fred:

`From now on I shall only be home at weekends. Southern Oceanic has put me in charge of the Freight Department at their emergency office. It's... ah... quite a feather in my cap.'

Garrick Barton dearly wished to impress Fred. For six years, ever since his wife died, Jean had looked after her father, but now there was Fred, a traveling hardware salesman, whom she had married.

After the honeymoon, Jean and her husband moved in to live with Garrick. With Fred in residence it did not feel like home, and it seemed to Garrick that he was no longer treated as the man of the house. It was Fred this, and Fred that.

`Fred will mow the lawn Dad. Fred will fix the sash cord. Fred!'

He was a lodger in his own home. At times they made him feel he was in the way and should find somewhere of his own to live. It therefore came as somewhat of a reprieve when he was sent to Barringdale and only had to go home at weekends. To his relief, when Fred was called up in March 1940 Garrick's visits home reverted to being almost like the old days. Once again there were the little jobs around the house, and it was just him and Jean again, with no Fred dominating the domestic scene.

During the weekdays at Barringdale, it was hard getting used to communal living. The only person he had ever shared a bedroom with was his wife, and sharing a room with two other men was embarrassing, even though one was Harry Stephens. Dressing and undressing in front of strangers; well, you could hardly call Harry a stranger but he had never spoken to the other man, Roger Dobson, before, except for business matters.

Then there were meals. For years he and Harry had shared a lunchtime table in a small city restaurant, and though they still sat together they were only two out of twenty at a long table. He felt awkward having to eat with men and women who were still no more than faces previously seen behind desks in other departments. In those first weeks at Barringdale he would watch the sky, dreading the possibility of rain. His problem was to keep himself occupied from the time he finished work until dinner was served.

The room where they sat at night was used during the day as an office, and was never rearranged until later in the evening. His solution, to go for a walk, was practical only in fine weather. His favorite walk took him to the far side of the school playing fields and into a narrow wooded strip of land that marked the boundary. This woodland, no more than forty feet wide, gave him a feeling of seclusion and a refuge from the outside world.

This was the way he felt in his own garden. In summer months, when he arrived home in daylight, he would spend a short while in the garden before mealtime. His wife had understood and would try to join him there for those few minutes. With her it had never been someone intruding into his private world, for Lottie had been part of that world.

Jean respected his desire to be by himself, but Fred was different. Fred would disturb his thoughts bringing brash conviviality to destroy the tranquil mood.

At Barringdale, when it rained, he had to mingle with the others who were waiting for the dinner bell. Upstairs, with nothing to do except sit on the edge of his bed, he felt foolish and undignified.

Downstairs, though constrained and awkward, he could at least maintain his dignity.

As Christmas approached, a more relaxed atmosphere began to build up. The girls no longer had to battle weather or the rush hour scramble, and this showed in their clothing. Now they wore more adventurous styles, and looked far more feminine and colorful than they had in town. The men, too, began to wear more informal styles.

Neither Garrick nor Harry felt comfortable in casual clothes. Sports jackets, polo neck pullovers and grey flannel trousers were something to wear on holiday, or at the weekend, never to the office. They remained somber, black-coated figures, looking more and more out of place as the days went by. It was not mere pig-headedness, but more that they feared to abandon the safe pattern of their lives. Standards were being attacked, and their outer shell was being stripped of its camouflage. Instead of giving anonymity, their formal dress now made them stand out from the throng.

Late in March, Harry arrived one Monday wearing a sports jacket and looking a little self-conscious. Garrick felt a sense of betrayal, but by now he had other things on his mind.

Since Lottie died he had never thought of any other woman in "that way". Well, perhaps there had been times when he allowed himself sexual fantasies but they had only been idle, dreamy thoughts. He had never for one moment considered making any direct approach to a woman, but now there were times when he seemed unable to think of anything else. The younger the girl the more she disturbed his senses, provoking erotic thoughts and leaving him hot with shame.

Each evening a fire was lit in the largest room, and the number of people seeking its comfort increased with the arrival of winter's chill. Garrick would find a place at the outskirts of the group around the fire and would settle down to read a book. A convention became established in which seats were left for the older people, and the younger ones, mostly girls, would sit on cushions inside the horseshoe of chairs. Already it was patriotic to save material by wearing short skirts, and many of the girls eagerly adopted this fashion.

Many evenings Garrick would catch himself reading the same paragraph over and over, failing to grasp its meaning, his eyes wandering to the girls who were arranged in a variety of poses on the floor. Some sprawled full length, others sat with hands clasped around their knees, but most favored lying on one side, legs curled up. Even with a cushion the floor was hard, and from time to time they would change position. At this stage of the war there was no shortage of nylon stockings, and Garrick found the smooth gleam of so many legs an irresistible temptation. When he sensed a movement, his eyes would search furtively. So often a girl would roll over, careless of modesty, seemingly unconscious of the flash of white thigh and taut suspender straps above her stocking tops.

The eagerness with which he anticipated these glimpses gave him an uneasy, guilty sensation, and a desperate longing to be accepted into the group. Beneath his remote and conventional exterior there was an insecure shyness. He tried to conceal his inadequacy behind a mask of self-sufficient composure.

* * *

Alan looked at the stars and tried to estimate the time. Dawn was still a long way off.

Those days at Barringdale were now far distant, yet Alan found them strangely near in time, though still distant in view. `Like looking the wrong way through a telescope,' he thought. He remembered sunlit days of delight, when he and Trina raced through tall grass to tumble into a tangle of arms and legs and laughter. Those moments of riotous bawdiness as they experimented with love, and Trina, in the snow, hurling snowballs at his head. Then later climbing into bed between ice cold sheets and clinging to each other for warmth until the chill was banished.

Trina's soft, husky voice saying `I love you', and the memory of his echoing answer.

`It must have been Spring 1940 when I was sent to Ocean Leader, on standby,' he thought. `I was away from Barringdale for about three weeks.'

* * *

Corncrake had been left with Trina, and she went to meet Alan at the station on his return. As they drove back to Barringdale he was brought up to date with the happenings of the last few weeks.

`You'll never guess. We've seen the last of the Penguins. Barton's finally given up his old plumage.'

`Did anyone recognize him?'

Trina laughed, and Alan realized just how much he had missed that low-toned laughter while he had been away.

`Just!' she said. `In fact he looked quite smart in a grey pin-striped suit.'

`Probably be another six months before he's game to wear a sports jacket.'

`I think he's trying to change in other ways too,'Trina continued. `He smiles more when someone speaks to him.' She moved fractionally, pressing a little nearer to Alan.

`I'm sure he's lonely,' she said, then explained; `While you've been away I've joined the crowd around the fire most evenings. Without you, I didn't feel like going to the Unicorn, even when some of the others went.'

Alan smiled and turned to glance at Trina.

`We'll go there tonight,' he suggested.

The Unicorn at Gallows Hill was their favorite pub, and the licensees were now counted as friends.

Trina nodded her agreement.

`Anyway,' she continued. `As I was saying, Barton's always in the big room every night, sitting just that little bit apart. I've noticed him sometimes, and I'm sure that often he's only pretending to read. He'll take a look around the room, and if he thinks anyone's watching him he'll pretend to be just resting his eyes, or turning a page or something. Then he'll bury his nose back into the book.'

It was true. Garrick had gone beyond just wanting to be accepted, and was reaching out, tentatively, hoping to make contact, but the slightest hint of rejection would freeze him into formality. On the other hand, a friendly word would produce a tendency to over expansiveness. He needed time to find the correct balance. The events of that summer were to unite the British people, and Garrick found that the stress of war helped him lower the barriers he had hidden behind for so many years.

Early June saw the defeat and withdrawal of the British armies from both France and Norway, and during the Dunkirk evacuation Alan was sent to one of the Company's ships. As on the previous occasion, he was only away from Barringdale a short time.

`This, is becoming a habit.'

Again, Trina was waiting for Alan when he stepped off the train, and had just been released from his greeting kiss.

`I'd call it a pleasant obsession,' Alan suggested as he bent to pick up his suitcases.

`Idiot! I meant meeting you at the station.'

Alan grinned at her happily. `How's everything here?' he asked.

`A few more men have been called up, and a couple of girls have left to join the women's services. Otherwise everything's much the same.'

`Barton bought himself any casual clothes yet?'

Trina laughed. `No, he hasn't gone that far, but he's certainly coming out of his shell.'

`Why? What's he doing now?'

`He doesn't sit apart so much, and he joins in the general talk.'

Trina considered for a moment before continuing.

`I think it was when most of us began to wait up for the late news bulletins that he really thawed out. After listening to the news, we'd go on talking, and he started to take quite a leading part in the discussions.'

Again Trina and Alan became onlookers. Secure in their relationship they could stand apart, and watch the intrigues that were going on; the liaisons, the jealousies, and among them the events that were leading Garrick Barton to become a willing, though unwitting, instrument of his own destruction.

* * *

Garrick Barton looked affectionately at the ivy-covered walls of Barringdale. It was good to be back after the weekend, for Fred had been home on leave. It was unfeeling, he supposed, to be so uncharitable about Fred, especially now he had been wounded and had returned from Dunkirk. Still, once again, Fred was the man of the house and with the added aura of a wounded hero. Garrick had to face the fact that he was jealous of Fred; jealous of the man who had taken first place in his daughter's affections.

Strange how he had hated Barringdale at first. Now it seemed more like home to him than his own house. He called greetings to several people, and was genuinely pleased to see them after the weekend. He knew them better now and was sincerely interested in what they had been doing. They, in turn, seemed glad to see him, asking after his daughter and her back-from-the-war husband. He could hardly credit how isolated he had felt here no more than three months ago.

He was less embarrassed with the girls now, not so guilty and furtive about looking at them. There were even times when he managed a few gallantries and flattering remarks. The girls, he discovered, did not object. One even told him;

`You really are quite a dear, aren't you?'

All the same, there were surreptitious affairs going on that made him feel uncomfortable. Some, he was sure, were more than mere flirtations. Even Harry spent more time with one twenty-year-old girl than was proper for a married man of Harry's years. When he remonstrated, Harry had laughed at him.

`Why don't you do the same? Scared you'll get trapped by one of the old harpies who's after a husband?' Harry grinned wickedly then added; `I know. Kate Headly, she'd be just right, pretty and married too. You'd be quite safe there.'

`Don't be ridiculous!' Garrick snapped, and stalked away angrily.

Harry's flippancy was made worse by the fact that Kate Headly was one of the girls who had caught his eye. Her husband had been injured in a car accident the previous year, and had been in an iron lung ever since. Kate went to see her husband each weekend, but he was filled with self-pity and her visits had become a tiresome duty.

Garrick was sorry for Kate, but knew she was now finding comfort with a clerk from his own department.

Living in close proximity was having its effect. Most of the men were married but some did not let this trouble them, and were encouraged by a few of the girls. The young single couples who had formed attachments did not trouble Garrick. It was the secret, illicit sex he disliked, and yet the sensual atmosphere aroused and tormented him. There was a dreadful fascination that made him want to be a part of it, and he found himself regularly stopping to talk to Brenda Holroyd. If the chair beside her was vacant it became natural for him to take it, and she in turn appeared to welcome his company. Garrick felt a pleasant warmth when he anticipated evenings to be shared with Brenda.

Brenda was older than most of the young typists, and yet a long way from becoming a career spinster. She was a mature twenty-nine, of comfortable appearance and with a good pair of legs. When he looked at her critically, Garrick had to admit that Brenda was over plump around the waist, but she did possess what he could only think of as "a magnificent bosom".

She, he was sure, had no idea of the effect she had on him. At times, when sitting together, Brenda would lean over to whisper in his ear. On these occasions he could feel her breast pressed against his arm, her scent in his nostrils and the soft brushing of her thick brown hair against his cheek. Confused by these sensations, Garrick would become tongue-tied and stammer some vague reply to her comment. To his mind, her casual, accidental touch was all innocence, and Brenda seemed amazed when Garrick mentioned his married daughter, refusing to believe he was no longer in his forties. `You don't look a day over forty-five,' she had said, and Garrick went to bed that night feeling much younger than his fifty-seven years.

* * *

France had fallen by the next time Alan returned to Barringdale, and it was to be several months before he was appointed to another ship.

When the bombing of London started, the searchlights could be seen and the guns heard, but it was rare for any plane to stray in the direction of Barringdale. In October the Luftwaffe changed its tactics, and for several nights in succession planes droned overhead. The basement at Barringdale consisted of a large central room, with narrow doorways leading to small rooms on either side. Southern Oceanic had strengthened the basement with timber supports, and insisted all staff go to these shelters during an air raid.

The first night the sirens sounded everyone trooped downstairs in their night attire, and Trina and Alan were astonished by the open intimacy of some of the married men with single girls. They were aware of what had been going on, but were still surprised by the blatancy and lack of discretion.

The cellars were lit by a dim red light, just sufficient to be able to see where to tread with safety, yet not bright enough to interfere with sleep. The bulb was in the centre basement, and little light filtered through to the other rooms. The areas furthest from the light became the precincts of passion. In this gloom, only indistinct shapes could be seen, but it was not hard to guess what was happening. With each air raid the atmosphere became more orgiastic.

On the night of the fourth raid, Trina and Alan were sitting in the main room, with their backs resting against the wall. They could hear muffled sounds, and half-stifled gasps from the next room.

`It's disgusting!' Trina whispered.

`Is it? We've been known to do that sort of thing.'

Trina jabbed Alan in the ribs.

`Not in public.'

`Perhaps not,' Alan agreed. `But they probably all guess what we get up to.'

`At least our behavior's only immoral, not adulterous.'

`My! We are righteous tonight,' Alan teased, and felt an indignant shrug.

Trina lapsed into an offended silence, and Alan waited a little while before taking up the conversation.

`You're right, I think, but our love isn't immoral.'

There was enough light where they were sitting for him to see her swift smile.

`I don't know about that,' she said. `It's certainly very enjoyable but I doubt if my mother would agree.'

`Agree about what? That it's enjoyable?'

`No! About not being immoral you idiot.'

`You had me worried for a moment,' Alan grinned. `Anyway, immoral's the wrong word.'

They were keeping their voices down to a bare whisper so as not to be overheard.

`Explain: what is the right word?' Trina commanded.

`Amoral,' Alan replied. `I'm sure that's a better word to use. It's largely a question of attitude, frame of mind that is. Amoral is a deliberate non-acceptance of convention, whereas immorality disobeys the convention and probably feels guilty in doing so. Do I make myself clear?'

`Sounds impressive. I'm sure you know what you're talking about.'

Alan was well aware that Trina was laughing at him, but having mounted his soapbox he intended to finish.

`Even if we made physical love just for the sheer fun and pleasure of the act, it could be classified as amoral, provided that was the standard we accepted. However, if there were any pretence, one to the other, then it would be immoral. Pretence or deception can't be part of any standard, moral or amoral. Anyway, what we do can't possibly be called immoral as we do it with love, physical and mental, and with no feeling of guilt.'

`I won't argue with that,' Trina agreed.

`Fortunately it's the only thing you don't argue about,' Alan retorted.

Trina sniffed, then demanded; `Why can't deception be any part of a standard?'

`Simple, if you make it standard that you deceive each other, then if you do deceive the other person you are only doing what is expected of you. Therefore you aren't deceiving that person and you aren't obeying the standard. You can only obey the standard by not deceiving. On the other hand, if not deceiving is the standard . . .'

`All right, all right!' Trina held up her hands in mock surrender. `I'm convinced. Both "not deceiving" and "deceiving" can only be kept by not deceiving.'

A squeal, followed by suppressed laughter, came from the next room.

`My God! They're the end.'

Trina's whisper contained a vast air of disapproval. Then she murmured;

`Just imagine what Boccacio could have made of this set up.'

* * *

In one corner of the shelter, Garrick Barton sat primly beside Brenda Holroyd. He had insisted that she take his blanket as well as her own.

`I don't need it, really I don't,' he told her. `My dressing gown is heavy wool and I'll be quite warm enough, probably too hot with the blanket.'

`Are you sure Garrick? I feel bad about taking it. Would you, I mean, couldn't we share it?'

Brenda lifted up one side of the blanket, inviting him to move closer so that it would cover them both. It was an invitation Garrick found hard to resist. She was really very thoughtful and kind, but people might get the wrong idea. They would not know how innocent she was.

Barton had heard the noises from the small rooms. He was shocked, and hoped that Brenda did not realize what was going on. The shameless sounds of sex play disgusted him, yet were exciting, and he clenched his fists, as he thought of Brenda in her thin wrap and nightdress. Hidden beneath that blanket he could, perhaps, have fondled that magnificent bosom. Garrick caught his breath with an audible hiss.

Brenda turned to him, startled.

`Is anything the matter, my dear?' she asked.

The words were spoken with such concern that, at first, he did not appreciate her exact words, not, that is, until well after he had reassured her.

That night it was less than an hour before the "all clear" sounded. Most of the staff returned to their beds, but some stayed in the shelter long after the rest had departed.

Garrick said goodnight to Brenda on the landing of the women's quarters and went, thoughtfully, to his own bed. He had little sleep that night. He must decide what his true feelings were for Brenda, and what hers might be for him. Had she meant it when she called him "my dear"? Had it been no more than a slip of the tongue? Probably it meant nothing. There was a shop assistant, where he bought his Sunday newspaper, who always called him "love" as she handed out his change. "My dear" might only be Brenda's way of showing friendship.

Did he love Brenda? There was something more than just wanting to touch her: he was sure of that. If he married Brenda he would be master in his house again. He was sorry for Jean, but she and Fred would have to find a place of their own. Brenda sharing his home, sharing his bed. He moved impatiently under the bedclothes. The picture was too vivid, too disquieting, and too attractive.

* * *

A fortnight later Garrick Barton and Brenda Holroyd announced their engagement.

`She's a selfish bitch!' Trina was emphatic. `None of the girls like her and they say she's twisted that poor man around her finger. One of them, who's known her for years, says she's been engaged twice before.'

`So what?' Alan asked.

'She's quite sure Brenda never broke off either engagement. She reckons the men must have woken up before it was too late.'

`Sure it's not general cattishness?'

`I don't think so. It's the way she's been behaving. She doesn't seem happy, in the sense of being in love. It's more like a triumphant happiness. She showed me her engagement ring this morning as though it were a trophy. She had the air of a cat with the cream.'

`I wouldn't think Barton was all that much of a catch for any girl.'

`You're wrong you know.' Trina was emphatic. `That's not the way Brenda would look at it.'

`Why? How would she look at it?'

`Well, for a start she's nearly thirty, and must have been wondering whether she'd ever marry. Without being catty you must admit she's not a beauty, and all she's ever achieved in the marriage stakes is a couple of near misses.'

`Even so?'

`Yes, even so. From what she said this morning, Barton owns his own home, and you should have seen how smug she looked. Then, as Head Clerk he's on a good salary, and he's been with the Company long enough to get a pension on retirement. When he dies she'll still get half of that, and I'll bet that Barton has a few quid in a savings account. He's one of the careful sort who spend their lives putting something away for a rainy day.'

`You never know. She may make him very happy.' Trina's answer was a disbelieving snort.

Garrick and Brenda were married at Christmas and Garrick returned to Barringdale the second week in January. Harry and a few others tried to pull his leg about his newly married status, but he did not enter into the spirit of their jesting. No one paid particular attention to this as Garrick was not noted for his sense of humor.

He left Barringdale as usual the following Friday and they never saw him again. He did not arrive for work on Monday morning, and someone remarked that he must be too exhausted after a busy weekend.

On the Tuesday morning they heard that his body had been recovered from the Thames.

The verdict was suicide.

CHAPTER FIVE

Light breaks where no sun shines;
Where no sea runs, the waters of the heart
Push in their tides.
Dylan Thomas

Alan sat at the tiller and looked at Jim Bristow who was, apparently, asleep. Alan and Jim had taken an instant dislike to each other the first time they met. The reason probably lay in the difference between their backgrounds, but there was also a conflict of temperaments. Alan tended to be flippant, taking few matters seriously, while Jim was intense and dogmatic in argument. Secretly, Jim envied Alan's ability to join in conversations that covered a wide range of topics. Apart from seamanship, his education had been very narrow.

* * *

Jim Bristow grew up in a suburban, semi-detached house in Burnham on Crouch. He was an only child and his upbringing was left almost entirely to his mother. He was lucky that she was a solid, no nonsense woman with plenty of common gumption, as she would have described herself. Her husband was a seaman, as was her unmarried brother. Her father and grandfather had also been seamen, so she had no illusions about the life of a seaman's wife. The lonely months with a young child as her only company she accepted as the natural order of things. You never found Mrs Bristow complaining about being deserted. She faced the world, hands on hips, and would set it to rights if need be. Her man supported them by going to sea, and that was that.

Jim's childhood seemed, in retrospect, to consist of long uneventful stretches, punctuated by the sudden arrival of his father or his uncle. For a few days the house would be in a turmoil of male laughter, tobacco smoke and excitement. Then it would be back to routine, with only an exotic present from some foreign country as a reminder of the visit.

There was never any doubt what Jim would be when he grew up. His father was Bos'n in a foreign going vessel, and insisted that Jim went to a maritime college. When Jim finished his cadet-ship, his Dad spoke to the Marine Superintendent of the shipping line he had served for so many years, and Jim was soon following the family tradition by joining one of the firm's tramp ships as Third Mate. He was the first of his family to go to sea as an officer, and Jim discovered that there were some disadvantages to sailing in ships where his father had been Bos'n. After two years he applied for jobs with several shipping companies, and when Southern Oceanic offered him a position he accepted immediately. Jim soon found that he was now faced with a new set of problems. On board a cargo ship dress had not been important and language tended to be frank and basic. In a passenger ship, Jim was expected to mix with people from all levels of society, and it was here he felt inadequate. His education had not prepared him to discuss such matters as music, politics, drama and other dinner table topics. He was trained in seamanship, not social chitchat.

In time, if he had been prepared to listen and learn, he might have been able to adapt. Instead he tried too hard, and attempted to cover his deficiencies with bluff. In doing this he developed a slightly pompous manner. Yet beneath his bluster Jim was unsettled and uncertain of himself.

* * *

A dusting of spray against his cheek startled Alan back to awareness, and he looked around in surprise.

`Must have been some freak movement of the boat,' he thought.

There was now the faintest suggestion of a breeze, but not enough to ruffle the water or alter the character of the long swell. Could it be the first hint of a change in the weather? Without rain they could not last much longer, and during the previous twenty-four hours they had watched scattered rain clouds with desperation. While these rainsqualls continued there was hope, but if they cleared...?

Alan and Jim had been surprised at how well they had got on together while in the boat. It was the circumstances that made all the difference; there was no room for petty argument and they had been forced to learn more about each other.

`Jim can't have found it easy,' Alan thought.

No one found it easy to deal with the arrogance of the Ticket Snobs, the people who bought affectation with their first class cabins.

Alan looked towards the eastern skyline, and now he was sure there was a change; no brightness yet but there seemed to be a fraction more definition at the border between sky and sea. The stars were shining brightly except in the west, which could only mean that clouds were building up in that direction.

Jim Bristow climbed to his feet and stretched. Although awake for the last hour he had remained quiet, and had noticed Alan's concentration on the sky. Alan, who was still looking to the west, heard the movement.

`Looks to be a bit of cloud building up Jim.'

`Hope so. It's our only chance.'

There was nothing dogmatic now in Jim's voice. The strain and anxiety could be heard, and there was no need to add anything to his remark. Almost thirty-six hours had passed since they had finished their water. The last drops were shared in the evening, and for the whole of the previous day they had been without water. It was not long before thirst became all-important.

`How will we get through the day?' Alan wondered. `It's bad enough now and it'll be worse when the sun gets up. We can't last long without water. It must be hell for Blacklock: thirst as well as the pain from his injuries. Best if he stays unconscious.'

* * *

In 1917 Terry Blacklock had been old enough to remember the telegram coming that said his father had been killed in France. His mother had stood, eyes wide open as she accepted the meaning of the words she had just read. Then came the sudden crumpling of her body as she fell to the floor, and the brightness of sunlight with the hard pavement beneath his bare feet as he raced to his grandmother's house for help.

Six months later his mother married again. Mervyn, his stepfather, was much older than his true father. He was a quiet, thoughtful man who was very kind to Terry, but his health was poor and during the time Terry knew him he was always, more or less, ill. Each morning Mervyn would go downstairs to open the doors of his small shop, while Terry's mother hurried through her housework and, at the same time, made sure her son was getting ready for school. When Terry had left she would go down and help Mervyn in the shop.

The war had been long ended, and Terry's school days nearly finished when Mervyn was taken to hospital for the last time. During the next few weeks Terry's mother ran the tiny green-grocery as best she could. Every night she went to the hospital, and each night would come home with her eyes red from weeping. One day she broke the news to Terry that his stepfather was dead.

For a few months they lingered on in the apartment above the shop, but without Mervyn the business was losing money. Even before Mervyn was taken to hospital the profit had been barely enough to keep them. The business was put up for sale and the day came when they had to leave.

For a couple of months they had enough money to get by, but when that was gone Terry's mother started going out in the evenings; and there were many nights when she came home with a man. The few shillings Terry earned as a delivery boy would not even pay the rent for their two small rooms. On those nights he would lie on a mattress under the kitchen table, curled up in impotent despair as he listened to the sounds from the adjoining room.

* * *

The small sounds of water lapping against the lifeboat nagged at Alan, reinforcing his body's craving for moisture. He tried to dull his mind by thinking of far off times and places, but with no success.

Alan was not the only one. The others, also, were watching the sky intently, seeing the stars fade as light spread upward from the horizon. The brightness was reaching out to the clouds, touching them with the rising glow of dawn. The change came gradually, from black to pink, to grey. Stealthily the sun crept up; creating a sparkling pathway that stretched towards them in a blaze of blinding light.

As the pink vanished, the clouds became a roiling mass of white and dark grey. Clouds, those all-important clouds. Now they could be seen clearly and their need drove them to watch anxiously. There, and there, and there, they were spilling rain in scattered curtains like wind-blown veils, misting down and breaking the line of the horizon.

`Be a while yet Alan,' Jim waved vaguely towards the nearest rain cloud.

Alan could only nod. He was too dry to speak. They had seen this sight before; and the rain had passed them by each time. Yesterday there had been rainsqualls in every direction, yet not a drop had fallen into the boat. Today might well be their last chance and Alan tried to concentrate, willing the clouds to move over them, but unbidden thoughts crowded relentlessly into his mind;

`Sun's getting up, I can feel its warmth and at this moment it's pleasant after the cold of the night; but we could do without it. We need to save every drop of moisture... if they hadn't sent us south we might be freezing up north... 'If we'd gone north we might've been on our way home by now. We've always gone north before... probably doesn't matter, it was just our turn, our luck changed. 'Which is easier? Dying of thirst or freezing to death? That argument standing around a bar. The bar was a comfortable place to discuss the merits of freezing, drowning and thirst. 'We decided thirst would be the worst. Could have been right. 'Those damn rainsqualls aren't getting any nearer... If we could get water... We've still got food. What's Jim doing? He's showing Huskins, Mahoney and Queenie how to hold the jib if we get rain.

'We've been through this time and again; everyone knows what to do. Len's looking really angry.'

`Christ! We're not kids!'

`Now Jim's upset... At least he's showing some sense and backing off. It's no use arguing with Len. Think I'll move into the bow before Jim comes back. He'll want to talk about it and I don't feel like talking.

`There that's better... Jim's sulking. Glad I moved.

`We're missing opportunities, minute by longing minute. Why the hell doesn't the rain come this way? Every bloody time it slips past and manages to miss us. Jesus! One time we could even hear the rain as it swept past, and all we got was half a dozen lousy drops. Half a dozen... bloody... useless drops.

`It's deliberate, it's got to be... It couldn't possibly happen like that... There must be some malignant force... some Olympian bastard steering the rain away.

`My God! Look at this one... It's coming. Please... Don't let it miss.

`I'm going to close my eyes... If I don't look... don't look... don't dare look!

`It's close... A breath of moist wind and I can hear it...

`It's raining!'

`Someone's trying to cheer... It's raining. At last it's raining.'

There was hardly any wind, just the beautiful hiss of rain, and Alan was content to sit in the bow a little distant from the others, so that he could listen and feel undisturbed. Listen to that wonderful sound whispering across the surface of the sea, and the even more satisfying sound as the heavy drops hit the stretched, taut jib. It was glorious, and his body was a sponge sucking up the freshness of sweet water.

They sat with faces turned to the sky as if in mute adoration, all except Jim who was guiding a stream of water into the drum. The rain battered their faces, trickling into mouths eager for the taste of clean moisture.

Alan realized that his shirt was soaking wet.

`Take it off and wring it out . . . it tastes of sweat and salt.'

And then the rain was gone; and it was all over.

Len was the first to laugh, and suddenly everything seemed hysterically funny. The rain had come... It had really come.

Alan looked back and saw that Jim was checking the drum and with an effort brought himself under control.

`How much did we get Jim?'

`About half full.'

`Damn!' Alan had thought it would have been more. Then, with a sudden surge of optimism, he wondered whether their luck had changed. Perhaps it would rain again. Perhaps they might yet fill the drum.

The excitement was gone, and they felt empty and somehow let down. It had been magnificent while it lasted, but now it was finished and they were wet and cold.

`What's Queenie doing?' Alan saw him bend over Blacklock.

Obviously something was wrong.

Queenie called Con Mahoney to come and take a look.

While it rained Con had joined Joe Hayter who had been sitting all morning, head bowed, silent and dazed. Queenie stayed with Blacklock and when the rain came had held his hands over Terry's eyes to protect them, allowing the water to run off his fingers on to Terry's face and into his mouth.

Con Mahoney stared at Blacklock for nearly a minute. At last he stood up, and there was really no need for Queenie to say;

`He's gone. He died while it was raining.'

Queenie's voice was quite calm, and Joe Hayter still looked bewildered, but there was nothing calm about little Mahoney's acceptance. He had turned outboard as if actually facing an enemy.

`You bastards! You shit-ridden lousy bastards!'

His gaze was fixed far and away over the sea. Then he turned and looked around the boat as if seeing each of his companions for the first time.

`Well, what are we waiting for? Let's get him over the side. The poor sod won't grudge us the extra space.'

Mahoney went to Blacklock's feet and signaled to Queenie.

`Give us a hand Queenie.'

For once his voice was soft.

No one said a word as they lifted the body and rested it on one of the thwarts. Mahoney gave the word.

`Now!'

`Hardly a splash,' Alan thought. `Twenty minutes ago that was Blacklock. Now it's a body...

`He's not sinking... Wait a minute, I think he's going under now.

I'm not going to look... The others aren't looking either.

`Oh God! What's Mahoney on about now?'

`I wish I could lay my hands on the bastards who did this to us!'

Joe Hayter had slumped down even further, and Alan wondered whether he even realized that Blacklock was dead? Joe was watching Mahoney, listening to what he was saying, his face blank and expressionless.

`All we do is sail around the world, a bloody great target for every fucking U-boat and stinking aircraft. Think of those bloody Germans. They'll be back in port now. What's the odds the bastards are pouring out champagne and singing "Deutschland up the Allies, we sank a big one this time. Heil sodding Hitler". Christ! In the bloody Navy you've at least got a chance of fighting back.'

Hayter, Mahoney and Blacklock... Inseparable shipmates, they were an institution in Ocean Monarch. Noise, laughter, friendly abuse and argument raged around them - Holy Joe, Horrible Con and Terrible Terry. It would have been unusual to see one without finding the other two nearby.

The wind was getting up a bit, and the movement of the boat became unpredictable. These facts Alan noticed automatically; but his mind was wandering again, thinking about the ship and those three.

Joe Hayter was the one who had really changed since the sinking. In spite of his pain Blacklock had been the hard, controlled man he had always been and they had been amazed at how long he had survived. Perhaps his injuries had not been quite as bad as they had thought. Mahoney though, he was no different, still a waspish little termagant.

Joe's morale had gone completely. He now looked pathetic, and he had always been so majestic with his nineteen stone starched into white smock and hat. All semblance of former authority had gone and his vast bulk slumped dejectedly. The flesh of his face and the fat of his body sagged wearily. He no longer responded to Mahoney's baiting, but every so often he shook his head slowly and the heavy jowls moved in an independent counterpoint of rhythm. He was the only one who did not look more cheerful since the rain... No; he was not the only one. Mahoney, too, was looking grim. Not surprising, Blacklock's death would have upset them.

Rapley and Basil Allward had certainly cheered up, and had even been talking about what they would do when they got home.

`What will I do if we get home?' Alan wondered. `See Trina, I suppose, and try to get things sorted out... I wish we could go back to those Barringdale days and start all over again.'

* * *

`Trina! I'm going to see if I can get into the RAF.'

It was January 1940, and Alan's conscience was troubling him. He could put off a decision no longer, not if he wanted to retain any self-respect.

Alan and Trina had just returned from a walk across the playing fields. It had snowed heavily overnight, leaving a two inch layer on the grass and their footprints trailed them in the otherwise smooth surface. There were only three people at Barringdale over the weekend and the third, Miss Fitzwilliam, was curled up in front of the fire lost in romantic fiction.

Trina and Alan had shed their coats and were perched on a table in the kitchen, waiting for the kettle to boil.

`I suppose you must, if you feel you have to,' Trina replied. `But why the RAF?'

`The army leaves me cold, so it has to be the Navy or the Air Force.'

`All right, but why the RAF?'

`Simple! The Navy goes roaming all over the world, but with the Air Force there's a fair chance of being based in England. That means I'd be able to see you occasionally.'

`Is that really the reason?'

`Can you doubt it? Anyway I'd like to learn to fly.'

`Now the truth comes out.'

`What do I have to do to convince you woman?'

`Make the tea, the kettle's boiling. I'll get the cups.'

A couple of weeks later Alan reported at Cardington for his interview and medical.

The interview was easy. There were the expected questions and Alan was accepted for training as Pilot/Navigator, subject to passing the medical. The one thing that had never occurred to Alan was that he might fail the medical. He was fit, and proud of it. However, to his shock, he was failed on a color vision defect. That night, somewhat shamefaced, Alan returned to Barringdale.

The vision defect ruled out any executive job in the Navy. With his school OTC training he could be sure of an early commission in the Army, but Alan felt he was not temperamentally suited to a soldier's life. He doubted whether his sense of humor would coincide with the Army's, as he explained to Trina.

`I've never trusted the Army since the day I landed in trouble for laughing, when no normal person had any option but to laugh. Anyone, that is, except the Army in the person of our Commanding Officer.'

Trina delicately raised an eyebrow.

`All right,' she said, `I'll buy it.'

Alan grinned back at her.

`It concerns a Major Craddock, retired from the Regular Army, who'd taken the part time appointment as Commanding Officer of our school OTC, and who prefaced the pearls of wisdom permitted to fall from his lips with a "Hooo!". This sound he produced from the very depths of his diaphragm. He'd a passion for TEWTs, and in case you get the wrong impression that stands for - tactical exercise without troops. He'd either use the sand table in his office, or take a select few of us to some distant hill in his ancient Ford. With a captive audience he'd expound, while we stood patiently eyes glazed and participating to the least of our ability. On this occasion some idiot decided to show a little interest, and asked a question about revolvers. The fact of a question being asked at all must have startled me into awareness; anyway I heard the gallant Major's reply.

"Hooo!" he said with more than usual gusto. "A revolver does more harm to yourself and other people than to anybody else."' Alan looked at Trina and grinned. 'Now I ask you, doesn't that remark justify hilarity?'

Trina had already burst into laughter but managed to say:

`Well... It would go a long way towards it.'

`Not in Major Craddock's eyes it didn't. To this day I doubt if he understands why I was laughing, and I made matters worse by saying: "I thought you were making a joke, Sir". He glared at me. "I never joke about serious matters such as handling weapons." Then he awarded me three extra parades as punishment.'

`I doubt if all Army officers are like that.' Trina was still laughing.

`It's a risk I'm not prepared to take, and that's final.'

It was all very well to joke about it, but Alan knew he had to make some decision. He could, of course, do nothing and wait for his call-up, but then he'd have to go wherever he was sent. The alternative was to volunteer and take his fate into his own hands; but volunteer for what? If he ruled out the Army he was left with only two choices: a ground job in the Air Force or something other than an executive job in the Navy. Hanging around an aerodrome would hardly be an exciting way to spend the war. It would have to be the Navy. As he told Trina:

`Volunteering's not being heroic or anything stupid like that. It's a very practical affair. At least it means having some small say in my destiny.'

Afterwards, Alan wondered whether it was just coincidence that Mr Carstairs, the senior executive at Barringdale, spoke to him a few days later and asked what he intended to do now that he had failed to get into the RAF. The question seemed so natural that Alan thought nothing of it at the time, and replied that he was thinking of trying for the Navy. Later, he remembered that Mr Carstairs was distantly related to the Marsdens. Trina was quite capable of a little behind-the-scenes manipulation. Although he never asked her, Alan sometimes wondered. Not that it mattered, as the final decision was his.

The day after that casual question Mr Carstairs sent a message for Alan to come and see him.

'Take a seat Alan,' he said when Alan entered his office. Unlike other executives, Mr Carstairs made a point of knowing, and using, the Christian names of everyone on the staff. 'I've been thinking about what you told me. Are you very keen on joining the Navy?'

Alan shrugged. 'Now that flying is out it doesn't matter too much, but I think I'd prefer the Navy to the Army.'

'What would you say to going away in one of the Company's ships?'

'I've never thought about it, Sir.'

'Well, think it over and let me know. Before long we're going to be short an Assistant Purser. Some ships haven't returned to England since the war started, and quite a few officers, including Pursers and Assistant Pursers, are in the Navy Reserve. They'll be called up when their ships arrive back. Then we'll be looking for extra staff.'

'Thanks very much for the suggestion, Sir. I'll certainly think about it.'

'Yes Alan, do that and let me know in the next day or so.' Alan was about to leave the office when Mr Carstairs called him back.

'If you do go into the Navy, there's a good chance you'll end up as a Paymaster. It's much the same job as you'd be doing in one of our ships, in wartime anyway, when there are no paying passengers.'

As Alan was again about to leave he added;

'Don't think it's a safe, cushy job. There's as much danger sailing in a merchantman as in the Navy, even more perhaps.'

'I realize that, Sir.'

'It could have its advantages. What you'd learn in one of our ships might help you after the war. I often feel there's not enough interchange between the shore and sea staff. It's worth considering.'

'Yes Sir, and thank you very much.'

Later, because of his friendship with Trina and thinking about the last remark by Mr Carstairs, Alan wondered whether the Marsden family was keeping a speculative eye on him.

That evening he told Trina what Mr Carstairs had suggested.

`Do you think it's a good idea?' she asked.

`I don't see anything against it. If I can't do what I want then this is as good as, probably better than, any job I'd get in the Navy.'

`You're going to take it then?'

`All right, I've made up my mind. Let's go out to the pub and celebrate. I'll see Mr Carstairs in the morning and break the glad tidings to him.'

The decision was made, but it was a long time before Alan was given a permanent appointment, and it was three months later before Mr Carstairs sent for him.

`Alan, you're to join Ocean Leader as a temporary replacement. The Assistant Purser has been sent to hospital with appendicitis. It's possible you may do a voyage in her, but if so it's likely to be a short one, no more than a few days. Curzon could well be out of hospital and back on duty before the ship leaves. You're only going up there on stand-by and won't be signed on, not unless the ship actually sails.'

`When do I leave?'

`You'll have to catch the early train from London tomorrow. Ocean Leader was in Scapa, but we've just been told she's on her way to the Firth of Forth. As soon as you get to Edinburgh, contact our agents and they'll see that you get on board.'

Alan checked the train times, and found that he would have to go to London that afternoon in order to catch the early train to Edinburgh next morning. At lunchtime he collected Trina, and took her across to the gymnasium where they could expect to be alone.

`I've got to leave this afternoon.'

`Why? What do you mean?'

`I'm going to Ocean Leader as a temporary replacement.'

`You can't be! They'd give you more notice than that.'

`Afraid not, the Assistant Purser's been carted off to hospital with appendicitis. I'm only going there until he gets back.'

`Suppose the ship sails before he gets back?'

`If she does it won't be a long voyage, or so Mr Carstairs says. I'd lay odds she's to make a trip to Norway.'

`What makes you think that?'

`Apparently she was up in Scapa, though what she'd be doing there I don't know. Anyway, I'm to join her in the Firth of Forth. She'd never be on the East Coast of Scotland unless she's to operate in the North Sea. Norway's the only place she could be going. According to the news broadcasts we've already got troops fighting there.'

`It's so sudden. I can't believe it's happening.'

Trina looked at him, her eyes wide with shock from the unexpected news, and neither of them knew quite what to say. They kissed, and Alan felt her hand clutch at his arm more tightly than usual. There was no time for long farewells.

`It won't be for long. I'll leave Corncrake with you.'

Trina nodded.

`I must go and pack,' Alan told her. `Can you arrange time off to run me down to the station?'

Again Trina nodded. `How long before you're ready?'

`About a quarter of an hour. I think I should go home and let my parents know what's happening, just in case I'm still on board when the ship sails.'

They separated, and Trina was waiting when he came downstairs with his suitcase. On the way, in the car and at the station, they said very little. Alan reached across and they held hands, the gentle pressure more eloquent than any words they could have spoken.

Trina did not linger at the station nor come to the platform. There were still ten minutes before the train left, but they both needed to get the farewell over quickly and cleanly.

`Look after Corncrake for me.' The words reminded Alan and he reached for his wallet. `I nearly forgot,' he said. `The petrol coupons; you'll need them. He's getting low.'

`I know how he feels.' Trina's words were rueful as she took the coupons.

`Not to worry. I'll be back soon.'

One quick kiss and Trina was walking out of the station. Alan picked up his bag and made his way to the platform. However it was indeed a short trip for him: as luck would have it, it was no more than a fortnight before he returned to Barringdale. Assistant Purser Curzon had rejoined the ship before she sailed.

Alan's next posting came only a few weeks later, when he was sent to join Ocean Wanderer at Southampton. The British army had fallen back to Dunkirk and the future seemed so very uncertain. This time he had a little more notice - two days. He was to join the ship permanently, not just as a temporary replacement. Mr Carstairs gave him the news on a Friday afternoon, and this meant that Alan and Trina had the Saturday and Sunday together before he had to leave. As usual they had Barringdale to themselves, except for Miss Fitzwilliam.

Much of those two days was spent beside the swimming pool. It was nearly midsummer and the weather perfect. On the Sunday afternoon they were sitting at the edge of the pool, their feet dangling in the water as they talked.

`I wonder how long you'll be away?' Trina murmured.

`No idea this time. Who knows what's going to happen? The way things are the war could be over in a week or two.'

`I know, it's too horrible even to think about.'

As she spoke Trina looked at him and Alan could see the worry in her eyes.

He shrugged helplessly. `It's almost impossible to believe, but I suppose it could happen and we'd have the Germans stamping about over here.'

Trina shook her head. `Don't let's even think about it.'

Alan rolled away from the pool and stretched out on his back. Trina swung around and sat with her arms about her knees.

`Strange how we take some things for granted without saying too much about them, and then, suddenly, it becomes a matter of urgency.'

Alan was watching Trina's face as he spoke these words, and she turned to look directly into his eyes.

`What do you mean?' she asked.

`Well, we've never made a habit of talking about, or planning for the future. It hasn't seemed necessary, and since we've met we've lived our lives in the present. I know quite well that I want to marry you but we've always agreed that it's not practical; that it's something to be postponed until after the war, something vaguely in the future. Just now though, that future seems entirely vague!'

Trina lay back on the grass verge so that they were lying side by side.

`It's something we've both taken for granted,' she agreed.

`Yes, and we've lived the way we wanted, in spite of family disapproval. We seem to have fallen into a code of conduct for ourselves, perhaps not in words, but an understanding that's grown of its own accord; and we've drifted along on that basis. Is it enough? Or is it, perhaps, even too much?'

Trina turned her head so that she could see the expressions on his face more clearly.

`What are you trying to say?'

`I don't really know. I don't even know whether I'm facing facts or just letting my imagination become too fanciful. I keep remembering that we may not see each other again for who knows how long, and not even knowing whether the other is still alive. Do you remember, ages ago it seems, we were talking about love and sex, the relative importance of each, separately and combined? Suppose...' Alan started to say.

`Okay,' Trina interrupted, laughing. `I'm supposing.'

`Stop behaving like that, you distract me' Alan complained.

`Like what?'

`You know quite well... enticing.'

Trina stopped laughing. `I'm afraid of being too serious. So much seems to be coming to an end. I don't mean just us, you going away that is, but the war and... I can't explain. It's not knowing, not even being sure there will be a tomorrow.'

Alan rolled on to his side so that he could look at her without twisting his neck.

`That's exactly what I was thinking about,' he agreed. 'Is there a future? No, that's a silly thing to say, of course there's a future. It's our future I mean. Do we have one? Life's a bit uncertain nowadays.' There was a silence that neither was anxious to break. Alan was trying to gather up his thoughts. They were just entering those unbelievable days when France was falling, and England was likely to come under the same threat. If England were to be defeated...?

Already Alan had heard a whisper that the ship's Captains had been given instructions about what to do in case of invasion and defeat. They were to head their ships for America or the nearest Commonwealth country.

If this should happen how long might it be? How would each know what the other was doing, or wanted to do? How much ought he to expect from Trina? Was it fair to bind Trina to some tenuous understanding? Suppose in one, two or even three years she should meet someone else; would it be right for her to feel in any way tied to the past? Should she not only be free, but feel free with no suggestion of remorse? Was it possible that he also might wish to feel free? Alan looked at Trina and did not think it likely; but could he rule out the possibility entirely? What about their theories of sexual freedom and equality? He knew what he wanted to say to Trina, but how to say it was the problem. The last thing he wanted her to think...

`You were talking about being apart. Is that what's worrying you?' Trina was looking at him quizzically.

`Of course it is, but it's more than that.' Alan stopped to sort out what he was trying to say, and Trina stayed silent waiting for him.

`I suppose I've been wondering what you'll be doing while I'm away. Who you'll meet and who you'll go out with.'

Trina moved as though about to say something, but Alan hurried on before she could speak.

`We've theorized about the difference between physical and mental unfaithfulness and agreed, again in theory, that physical unfaithfulness might, in some circumstances, be unimportant, a momentary release with no deep or lasting implications.'

`Oh yes! I remember. We'd been drinking rather a lot that night.'

`Had we? You had perhaps, but I'm sure I was sober.' Alan grinned and waited for her reaction.

`I'm never drunk when you're sober, which is more than you can say.'

Alan was tempted to take her up on this slanderous claim but he had other matters on his mind, so merely attempted a look of amazed disbelief.

`I've come to a conclusion,' he told her.

`Good! Let's talk about something else.'

`I meant that I'd come to a conclusion, not come to a conclusion. So shush and listen.'

`Well stop being ambiguous then.'

`Exactly what I intend. I've decided there's no way I can say what I want without the possibility of being misunderstood, so first I must make one thing clear.'

`What's that?'

`In simple, straightforward terms it's this. I love you, and intend to go on loving you.'

Alan was aware that Trina was studying his face and that her eyes were glinting wickedly.

`But?' she prompted.

`But!' he confirmed. `Let's face it. We may be separated for ages, even assuming nothing worse happens to either of us. Let's suppose you or I meet someone who is, or seems, as desirable as we now find each other. Should we have any feelings of guilt or be inhibited by our present arrangement?'

`It sounds horrible when you say it like that.'

`I know. That's what I meant when I said it was difficult to explain. I know I've been incredibly lucky in finding you, and I've no desire to go looking for anyone else; but it's stupid to claim that in the whole wide world there's only you for me and me for you. There must be hundreds, thousands of other people whom we could love and marry. It's largely a matter of decision. One day you meet a certain person and something clicks, so you get married. If you stick to that vital decision and work at it the marriage is successful. If you don't, it means separation and divorce.'

`Logically, yes, I agree. Illogically I just don't feel that way.'

Alan leaned over and kissed her. `I'm glad of that.'

Trina responded, and a few minutes passed before Alan rolled away to lie on his back, hands behind his head, to stare at the sky and finish what he had been trying to say.

`I find it hard to put into words, but if the situation arises I would want, no not want . . . expect perhaps. Yes, I would expect you to feel free,' he said. `In spite of those ideas of amorality we've talked about, what worries me most is how I'd feel if you had a light-hearted affair, which had nothing to do with your feelings for me. Sensibly, logically, I should accept that you have a right to do what you want with your body, and that there's no harm done. Yet, basically, I'm afraid I'd be as jealous as all hell! What I want to say is that I'd try not to be ridiculously so.'

Trina sat up and clasped her knees again before replying. This time she seemed to be taking his remarks more seriously.

`If you stray I think I could accept it. Provided I didn't know about it,' she replied, and then started laughing again.

`That sounded like one of my more stupid remarks. Now I'll have to explain. I could accept it if I knew it was just a lighthearted fling, or as you put it, an affair that didn't affect the way you felt about me. What I mean by not knowing, is the gory details. You know, names, dates, places: they'd make it all too real and then it might be difficult to accept.'

Alan nodded. `That about sums it up, but...' It was his turn to sit up.

`I'm sorry! I shouldn't have started all this. It's much too serious a conversation for us, especially on my last day.'

Trina was smiling back at him.

`Thanks for trying,' she said. `There's one other thing though. I'd like to think we'd be honest with each other. If something does happen to your feelings, or mine for that matter, we should be able to trust each other sufficiently to talk about it and remain friends.' It was a strange conversation, yet, to both of them, it seemed to make sense in those menacing days when their world was so likely to come apart.

* * *

Ocean Wanderer was in Southampton, at short notice to sail. Two days after Alan joined her they left for St Nazaire to evacuate British troops and civilians. It was not a pleasant introduction to life at sea. In St Nazaire confusion reigned, and they were able to get no reliable information about what was happening. For two days and one night they lay at anchor and, at intervals, launches would come alongside bringing a few more people to embark. In dribs and drabs they took just over three thousand on board. With monotonous regularity German planes would come over and drop bombs and gradually the attacks intensified.

They were lucky, if being hit by a bomb is lucky. The luck was in the small amount of vital damage done. That is to say the engines were left intact and the ship could be steered from the aft steering flat. Although the bridge was hit, only three were killed and about a dozen injured.

The Lancastria was doing a similar job and she was not so fortunate. She had almost completed embarkation when she was hit and sunk. A large number must have been killed outright and thousands ended up in the water. Ocean Wanderer's boats picked up as many as they could. Some survivors had life-jackets but most did not. Even those with life-jackets were weighed down by heavy clothing and found it difficult to keep afloat. Men disappeared, dragged down within yards of rescue, and their last despairing cries would hang in the air over a swirl of water.

Later one of Lancastria's officers told Alan that he thought they must have had nearly five thousand on board when they were hit and he thought it likely that at least half had died. With the Lancastria survivors, Ocean Wanderer was carrying over five thousand persons and conditions on board threatened to become chaotic. Not long after the Lancastria disaster, orders were given to sail. While still weighing anchor they could see German tanks rolling down the road into the town. It was nearly dusk, and in the gathering darkness they were able to clear the harbor and head back to Southampton.

The damage was assessed, and Ocean Wanderer sent to the Clyde for repair. She was out of action for many months. Again Alan returned to Barringdale. When Trina met him at the station she remarked;

`This, is becoming a habit!'

CHAPTER SIX

Footfalls echo in the memory
Down the passage we did not take
Towards the door we never opened.
T.S. Eliot - Four Quartets

`Blacklock's gone, and in his place we're left with an illogical sense of guilt.'

Alan sensed this feeling among his companions. The unceremonious disposal of the Storekeeper's body had aroused an atavistic feeling of wrong doing. There was silence and they avoided each other's eyes. Each wondering if his body would be thrust over the side, or whether he would be the one to rot in a derelict boat.

For fifteen days they had been drifting, in an empty sea with not even the trace of a distant smoke plume. Although he said nothing to the others, Jim Bristow was not surprised. Ocean Monarch had been routed well clear of the usual convoy lanes, and the drift was likely to have taken them even further away. Also, they were likely to be beyond the patrol range of Sunderlands and Liberators.

With Peter and Terry gone, only ten were left to share the collected rainwater. With luck it should last a week. The most pressing problems now were the hard wooden seats and the constant movement. The sea had continued to build up, and it was impossible to relax. There was no danger, but they were all developing body sores and weariness troubled them.

Alan shifted slightly. `I suppose it's the way our muscles react to the movement of the boat which tires us,' he thought. `We're all so much weaker now.' The dull depression which now gripped him was hard to conceal and harder to throw off. ` Blacklock's death has upset me more than I thought,' he rationalized. `I haven't seen death since that day in St Nazaire. It has passed nearby a few times, but not as an intimate presence. When another ship is sunk the human agony can be imagined, but it's a mile or more away. We sail on and leave the horror behind. Even the air raids in London and Liverpool gave only second hand knowledge of pain and death. It's so much easier to accept things at a distance, the difference between knowing and seeing.'

* * *

The thought of St Nazaire reminded Alan of his return to Barringdale after the voyage in Ocean Wanderer. He brought the shock of so much slaughter with him, and the remembrance of his first taste of real fear. A fear that gripped the body with paralyzing force. Fear fighting its own battle with pride that feared the shame of fear, and forced unwilling feet to take the first steps into action.

Action, Alan learned, helped to tame jangled nerves and bring them under control.

The familiar office surroundings were now the unreality, and Alan found difficulty settling back into the routine. The quiet manipulation of book entries, the columns of figures and the tap-tap tapping of typewriters seemed remote and pointless. The atmosphere was completely divorced from those men who had died, some as heroes, a few as cowards, but most dying surprised, disbelieving victims of war's futility.

Trina found Alan unwilling to talk about St Nazaire. She saw the difference in him, yet knew that his feelings for her were unchanged. In many ways Alan was now uncertain; the stark contrast between love and hate, life and death, left him vulnerable and confused. He was seized with a revulsion against war, believing that most of those taking part were deluded victims. His upbringing and conditioning made conscientious objection impossible, something he could never consider. The cowardly fear of being thought a coward was far too strong.

He was lucky in having Trina. The face she commonly wore was one of laughter, yet her lighthearted approach to life concealed a sensitivity that was easily moved. While Alan readjusted she drifted along accommodating her pace to his, sensing his moods and responding to them.

Was the weather of that summer of 1940 the most glorious that ever was? Or was that merely the way it seemed? Was the beauty of the country, the lush green of the hills and the flawless blue of the skies a mirage? A mirage created by a heightened awareness? Awareness that sought for something other than the hate that was now unleashed; a hate written in the twisted contrails above their heads, an insidious hate nurtured by propaganda.

It was hard to remember that hate was the prerogative of a diseased few who had the desire, and the means, to spread their infection. In action Alan had not been able to accept this, and now thought it a weakness that he had felt hate for the pilot of a plane diving to bomb. He had found it easy to forget that the German had been conditioned to hate the enemy. To that pilot, Alan would be seen as a ruthless opponent who must be destroyed. Alan did not feel bloodthirsty and doubted that most Germans did. It was the inevitability of what must happen, of what was happening, that was so frightening.

Time had become precious, and, paradoxically, something to be squandered recklessly. Not for Alan and Trina the luxury of allowing the seconds to trickle away while trying to extract some deep meaning from their passing. They did not wish to stop and think. All they wanted was to pack each instant with a lifetime of love and experience, within which they might seek, and create, their own world. One night, as they lay in bed, Trina whispered as though to herself;

`We must make today yesterday, as well as tomorrow and the day after. Tomorrow there may be no day after to follow, and today may be the yesterday left for us to remember.'

`That sounds profound,' Alan teased. `Do you know what you're talking about?'

Trina laughed, then raised herself on one elbow so that she could look at him.

`I probably don't know what I'm talking about, but I do know what I mean.'

In spite of Alan's teasing, her words seemed to sum up the whole urge of their life together.

Southern Oceanic had no immediate shipboard vacancies, and Mr Carstairs told Alan that he would probably have to wait until Ocean Monarch completed her second conversion to a troopship. Her first conversion had been hasty and incomplete. Now, with Ocean Wanderer out of action, and survivors from Ocean Queen, which had been sunk, there was a surplus of experienced crew. In addition, Ocean Leader had been lost on her voyage to Norway.

However, Mr Carstairs assured Alan that he would still be needed, and meanwhile they could make good use of him at Barringdale. The accounts department was in a mess, and still had not finalized the thousands of bookings cancelled by the outbreak of war. There were refunds and commissions to be sorted out, and tidying up to be done.

These were frustrating, unsettled and happy days. Frustrating because Alan felt he should not be sitting at a desk reducing a jumble of figures into their final, irrefutable, conclusion. Unsettled because at any time he could be sent to join a ship with only a minimum of notice. Happy? Yes, with Trina there was sanity and contentment. Death was no longer an abstract possibility. He had felt it at his shoulder and whispering in his ear. There was nothing to be done except close his mind to its threat. Strange twilight days, when reality seemed unreal and they accepted unreality as normal.

* * *

'For we alone create
and make, of love, our will.
Deny the barbs of hate.
Defy death's icy chill.'

Were these the words Alan scribbled on the back of an envelope when trying to sum up his feelings one noisy night in London? Later, when his thoughts returned to that night, he could not be sure if he was remembering them correctly.

The air raid siren had awakened Alan, but Trina did not stir when he slid out of bed and pulled aside the blackout curtains. The searchlights were thrusting in and out of the clouds, and he watched their probing wands of light weave seemingly aimless patterns over the threatened rooftops. The guns started a barrage and the drone of engines could be heard. Then came bombs, each screaming its threat of destruction; and finally the quiver from each stabbing plunge and the shaking violence of a purpose achieved.

A hand slid over Alan's back to rest on his shoulder. He looked down at Trina who was beside him. They stood silent and naked, spectators at an inferno.

`Pull the curtains and come back to bed Alan,' Trina gestured at the scene outside. `This has nothing to do with us.'

Nearby a building was on fire and its flames were lighting the sky. The eerie, flickering glow bathed Trina's body, and Alan turned to her, his hands feeling for her waist. Trina's skin was warm and smooth beneath his fingers, and there was an erotic excitement in the pulsating orange light, which enveloped them. Nothing else mattered. There was a magic beauty, which defied its deadly origin.

They kissed and desire flared.

`No,' Alan agreed. `It's nothing to do with us.'

The curtains were left apart, but it was only the savage beauty that was allowed to enter. The ugliness of war had no place where they were making love.

The early morning light woke Alan, and he sat on the edge of the bed trying to crystallize his feelings into verse. Feelings now shadowed by the distance of time, their detail converted into a sense of loss. The words he wrote were lost too, except for an indistinct snatch of memory.

* * *

Corncrake was growing weary. To keep him operational would require a lot of work and expense. It might be cheaper to trade him in.

`You can't get rid of Corncrake!' Trina was horrified.

`That wasn't your opinion a few days ago when we had to get out and push. You were positively insulting.'

`I was no such thing. I'd never hurt Corncrake's feelings.'

`If calling him an uncoordinated heap of scrap iron isn't insulting, what is?'

`Oh that,' was Trina's airy reply. `Corncrake knew I didn't mean that personally. I was just trying to annoy you. You were being so bad tempered.'

`Never!' Alan protested.

`Never nothing. You were the one who was threatening him with the wrecker's yard.'

`That was for his own good, to make him pull his tires up. He's been misbehaving far too much recently. Seriously though,' he added, `If I don't patch him up and trade him in soon, the wreckers will be the only people who'll take him.'

`Must we? I'm really fond of poor old Corncrake.'

`We must, and so am I. But sentiment wears thin when I have to get out in the rain and push. I'm the one who gets wet. You stay inside and steer.'

All very well to say `Corncrake must go,' but there was the problem of money. They were paid monthly and the time between checks was almost intolerably long. There were always a few days each month when they were completely broke.

The situation was desperate, and Alan committed sacrilege. Soon after he was born, his grandmother had placed one hundred pounds into a savings account that she opened in Alan's name. It had been untouched, almost forgotten for eighteen years, and had increased until there was now more than one hundred and fifty pounds. Alan had been taught to regard this money as nearly sacred, never to be touched except in case of emergency. However, the old rules no longer applied. Alan needed money now, not in a future which, for him, might never exist. It was time to violate the savings account and he drew out twenty pounds.

The next Saturday Trina and Alan set out to visit second hand dealers' yards and showrooms.

`It's not tactful taking Corncrake with us. Just think how he must feel.' Trina reached around the windscreen and patted Corncrake on the bonnet.

`He,' Alan said emphatically. `He is not one of your horses. He doesn't have to suffer his fate with, shall we say, equanimity?'

Trina shuddered and curled her lip in disgust.

`Anyway,' Alan asked; `How could I get a trade-in if he's not with us?'

`You'd probably get more if they didn't see him.' They were going down hill, and Alan spoke to Corncrake.

`Did you hear what she said? Isn't she rude and unkind?'

He eased his foot off the accelerator, and Corncrake obliged with a series of backfires. Trina apologized hastily.

`I didn't mean it Corncrake. The nasty man provoked me.'

They bickered amiably all morning as they examined the merits and demerits of various second-hand cars. Trina distracted the salesmen with flirtatious smiles, and broke up their smooth talk with unexpected questions.

`Does this car have a clutch?' Or, pointing at the spare wheel,

`What's that one for?'

She contrived a look of such apparently genuine interest, both in the cars and the salesmen, that they could never be certain whether they were having their legs pulled, or were dealing with a nut case.

By the time a final decision was made, the last unfortunate salesman must have been quite unbalanced by Trina's efforts.

Probably fearing for his sanity, he offered twelve pounds trade-in for Corncrake against a two-seater Morris 8 that was for sale at twenty pounds. Alan and Trina made a fond farewell to Corncrake, handed over eight pounds, then set off to become acquainted with their new purchase.

The Morris was luxury after Corncrake. It gave a smoother ride, and it was possible to carry on a conversation without shouting. It was a sporty looking car, a bit like a cousin to an MG, and with a snug cockpit. The paintwork was a smart bottle green, and the black hood well preserved. Best of all, it had weatherproof side screens.

Long before they got back to Barringdale Alan found that their new car had one bad habit. A habit that could be extremely painful until the appropriate evasive action became second nature. The gear lever was liable to snap down into neutral when Alan accelerated in third gear, and its hard knob was accurately placed to hit an unwary driver on the left kneecap. Three times this happened in the first half hour, and on each occasion Alan had a few words to say. It was an act which won applause from Trina, who was highly amused by the whole performance.

The hammering Alan's knee received prompted her to christen the new car `Mr Bumps'.

Now that the savings account was no longer inviolate, it became easy to draw money from it. Many Saturday afternoons they left Mr Bumps in the station yard while they caught a train to London. There they would go to a theatre, and after the show have a meal at a Greek restaurant in Soho, before returning to their hotel.

`Dear, intense Trina,' Alan thought. Trina had an uncanny ability to shut out from her mind anything she decided to reject. She showed no nervousness on nights when there were air raids, and they stubbornly refused to make any concession to the danger. They had no intention of paying for a room and then spending the night in a crowded hotel bomb shelter with other guests. They resolved to ignore the war and were surprisingly successful. The sound of falling bombs lent a peculiar excitement to their caresses.

* * *

Alan's eyes were open, but with his mind in the past he had not been aware of the scene around him. When he returned to the conscious present, he saw Len Huskins glaring at Jim with concentrated hate.

`Len's been worse the last day or two,' he thought. `When not quarrelling with Mahoney he mutters to himself, and he's taken an intense dislike to Jim since that argument about catching the rain.'

* * *

Len Huskins could just remember his mother and father. He could remember them both, drunk and lying in their own vomit. He could remember the dirt, the cold, the hunger and the squalid hovel where they lived. That was all he could remember before the day when he was taken from his home by strangers who fed him and put him to bed, yet who treated him as an object. It was the same with the foster parents with whom he was later boarded. They were not cruel, but he was just one more in a series of children they had been paid to look after. There was no love given to him nor did he have any outlet where he might give affection, and consequently was driven in upon himself.

Even when he was apprenticed it was an act of charity, a salve for the Sunday-Church-going consciences of the Board of Directors at the local ship building yard. Unlike most of the other children, Len was happier at school than at the place he now called home. He was quick and clever with his hands and also had an aptitude for figures. One of his teachers brought him to the attention of the Minister, and he in turn spoke to an Elder of the Kirk, a man of self Esteem, conscious of his own dignity and position, who was a major shareholder in the shipyard.

At thirteen, Len was brought and made to stand in front of a row of solemn and severe gentlemen. Feeling small, nervous and bewildered, he answered their questions as best he could and was told to await their decision. Brought back in front of his judges, he was told;

`If we gie ye the job ye'll have to work. Ye'll no get any second chance here.'

Even at that age, Len found it difficult to be properly grateful to the imposing men who had given him this special apprenticeship. As an apprentice he received no pay. Money was paid to his foster parents for his food and clothing, and to recompense them for providing him with accommodation. He had been working for nearly two years when his old teacher suggested he go to night school and take a course in engineering. After some discussion the firm agreed to pay the expenses. He was a bright lad, and they decided his training could be a good investment.

For Len it was different. It was the first time he had seen any hope of escape from the environment where he was trapped. Somewhere, he was sure, there must be a better life. He plunged into his studies with dour determination. Len was still only eighteen when the world-wide depression closed the shipyard and he joined the queue of unemployed. Not for long; again he found a friend to help him. One of the engineers at the shipyard, an elderly man just on retiring age, had taken an interest in the youngster, giving him help and encouragement with his studies. This friend now wrote to an old colleague who was Chief Engineer in a cargo ship. Through this intervention Len was offered a job as a junior engineer on board ship.

It was another first in his life when he left his birthplace. Len had never been on a train, and the journey from Glasgow to London was a plunge into the unknown. London, itself, did not surprise him. Except for the different accents it might have been a larger version of Glasgow. True, the journey across London to the Surrey Docks seemed never ending, but once there the atmosphere, ships and docks, was familiar. For the last five years he had worked on the Clyde, helping to build and repair ships of all sizes. Duffle bag on shoulder, he enquired at the dock gates for his ship, and five minutes later was climbing the gangway to start a new life.

On board, his studies continued and, between voyages, he would attend the School of Marine Engineering and sit for his examinations.

During one of his leaves Len met Rosie, and fell hopelessly in love. Rosie was a bright, fragile creature, and Len pursued her single mindedly. Even from the start she was a little frightened of him, but all the same he held a fascination for her, the fascination a child may feel when playing with fire. She agreed to marry him, and then was afraid to go back on her word. Almost exactly twelve months after they married, a daughter, Ailie, was born. Len was twenty and Rosie barely eighteen years old.

Six years later the marriage was staggering. Money was not plentiful and, feeling neglected by Len's long absences at sea, Rosie was becoming petulant. Knowing this, Len put his name down with Southern Oceanic for consideration should a vacancy occur. In 1938, when he had almost forgotten about his application, he was offered a position as Fourth Engineer in Ocean Monarch. His new job did not mean any increase in pay, but it did offer regular, scheduled voyages and more frequent leave periods.

When war broke out, Len's first thought was to persuade Rosie to take Ailie into the country, away from London and the threat of air raids, and he had time to make arrangements while Ocean Monarch was laid up for conversion to troop carrying. By the time he returned to sea, Rosie and Ailie were settled at Whittlesford, where Rosie found herself a job as a sorter in the nearby paper mill. With the job to keep her occupied, Len hoped she would be more contented. When he left Whittlesford Len did not know that for all practical purposes his marriage was ended.

For Rosie the past two months had been almost unbearable. This was the first time she had lived with her husband for more than two or, at most, three weeks continuously. She found his constant presence distressing. From the very beginning she had never felt entirely comfortable with this moody, silent man; and in the evenings she would sit and look at Len, wondering what on earth had made her agree to marry him. While pretending to read her book, Rosie would watch him as he sat in front of the fire, doing nothing but sit and gaze at the flames. The dancing firelight flickered on that craggy face with its prominent, bushy eyebrows, his head crowned by a shock of stiff, sandy hair; and Rosie would realize how little they had in common. Above all it was his eyes that made her feel nervous when he looked in her direction. They were a pale, pale blue and gleamed, with an intensity, which managed to give him a fanatical appearance. In bed, his-love making was urgent but ignorant, and he gave her no pleasure.

The ship, no longer on a passenger run, was sent to ferry Australian troops to the Middle East, and did not return to England for twelve months. It was only then that Len discovered his wife had left him. Rosie had disappeared, and Ailie was now living with her grandmother.

When he called to see Rosie's mother and asked where his wife had gone, he was handed a letter. It was very brief. In it Rosie told him she could not continue with the marriage and asked him not to try to trace her. She gave no reasons, nor did she say what she planned to do; all Rosie said was that her mother had promised to look after the child. Her mother, Mrs Thomas, had never liked Len and could not, or would not, give him any more information. Ailie seemed happy with her grandmother, and Len arranged with Mrs Thomas to send money for his daughter's support.

Never a sociable man, bitterness now became a part of his life. On board ship he had no friends, and it seemed that he wanted none. Len Huskins had experienced hurt too often during his life. He was no longer prepared to trust anyone.

* * *

`Len may be looking sour but Basil Allward can still find something to laugh at. Wish I could hear what he's telling Rapley.' Alan strained to catch what was being said but he had missed the first part. Obviously it was something to do with an Army fatigue party bringing cases of soft drink from the storeroom to the Wet Canteen.

Basil was trying to stand to attention and imitate an Army officer, not easy in a rocking boat.

`You stupid, stupid fellow.' Basil was imitating a plummy high-pitched voice.

`I wonder what that was all about?' Alan had missed too much of the story to understand the point, but Rapley was finding it funny.

`I suppose you find them everywhere, but the Army does seem to have more than its fair share of bone heads.' The story, obviously, had been about some officer's idiocy, or so Alan concluded.

* * *

In January Ocean Ranger docked in Liverpool. She had cracked a turbine when her engines were thrown into emergency full astern to avoid a collision. Heavy fog had blanketed the ships in the convoy and an error had been made.

Ocean Ranger was to be in port for some weeks while repairs were made, and her Purser, only a few years off retiring age, was a sick man. When the ship docked he was taken straight to hospital and it seemed unlikely he would ever be fit enough to return to sea. His deputy was inexperienced, and though the company was reluctant to promote him they had no one else available. The problem was solved when Ocean Monarch arrived and also docked in Liverpool. A general re-shuffle of staff was organized.

Early in February Mr Carstairs sent for Alan.

`Some news for you at last.' Alan was greeted with this statement as he entered Mr Carstairs' office.

`We want you to join Ocean Monarch next week.'

Although Alan had known that this must happen one day it still took him by surprise. He thanked Mr Carstairs, then went to find Trina and break the news to her. They had ten days ahead of them before he had to leave. Ten days before they had to face the probability of a lengthy separation.

The night before Alan left for Liverpool, he and Trina went to London so that they could have a few more hours together. That night there was a long, intermittent, air raid as waves of bombers came and went.

They left the bedside lamp switched on and, against the wall, Alan's two half trunks stood strapped and ready for departure in the morning. They had made love and were resting quietly, the only physical contact being their fingers that were interlaced as they held hands. Temporarily the planes had passed from overhead, and the noise of battle receded into the distance. Above the bed was an ornate plaster centre-piece in the ceiling. Alan looked up at it idly wondering whether a nearby bomb might shake it loose, and, if so, whether it would fall on them in one solid lump. Without taking his eyes off the plaster whorls he said to Trina, as he so often did;

`I love you.'

She moved slightly, and he felt her free hand glide onto his chest.

He could sense that she had turned her head and was watching him. Lying there, he became intensely aware of how they had come to accept their love as something permanent, but had still made no formal promises to each other. He moved so that he could see her face and knew, with complete certainty, that if he asked Trina to marry him, to commit herself irrevocably, she would say `Yes'. The mood and the moment could have brought no other answer.

Yet he did not ask it of her.

They loved each other and expected to stay together, but did not believe one person should own another. Occasionally they had skirted around the question in an abstract form, and had claimed that when, and if, they married, it would be because it was time for them to obey society's dictates. They refused to accept the engagement condition, which tended to symbolize that a woman belonged, and a man possessed. In their youthful certainty they had no doubts. They were two individuals who shared each other, because it pleased them that this should be so. There could be no question of rights. If love proved insufficient, so be it.

This was how they argued, and these were the thoughts that went through Alan's head as he looked into her eyes. How could he sweep away this reasoning, and claim a commitment from Trina's vulnerability? At that moment, facing the prospect of lengthy separation, emotion ruled; yet, once given, Trina would never go back on her word. Her pride would not permit her to break a promise, even should doubts arise later after Alan had left. For himself, Alan had no doubts. He was certain he would always want to honor such a commitment.

He was tempted, but hesitated, and the moment passed. Time enough when the war and the future were resolved. Or was there time? Perhaps that was the moment when he should have abandoned theory, and, instead, given Trina the choice.

The next wave of bombers was approaching. It was time to make love again.

CHAPTER SEVEN

Fare thee well, for I must leave thee
Do not let this parting grieve thee
Anon

`I wonder if anyone got away on a raft?'

Alan looked at Jim, unsure whether he was being spoken to or if Jim was talking to himself. He decided to respond anyway.

`Don't see why not. Some of the rafts must have floated free.' Jim nodded. `They'd never last more than a day or so. Not unless it was one of the big rafts with supplies.'

`What are you getting at Jim?' `Nothing really. Just clutching at straws. A raft wouldn't drift the same way as a boat, and could be miles from here by now, but if found it might help us.'

Alan began to wonder what the odds were? The odds that some of the crew managed to get on rafts. It was something to do, and he started by working out how many had sailed in the ship.

'Four hundred and fifty-three.'

`What's that Alan?'

Without thinking he had spoken aloud.

`I've just been trying to add up the number on board: crew, Army staff, Navy gunners and so on.'

`Well what about it?'

`Just trying to work out probabilities,' Alan replied. `There are ten of us here, and we know what's happened to another two. That leaves four hundred and forty-one.'

`OK, so what?'

`It's like this Jim. I know there was little warning, but possibly up to ten percent got clear of the ship. We know we weren't the only ones; there were those we saw in the water. Sure, some drowned, but others couldn't reach us. That doesn't mean they didn't find something else to hang on to, and there would have been others we didn't see; but let's stick to ten percent, say forty-five. Excluding the twelve who reached this boat, that leaves thirty-three. Surely it's likely that one or two would find a raft?'

`I'd agree with that as far as it goes. In fact, when you weigh it up, it's possible, even likely.'

`Yes, that's about it, Jim. As you say, as far as it goes.' Jim was stroking his straggling beard, steadily, rhythmically, and Alan found this extremely irritating. It seemed an age before Jim spoke again.

`As you know, the small rafts stacked on deck were just something to hang on to for a few hours. With troops on board we'd be in convoy and small rafts would be useful, as Destroyers might be able to pick up survivors. The big rafts, on launching frames, were locked down, and needed someone to knock out the pin.'

`Would there be any chance of one breaking clear when the ship sank, the same way this boat must have done?'

`I'd like to think so, but it's unlikely. There must have been quite a series of coincidences to let this boat get clear. One fluke is probably all we can expect.'

Alan nodded. `Suppose so. Looking at it logically the odds must be pretty slim.'

`Yes, not much hope. You could be right though. Probably quite a few of the crew ended up in the water, but they wouldn't have a hope in hell of lasting for very long.'

Alan's imagination took hold, bringing images of despair into his mind.

`Pity any poor devil clinging to one of those rafts. What would I do...? Hang on like a limpet, fighting fatigue, using every last little bit of will power to prolong life? Would I struggle to defer for another instant the inevitable inrush of salt sea... the ultimate despair of light being strangled into darkness? Or would I let go when the hopelessness of it was obvious? I've a horror of drowning... Used to dream about it as a small child.'

Alan looked around at his companions and wondered whether they were so much better off in the boat? Perhaps the only difference was that it was taking them too long to die, and they were bored by it. There was plenty of room, yet it was strange how they tended to group. He and Jim sat in the stern, and then came a barrier of space to where Len was sitting on the starb'd side with Higgins opposite him. Another space barrier beyond Len separated him from Mahoney and, next to Mahoney, towards the bow, Joe Hayter and Queenie. On the port side Rapley sat next to Higgins, and beyond him the Allward brothers. Queenie was the only one who ever changed position, sometimes moving across to talk with Rapley and Basil Allward.

`Yes,' Alan decided, `Boredom's our enemy now. We've nothing left to say to each other. The effort's too great. Jim's eyes have become hollow looking, haggard and sunken into their sockets. Is it the strain of being in charge? Yet he has no decisions to make. Perhaps that's the trouble. If we had a mast and a sail it'd be different. He might be happier... All the same he'd have trouble trying to make this bathtub go anywhere. Better try to dream away the time Jim, the same as I do.'

Joe Hayter now looked to be more affected than any of the others, perhaps more mentally than physically. For one who had always looked so competent and majestic, he was a pathetic sight.

After distributing the water ration the previous evening, Alan had stayed up for'ard for a while talking to Con, who was telling how he, Joe and Terry had managed to get away from the ship. `We was in the galley see. Trying to find jobs to keep the lazy bastards there out of mischief. With just crew on board I only had half a dozen getting breakfast cooked. The others I had stripping down some of the ranges and steamers, when bloody old Joe waddled over. He was out to stir me up, and claimed he'd found a cockroach in the bakery, swore he'd seen it walk in from the galley. Said it didn't surprise him, seeing as I kept the place like a pigsty.'

Con's eyes gleamed as he glanced at Joe and remembered the insult. `I'd picked up a cleaver and was demanding an apology when

Terrible wandered in. "Can't you two find something useful to do?" he says, and then says; "Fine example you're setting, doing nothing except loll around and chatter." Joe and me told him to go and stuff himself.'

Alan had to laugh. He could readily imagine the scene. Con went on with his tale.

`I was pissed off and said, "Let's get out on deck, I'm fed up with the stink of food." We all went up and we was standing in the for'ard well deck when it happened. We linked hands and jumped. When we hit the water I think Terry must have landed on something. By the time we surfaced he'd let go of my hand, but I could hear him swearing a few yards away. It was a minute or two before we joined up again. He didn't seem too bad though, not then.'

Con paused for a few seconds, lost in recollection, then came back with a jerk.

`I'd say it'd be about twenty minutes before we found the boat. I got in easily; it was so low in the water. Then, with me in the boat and Joe in the water behind him, we got Terry in.'

`How did Joe manage to get in?' Alan asked.

`Him! He's so full of blubber he swims like a fish. He just slithered into the boat like some bloody great whale.'

Alan smiled as he recalled Con's vivid description. `Amazing how tough little Mahoney must be,' he thought. `Never realized it before, there's not much of him, but what there is, is hard as nails.

Higgins now... He's a complete contrast.' Higgins the invisible, the most self effacing person one could possibly meet. Every word, every movement seemed to express an implicit apology. An apology for something he might be thought to have done, or that he might do, or perhaps for just being there, taking up space that someone else might have used to better advantage. One never knew what he was apologizing for, or why he was apologizing. It was simply his nature. As a person he was entirely amiable and anxious to please, and his meekness was so complete that it was often embarrassing to other people.

Although a bachelor, he was not one of the homosexual clan. It could be that the thought of any form of intimacy with another being was more than his nature could stand.

Alan looked across the boat, still considering Higgins `What's he feeling now? What does he think about? I've no idea, not even the faintest clue. Being in the boat has made no difference, his tentative, ingratiating manner hasn't changed.'

* * *

Meat! There was always the smell of meat, on his hands, on his clothes, drifting through from the shop and the cold rooms next door. Paul Higgins stood for a moment at the window of his bedroom, and stared down at the stream of traffic in the High Street below, before turning away to finish dressing. He would have to hurry; Bill and the other two members of the Band would be arriving any minute now. Tonight was their first engagement to play at the Black Diamond Roadhouse, and it would never do to be late. It was a long-term engagement and a big step in their progress. Until now their only bookings had been casual, for weddings and private parties.

Paul looked at his reflection in the mirror, another first. Tonight they would be wearing matching clothing; black trousers and shoes, with loose gypsy-style white silk shirts. Professional looking without being too ostentatious.

He checked the mound of sheet music stacked on a chair, then piled it into a leather satchel and ran downstairs. Of course, Dad had to be there. Too early for him to go to the pub, but with luck he might be so absorbed in the evening paper he would not even look up.

`Christ boy, what the hell are you dressed like that for? You're not going out in that fancy dress are you? My God! I don't want people thinking I've got a bloody pansy for a son.'

`It's the Band, Dad. We're all dressing like this, stage clothes, a sort of uniform.'

`For God's sake put on an overcoat or something. Cover up so it can't be seen. Why you want to mess around with those so called musician friends of yours I'll never know.'

`We've been through all this before Dad.'

`Don't I know it.'

`Oh let him be Dad. You know what he's like about his music.' His sister's arrival created a diversion, and Paul took advantage of it to sidle towards the door. As he slipped out he heard her say, viciously:

`Better than coming home stinking drunk, like some people.' Millie, a year older than he was, ran their lives, his and his father's as well as her own. Only eighteen when their mother died, she had taken over the running of the house. Millie also worked in the shop as cashier.

Paul knew that his sister despised him. She always had, from the time they were small children. She never forgave him for the fate that made him a boy and her a girl. Even in the shop Paul could sense her critical eye, watching as he went about his work. Millie was a real professional with knife and cleaver and Paul was just competent. But it was not seemly for a girl to work at butchering, not when customers were in the shop. Instead Millie had to sit behind the cash register, and conceal her boredom as she handed customers their change.

There were times when Paul almost hated Millie. When he was only twelve and had started music lessons, she would torment him as he practised. Often he would be driven into a rage, and Millie would scream for help when he turned on her. At times his frustration was so great that he would burst into tears, only to have her chant;

'Cry baby! Little Paul's a cry baby.' His mother had played the piano, very badly it is true, but the piano was hers, bought before she married. When Paul first showed interest in the instrument she talked her husband into paying for lessons, but not even his mother had expected this childish desire to become his one great passion. Paul now knew he would never become the virtuoso of his dreams, and had accepted that the most he was ever likely to become was an accomplished, all-round pianist. However, it did not lessen his desire to work as a musician, and he jumped at the chance to join a small group which was looking for a pianist. He and his father had argued about it so many times. His father wanted a son to carry on the business, and even had the sign over the shop front altered to "Higgins & Son". Millie had been furious, but, pathetically, his father hoped that it would arouse some sense of pride and satisfaction in

Paul: the same pleasure he himself felt in the prosperous business he had built up from nothing.

If Paul had drunk, and smoked, and swaggered all night at the local boozer his father would have been proud of him. Another "Higgins Quality Family Butcher" to carry on the name. Paul knew that it was no use. Soon he would have to make a break. He was twenty-two and already had several years of butchering behind him. He had hated every minute of it. In the evenings, before his father went out, Paul would keep silent trying to make himself as inconspicuous as possible, and hoping to avoid conflict. At seven o'clock, on the dot, his father would leave to go to the pub. Most nights, Paul would then go upstairs. If he stayed beside the fire he would have to face Millie's scorn. `Well? Are you going to sit there all evening saying nothing? Fine company you are.'

Paul had nothing he wanted to say to Millie. What could he possibly say? Nothing ever happened, nothing interesting, except the thrill of making music. He could have talked to Millie about his music, but she would not have listened and he certainly was not going to talk about sausages or pressed beef. So what did they have in common? He would wait until his sister was occupied and then quietly leave the room.

Eleven o'clock and Paul would hear the front door slam as his father came home. Most nights he was only slightly the worse for wear; but at least once a week, and sometimes several nights in succession, he would come home drunk, staggering and assisted by his boozy mates. It was Millie who would help her father to bed, unless Paul was needed to carry him up the stairs. However, some nights Paul was forced to confront his father: the nights when Paul himself returned late after playing with the Band.

Usually the house was dark and silent when he unlocked the door, but not always. Some nights he would find his father brooding over the remains of the fire. These were nights when his father returned from the pub having drunk enough to be melancholy, yet savagely argumentative. He would refuse to go to bed, forcing himself to stay awake, sure that this time he could convince Paul; talk some sense into him, talk him into giving up his foolish ideas of a musical career.

Each time he would greet Paul with heavy sarcasm, and turn to abuse when Paul refused to respond. 'Had a good night with the girls have you? Wouldn't be surprised if you've been drinking. You want to be careful son.' When Paul said nothing, his father would continue taunting him.

'Come on, don't be shy. You can tell me what you've been up to. I expect a son of mine to come home pissed sometimes. Show he's got some real man's blood in him.'

`I've been playing Dad,' Paul would say.

` "I've been playing Dad". Is that all you can say? For God's sake, don't you ever want to do anything except fool around with those pansy mates of yours?'

`They're not pansies Dad. They're musicians.'

`Musicians? The whole bloody lot of you . .. you . . . you'd fall down like a bunch of frightened jellies if a girl so much as poked her bum at you.' Paul would stand silent waiting for the next assault. `You're going to give up this Band of yours. I won't have you wasting your time.'

`I'm sorry Dad. I won't do it.'

'Won't do it? What do you mean, won't do it? You'll do as I say.'

`You can't make me. I'm twenty-two, nearly twenty-three, and I'll live my own life the way I want to.'

By now his father would be on his feet, shaking with rage and shouting;

`You'll do as you're bloody well told. I can still handle a namby-pamby thing like you!'

Paul was not frightened. Meek he might be and with a horror of scenes such as this, but he was no weakling. Years handling sides of beef had seen to that. When drunk, his dad forgot those other times when Paul had put an arm lock on him. The humiliation of being held, helpless, by his milksop son infuriated the older man.

He would have preferred Paul to slug it out, man to man. Defeat would not have mattered so much. He could have boasted to his mates about what a tearaway bastard his son had turned out to be, and perhaps have hinted that the lad had not had it all his own way. The care Paul took not to cause pain gave him no reason to feel pride, either for himself or for his son.

The noise always disturbed Millie, who would come to the head of the stairs and listen. When the argument threatened to become violent she would intervene, to save her father rather than Paul.

`Come on Dad. Off to bed with the pair of you. You're waking the neighbors.'

In spite of everything, Paul was reluctant to leave home. There was heavy work in the shop handling carcasses, and he had seen how his father had to struggle. Although Tom Higgins would never admit it, Paul could see that his father was only too willing to find some other job that needed attention when bulk meat was arriving. Millie had become engaged, though there was no talk of any date being set for the wedding, but when she did marry and leave home the butcher's shop would have to be sold if Paul were no longer there. Paul knew just how much "Higgins & Son" meant to his father and could not bring himself to that final, hurtful act. Although he felt little affection for his father it was difficult to abandon him altogether.

Release came when his father suffered a stroke that left him in need of permanent nursing care. For once, Paul and his sister discussed the future without personal rancor. They decided to sell the business and place the money in a trust fund to pay for their father's care. When this was done Millie fixed the date for her marriage, and Paul was left free to do whatever he would. The two nights each week playing at the Roadhouse brought a pittance that was not enough to live on, and Paul was forced to leave to try his luck in London. For three years he went through a variety of jobs, some full-time, some part-time, but always he could be found playing a piano, somewhere, sometime during each day.

One night, Paul was playing in an East End pub when one of the customers came up and offered to give him a spell. This was not unusual. Often it was the beer prompting someone to try out his party piece. Still, it was sometimes good for a laugh.

The customer introduced himself as Frank, and as soon as he sat down to play, Paul realized he was a professional. For the rest of the evening Paul and Frank shared the piano, chatting as they played, and in this way Paul learned about the life of a shipboard pianist. `At least you're guaranteed your bed and board,' he was told. `Once you get taken on, the job's yours as long as you want it. Provided you keep your nose clean that is.'

`What do you have to do?' Paul asked.

`You're responsible for the Band, especially their behavior; that's the hardest part of the job.'

Paul nodded his agreement. By now he had met many musicians, and it needed no great imagination to understand what Frank meant.

`Drink's the worst problem,' Frank continued. `Not that I can talk. I've been in trouble often enough for having a few too many when I've been ashore. The rest of the job's not too bad; you have to arrange the light music in the afternoon, and, of course, the music for dancing each night.'

`Is that all?' Paul asked.

Frank laughed. `Not quite, you don't get Sunday off. You're expected to play for Church Service.'

`What's the pay like?'

Frank wrinkled his nose. `Not good, but there are no living expenses and cigarettes are dirt cheap. Oh yes, you have to work in the Purser's Office for a couple of hours each morning, selling postage stamps. In port, you and the Band have to sort and hand out the passenger's mail.'

They were interrupted for a few minutes by a customer who wanted a couple of songs played, and who insisted on telling a long story to explain his request. After he had gone Paul asked; `What do you think? Is it worthwhile trying to get a job as a ship's pianist?'
`Nothing's worth while,' Frank smiled a trifle cynically. `Not unless you're lucky. Pianists like you and me are ten a penny. Honestly, do you find what you're doing now worthwhile?'

There was no need to answer and Paul shrugged. The very fact of playing all night in a smoke-filled Bar while trying to be pleasant to all comers, friendly or unfriendly, was answer in itself. Ship's pianist was certainly worth a try. Paul felt it could be no worse than what he was doing and, in the event, it had not turned out too badly. The Purser rarely interfered, and Paul found that he ruled a little world of his own. He filled his off-duty hours composing music, which would never be published. He lacked the spark of inspiration, and knew it.

All the same, he kept on trying, and sometimes, during an afternoon music session, would slip in one of his own compositions. With his modest aspirations, this was sufficient.

The war had interrupted this pleasant sinecure. He now worked full time as a clerk in the Purser's office and the ship had become his home. Leaving it was unthinkable. He was grateful that he had been kept on by the Company and could still go on living in his sheltered world.

Now his home had left him, and he retreated inside himself the way he had always done when faced with difficulty. If spoken to he would reply, but he felt no desire to take the initiative and start a conversation. There was a need to isolate and insulate himself from all unpleasantness.

Would he be able to get another ship? He would have to stay with Millie when he got back. He always spent his leaves with her and she was happy to see him. Happy, perhaps, because he brought parcels of rationed items such as sugar and bacon and butter. Millie would welcome him when he arrived, but Paul felt sure she was glad each time he returned to his ship. Millie would find him to be an encumbrance if he stayed more than a few days.

* * *

The night was clear and cool, and Alan was finding it hard to keep warm. Jim was taking first watch, and Alan tried to get some rest but doubted that he would get much sleep. Another long restless night was ahead and he thought;

`Time for me to number myself among Ben Johnson's " . . . patient fools". To sing: ' "My mind a kingdom is When the lank hungry belly barks for food." Except that it's not my lank belly which troubles me most. Perhaps I should adapt his lines:

' "To save my wisdom I will be a fool.
Then mind, in dream, a kingdom is
When the festered body aches for ease."'

* * *

On that last night they shared before he left to join Ocean Monarch, Trina and Alan slept very little. Even when the "All Clear" sounded and the dark morning hours were quiet, they lay awake and chatted about nothing in particular.

Mr Bumps had been consigned to her care, but Trina never felt the same towards him as she had to Corncrake. Talking that night, she seemed obsessed by memories of things they had done together and recalled, particularly, Corncrake and his quirks. Mr Bumps was different, and when Alan said something in his defense Trina would have none of it. `He's vicious!' she claimed.

Trina never apologized to Mr Bumps. With Corncrake she would pat him on the radiator and explain all about rationing, excusing her lack of lump sugar. Contrarily, when Alan was watching, Trina would give Mr Bumps a wide berth as she walked in front of him and would say, flatly; `I don't like the way he looks at me. I'm sure he'd bite if I gave him half a chance.'

It was her own fault. Trina never did remember to hold him in third gear. Each time she drove, the gear lever was certain to snap out at least once. Later she would show Alan the resulting bruise, and be indignant about it. But then, of course, it was Alan's fault. `You can't expect him to have any manners. You've never broken him in or schooled him properly,' she would complain.

`There's nothing I can do about it. He was too old and set in his ways when I got him. Blame his first owner.' Alan's excuses would be treated with disdain.

`I do blame his first owner, but it's still your fault. You've never made any real effort to get him to change his ways.'

`Rubbish,' Alan would reply. `It's the rider. He never plays up with me . . . Well hardly ever. You must have hard hands, or whatever it is you horsy people shouldn't have.'

After such a remark Trina would lapse into hostile silence, which usually lasted all of half a minute.

Despite Trina's rudeness, Mr Bumps served them well, and certainly had a more dashing, sporty image than Corncrake.

Alan's train was to leave at eight that morning, and it was half past six when he reached for his watch to check the time.

`Another half hour and I'll have to get moving.'

He replaced the watch and turned to Trina.

`Don't get up and come to the station with me,' he urged. `I'd rather say goodbye here. I can walk out of that door and get it over with quickly. Better to leave you in bed than standing on a bleak, cold railway platform. It's a much nicer way to remember you.'`Are you really going to miss me?'

`Now what sort of question is that? You know damn well I will. You're just fishing for compliments.' Alan had misjudged her mood. Trina was being hit harder by the parting than he had realized, and needed comfort. All he could do was hold her. There was nothing helpful to be said that did not sound trite or forced. After a couple of minutes Trina regained her self control and managed a smile.

`Sorry, that was silly of me.'

`Was it? I don't like seeing you sad, but I must confess it's nice to know that you are going to miss me.'

He stroked her cheek before continuing.

`And the answer to your question, as you very well know, is; Yes, I am going to miss you. I'm going to miss seeing you every day, having someone to argue with, someone just to be with, as well as someone to race off to bed at every opportunity.'

`Particularly the last qualification, I've no doubt!'

`Where you're concerned it's no qualification, it's a requirement.'

`That's an ungentlemanly insinuation.'

`Whatever sort of insinuation it is, it's very pleasant.'

Trina laughed.

`I laid myself open to that one didn't I?'

`You always do darling. That's what I like about you.'

`Alan! You're . . . you're incorrigible.'

She continued laughing for a few seconds, then became serious again.

`Alan?'

`Yes?'

`I don't think I can go back and work in the office.'

`Why not?'

`It just wouldn't be the same. I couldn't go on as though nothing had changed. I'd be reminded of you all the time. I'd look up when someone came in, expecting it to be you . . . I don't know how to explain it. I'd like to be able to think about you when I want to . . . not to be tricked into remembering. Do you know what I'm getting at?'

`I think so. But if you don't go back what will you do?'

`I've been thinking about it for the last week, ever since we knew you'd be going. Every day, when we did something together, I'd be wondering what it would be like when you weren't there.'

`With any luck I won't be away too long.'

`I hope not. But even if you do come back in a couple of months or so it'll only be for a few days, and then you'll be away again. We can't count on anything until the war's over.'

Trina was starting to sound miserable again.

`Well, what will you do?' Alan asked.

`I've made up my mind.'

Alan was watching her as she spoke, and saw the small determined nod.

`I'm going to join the Wrens.' She tried a smile, then continued.

`I think they have the nicest uniform. I feel . . . I want to be among strangers I suppose. I don't want anyone asking me if I've heard from you, or being sympathetic and asking if I'm missing you, reminding me when I don't want to be reminded.'

Trina sounded so doleful that Alan shifted his position and pinned her arms while he kissed her.

`Good idea, it'll make it much easier to forget me,' he teased. `Beast!' She struggled playfully, but his precaution paid off and Trina could not free her arms. The struggle ended in laughter, which somehow took the edge off her tragic scene. It was time to get moving and Trina sat up in bed watching while Alan shaved and dressed. Those last minutes flew past, and in the end their final farewell was hurried.

`Goodbye, don't worry.' This was all Alan was able to say as he leaned across the bed to kiss her.

`Goodbye,' Trina replied in a whisper.

Alan picked up his two heavy trunks. In the doorway he paused and looked back. Trina still sat, huddled in the sheets, her face solemn.

`Goodbye,' he said again, and left the room quickly.

Downstairs, he asked the night porter to help him get a taxi; and for a little while was occupied in the business of getting himself, and his baggage, first to the station and then on board the train. After he was settled in the carriage it really hit him. He could picture Trina, as she had been when he looked back from the door of the hotel room, and knew that she was only waiting for him to leave before allowing the tears to fall. How long would it be before he saw her again?

For Alan there was no excitement in going to war. He had no eagerness to go and do his duty. It was more a feeling that it was something unpleasant that had to be done. Something that had become necessary, but should never have been allowed to happen. He remembered his experience in Ocean Wanderer, and did not feel too happy, nor any too brave.

It was still early afternoon in Liverpool when the train pulled into Lime Street station, and after queuing for half an hour Alan was able to get a taxi to take him to the Gladstone Dock. He paid off the cab and looked up at Ocean Monarch, drab in wartime grey, huge and slab sided, seemingly a fixture at the dockside rather than a seagoing vessel. The wharf was deserted, and a cold wind howled between the ship and the cargo sheds. There was the tang of oily water, of tar and hemp, as well as the distinctive smell from the sheds: a combined odor from hundreds of cargoes over many years. The wind picked up swirls of dust, which it chased down the wharf together with pieces of paper and scraps of rubbish. It was a Sunday afternoon, and war or no war the dockside was barren and desolate.

Alan staggered up the gangway with his two cases. The general layout of Ocean Monarch was similar to Ocean Wanderer, and he had no difficulty in finding his way to the Purser's office. It was closed. He left his bags outside, and set off to look for the Purser. As he turned for'ard into the starb'd alleyway he saw a steward coming towards him, and that was how he met Rapley for the first time.

`Can I help?' Rapley looked at Alan with an element of curiosity, wondering who he was and whether he had any right to be there. He had waited until he was only three or four feet away before speaking.

`Yes!' Alan was happy to have found someone in this, apparently, empty ship.

`My name's Anderson. I've just joined as Assistant Purser.'

`Pleased to meet you Sir, I'll let Rankin know you're on board. He's your cabin steward.'

`Thanks for the help,' Alan said. `Can you tell me where I'll find the Purser?'

`You'll find him on "A" deck Sir. When we're in port he spends an hour walking on deck each afternoon at about this time.'

Rapley showed Alan to his cabin, giving him a hand with his baggage, and after he had gone Alan went to look for the Purser. When Alan stepped out on to "A" deck there was no sign of Purser Redpath, and he thought Rapley must have been mistaken. Then a movement caught his eye. Peter Redpath was in one of the bays beneath the lifeboats, and was almost hidden from sight behind a winch. He was standing at the rail, and looking across the dock to where the new battleship, King George V, was completing her fitting out. Peter turned as he heard Alan approach and waited for him to speak.

`Purser Redpath?'

`That's me.'

`My name's Anderson, Sir. I expect you were advised. I've just joined.'

There was no welcoming smile, just a brief nod. `Glad to have you on board Anderson. I expect I'll see you later.'

He hesitated awkwardly, then with another infinitesimal nod walked away and left the deck. This was Alan's first experience of the shyness that so embarrassed Peter at times.

After the Purser had gone, Alan went to the rail where Peter Redpath had been standing. The power and menace of the battleship that was so near fascinated him. With her low profile, Alan was able to look down on her from the height of Ocean Monarch's boat deck. He did not stay long: on the open deck the wind was cold and blowing strongly.

Back in his cabin he found Rankin waiting.

`Rankin Sir, I'm your cabin steward. Rapley told me you'd arrived on board.'

`Good of you to come up Rankin. You'll be off duty now I expect.'

`Yes Sir, but I wasn't doing anything. There's nothing much to do in fact. I wondered if you'd like any help unpacking?'

`I don't think so thanks. It'll only take a few minutes, and I don't want to cut into your off-duty time.'

`It's no trouble, Sir. I'd be glad of something to do. I know, would you care for a cup of tea?'

It was obvious that Rankin wanted to check on him, to find out what sort of person he was, and Alan decided he might as well string along with him.

`Fine, I'd like that.'

While Ranking was fetching the tea, Alan made a start on unpacking, but when he returned Rankin took over, emptying the trunks, sorting and placing Alan's clothes and personal possessions in various drawers and the wardrobe. Alan drank his tea and had to admit that Rankin did a much neater job than he would have done himself.

When Rankin left, Alan was at a loss what to do. The other cabins in the alleyway were empty and the office still closed. He wandered around the ship looking through the public rooms, the lounge and galleries. All the cabin accommodation areas were silent and empty, as was to be expected. He felt very much alone in alien surroundings and wondered whether Trina was back at Barringdale. At least he could write to her. It would be something to do. He returned to his cabin, pulled out a writing pad, and settled down to give Trina an account of how he had spent the day since leaving her that morning.

Was it only that morning? Already the hotel room belonged to a previous existence. He was still writing when there was a knock at his door. It was Peter Redpath.

`You'd better come and have a drink. I expect there are one or two things you'd like to know.'

This was the beginning of their friendship. Over a few drinks Peter's shyness wore off. They went down to dinner together and continued drinking afterwards.

Alan was not entirely sober when he went to bed that night.

CHAPTER EIGHT

To mourn a mischief that is past and gone
Is the next way to draw new mischief on.
Shakespeare `Othello'

`I'm bored to death.'

For the listless survivors in the boat the cliché was a little too true, and was, perhaps, the worst part of waiting for the end.

Alan wondered what the others did to pass the time. He tried many things, but, mostly, he sent his mind off to far scenes, distant in time and place. He lingered over memories, holding to the ones that he liked to remember. It did not always work. Events he would have been happy to forget too often claimed his thoughts, and brought their own regrets. He was afraid of squandering memories, wishing to eke them out and keep them as a place of retreat, only to be used when the monotony of waiting became unbearable.

Poetry was another game, sifting the corners of his mind for a snatch here and a line there, trying to rebuild a poem from memory. When this failed he would turn to creation, looking for words to paint their plight. There was much that was somber, and much that still shone in the human spirit. Their inner solitude was that of the condemned who must make peace with themselves. Their minds and their bodies drifted aimlessly, dwarfed by the emptiness of their surroundings.

Alan felt cheated. He had always assumed that the prospect of death should prompt deep and significant thoughts. Now he feared that this was not true, at least as far as he was concerned. It seemed that his faculties were attracted by trivia. He could no longer construct without pencil and paper, and, unable to concentrate, his wits would wander and his theme vanish, his mind becoming a frustrated blank.

He now tried to trickle away a few more minutes of time by recalling his early morning musing, but could remember no more than the last lines;

'So where lies truth? Or does truth lie?
The poet's mind enacts
a meaning varied, as needs be,
to suit his fancy's facts.'

`Nothing fresh in poets claiming license. Even Horace, two thousand years ago, said: "Painters and poets... have always had license for bold invention" or something like that anyway.'

Con Mahoney and Joe Hayter sitting in the bow, what did they think about? Did they take time to remember the parties they used to hold in their cabins? Did Joe remember the obscene cake he baked for Con's last birthday? Even Con was taken aback when it was unveiled.

They had talked Joe into doing his party trick that night; getting him to squeeze through one of the tiny "F" deck portholes. To look at him you would swear that he could never get his bulk through so small a hole. Nevertheless he won many a bet proving that, where the head and one shoulder would fit the rest of the body would pass. How did Con describe it?

`Like a bloody great tube of toothpaste. One day he'll burst himself and we'll be left to clean up the mess.' Then with an evil grin he added, `You never know. He might slip right out sometime and fall into the sea. Gawd, wouldn't that cause a tidal wave?'

Mahoney himself, was he still constantly thinking about women? Perhaps it was all pretence, the succession of women he claimed to have bedded. A confirmed bachelor, he was randy in word but suspect in performance. In talk he always had some woman in his sights, but whether he ever got around to pulling the trigger was another matter.

Unlike the others in the boat Con always seemed aware of what was going on around him. In spite of everything that had happened, he looked more like an animal about to spring than a castaway chef. Since Blacklock died he had been a bundle of hatred set against the world. Still the same cocky little man who ruled his galley as a foul mouthed tyrant; yet, surprisingly, the galley staff never resented his abuse, and seemed to take pride in having such a fierce little tartar as their boss. If a new assistant cook lost his temper and threatened Mahoney with violence, inevitably someone would stand by him. `Leave the little bastard alone. Find someone your own size.'

As Joe would say: `It's a bloody miracle you've lived as long as you have.'

Alan came out of his reverie and looked around the boat. `Hell!' he thought. `We're a shaggy, unlovely looking lot. Is this the way people face the prospect of death? Are we all looking for comfort in the shadows of the past, unwilling to face the shadows of the future? There are no dramatics, no fine gestures, but is there resignation? All protests internal, secret to each individual mind.

`How do I feel?

`I don't want to die: that's sure. There's a core of anger, but not directed against the Germans who sank us. At least I don't think it is. Hard to say what it's directed against; fate perhaps. It's this frustrating inability to do anything to help ourselves, of being forced to sit and contemplate, regret, and wish. I reject the approach of death. It's too slow, too much time for thinking, and too quick... Too quick for my dread of the unknown.

`Does my face tell the others what I'm thinking? Probably no more than I can guess their thoughts. Take Higgins, he seems the one least affected. Or is he? It's difficult to remember what he was like before. He's still practically invisible. If someone stumbles over his feet he hastens to apologise, blaming himself for the other's clumsiness.'

Yes, each face, each mannerism, each attitude had become screamingly familiar, yet each man had own private quality hidden from his fellows. There were changes though, and not just physical deterioration, but elusive differences in behavior. Hard to pin down, for on the surface everyone tried to behave and talk naturally. Was it perhaps like the dull look in a condemned man's eyes, in some way already dead and concealing inward thought.

If Alan could see changes in the others, they would see changes in him; but these were mainly physical changes. There were also character differences, but whether brought about by the experience in the boat Alan could not be sure. He was still too close to the individual who had jumped from the dying ship to know. `I wonder…' and with that question he was caught in the toils of introspection. `I do know this: I'm no longer the same person who left Trina that cold February morning to begin my life at sea. It's not just that I'm two and a half years older; many scenes, hopes, fears and yes, hurts too, have made me a stranger to that youth.

`I had little humility then... No, be truthful. I still have little humility. The difference is that now I realize it. The treatment I received as a football player encouraged an inflated opinion of myself. Such good points as I had were matched by bad points. I learned quickly and easily, and that made me intolerant of people whose minds moved more leisurely.

`Hell, perhaps I haven't changed much. I must be honest with myself otherwise this game won't work. I'd just be making up a fanciful story for my own benefit.

`I have changed. I think. I've learned to be less trustful, which may not be a good thing.

I've found that it's not possible to go through life being polite and courteous at all times. Not for me anyway, and not when dealing with a certain type of person. Within the confines of a ship there are situations which must be resolved, situations which can't be sidestepped with a polite smile: moments involving defeated people; people made desperate by fear, bereavement, drink, and sometimes even hate. A handful of crew refusing to sail because they'd lost their nerve... refugee women and children bereft of husbands and fathers... the violence of witless drunks... and hate. Yes, that too. Prisoners of war, puppet victims programmed by propaganda.

`So, I've also learned to be brusque when there is no time for kindness, and I've learned to be bruisingly abrasive when it's a waste of time to try persuasion.

`What have I lost? A portion of idealism, a little of trust, and some of the old confidence in my philosophy of life.

`Am I a better person? I doubt it.'

* * *

Eleven days after Alan joined her, Ocean Monarch moved from Gladstone dock to the landing stage. There they embarked troops and anchored in the Mersey, waiting for the convoy to assemble. Just before leaving, a short note from Trina arrived, telling him she had enlisted in the Wrens.

With troops on board, the empty echoing alleyways and deserted decks of the previous few weeks became a noisy bustling metropolis. Everywhere peace was shattered by the clatter of army boots. Bewildered subalterns searched for missing platoons, and below decks many lost all sense of direction, unable to sort out port and starboard or fore and aft. Sergeants, equally bewildered, maintained an air of confidence, while searching for their lost sheep in the maze of troop decks. Within twenty-four hours the chaos subsided and five thousand troops settled into a routine.

In time, embarkations and convoys became an everyday occurrence, but none ever left so vivid an impression on Alan as this, his first experience of a large troop convoy. Many ships, whose names were household words in pre-war days, sailed, drab but dignified, in their wartime grey. Ships from the halcyon days when the big passenger liners were the aristocrats of the high seas. Vessels of the P&O and Orient Lines bore an aura of romance enshrined in a thousand novels, with tales of Australian cattle kings and mining magnates, Sahibs and Viceroys, Nabobs and Anglo Indian society. Union Castle ships, impressed from their peacetime voyaging between England and South Africa, brought images of Zulu Impis, the wide veldt, diamonds and gold, and empire builders like Rhodes. Next the "Drunken Duchesses" of the Canadian CPR Line, bringing reminders of the great inland waterway of the St Lawrence, and the vast plains and tundra of Canada, trappers and dog sleighs, Redcoats and Indians. "Drunken" because their design, essential for navigating shallow water, made them prone to roll in the slightest sea.

There were Atlantic liners. Ships which had ferried the New World wealthy to their Old World playgrounds, and returned with Migrant-crowded lower decks where hope blossomed, though tears told of sorrow for loved ones left behind.

Dutch ships of the Nederland Line evoked the exotic flavor of the Far East, the fabled Indies lands of spices and strange customs. All were proud descendants from the age of buccaneers and merchant adventurers.

The convoy spread over many miles of ocean, the ships sailing in columns distanced by half a mile. In the centre of the convoy the battleship Revenge, majestic in spite of her age, ploughed through, rather than over, the waves. On the perimeter of the convoy, escorting Destroyers cast their sonic web, protecting the soft merchantmen from hunting U-boats, while Revenge gave insurance against any marauding enemy raider.

They moved with a stateliness that disguised progress. Each day the formation remained untouched, and it sometimes seemed that this mass of ships was fixed in one position, divorced from the rest of the world.

The illusion crumbled when they arrived at dawn off Freetown, in Sierra Leone. Alan and Peter Redpath were already on deck watching a shadowy fringe on the horizon that soon resolved into trees and a low-lying coast. By now the breeze was bringing a distinctive, earthy, almost fetid smell of land. It was like entering a Turkish bath with several years' accumulation of sweat hanging in the air. Two days in Freetown, two more days in Capetown, and on through the Indian Ocean and the Red Sea to their destination, Port Tewfik, at the eastern end of the Suez Canal.

On the homeward voyage they called at Durban for re-fuelling and storing, and Alan took the opportunity to meet Wyn, a distant relative. Wyn invited Alan to a party where he met Helen, an intelligent, attractive blue-eyed blonde whose husband had been killed in the Middle East a few months previously. Helen had a life to begin all over again. She was the first woman Alan had met, socially since leaving Trina, and Helen was desperate to prove that life was still worth living.

Trina was a long way away, and it was a pleasant interlude.

* * *

`The sun's nearly down. Soon I'll have to help Jim measure out the water ration.'The knowledge registered automatically with Alan, but his mind was elsewhere.

`That girl in Durban. It meant nothing to my feelings for Trina. It wasn't at all important. It was just... temptation I suppose.' Alan shook the thought from his mind and looked across to Jim.

`What's he thinking about? None of his confident bounce left. It must be his mouth that makes him look so gloomy. Instead of the usual hard, firm line his lips are slack. I suspect he's daydreaming.

'Could he be seeing himself as Bligh or Shackleton, making an historic boat journey? If so it'll be a sad blow when he returns to reality. We're making no journey... in that sense anyway. We're at the mercy of chance with no control over our movement, so there's no hero's role for Jim.

`What could Jim write in a log, if he had the paper and pencil to keep one?'

TODAY MONDAY: (if it is Monday) Len's beard is definitely the fastest growing. The sandy bristles jut pugnaciously and he looks angrier than ever. Queenie's beard does not suit his character.

LATER MONDAY: Clouds building up, but I fear too high to bring rain. Mahoney and Huskins were quarrelling, nothing serious though.

MONDAY AFTERNOON: Usual routine. Taking it in turns to go over the side. It seems to help with body moisture and, at least, keeps us clean.

MONDAY AFTERNOON LATER: Had to speak to John Allward. His morale is cracking badly and it affects the others. Alan is away in dreamland as usual.

MONDAY AFTERNOON LATER STILL. Clouds increasing but still too high. Dare we hope for a change and the possibility of more rain?

`No, there's not much that Jim could enter in a log. Perhaps a few technical guesses about wind force, direction of drift, or a report on the condition of the boat: Slight seepage, and we have to bail for ten minutes night and morning.

`What would I write about if I had pencil and paper?'

`Nothing practical that's sure. Silly little poems? Or I might try to describe the others in the boat, capture something of their characters, showing how they became what they are. If, one day, some scraps of paper were found in a drifting boat, these few might live again, shadowy images in the mind of a reader.

`Take Rapley, the formerly ageless, dapper steward, well past the time when he should have retired, but falsifying his age so he could stay on at sea. I never realized how white his hair had become. Slicked down neatly on the bald dome, the few sparse wisps seemed colorless, but now the white is emphasised by his beard, making him ancient and patriarchal. Each time I look at him I have to tell myself that it really is Rapley. He's weak too. We're all weak now, and age is telling on him, but he's never complained. When I catch his eye he tries to produce that familiar, perky grin.'

* * *

`Jack Rapley, How often have I told you it's time you settled down. Leave it to the young ones. There's no need for you to keep on going to sea. With our few savings and the pension we've got enough to get by.'

Jack had looked at Annie and felt a sense of guilt. It was not fair to her, yet how could he stay home? It was a nice enough little house, and most of their friends lived nearby, but they were Annie's friends, not his. His friends were at sea. Well, perhaps there were one or two who were now ashore, content to exist on the pension, but no one he would want to spend time with day after day. What could he do? He drank little and the pub held no attraction. It was different when he went ashore with a few shipmates: then it would have seemed miserable not to have a drink.

His old standby of rug-making was a good way to pass the evenings on board, and there was pleasure in producing the completed article when he got home at the end of the voyage. It would never be the same with Annie and the girls fussing around, able to watch the rug grow. He had known many seamen go to pieces after six months ashore. Jack knew he was being selfish, thinking of himself rather than Annie, but that had been the way of it all their married life. Annie had been the one to make sacrifices. He still remembered with wonder that day when, in spite of everything, she had joined him in church for their wedding ceremony. Her father and mother were there, grudgingly, but they had resigned themselves to the inevitable. What uproar there had been when, in 1888 and at the age of thirteen, he had run away to sea. His father was senior clerk with a produce wholesaler where Annie's father was the senior salesman. Jack and Annie had known each other since they were children, but he had always felt this yearning for the sea. What started it, he could no longer recall. It was a part of him, deep and uncontrollable. Annie's father thought Jack a ne'er do well, and pressured Annie into becoming engaged to Ben, his junior salesman. Annie was in no hurry to wed and was happy for the engagement to continue indefinitely. This suited Ben, who was studying at night, and wanted to qualify as an accountant. When the Boer war broke out, the patriotic Ben volunteered to serve in South Africa and never returned. When news of his death arrived, Annie was upset, for Ben, too, had been a childhood playmate, but mingled with sorrow was an element of relief. Marriage to Ben would have been comfortable, but with little passion.

From that time on there was no doubt that she and Jack would marry. Annie was now old enough to resist her father's pressure and never regretted her decision. Even though she would have liked to see more of Jack she knew he would never be happy in a shore job. Money was no problem. Jack was now a cabin steward, and although his pay was small his happy manner made him a favorite with the passengers. Their tips were always generous, and made him one of the more affluent members of the ship's company. Annie made friends easily and soon there were children, so she was rarely lonely when Jack was at sea, except, perhaps, at night.

In most ways she was content, and each time Jack came home it was like a fresh honeymoon. They genuinely loved each other, and neither could now imagine a life married to anyone else. If Jack stayed home he might not be happy, and the harmony between them might suffer.

Annie made Jack's life complete. He missed her presence and her smile, but it was emptiness tinged with a pleasurable sense of anticipation. He had a sure confidence that she would always be there, waiting for him, and eager to welcome him home. Forty-two years they had been married, with a family of two boys and two girls, yet he still thought of her as the girl of twenty-one who had taken him as her husband.

Sometimes he felt a sense of guilt that she had been left so much on her own, his own visits home only serving to disrupt the household, the signal for excitement and presents. There would be a few days of special treats, love and laughter; and then he would be gone. Annie would smile tolerantly; allowing some of her rules to be broken as the children made the most of every hour with Jack. `The sooner you get back to sea,' she would say, `the better I'll like it. Takes me all of a week to get the children settled after you've gone.'

Annie would laugh as she spoke, but her eyes told a different story. All the same she did not envy her friends whose husbands came home every night. She listened to their complaints, and came to the conclusion that it was better to have a man she loved, but who was rarely home, than to risk suffering constant domestic irritations.

`I'm a fool,' Rapley thought. `Annie was right. I should have retired when war broke out, and stayed home to keep her company.' He thought of Annie alone, busying herself with small chores.

`I'd do anything for her, yet...'

He was saddened as he realized the futility of regret. In the last war he had been torpedoed, but then he and most of the crew had been picked up within a few hours. Annie had known nothing of it until after he returned home. This time was different, and Jack knew that he was not going to make it. His strength was failing, and, though he tried to hide it, he knew the others were aware of his weakness. The knowledge made him more sad than apprehensive. Sad for Annie, for, though she never nagged him, he knew she wanted him home to share their last few years together.

At least she would have the girls. They lived nearby and Annie was able to enjoy her grandchildren. As long as the two boys came through the war safely he did not care so much about himself. He could not even write to her. Write a few words to say goodbye... to explain. Perhaps Queenie or Basil would go to Annie…

* * *

`The slackness has gone from Jim Bristow's mouth and his familiar stern expression is back. Could he be hanging a mutineer, or flogging a minor offender?

`Jim Bristow went to sea...'

Alan was finding it hard to maintain concentration. He would drift off, losing all sense of time. Then would come a moment of intense awareness of the others, seeing them in sharp focus, noting every little detail in appearance and behavior. Then, without warning, he would lose interest, and his mind veer off into some by-way or blind alley.

He would try to make his mind blank, to listen to nothing, to think of nothing except the slop of waves against the side of the boat. Could he hypnotize himself into forgetfulness? Forget where he was? Forget his soreness? Forget even Trina . . .? No!

`Forget, how could that be? past love is yet a part of me.'

* * *

`Jim Bristow went to sea . . .

'I must be going crazy. My mind's running around in circles. 'Jim Bristow went to sea! 'Of course he went to sea you silly bastard. Why keep thinking that absurd phrase?

'Jim Bristow went to sea a big bold man was he.

He went to sea to win a bet, fell overboard and got quite wet then hurried home to tea.'

`There I've made a stupid rhyme. Perhaps now it'll go away instead of repeating itself, over and over.'

The rhyme worked or, perhaps, his mind had slipped into another gear. To Alan it seemed that he was once again on board Ocean Monarch, sitting in his cabin and reading a letter.

* * *

Before leaving Durban a letter arrived from Trina. It said that within a week of joining the Wrens she had been sent on an officer training course. With the letter she enclosed a snapshot of herself, wearing an ill-fitting uniform and with none of her usual elegance. The figure, standing in front of a brick wall, seemed remote, anonymous. The coarse serge took away her individuality, and transformed her into the stereotype of a Wren Other Rank. Alan smiled as he examined the photograph closely. There was no doubt in his mind that she would qualify as an officer, and he was sure it would not be long before Trina was wearing a well-tailored officer's uniform. Her mother would see to that. Trina's letter made Alan realize how much he had missed her during the past weeks. The convoy had taken two months to reach its destination. Then there had been a long stay in Port Tewfik while the ship had been unloaded by lighter. When Ocean Monarch was finally cleared, she left for Durban to refuel. From there she was ordered to sail to the UK without escort.

Ocean Monarch was to go straight home, or so they thought, but two days out from Durban she was diverted to Trinidad. U-boats were concentrating off Freetown and the longer way home was safer. They waited in Trinidad until fresh orders were received, then sailed on a course plotted to take them clear of the latest U-boat sightings.

The ship docked in Avonmouth and, half an hour after arrival, Alan was reading a letter from Trina written only ten days earlier. The news was that she had been commissioned, and was stationed at Portsmouth. There was a telephone number where he might contact her or leave a message.

Seven days leave was being granted, and half the ship's company was to go almost immediately. The other half would take their turn when the first leave returned. Alan was on the second leave, and went ashore as soon as possible to ring Trina to let her know when he would be able to visit. The girl who answered the phone told Alan that Trina was not in the office, and that it would take a few minutes to find her. Time went past and Alan feared he would run out of change before she was found. When the operator came back and said they were still looking for Trina he left a message saying he would call again, but possibly not until the next day. The crew was being paid off and re-engaged for the next voyage, and Alan was kept too busy to try again that day. Next morning the dockside call box was out of order, and the nearest public phone box was about two miles away. Being on duty, Alan could not leave the ship for more than a few minutes, and could not be sure when he would have a chance to ring. Instead he gave the Ship's Agent a telegram for Trina, saying he would call when he reached London.

The week passed slowly for Alan, but at last it was Sunday and he caught the train to London. When he arrived home it was late afternoon and he tried to phone Trina, but again he was out of luck. Trina was off duty and could not be contacted. Next morning he rang again to find that Trina was not immediately available. The switchboard girl took a message from Alan to let Trina know that he would call back in half an hour. Before he rang off she asked; `Was it you who called and left a message last week?'

`Yes.'

There was the suggestion of a giggle in her voice. `I'm sure she'll be here when you call back; she was cross the last time, when she found she'd missed you.'

As soon as the half-hour was up Alan rang again, and this time there was little delay before Trina came on the line. There was no mistaking her voice.

`Hello?'

`Trina!'

`Alan, how lovely to hear from you.'

`It'll be even better seeing you. Any chance of getting leave?'

'Not much. I'll try, but I've only just arrived here, and they don't grant leave on passionate grounds.'

`In that case I'd better come down to Portsmouth.'

`That'll be good. Oh, I don't think you'll be able to.'

`Why not?'

`The entire coast down here's in a restricted area. Only residents and service personnel are allowed into this, so called, invasion zone.'

`How strict are the checks?'

`I don't know. I came down by train with a draft and there were none that I saw. There were guards at the platform exit, but they took no notice of us.'

`I don't believe that. Not unless they were blind or dotards.'

`Idiot! I didn't mean that way. Anyhow, I'm just a dowdy Wren now, not worth a second glance.'

`If that's the case I'll have to pluck your feathers.'

`Will you indeed?'

`Well, what do you expect after six months at sea?'

`I'd rather not say. You never know who's listening on these phones.'

`I'll come down tomorrow, and you'll have a chance to find out if you've guessed right. I'll phone when, or should I say if, I reach Portsmouth.'

`I hope you make it.'

`I know. You always do!'

`Alan! Goodbye.'

He was left grinning into a dead phone.

Next day Alan wore his Southern Oceanic uniform which, he hoped, would get him through to Portsmouth. When the train arrived, the passengers streamed through the exit and past the bored guards who asked no questions. His next problem was to find accommodation; he chose an hotel at random where he was asked to register and his identity card was examined. A merchant seaman registering into a Portsmouth hotel was surely not unusual. In the entrance hall there was a phone booth connected to the hotel switchboard, and Alan asked the receptionist if she would put a call through for him.

Trina was soon answering.

`Alan! You've made it then?'

`Not yet I haven't.'

`Where are... Oh shut up!'

After telling Trina where he was staying, and arranging how and when they would meet, Alan talked with the receptionist. She was an attractive brunette with a pert manner, and it helped pass the time. Trina had taken Mr Bumps to Portsmouth, so was able to drive to the hotel and there was no need for Alan to meet her.

When she arrived he was waiting just inside the main entrance and immediately jumped to his feet. They stood facing each other, and in those first moments neither seemed to know quite what to say. Alan reached for her hands and with the touch their tongues were set free. Afterwards Alan was not sure what his first words had been, but Trina swore that they were;

`Let's go to my room.'

He did remember that Trina had burst into laughter.

They headed for the stairs and Alan glanced across to the desk.

The receptionist caught his eye, and with a wicked smile raised her eyebrows.

Trina was only able to get away for a few hours each evening and during the daytime Alan wandered aimlessly, just wasting time. He had arrived in Portsmouth on the Tuesday, and would have to leave early Saturday in order to get back to Avonmouth that same day. On the Thursday afternoon he was standing outside the hotel waiting for Trina, and sensed her excitement the moment she stepped out of Mr Bumps.

`Guess what.'

`What?'

`I've got a twenty-four hour pass. I don't have to get back until Saturday morning.'

`How d'you manage that?'

`Don't really know. I just put in an application and it was granted. The reason I gave was "personal matters that need my attention". I thought I'd be called up and questioned; instead I was told my request was granted.' Trina paused while she laughed. `Maybe they do give passionate leave. Somehow the word has got around, and it seems everyone knows that my boy friend is here on leave.'

`If that's why it's been granted we'll have to justify it!'

`I knew I could rely on you. That's why I accepted the pass.' Trina was smiling at Alan and looked positively radiant.

`Come on,' he said. `Let's get rid of the dowdy feathers.'

At the desk Alan stopped for a moment to speak to the Receptionist.

`My wife will be staying with me tonight.' The eyebrows flickered, but the receptionist kept a straight face.

`Very good, Sir,' she said, accenting the "very".

They walked across the hotel foyer, and Alan could hear Trina muttering.

`As the actress said to the Bishop.'

Next day they left early, heading for the New Forest. Alan was becoming used to the sight of Trina in uniform, and had been correct in his guess. The cut of the uniform was immaculate, giving her exceptional smartness even for a Wren officer. The crisp white collar and black tie, together with the severity of the dark uniform, emphasised that cool, distant look so characteristic when her features were in repose.

They had no worries about fuel for the car. Before leaving London Alan had collected his leave allocation of petrol. He filled Mr Bumps' tank and gave Trina the surplus coupons. There was no hurry and they drove slowly, talking and sightseeing. They stopped for a few minutes near where Sir Walter Tyrrel accidentally shot King William, Rufus, with an arrow, and debated whether Sir Walter was bawled out, or whether he was congratulated by Henry, who succeeded the unfortunate Rufus. They could not remember reading any history book that made this clear.

Lunchtime found them at Brockenhurst, where they stopped to eat at a delightful pub. For wartime it was an excellent meal, and after lunch they drove on for a mile or two before leaving Mr Bumps and walking across the open, lightly wooded country. It was a still summer's day, a day to luxuriate in, and a day for escape and carefree living. They were determined to make the most of the interlude fate had granted them. Tomorrow it would end. Their paths would separate, and who knew when they might rejoin.

They sat beneath a tree, their backs resting against its trunk.

`Remember that last night in London?' Alan said. `Remember asking me if I'd miss you?'

`Uh huh.'

`Well I did.'

`Did you now?'

`Yup, it started as soon as I left you.'

It was warm and they were drowsy after their lunch. A half minute or so went by before Trina got around to replying.

`I missed you, too.'

`You don't say.'

`I did say.'

`So you did.'

The effort of making conversation was too great. Trina shifted, so she could rest her head against Alan's shoulder. Once settled, the silence continued.

'I'm uncomfortable.'

Five minutes had elapsed, and now Trina sat up and stretched.

`Go behind the tree. I don't care.'

`Not that sort of uncomfortable. There's no room to stretch out here. There's not enough shade. Let's go to that big tree over there.' Trina pointed to an oak some fifty yards away, heavy with wide leafy branches and throwing a solid circle of shade.

Alan stood and reached down for her hand. Trina came up into his arms easily, and they paused to kiss before strolling over to the oak tree. For about half an hour they lay quietly, sprawled on the grass, and for most of that time Trina kept her eyes shut. She was not sleeping. Every few minutes her eyes would open slightly, and, seeing Alan, would smile. For his part he was happy just to look at her. Eventually she began to show some signs of life.

`That's better, my lunch is now digesting nicely.'

She rolled over.

`Don't tell me you're getting hungry again?' Alan demanded.

`I don't think I'll be hungry for quite some time, not after that meal, but at least I don't feel bloated now.' In the mood that had overtaken them they did not really need conversation, and Alan was thinking; `Why can't every day be like this?'

On impulse he leaned over and tickled the back of Trina's neck.

`Will you marry me?' he asked. Trina was lying on her stomach chewing a blade of grass, and glanced at him quizzically, raising a delicately penciled eyebrow.

`Probably.'

`Supposing we get "probably" officially engaged,' he suggested.

`Why?'

`God! What a depressing question to my question. Here am I, expecting you to be in a flutter, and all you do is lie there chewing the cud and saying "Why?"'

Trina took the grass out of her mouth and gazed at it reflectively.

`Are you suggesting I'm a cow?' Alan laughed back at her.

`If I don't get a sensible answer soon, I may start thinking of something canine and female.'

Trina sniffed insultingly at him, then said: 'Seriously though, why? What's the advantage in getting officially engaged? I don't see it matters. We know what we mean to each other, and surely that's enough. We've always reckoned an engagement was - unnecessary.'

`For us, yes,' Alan replied. `But I was thinking it might be easier for you to get leave next time if you could claim a genuine, gilt-edged fiancé who was home after braving the perils of the deep.'

`Oh! I see. I thought you wanted to marry me.'

`Why? What would I get that I'm not getting now?' Trina regarded him thoughtfully.

`You,' she said equably, `are a bastard.'

`Would you like me to start all over again, down on one knee, with protestations of undying love?'

`Might be fun at that.' Trina looked at him wickedly, then sighed.

`No, don't bother. I'd look stupid lying down while you proposed formally, and it's far too much trouble to stand up.'

`Oh well, forget I ever suggested it.'

Perhaps there was a slight edge to Alan's voice. Trina's manner changed immediately, and she reached over to him.

`Can't we go on as we are? All I was thinking was that it could cause problems with our families, mine especially. We're still only twenty and they'd be telling us we're too young, and they'd worry that we were rushing into a hasty wartime marriage.'Trina hesitated, looking questioningly into Alan's face, then said;

`If you really want to...' Alan pulled Trina towards him and held her.

`Of course I want to. I wouldn't have asked otherwise. Still I think you're right, but it suddenly seemed like a good idea and I just had to ask.'

He kissed her, then added:

`Getting engaged certainly wouldn't make the slightest difference to the way I feel about you.'

He looked into those cool grey eyes, and unbidden there crept into his mind the memory of a pair of blue eyes that he had also looked into. He had not told Trina about them, for they did not seem important. It had been one wild, carefree night, which had left nothing more than pleasant recollections.

Trina and he had agreed...

Why then this shadowy sense of guilt?

CHAPTER NINE

Chewing the food of sweet and bitter fancy
Shakespeare - Coriolanus

Trina closed the door, then leaned against it. Her body seemed numb, yet there was a deep ache lurking, ready to pounce the moment she relaxed her self-control. She looked around the room, remembering that first excitement of ownership, and the planning and pleasure she had taken in buying the furnishings. In her letters she had said nothing to Alan about the flat. It was to be a surprise. It must be true; true what her cousin, John, had told her. There would be no surprise, no Alan. It did not seem possible.

Alan was sometimes so confident, sometimes so unsure of himself. He had surprised her in Portsmouth in more than one way. In her thoughts she had never visualized him in uniform.

Had he really been hurt when she evaded his proposal? She had been scared, scared that later he would regret being tied. That was why he was so touchy about her prospects. No, not prospects, it was her connections which were the problem, her Marsden relationship, and now...?

She had planned everything. After the war she would not work for Southern Oceanic, and it would be entirely up to Alan whether he stayed with the Company. None of her mother's shares would come to her, they would all go to her brother. She would have some money, of course, though not a fortune. Perhaps she had hugged her plans too much to herself, and now she had nothing, not even a photograph of him in uniform. Trina looked at her bare hands and smiled ruefully. If he had given her an engagement ring she would have worn it, and not cared about any bondage idea.

Trina shivered and walked over to the table, pulling off her tricorn hat and throwing it down. It landed next to the last letter she had received from Alan, and she picked up the envelope, taking out the note he had written. His letters were often short, as there was so little that security rules allowed him to say, but he wrote regularly.

Even so, she would sometimes go for weeks without hearing from him, and then half a dozen letters would arrive all together.

This was one of his nonsense letters, rhymes or silly stories. Sometimes, as in this one, there was a hidden reason. She read again:

'Hi there Trina!
Since I seenya
I've been hither,
if not whither.
Shall I wander
far beyond a
blue horizon?
Hear my sighs an'
know I missya.
(Rhymes with kissya!)
Leave trochaic
try iambic.

I wonder when
I'll see my Wren?
I love my bird! (double entendre - ref: OE bird & bridda)
It's quite absurd
to say I don't
and so I won't.
Instead I'll say,
from far away,
I want you dear,
and, were you here,
I'd make you know

that this is so.
I wonder when
I'll see my Wren?'

There were a few clues in the rhyme. The "I've been hither" in the first verse alerted her to look for the hidden message, and the "Shall I wander" hinted that he was not homeward bound. The second verse with its "wonder when", and "were you here" reinforced this, but it was the postscript which gave her the answer.

'P.S. I must confess that, when I read what I have written, I fear `Tis a poor creature but mine own'. As you see, unlike the songs the Bard sings, there is no doubt that the song I sing is a poor thing!'

Trina looked at the date: nearly three months since it was written. The way Alan had used the words "sings, song and sing", and the repetition in "'Tis a poor" and "sing is a poor" left no doubt that he meant Singapore.

Her movements were still carefully controlled as she folded and replaced the letter in its envelope. Loneliness started to gnaw at her calm. The flat was so quiet... some music might help. Trina walked to the radiogram, and then...

The neat package lying on the record cabinet. The whisky flask, her present for his twenty-first birthday, engraved with his initials. Bought on the actual day of his twenty-first, some three weeks ago.

Was he drowning at the moment she bought it?

The ache pounced, and Trina crumpled on to the settee.

* * *

`Today's the twenty-second day.'

Jim was conscientiously keeping count of time, and Alan wondered whether he was talking to himself or if he expected a reply.

Alan did not want to start a conversation so confined his answer to a nod.

None of the others seemed to have heard, and with a sudden swell of irritation Alan found himself thinking: `What the hell does it matter? What difference does it make whether we survive for twenty-three days or twenty-four? Counting them's not going to make any difference... perhaps the sooner the better.'

The irritation died, yet it sparked a memory.

`I might have have had to live another morn.' Gilbert and Sullivan, Yeomen of the Guard, and for an instant the recall was vivid. The last time he had seen it was with Trina at Lewisham.

The moment passed, banished by his immediate need. `God! I can't think of anything except water.'

Jim was checking his count of the days once more and Alan felt an unreasoning anger. It took all his remaining self-control to refrain from shouting;

`Stop it Jim! We're not interested. We don't care.' Then his mood changed to apathy. `He doesn't know what I'm thinking, and I'm too dry to tell him.'

Alan looked at Rapley, who was obviously past caring. His face was putty colored and it was surprising that he still lived. They had given him the last drop or two of water and had expected him to die before the day was out. That was yesterday morning and it seemed longer... a lifetime ago. Queenie had been cradling him for hours, shading Rapley from the sun with his own body.

The sun had gone now, hiding behind the clouds, but Alan was gripped by desperation; `Thirst... water. I've got to get away from here. Where shall I go?

`Lewisham, that's it.' It had been cold and clear, and freezing when he and Trina drove up from Barringdale to Lewisham where the D'Oyly Carte company was playing. He had booked tickets without asking which opera would be on, and was happy to find that it was Yeomen of the Guard, one of his favorite Gilbert & Sullivan operas.

`I have a song to sing O!... Only in my mind though...

'Moping mum? ...I've lost my Merry Maid... Poor Merry Maid.'

Alan's mind was wandering and he tried to snatch it back.

`Stop it! Stop... Stop.'

* * *

Trina snuggled against Alan as they drove, and nibbled against his ear.

`How can I concentrate on driving when you're doing that.'

Trina wrapped her arms around Alan even more tightly and slipped a hand inside his shirt.

`You don't suggest you're driving without due care and attention do you?' she queried, and there was a touch of laughter in her voice. `If so, what more do you want?'

It all depended on the point of view. Anyway body contact helped ward off the cold.

Warmth enveloped them as they sat in the theatre. Warm air, warm music and warm laughter... Martyn Green as the tragic Merryman.

After the show they froze again. Rotten Mr Bumps! His fuel pump played up and he refused to start. Luckily it was a clear moonlit night or Alan would never have been able to see what he was doing.

After an hour of frustration he got the car moving. By then his fingers were frozen and an air raid had started.

When they reached the hotel they found that the hot water system was out of action. No hot bath, the bed was like ice, and so were they.

* * *

`He's gone.'

The words brought Alan back to the present.

Queenie was looking at Rapley, whose staring eyes and open mouth left no doubt that he was dead. All the others seemed stunned and incapable of reaction. Jim's eyes were fixed and unfocussed, and Alan reached out angrily to attract his attention. It was not decent to look like that, not when someone had just died.

`He's seeing now,' Alan thought as he took his hand away from Jim's arm. `But not understanding, and he's not doing anything...'

'Someone's got to help Queenie. I don't want to but suppose I must.' Queenie tried to move, but was too stiff and cramped. Alan told him to stay where he was, and beckoned Basil Allward to come and help as he took hold of Rapley's arms.

`Basil, you take his feet... That's right. Quick, let's get it over with. There...'

`He's gone, really gone this time. There was no weight to him...

'I hated that splash. Don't look, turn the other way.

`Damn you Jim, that should have been your job. Captain Bligh wouldn't just sit there.' They had not been able to get rid of Rapley fast enough and this thought kept nagging at Alan. Why had it seemed to be so necessary? Was it that they were frightened by this threat to their own mortality?

Alan shivered. It was some few moments before he understood that a new chill in the breeze and not his brooding thoughts caused it. The sky was getting murky, and the clouds were heavier.

`All that water up there.'

Alan closed his eyes, willing it to fall. `If I just keep my eyes closed it'll rain; if I don't think about it perhaps it'll happen again. Try not to think... Especially not... I let go before Basil, and Rapley went in headfirst.

`Eeny meeny miney mo
Basil held on to his toe.'

`Pull yourself together. Don't be stupid... Open your eyes.'

With an effort Alan brought himself under control, but his dark mood persisted, and now he could not keep his eyes away from Joe. Joe Hayter had the look of a man who is condemned and is afraid, and Alan wondered if Joe would be the next to go. So much fat had melted away that he looked like an empty sack.

Alan glanced at John Allward and decided that he, too, had that condemned look, but without the fear. `Strange,' he thought. `We still have hard rations but no one wants them. We're too dry to eat. But then I don't feel hungry and I don't think the others are... '

* * *

An inch or two of water slopped between his feet in the bottom of the boat. Joe Hayter could not take his eyes off this movement. For how much longer would he watch it run from side to side? It was not fair. It was not bloody fair. He should not be here. All those years saving money, and Tom, his brother, working and saving as well. By now, but for the war, they would have had a nice little business.

All those years while Tom built up the Pie Shop trade in Hastings, waiting for the lease they had been promised on the shop next door. They planned to make the two shops into one big shop and had saved enough to put in modern ovens. Tom would have continued with his pies, while Joe looked after the cake side of the business. Now it was all over, and even Tom's business was almost finished. All the houses and hotels were closed or taken over by the army, and rationing had slashed his output. Even with staff cut right back it was all Tom could do to keep up his rent payments. It was not bloody fair. It just was not bloody fair!

* * *

`If only I'd been able to see you Trina... just once after that last disastrous night before we left for Malta. Surely everything would have sorted itself out. If... perhaps not... perhaps it's better this way. I don't know.

`That's water... a great big spot of water. Water on my knee? And there's more.

`My God! It's raining.' It was as if Alan had received a shock. Although the others were now showing signs of excitement no one had moved.

`They don't seem to understand,' he thought. `The jib you fools.'

'Hurry! Hurry!'

Alan stood and staggered for'ard. `Give me a hand.' His voice cracked from excitement. `Spread out the jib.'

To his relief he saw that they were beginning to respond. Jim had followed him and was now holding the drum ready to catch the rain.

`Rain, rain, rain like hell and don't stop. Don't ever stop.' It was driving, heavy rain, flooding the drum and overflowing. Rain which beat on them painfully. With the drum full, Jim reorganized the jib so that it sagged and held a pool of water. In turns they buried their faces into this pool, sucking up the precious fluid until they could drink no more.

There was no laughter this time. They sat, shivering, and waited for the rain to end. It stopped, and they watched, glassy eyed, as the remaining water soaked through the sail and dripped into the bottom of the boat. Another twenty-four hours without rain and they would not have survived. Was it an omen?

Con Mahoney dropped the corner of the jib that he had been holding, and glared around the boat.

'First Blacklock, now Rapley, does that bastard up there want a sacrifice for every sodding drop of rain?'

It had to be little Con, putting into typically lurid words the haunting thought that no one else had dared mention.

Alan felt drugged with water but found that he could think more rationally now, except that he felt so sleepy.

* * *

There were four seated at a table in Capetown's Del Monico; Peter Redpath, Alan and two army officers who were traveling in the ship. Built in imitation Spanish style, the Del Monico was the best known beer hall in Capetown. The large floor was a mass of small tables and chairs, and when a convoy was in port every chaotic inch of space was crowded with clamoring, thirsty bodies. In the mad crush, the Del Monico staff strove vainly to meet the demands for service.

The four had been sitting for over five minutes, waiting to order drinks, and were thinking of moving on.

`With our compliments, Sir.'

Peter and Alan turned at the sound of the familiar voice. Somehow Rapley had acquired a tray, loaded it with drinks, and was standing behind them grinning. The tray, held high above his head, was balanced on his fingertips, the way he had been forced to hold it while he worked his way through the crowd.

`Our compliments?' Peter queried. Rapley turned his head, and gave a nod to indicate a table a few yards away. Several of the group sitting there grinned and raised their glasses. They had pushed two tables together and made a compact gathering of experienced, hard-cased shipmates. Even if Alan and Peter could not have seen them, they would still have been able to make a fair guess at the bunch of cronies who had gone ashore together.

Bow legged Spinks, the Bos'n; tall skinny Baker, a Quartermaster; bustling Selkirk, 2nd Steward; Bill Martin, Able Seaman who had no ears. They had been cut off at the siege of Kut, or so he claimed; funereal Monkton, Headwaiter; and Slasher Salter, Ship's Butcher. They were a hard-bitten crew who had sailed together for many years and were now no more. Rapley had almost certainly been the last survivor of that close knit gang.

It was Alan's second voyage in Ocean Monarch. It was one that had been most eventful from the time a steering mechanism failed in the battleship that accompanied the convoy. On Ocean Monarch's bridge the officer of the watch realized the danger and took urgent avoiding action. His swift decision minimized the damage and the damage, though serious, was not disastrous.

The battleship spent six months under repair in Simonstown, and Ocean Monarch's bows were sealed with concrete so that she could complete her voyage to Port Tewfik. From there she was sent, via Karachi, Bombay and Colombo, to Singapore, where a dry dock was available at the Keppel Harbor. She arrived in there a few days before the Japanese attack, made at the same time as the assault on Pearl Harbor.

At first it promised to be a pleasant holiday, as shipboard duties were nominal and Alan had plenty of spare time. Not far from the dry dock was a nine hole golf course and the ship's officers were invited to become honorary members. There was heat and there was rain, but unlike the miasma of Freetown it was not oppressive. When it rained, which seemed to happen at least once every day, a freshness was left in the air. Perhaps it was the scents released from the tropical vegetation, or the clean lush foliage sparkling with raindrops that gave a feeling of well being. Then the heat would take over again, and build up, until the next downpour.

The Japanese spoilt their relaxation. On the night when their bombers made the first, surprise attack, Ocean Monarch was trapped in the glare of floodlights, exposed and vulnerable. Soon they had real reason to be worried. Much of the damaged bow had been cut away, and until it was rebuilt the ship would be unable to sail. It looked as though it could be a race between the dockyard workers and the advancing Japanese.

By the end of the third week in January the repair was completed, but the battleships Prince of Wales and Repulse had already been sunk, and Ocean Monarch would have to escape through what were now Japanese dominated waters. They took on board as many women and children as possible, but embarkation was a miserable, harrowing process. It was a day when fear for the unknown future could be seen in the faces of the women and older children. It was also a day of tears and emotional farewells as wives parted from husbands, not knowing if they would ever meet again. A series of air raids added a sickening emphasis to these individual tragedies. There was no escort, and their only hope was to slip away unobserved. The first twenty-four hours were tension packed. The human cargo was so vulnerable that no one dared think of what would happen if they were attacked. Luck held, and in a few days they reached Australia, where their passengers were landed. From Australia they crossed the Pacific, then sailed through the Panama Canal and on to Bermuda.

The barometer was falling when the ship left Bermuda, and almost immediately they ran into a hurricane. The seas forced Ocean Monarch to cut her speed, but the two Destroyers that now escorted her were fighting for survival in the high seas. After a further reduction in speed, to allow the escort to keep in touch, a decision was reached to part company.

There had been a party for Alan's twenty-first on the night they spent in Bermuda, and when they sailed, Alan felt it unfair that his hangover should be compounded by a hurricane. He went on deck and tried to find a reasonably sheltered spot, hoping the fresh air would help clear his head.

This was his first experience of such a gale and he was amazed by its power. It was an awesome sensation when the twenty-eight thousand ton ship was tossed about as if she were a small boat. The howling of the wind was intense and eerie. The tops of the waves were snatched away, then swept violently into a dense layer of spume, which filled the troughs. It looked as if the whole surface of the sea had been beaten into foam and raised some forty feet above its normal level.

It was then, while she was battling the hurricane, that the Admiralty lost Ocean Monarch.

The Navy office in New York sent orders by radio diverting the ship to Halifax, Nova Scotia. However, in England the Navy believed that Ocean Monarch was still heading direct to Liverpool. When she failed to arrive, it was assumed she had been torpedoed, or had capsized during the hurricane. At that time U-boats had intensified their attacks off the West Coast of America, and the loss of Ocean Monarch was accepted without question.

Halifax was under an eight-foot blanket of snow, and lanes had been cleared down the centre of each street. From these lanes narrow alleyways were cut leading to shop entrances and buildings. The ship stayed in Halifax for more than a week before embarking Canadian troops and joining a convoy to cross the Atlantic. In spite of the snow Alan found it a friendly town, the welcome being much warmer than the weather.

* * *

'Where have you been? You were supposed to be here nearly three weeks ago.' The Liverpool branch manager appeared to be quite indignant, as if the ship had been absent without leave. With Ocean Monarch listed as missing, presumed sunk, her arrival caused quite a stir. Luckily, although the advice notices to next of kin had been prepared they had not been sent, and, apart from the branch manager's feelings, it seemed that little harm had been done.

Before leaving Singapore Alan had received two letters from Trina. In the second she had told him that she was leaving Portsmouth and going to a new posting. Trina could not give any details but promised to let him know how to contact her when he returned home. Mail for the ship's company would normally have been brought on board when they docked in Liverpool, but this time it had been sent back to London when it was thought the ship had been lost. Alan arranged to go on second leave. Until he had some idea of where Trina was stationed, he preferred to wait on board.

Two days later, when the mail arrived, there were three letters from Trina, but with little news. Security limited what they could write, and letters tended to be; `I'm well. Hope you're well,' and `I love you.' A frightening sameness threatened their correspondence. To relieve the monotony Alan would write fictitious tales about impossible happenings. Trina, in turn, transformed the repulsive toy dog, which Alan had given her more or less as a joke, into an ostensibly living Pekinese of uncertain temper. Alan now had to wade through the latest misadventure of Wat Ah U before finding the information he wanted.

`Glory be, there it is.'

Trina was stationed in London, and gave a telephone number where he could get in touch with her. Alan skimmed through the other details. She had nowhere to park Mr Bumps so had left him at Alan's home. Her weight had increased by a whole two pounds, an event treated as catastrophic and blamed on mess caterers. He put down the letters. It was already after four, and he had better hurry.

The first call box was, as usual, out of order, and it was nearly quarter to five before he got through and asked for the extension she had given. There was a short pause before Trina came on the line, and although she did not give her name Alan recognized her voice. `Would you have a second hand Destroyer for sale? Preferably one that's only been driven by a little old lady.'

`Alan! What... what... Is that really you?'

`If it isn't I'm awful confused.'

`What's happened? Where are you?'

`What do you mean? What's happened? I'm in Liverpool and I've got a few days leave, starting Friday.'

There was no reply, and after a few seconds of silence he asked:

`Trina! Are you there?'

`Yes, yes... I was just surprised.'

Her voice sounded flat, and Alan had a sudden shattering thought. `Has she found someone else?'

`Don't you want to see me?'

`What do you mean? Why do you say that? Of course I want to see you.'

Her words were emphatic, indignant even, and there was eagerness when she asked; `When did you say you'd be home?' The leaden sensation left Alan's stomach.

`I'm coming down Friday afternoon, but I'll have to go home and unload the food parcels I've brought. Can we meet on Saturday? I'd better spend Friday night at home.' There was no doubting Trina's enthusiasm now.

`Alan! I just can't believe it. It... it's been so long.' Alan realized that he was laughing. That sudden moment of doubt had left him feeling quite weak.

`It has. It's seemed an awful long time. I began to wonder if we were ever coming home. When and where shall I meet you?'

`Saturday... I'll be working until half past three, or perhaps four. Make it say four in Trafalgar Square, over on the Whitehall side. I may be a few minutes late.'

`So? What's unusual about that?' Alan demanded, and without giving her a chance to reply added; `OK I'll wear a grey pin stripe suit and a top hat, so you can recognize me.'

`Shouldn't you carry something as well, to make it easier?'

`How about a torch for you?' he suggested.

`If you really want to.' Trina laughed shakily. `Oh! Something else... but I'll tell you later.' Quite suddenly Alan had the feeling that Trina was crying.

`Alan... I'm so... '

`Three minutes. Are you extending?' a voice cut in.

`Yes please,' said Alan, but simultaneously heard Trina say; `No, no thanks.' Then speaking quickly she said; `See you Saturday.'

The line went dead.

Alan walked back to the ship. Hearing Trina's voice had increased his longing for her, and Saturday seemed a long way off.

CHAPTER TEN

With a smile on her lips, and a tear in her eye.
Sir Walter Scott

Alan's first evening at home was spent answering his parents' questions, and next day time moved too slowly for his impatience. Servicing Mr Bumps did not take long and by half past ten the car was ready to go. Alan's father had gone out and with his mother busy around the house he was left to entertain himself. Lunch helped pass the time and afterwards Alan tried to bury himself in a newspaper.

At a quarter to three he could wait no longer, and set off for the West End. Being a Saturday afternoon, the City streets were almost deserted, their traffic-smoothed surfaces gleaming in the light drizzle of rain. Although he drove slowly Alan still arrived far too early. He left Mr Bumps in a car park near Piccadilly Circus, then walked down the Haymarket to Cockspur Street and through to Trafalgar Square. The rain had become heavier and Alan was glad he had borrowed his father's umbrella. He moved down the Square to stand where he could see down Whitehall, but there was no sign of Trina. In spite of his time wasting it was still only twenty to four.

Alan had waited for Trina at many times and in many places, but never before had he felt so anxious to see her. He knew her well enough to know that there had been something wrong in her voice and manner when he had spoken to her on the phone. By ten past four he was in an agony of impatience and twice made a move to walk down Whitehall, then checked himself. Although implied,

Trina had not said she would be coming from that direction. At last he saw her, a slight, uniformed figure hurrying towards him. Even at a distance he could see the tiny quirk of a smile. He knew that smile, and understood that Trina was trying hard to keep her emotions under control. He ran to meet her.

`Wren officers aren't supposed to be kissed passionately, not in public that is,' she protested as he released her.

`Tell them Wren officers sometimes don't have any say in the matter,' he replied.

They stood, facing each other and holding hands. Alan saw no sign of added weight, indeed her face looked thinner and more strained than when he had left her in Portsmouth, but the look in her eyes was the same. He knew then that everything was still all right between them.

`Have you been waiting long?' Trina asked, still slightly breathless from hurrying.

`About seven months.'

`Idiot! Usually I get away by quarter to four on a Saturday. Of course, today had to be different.'

She tried to slip her hands out of Alan's, but he held them and tried to pull her towards him again.

`Not now - later.' Trina was holding back and Alan let her go.

`Better not make a welter of it,' she cautioned. `There's too much brass around this area.'

`Then you'll just have to imagine I'm kissing you, and arousing your worst and most passionate instincts.'

`You must be losing your touch. I didn't feel a thing.' Trina was smiling openly, and Alan wondered why he had been so worried.

`You're a cold unfeeling creature,' he complained. `Come on, I'll buy you a drink to loosen you up.'

`No, you come on. I'm loose enough and I want to show you my flat.'

`What's all this? What flat? How come? Don't the Wrens keep you within their cloistered confines?'

`Not in the job I'm in now. Come on, let's go.' Trina tucked her hand inside his arm, and Alan looked down.

`Isn't that forbidden?' he asked.

`Not really. It's the complete bodily surrender bit they don't like.'

`Where's the flat?'

`Chelsea.'

`Sounds interesting. We'd better go and get Mr Bumps, I deserted him in the car park at Piccadilly.'

`Poor Mr Bumps, ' Trina exclaimed. Then added: `I thought I'd better leave him at your home. There's only a courtyard where I'm living. There's nowhere to lock him up, and I didn't like leaving him in the open all the time. Anyway, when it's fine I like to walk to Whitehall. I cut through past the Palace and along Birdcage Walk, and take a few pieces of bread to throw to the ducks.'

`How come you're able to do this?'

`You remember, last time you were on leave, I told you aunt Margaret had died?'

`About a couple of weeks previously, wasn't it?'

`That's right. Well, the old dear left me quite a bit of money. Not an enormous amount, but it's all invested in something safe that brings in nearly three hundred and fifty a year.'

`I see, very useful, but how about the flat? I thought the Navy locked up the Wrens at dusk, and didn't let them out again until next morning.'

Trina laughed. `Hardly, though there are times when I've thought it mightn't be a bad idea. Not referring to myself, of course.' The rain was now falling heavily, giving them an excuse to huddle under the umbrella, and Alan slipped his arm around Trina's waist. She continued her explanation.

`It's like this. I'm now in a confidential job as secretary to one of the top brass and often have to work back late, usually after he's been at some conference.'

`You'd better not work late while I'm on leave.' Alan tightened his arm pulling her closer. `Tell him to postpone the war, or some such.'

Trina brushed away a spot of rain that had blown off the edge of the umbrella and on to her cheek.

`I'll have tomorrow off anyway. The Chief nearly always manages to organize his week so that he can get away to the country on

Friday afternoon. It means that I get Sunday clear, and can usually get away without too much trouble on a Saturday afternoon. I go in on Saturday in case there are any urgent messages, and it gives me a chance to get odd jobs done and tidy up while he's away.'

`What about Sunday? Does the war let up by some special arrangement?'

`More or less, but no, things still wind down a bit in Whitehall at the weekends. Of course there are duty officers rostered to take over at night and on Sundays. Oh, that reminds me. They've just put a phone in my flat so I can be called if there's a panic when I'm off duty. Unless I'm on leave I'm supposed to be on call, and, if I'm going to be away from the flat for more than an hour or two, I have to leave a message saying where I can be contacted. Either that or ring in regularly.'

`Sounds important.'

`Not really, it's just that most of the work's confidential. It'd be pretty difficult for someone else to take over, unless they'd had a couple of days with me first. It doesn't need all that much intelligence. It's more a matter of knowing what's going on and where everything is.'

`Yes, but why the flat?'

`My boss fixed that. We were working late one night and stopped for coffee. He asked me how I liked the job. I said something about the inconvenience of the quarters, and that I wished I could live out. He knows I'm related to Uncle Harry, and I think that helped. Anyway, next day he told me I could make my own arrangements, provided I found somewhere close by.'

At the car park Alan handed over the ticket, and it was a few minutes before the attendant brought the car down in a lift from an upper floor.

`Always Uncle Harry in the background,' Alan thought. Whenever the Marsden relationship came up he had this uncomfortable feeling. Even Trina's new job in Whitehall; perhaps a word had been spoken in the right quarter. Immediately Alan felt ashamed. Trina's ability would qualify her for any job on her own merit. All the same, there was this background feeling of power and wealth, with the influence it carried. Even Trina, who could never be accused of snobbishness, still took certain things for granted. With her expensive education she could easily have become a social butterfly. That this had not happened was due to her own common sense and the influence of her father. Of course, her mother was no socialite. Mrs Grant was a clever, scholarly woman in her own right, but was always aware that she had been born a Marsden.

For his part, Alan would have been happier being with Trina if Uncle Harry had not been lurking in the shadows. He always felt that the Marsdens were weighing up whether his genes were suitable for an alliance with Trina.

`Poor Mr Bumps!' Trina's voice was shocked. In that car park, cars were moved by lift between the various floors and they had often left Mr Bumps there. This time the attendant had driven Mr Bumps out of the lift at more than the usual speed. With a loud clang and a squeal of brakes he was stopped, abruptly, on a large revolving steel plate in the centre of the ground floor. The momentum and sudden braking set the disc turning. When Mr Bumps had swung around to face the entrance the attendant let in the clutch, and there was a second metallic thud as his wheels passed over the edge of the turntable and brought it to a halt.

Trina walked across to the car, then flicked a glance to make sure Alan was watching. Satisfied she was observed, Trina made an exaggerated detour, to give Mr Bumps's bonnet a wide berth. This was not to be tolerated, and Alan promptly went over to pat the radiator and murmur words of comfort. They drove off, leaving a parking attendant who surely thought they were both mad.

Trina guided Alan as he drove towards Knightsbridge, cutting through to Kings Road and the turn-off to her flat. He parked in front of a four-storey block, and Trina, impatient to display her new home, waited while he immobilized Mr Bumps.

`No one seems to bother much about that nowadays,' she said. `Hordes of German parachutists aren't likely to arrive any minute. It's not like a year ago.'

`Force of habit,' Alan replied. `Anyhow, it's still the law isn't it?'

`Come on, I want you to see the flat.' The lift was not working, and they had to climb four floors to the apartment.

`This was the reason I got the flat,' she explained. `The couple who had it got fed up with climbing the stairs. By sheer luck I happened to contact the agents just after they'd given notice they were leaving.'

Trina stopped in front of a door marked "4-8", and already had the key in her hand.

`This is it.' She threw the door open and led the way inside. They stepped into a large sitting room, and the first impression Alan had was of light and airiness, created by the size of the big glass doors that led to a small balcony. Through these doors was a view he had not expected. Over the rooftops of nearby buildings, and through a gap between two office blocks, he could see the Thames gleaming like shining lead under the grey skies.

`It's terrific!' he said, and to his surprise Trina promptly burst into tears. For a moment Alan was too startled to do anything. Then he caught her to him.

`Darling, what's the matter? What is it?' It was some minutes before he could make any sense of what she was saying, and by then they were sitting on the settee.

`I'm feeling better now,' she said at last, then added. `I'll light the gas fire first, and then explain.'

From the few strangled words between her sobs Alan realized that Trina had believed him dead. What had she heard? Who had told her Ocean Monarch was lost? Uncle Harry perhaps?

She came back to him and he led the way to the settee. `I'm sorry I was so silly.' Trina settled into Alan's arms and smiled; though her eyes remained a little watery.

`I'd been so looking forward to showing you the flat, and then I heard that Ocean Monarch was sunk. When we came in just now it brought it all back to me, and how miserable I'd felt. You've no idea what a shock it was when I heard your voice on the phone.'

`Who on earth told you, and why didn't they tell you we'd turned up in Liverpool? The Navy lost us... '

`Yes, I know now,' Trina interrupted. `After you rang I got through to Uncle Harry and he gave me the whole story.'

`But where did you get it from in the first place?'

`My cousin, John told me.'

`John? Why John? And if he told you, why didn't he let you know it was all a mistake?'

`Poor John, he thought I knew. That's why he mentioned it. He's not living at home now, and didn't hear you'd turned up until after you'd called.'

`But what the hell did he want to tell you for in the first place?'

`He didn't, not really want to, that is. It was just that I bumped into him about a week before you got back. I would have walked past if he hadn't called; "Hi Trina". I turned around and saw him, but before I could say anything, he said; "I was sorry to hear about Alan".

` "What do you mean?" I asked and immediately he looked embarrassed. "Haven't you heard?" he said.

` "Heard what?" I demanded. "Oh damn, I'm sorry Trina," he said. "I shouldn't have said anything I suppose."

`By this time I was beginning to panic. "What's this all about?" I asked, or more likely yelled.'

Trina paused, giving Alan a faint smile before continuing.

`Because he said: "Take it easy now Trina."

`I was absolutely furious and said: "To hell with that John." Tell me, what is it? You can't stop now.

`He hesitated, looking uncomfortable and then said: "I saw Dad last night. He told me Ocean Monarch was nearly a fortnight overdue. There doesn't seem much doubt that something's happened to her."

`I don't remember leaving John. I must have gone back to the office, because I had to try to pull myself together when the boss sent for me. I suppose I looked dreadful. Anyway, he saw that something was wrong and asked me what was the matter. I couldn't face explanations and said I wasn't feeling well. He gave me a long, hard look, and told me to take the afternoon off.'

Trina had been gazing out of the window as she talked. Now she turned and smiled to Alan before continuing. `That was when I came back here and felt so miserable.'

`Why didn't anyone tell you when they knew we were okay?'

`Uncle Harry didn't know I'd heard anything about it. Before I left Whitehall that day, I rang to find out if he could tell me any more than I'd heard from John, but Uncle Harry wasn't in the office. I spoke to Miss Paisley, his secretary, and asked if they'd had any more news, but she was only able to tell me the same bare details John had heard.

`I asked if next of kin had been told, and she said they were preparing notices but wouldn't be sending them out for a few days. They were waiting for an Admiralty check, just in case any of the original crew members had been landed sick at some port during the voyage. Also, with so many of the crew living in Tilbury, they wanted to make sure all notices would be delivered in the same mail. They had to be certain there'd be no mistakes. It's not the sort of thing you want to slip up on.'

Trina paused, and Alan was about to speak when she said; `I was going to see your parents, but I didn't want to be first with the news. Apart from being a coward about it, I didn't think it right they should feel I'd been told before they were.'

`Why didn't Miss Paisley let you know when we arrived in Liverpool?'

Trina shrugged. `I expect she thought Uncle Harry had given me the news in the first place. Naturally she'd think he'd tell me himself. It was hardly her business to interfere in what she'd regard as a family matter.'

Alan gave her a consoling squeeze.

`I'm sorry, darling, it can't have been very nice. Still it's all over now.' Trina nodded, but Alan could see her lips were still quivering, and her body was tense.

`That's not all though.'

In spite of her desperate attempt at control, the tremor in her voice could not be disguised. Alan's left arm was still around Trina, and her fingers, which had been resting in his right hand, balled themselves into a fist.

`What else has happened?' he asked, and once more tears were trickling from the corners of her eyes.

`It's Ian,' she said. `My brother. The day after that news about you, my mother arrived late in the evening. I knew at once that something was wrong, and I don't know why, but for some reason assumed that it was Dad. She'd come all the way from home to break the news to me herself. They'd received a telegram early that morning saying Ian had been killed, somewhere in the Middle East.'

Trina unclenched her fist, and turned her hand so that her fingers could grip Alan's.

`Mum was very controlled, you know how she is, but she'd been hit very hard. She stayed the night here, and left first thing next day as she didn't want to leave Dad on his own for longer than necessary. I wanted to tell her about you, but for some reason I just couldn't. We were both trying so hard to be brave, and... well... I thought it might be easier for both of us if - if I left it until we'd had a chance to recover from the shock.'

Trina was now crying quietly, and Alan did his best to comfort her. Within a few minutes she was brushing away the tears, determinedly.

`I must look a mess.'

Trina looked at Alan and he knew that she was signaling for help, wanting him to assist by bringing the conversation back to normal.

He did his best, and pretended to look at her critically.

`We-ell, perhaps your image as a prim - in inverted commas, immaculate - in even more inverted commas, Wren officer has slipped a fraction, but don't let that worry you.'

Although he tried to use a flippant tone, the result was not very convincing. He was feeling far too upset after listening to what Trina had been through.

`When you rang from Liverpool...' Trina spoke as though the words were being forced from her. `Do you know why I had to ring off so quickly?'

`I had a feeling you were crying, and wondered what I'd done to have that effect on you.'

`I was crying, and then saw the boss standing in the doorway watching me. He made me tell him what it was all about. Normally he's friendly, but keeps a little distant from the staff. He's quite nice when you get to know him.'

`Is that so, well don't get to know him too well. No extramural secretarial antics.'

Trina made a face at Alan, then said: `I'll be back in a minute,' and went to put in some work on her appearance. Alan walked across to the window, looking out over the Thames to the distant shapes of Battersea in the dusk. The light was switched on behind him, and he turned to find that Trina had taken off her jacket and tie. She looked softer, younger and even more vulnerable. She joined Alan at the window and he helped her lift the blackout boards into place. With the last board fixed into position he stood behind her, his hands resting on her waist, while she adjusted the heavy curtains. When she had finished drawing them, Trina looked back at Alan over her shoulder, then turned, placed her hands behind his neck and rose on her toes tilting her head in a demand to be kissed.

When the demand had been met to her satisfaction, Trina took Alan's hand, and pulling gently, said `Come and see the rest of the flat.'

There were shadows under her eyes, but Trina's make up was repaired and she had regained control of her emotions. Alan lifted his hand to her cheek, and brushed back a wisp of hair that had somehow managed to escape from its appointed position. Looking into her eyes, Alan knew an intense desire to wipe out the pain she could not disguise.

Trina made him examine the kitchen, separated from the dining area by an open doorway and a serving hatch. The dining area was at one end of the long sitting room. There was no dividing wall and this helped with the spacious feel of the flat. Next she showed Alan the bathroom. Every move was unhurried and deliberate, prolonging their anticipation. Desire had flashed between them when Alan had brushed her cheek. At the bedroom door they paused and Trina murmured 'Alan', before leading the way into the room.

There was a change in their behavior towards each other during the few days Alan was on leave. The change was subtle, and would not have been noticeable to an outsider. But it was there. Though Alan and Trina seemed to talk and argue in the same old way, the careless, light-hearted mood had gone. Often, after a few exchanges, they would sense a false note in their banter, a lack of spontaneity in their words, and suddenly there would be a silence.

Perhaps they drank a little more than usual, trying to find their lost badinage through artificial means. It never worked. Instead, they found a new degree of tenderness, with Alan becoming far more protective than in the past, and there were times when he wondered what was happening to them. Trina accepting such solicitous behavior was quite unlike her normal self. The Trina of old would have laughed if he had tried to treat her as delicate and fragile, yet this was how Alan now behaved. Not openly perhaps, but in small everyday happenings.

For Alan, Trina's independence and strength of mind had been her greatest attraction. She had an integrity of spirit that he loved. Now the vixen in her seemed to have been tamed, and he could only hope that its wildness would soon revive. Meanwhile, he worried about her possible reaction when he returned to his ship. This time there was no question of Trina being able to get leave. Except for the Sunday she had to work each day. In the early morning the flat would be cold, and they would lie in bed talking until the last possible moment; then came a mad scramble to get her to work on time. After dropping her in Whitehall Alan would return to the flat to shave and clean up. Shortly before midday he would take sandwiches and a flask of coffee, then stroll through the Park to Whitehall and wait for Trina. Each day they went to St James's Park, and fed crusts to the ducks while eating their own lunch. After that first day Trina was able to talk more calmly about her brother. Alan had not realized before just how close she and Ian had been. Ian was almost five years older than Trina, and had gone directly from school into the Regular Army. Alan had not met him, and Trina had only ever mentioned Ian in a casual manner. Now, as she spoke of her earliest memories, there was a distant, fond look in her eyes that told, more than words, of her love for an idolized big brother.

'It's almost exactly two years since I last saw him,' Trina said. 'Ian was sent out to Egypt early in 1940, to join his regiment which was stationed there. They'd been moved to Egypt just before war broke out; but Ian was doing a course, so it was several months before he rejoined them.' Another time when talking about Ian she had said:

'I wish Ian had married. He'd a girl friend, Diana, who I thought was lovely. They were engaged at one time but something must have gone wrong, and they broke it off when he went overseas. I never could understand why, and Ian never gave any reason.'

`Perhaps they felt life was too uncertain,' Alan suggested. `Ian may have thought it unfair to get married and then leave her almost immediately.'

`That still doesn't explain why they broke the engagement.' Alan shrugged. `Are you sure they didn't, perhaps, feel much the same way we do about it?'

`Perhaps, I don't think so... Oh, I just don't know.' There was a touch of impatience in Trina's voice.

Alan could only guess at the sorrow she was fighting. All he could do was listen, and hope that talking about Ian would help her accept what had happened.

Thursday arrived before they were prepared for it and Alan had to catch the train back to Liverpool in the afternoon. In bed on Alan's last night of leave, Trina talked again about those few days when she had been sure that he was dead.

`Promise me you won't go missing again.'

It was tempting fate, but Alan crossed his fingers. `I promise,' he said, but when he kissed Trina her cheeks were damp. In the morning he was packed and ready by the time Trina had to go to work. Although they would be meeting later, they said a private goodbye before leaving the flat. As he held her Alan could see that the strain was back in her eyes.

`Try not to worry,' he told her. `It doesn't help.'

It was a useless remark, and he knew it even as he spoke. After dropping Trina in Whitehall, Alan took his bags to the Left Luggage office at Euston. Then he drove Mr Bumps home, jacked him up and put him back on blocks. There was little to be discussed before saying goodbye to his parents. During his leave he had spent many hours with them in the afternoons while Trina was working.

Alan caught a bus back to Whitehall, and was waiting in the usual place by the time Trina came out of her office. Although they said little during that lunch hour, their need for each other linked them firmly. When the time came, Alan walked Trina back to work. At the entrance to the building he took her hands, giving them a quick squeeze.

`Goodbye,' he said. `I'll be thinking of you.'

For one dreadful moment he thought she was about to cry, right there in the middle of Whitehall. Alan should have known better. Trina's pride and self control won out, but there were a few seconds of silent struggle.

`Take care of yourself,' she said, and though her voice was quiet it was also steady.

Trina slipped her hands from Alan's, turned, and disappeared through the door.

CHAPTER ELEVEN

I seemed to move among a world of ghosts,
And feel myself the shadow of a dream.
Alfred, Lord Tennyson

The breeze was strengthening and the sullen swell of the last few days had gone. The steady rise and fall had been replaced by a quick, uncertain reaction to wavelets that now slapped and hissed against the boat's sides.

For the weary survivors this irregular, jerky movement was a cruel addition to their woes. They were tired with an aching exhaustion that seeped right through their bodies and their bones. Every lurch and buffet was agony, and in his weakened state Alan was losing control of his thoughts. They wandered as if with a will of their own.

`Six little nigger boys now - there were nine when darkness fell last night.

Nine little nigger boys
sitting up so late.
Higgins went to sleep... I think:
Then there were eight.'

`Three dead, one after another this morning. This must be the beginning of the end. I wonder... I suppose they must be... No reason why mine should look any different. It's the eyes, sunken and hollow.

`Wonder why Higgins went first? Seemed all right yesterday... unlike him not to wait his turn. I was sure Joe Hayter would be first... never even considered Higgins. Typical of him to go unobtrusively. No one saw him die. Until Jim noticed no one realized, and it had then been light for quite a while.

`We can't last much longer... Just helping to shift Higgins exhausted me. We rolled him over the side... I'm sure he apologized for the trouble he was causing.

`It took four of us to get the other two out of the boat. If Joe Hayter hadn't lost so much weight we'd never have got rid of him.

`There's little pain in dying this way, just listlessness and weakness. John Allward and Joe seemed to fade away. No struggle... nothing.

`Queenie realized that John was dead about an hour after dawn.'

> 'Eight little nigger boys
> far south west from Devon,
> watched the wily Johnny go.
> Then there were seven.'

Alan's mind went blank, refusing to accept what had happened or was to happen. For some minutes he sat with wide, unseeing eyes, and appeared to have retreated to some far distant place. When he came out of his trance he seemed bewildered, and for a few seconds was unsure of his surroundings. Reality grasped, and with reality came memory.

He remembered John Allward's wife. How would she take the news? Was she fond of John? Was he fond of her? Neither seemed the type to love anyone except themselves. Difficult to tell, they weren't people to show emotion. They had no children. Which came first? Did having no children make them selfish, or was it the other way round?

One night, in Liverpool, Alan had chanced to meet John and his wife in a restaurant, and his impression was of a cold, enameled person. She was a big woman, not fat but well fed, and with large breasts firmly supported. She was pinched into a tight fitting dress, as if trying to cling to the obvious sex appeal she must have had as a young girl She made a good foil to the hard-eyed, calculating John.

Unlike his wife John was conservative in dress, his suit expensive and well cut.

`Thoroughly disliked by most of the crew.

`Is that his epitaph?' Alan thought. `Shouldn't speak ill of the dead? Maybe... No taboo on thinking though. No one can hear.'

'Seven little nigger boys
all in a fix.
Said goodbye to Joe today;
now we are six.'

Alan felt sorry for Con Mahoney. First Terry, now Joe. Basil too... having to help dispose of his brother's body.

Con Mahoney had moved to sit next to Len Huskins, which was strange as they made a most unlikely combination. Obviously they hated each other, and Alan wondered if they found stimulation in their hate, but there was a difference in their attitudes. Con's eyes were angry, but with an outward-looking anger. With Len it was different. There was anger there but it was more inward, bad tempered and petulant.

The six now divided into three groups. Len and Con were sitting midships on the starb'd side with Basil and Queenie opposite. Jim and Alan remained in the stern. There was silence, but Queenie reached up to pat Basil on the shoulder.

* * *

When he felt Queenie's hand touch him, Basil appreciated the gesture, but it was not necessary. Odd that he should feel so little. He had even helped put John over the side. It was no lack of feeling; rather it was a sense of hopelessness that acted as an anesthetic. The knowledge that he would soon follow his brother destroyed the need for grief.

He knew many of the crew disliked his brother, some even hated him, but that made no difference to his own feelings. John was hard, sure. He had been like that even when they were kids. John always played to win, but there was another side to him that few people were allowed to see.

There had been a side to his personality that John kept hidden, as though it were something shameful. John never talked about it, but Basil suspected that John was unwilling for the world to know that he, John Allward, had fathered a sub-normal child. It was something never spoken about, not even within his family.

The girl had been born while John was away at sea, and as soon as the ship docked in Tilbury, he had rushed to hand over to his relief barkeeper. John had arranged to take a voyage off, expecting to be home when the child was born, but little Margaret was four weeks premature, and a cable arrived eight days before they were due to dock telling him that he was already a father.

Even in those days he was secretive, and the few on board who knew soon forgot the existence of his daughter. In those early days of their marriage, Emily had insisted on living in Whitby, close to her parents. If she and John had lived in Tilbury it would have been different; there, with so many families dependent on the Southern Oceanic ships, everyone would have known.

When John returned to sea Margaret was five months old, and already they suspected she was different from other children. Margaret, always sickly, died shortly before her second birthday. John showed little emotion, and seemed to agree with the doctor that, perhaps, it was for the best that Margaret had not lived.

`If it's any comfort,' the doctor had said; `your daughter would never have been able to live a normal life. Try to accept this. After all, there's no reason why you and your wife shouldn't have another child, and the chances are that the next one will be perfectly normal.'

Emily wanted another child, but John's mind was made up. His feelings for Margaret had been a queer mixture of love and revulsion, and he was unwilling to risk the same thing all over again.

The experience haunted John, and left him with a feeling of guilt he could never escape. No one knew, not even Basil could guess, how much money John had given to homes for handicapped children. It was as if he were trying to buy absolution for his invidious feelings about Margaret. He tried to make up to Emily for her lack of children by giving her everything material she could desire. On the surface they looked to be a well-matched couple, but love had died with Margaret. Oddly, in some strange way, it was this shared tragedy that had kept them together.

Basil could remember the bright girl Emily had been, vivacious and outspoken, although a little too brittle in manner for his own taste. She had been pretty, and with loads of sex appeal. It was no wonder that John had fallen in love, almost at first sight, when she and her mother joined the ship for a Norwegian cruise.

Emily was still brittle, but now it was in a harder, less fragile way. She and John had behaved politely to each other, more like old acquaintances than man and wife. Perhaps the news of John's death would break that elegant facade. She would be a very lonely woman in future; her parents dead, no children, no husband and few friends. She knew many people yet, since Margaret's death, seemed unable to love or to accept love.

For himself, Basil knew that there was no one whose life would be disturbed by his passing. He had never married. Sure, there had been girls; but never one he had wanted to marry. His home was with John and Emily, where he had his own room, and Emily treated him in much the same way she dealt with John.

It had been John's idea that he should live there. Big brother John, that was how it had been as long as he could remember. With their father away at sea, it was John he always turned to whenever he was in trouble; and John had never failed him. John's rough impatience concealed a genuine affection for his young brother.

It was John who decided that Basil should follow him to sea. Listening to their father talking about his own job had made up John's mind. Their father had been Chief Steward in one of the Orient Line ships. 'If I had my time over, knowing what I do now,' he would say, 'I'd never be Chief Steward. Too many responsibilities, and you're first in line to take the blame if anything goes wrong. It's all very well for the Purser, he can issue his orders; but I'm the one who has to see they're carried out.'

He would lean back in his chair, puffing at the vile old pipe that gave him so much satisfaction.

'No John,' he would continue; 'Take the advice of someone who knows what he's talking about. Aim to be a Head Barkeeper, if you want to go to sea. That's the job. That's what I'd do if I was starting out again.'

John and his father had much in common. They had the same streak of ruthlessness, and the old man had no cause to complain about what he had achieved. He had more money quietly salted away than most people would have thought possible, judging by his modest life-style.

When John went to sea, he too started with the Orient Line. For the first few years he had to prove himself, and then with one or two gentle nudges, a word dropped here and there, his father took a hand in his career. Soon the vital promotion to Assistant Barkeeper came, and from then on it was only a matter of time.

Through one of his father's contacts he was offered the job of Head Barkeeper in Ocean Monarch, and John was glad to switch from the Orient Line to Southern Oceanic. With a different shipping company he was starting afresh, having no obligations. No one had any claim on him for past favors; he could start as he meant to continue, and had remained with Ocean Monarch ever since. Basil just tagged along. Automatically, it seemed, he became Assistant Barkeeper under his brother. John was still keeping an eye on him, and, from John's point of view, it was invaluable to have at least one assistant who would do as he was told and ask no questions.

When John died Basil felt naked. There was no one now who would tell him what to do, or when to do it. Not that it really mattered, not even John had been able to find an answer this time; except the one final answer.

* * *

`Strange how much calmer I am,' Alan thought. `I think I've stopped fighting, even stopped caring. It seems easier to think clearly. Or is that an hallucination too? Do I only imagine that I'm thinking logically?

`No,' he decided. `I'm not mad... yet. The memories have become so vivid. Trina will be upset: I must still have some part in her life, and it hurts to know I'll never see her again. My death will make her unhappy, especially since...'

Alan tried to turn his mind aside.

During these last few days it had become easier to forget, to close his eyes, to leave his body and float away. So often, when his imagination roamed and unfolded a memory, his body would dissolve and set his mind free.

`Sometime... soon, I'll float away and I won't come back. It'll be easy - I think. Not yet though, I'm not quite ready.'

Trina would know by now. Next of kin must have been told; and Uncle Harry, surely, would have told her. Had she been to see his parents? It would be hard on them. They had never known about that other time when the Navy had lost Ocean Monarch

For Trina it would be a repeat performance but with a different ending. She would know by now that it was foolish to hope. The `SSSS' radio signal must have been noted and the fact of a submarine attack plotted. They had seen no sign of a search, but the Atlantic was a big chessboard and they were only one pawn in the contest.

`Last time,' Alan thought, `was just a rehearsal; and I can see Trina as she was before, outwardly calm, but with the tell-tale smudging under her eyes.... regretting perhaps... even as I do.

`Bruised eyes? When was it? 1942, August? Bruised eyes... Whitehall... unhappiness. Both times I saw her there.'

* * *

Alan's third voyage was uneventful, around the Cape to Suez and returning to dock in Glasgow.

Only four clear days of leave could be granted and Alan traveled through the night, arriving in London in the early morning. At Euston, Alan needed a porter to help with his baggage and the boxes of food he had brought. Afraid to leave his cases while making a phone call, he went straight to the taxi rank, expecting to get home in time to catch Trina before she left for work, but just missed her. Alan waited half an hour and then tried to make contact through the Whitehall number.

The Wren on the switchboard asked his identity and Alan had to explain that it was a private call. He was told, politely, that no personal calls could be taken. It seemed that security had been tightened and

Alan's first thought was that he would have to wait until Trina had finished work. But then, he told himself, she might be working late, or going out that evening. It was worth trying another way.

* * *

`Nylon stockings...' Alan's mind skated away down a side-track.

`Black Nylon stockings, how she always drools over them.' There were none in the shops, and WRNS issue stockings were hardly elegant. Among Wrens, black Nylon stockings were a symbol, a statement of a sea-going boy friend able to buy them overseas.

`Where will Trina get her Nylon stockings now?...What the hell was I thinking about?... Oh yes, that was it, crashing the barricades in Whitehall.'

* * *

By late morning Alan was walking down Whitehall wearing his Southern Oceanic uniform. There was no security check at the street entrance to the building where Trina worked, and a narrow spiral stairway led to an ante room, where a Marine corporal sat at a desk between Alan and two swing doors on the far side. Alan walked across the room with a confident air. Would there be a challenge? The Marine looked curiously at Alan's uniform but did not say anything.

On the far side of the swing doors was a large room with Wrens working at a number of desks. Alan went to the nearest girl and asked if she could give a message to Second Officer Grant. She looked surprised, but said;

`Er... yes,' and, after a slight hesitation while she looked at Alan's uniform, added: `Sir'.

`Please tell her Mr Anderson is here, and wonders if she can spare a moment.'

The girl left, and within half a minute a rather flustered Trina arrived. She did not say a word until she was close enough to whisper.

`Alan, you shouldn't be here.'

`I know, but I couldn't get through to you on the phone.'

`You mustn't stay.'

`Okay I'll go, but meet me for lunch.'

`One o'clock then. You'd better go.'

Trina turned and hurried away, leaving Alan standing. He took his cap from under his arm, pulled it on, and shouldered his way through the swing doors.

`What the hell's the matter with Trina?' he thought. `She looks so thin and pale, and why so jumpy? All right, perhaps I shouldn't have gate-crashed; but it was up to their security to stop me. If they let me through that's their fault.'

It had been unlike Trina to let something like that worry her. Fair enough, she might have said; `Get lost quickly.' But it would have been with a grin.

Alan went to buy sandwiches, then returned to wait for her.

Trina was about two minutes late and Alan could not kiss her, not while they were standing on the pavement in Whitehall. He had to content himself with studying her face, and in the daylight saw the signs of tension. She was pale and the skin over her cheekbones seemed tightly drawn and worse, her smile did not come easily.

`I'm sorry,' were her first words.

`Why so?'

`I was startled when I got your message. I... I didn't say I was glad to see you.'

`I didn't say that to you either, but I was, and am.'

'Me too, let's go.'

`Hardly exuberant,' Alan thought, as they crossed the road and entered St James's Park.

`I bought some sandwiches,' he said.

`Oh, I'm sorry. I don't feel like eating.'

`What's the matter? Aren't you well?'

`No.'

`Is something wrong?'

`No.'

Something was, obviously, wrong. A monosyllabic Trina was an entirely new experience. Alan wondered whether his storming of her office had caused trouble.

`Have I done anything to upset you?'

Trina shook her head.

`Please, it's not you,' she said. `I just don't want to talk.' Alan was at a loss. Trina's behavior was so odd, so strained, so worried, and yet for some reason she could not, or did not want to explain. They sat on one of the seats and Trina pressed close to Alan. He wanted to comfort her but could not take her in his arms, as he would have liked, not there, not with Trina in uniform.

She was sitting quietly and appeared to be lost in thought. Her hands were clasped lying in her lap, and Alan moved to rest his hand on hers.

`Hey!' he said.

Trina looked at him turning her hand so that their fingers could clasp, while a lack-luster smile slowly came and went. Alan put the packet of sandwiches down on the bench and they sat silently.

`What am I to do?' he thought. `If Trina doesn't want to talk, perhaps it's best to wait and see what happens. No point in forcing conversation.'

Alan was worried; he had never known Trina to be like this. Clearly her thoughts were far away, in some time or place where he was not allowed to be. Trina's whole body was taut, and he sensed strain and tension flow to him through the nervous touch of her fingers. Perhaps it would be better to do something, anything, rather than let her sit and worry over a problem she was unwilling to share.

`Come on, let's feed the ducks. We've got to get rid of these sandwiches.' He pulled Trina to her feet and they walked over to the pond. Even then, it was not until Alan put a sandwich into her hand and the ducks started clamoring that she showed any response. Mechanically, Trina threw the bread but still remained silent, and Alan tried organizing the proceedings.

`No, don't feed him. He's got a greedy look... Watch out for that one over there. He's a bully: don't give him anything.'

Such remarks usually started an argument, but not that day. Trina merely gave a half smile, and ignored Alan's instructions. Again her actions became semi-automatic, and Alan said no more.

Above them, clouds scudded across the sky, bathing Trina in alternating moments of sunshine and shade as she stood with the cluster of urgent ducks at her feet. Yet she remained divorced from this familiar scene, withdrawn and solitary.

With their hands empty, Alan watched the ducks disperse about their business. Trina showed no reaction, standing with fists clenched, and Alan was pained by her obvious wretchedness. He suggested, quietly:

`How about I take you out tonight? Or we can have a quiet evening in the flat? I've brought heaps of food, so we can easily scratch up a meal.'

Trina nodded but said nothing, and Alan continued:

`That's why I barged in today, to find out what you wanted to do. I thought it'd give us a chance to sort out the next three days. That's all the leave I've got, and I'll have to organize a bit of time to spend with my parents.'

`No,' Trina's voice was sudden, flat and colorless. `I'll be better on my own tonight. Anyway, your mother's been missing you, especially since your brother was sent overseas.'

At that moment Alan did not give a damn about formalities, or whether every brass hat in Whitehall was watching. He could not stand that look any more. He reached for Trina's shoulders, turning her to face him and let his hands drop to her waist. As he looked into that pale face he felt her tremble.

`Can't you tell me, darling? I can't bear seeing you like this.' Trina returned his look, more steadily this time, but her eyes were wide, and she gave a small, tight shake of her head.

`I'm sorry Alan. It's... it's to do with my job. I know I'm being horrid. It's nothing to do with us.'

She started to pull away, and immediately Alan let his hands fall away as she took a step backwards. Trina took just the one step, then stopped and stood quite still, a new look of distress showing in her face.

`I… I didn't mean to do that. Please don't think... I didn't mean to. I wasn't rejecting you, nothing's changed. It's just that... it's just something that's happening. I can't explain. Everything seems to be going wrong and it's... awful.'

She moved back towards Alan.

`Please, don't ask any more, not now. Just take me back to the office.'

They walked across the road, with Trina gripping Alan's arm. They were waiting to cross Whitehall when she said:

`I do love you Alan. It's not us I'm worried about.'

They paused a few yards from the entrance to her office.

`Shall I wait for you at the flat tomorrow, or meet you here?' Trina thought for a moment:

`No, at the flat. Better not wait here in case I have to work late.'

When she had gone, Alan walked up to Charing Cross. He would go home and get Mr Bumps mobile. In the bus he worried about Trina. It must be something very strange to affect her like that, and, whatever it was he hoped it would not last too long.

Next afternoon Alan let himself into the flat soon after three. He did not expect Trina much before six, but he knew that she did occasionally get away early. He had brought the food packages with him, and took these into the kitchen to unwrap and store in the tiny pantry. Afterwards he wandered through the flat, and found a magazine to help pass the time. Three quarters of an hour later he had read enough, and threw the magazine on to the settee with a gesture of impatience. He looked at his watch and saw that it was only twenty past four.

The sunlight streaming in through the open glass doors beckoned him out into the fresh air. Alan crossed the room and stepped through to the balcony. He was still standing there, leaning on the railing, when he heard the door of the flat being opened. Moving quickly, he went back into the room.

Trina was standing just inside the front door. She looked terrible, and Alan ran across to her

`Trina,' he said, and took her in his arms.

She did not resist, but her body was stiff and unyielding. It seemed as though Trina did not care, one way or the other, whether she was held.

The thought came into Alan's mind:

`She's like a zombie.'

He drew her further into the flat.

`Trina - darling, come and sit down.'

She allowed him to lead her to the settee, and sat, obediently, as if she were a puppet. Alan removed her hat, unbuttoned her jacket, and lifted her feet on to the settee. While he did this Trina said nothing, nor did she speak when he slipped off her shoes and placed cushions behind her back.

`Is there anything I can get for you?'

Trina shook her head.

`How about tea or coffee?'

Again that disinterested headshake. Something had to be done, but what? It was then Alan had an idea.

`Trina, don't you dare move. I'll be back in ten minutes.'

He ran all the way, and almost made it in the promised time. Fetching a glass from the kitchen, he opened the bottle he had bought and poured a sizeable brandy. At first Trina turned away when he offered it to her, but Alan was determined and would not accept a refusal. Placing the palm of his hand against the side of her chin he made Trina look at him.

`Stop it Trina, do as I say. You're to drink this.'

She took the glass in her hand but made no other move.

`Drink.'

Trina shuddered, and for an instant Alan thought she would throw it at him. Instead she turned her head and gave him a look that seemed to say: `How can you treat me like this?' Then she lifted the glass, and swiftly gulped it down as if taking medicine.

Alan took the empty glass and knelt beside her, wondering what to do next. Trina had put her hand to her throat and was swallowing convulsively. Alan feared she might vomit, but the nausea subsided and Trina seemed to relax slightly.

Previously he had noticed that her hands were like ice, and now he tried to warm them. Since arriving, Trina had not spoken, she had either nodded or shaken her head. Now she said the one word:

`Thanks.' Alan moved to sit on the edge of the settee where he could put his arm around her, but Trina was still stiff and unyielding, her eyes lost and lacking any spark of life. She lay with her hands clasped while Alan held them, trying to bring some warmth to those chill fingers. Quite suddenly she moved to clutch his hand, holding it with painful intensity.

They sat like this, neither speaking nor moving, for what seemed to Alan to be an age. Occasionally he would murmur an endearment, but otherwise there was silence. Alan was becoming cramped, and had just decided he would have to change position when he heard her say:

'Alan?'

Trina was looking at him and, heaven be praised, seeing him.

Without warning she burst into tears, and Alan lifted her so that she rested against him instead of on the cushions. As he did so, she turned towards him and pressed her face against his chest, wrapping her arms tightly around his body. For a long time Trina lay like this and sobbed. Gradually, very gradually, the sobs eased and finally stopped altogether. Alan was stroking her head when, after a deep breath, her body went quite limp.

'Trina?' Alan whispered. There was no answer, and he realized that she had fallen asleep.

She did not wake up when he carried her into the bedroom, and did little more than stir as he undressed her. After settling her in the bed Alan pulled the curtains, then stood looking at her and wondering. She lay, curled up and still. There was no doubt that Trina was exhausted. The time was quarter past seven.

In the sitting room, Alan poured himself a brandy and while drinking it rummaged around the kitchen. He found the best part of a loaf of bread, and using some of the cheese he had brought made himself a Welsh Rarebit. Even after he had cleared away it was still only a few minutes past eight. The events of the last few hours had left a multitude of questions unanswered, and he felt disturbed and restless.

Alan poured himself another brandy, then looked over the bookshelves. Trina's taste showed in the anthologies of poetry and the well-worn collection of Shakespeare's plays and sonnets. Alan needed something easy and escapist, and selected a murder mystery. For the first half-hour he was able to give only a part of his attention to the book. At the slightest sound he would be alert, and several times went to the bedroom to check, but Trina had not moved. Soon after eleven Alan finished the book and decided it was time for bed. He turned on the taps to run himself a bath, and while it filled looked in on Trina. She had still not moved, and as far as Alan could tell was in the same position as when he first left her. Rather than risk disturbing Trina, Alan found a couple of blankets and made his bed on the settee.

Daylight was streaming into the sitting room when he awoke to find that Trina was leaning over the back of the settee, her face only inches from his. She had been tickling his ear and now bent down to kiss him.

`Breakfast's ready,' she said. `I've got to leave in a quarter of an hour.'

Alan followed her to the kitchen where she had made toast and coffee and was now taking boiled eggs out of the saucepan. When they sat down Trina was facing the light, and Alan was able to get his first good look at her. There were dark circles shadowing her eyes, but there was life in them again. She looked haggard, frail even, but the haunted look had gone and Trina had come to terms with herself.

`I can tell you now,' she said, when Alan asked her how she was.

`The news will have been released. The day you arrived was the start of a big raid into France, at Dieppe. When you walked in we'd just had news that everything was going wrong, and yesterday the casualty figures started coming in. It's been a complete disaster.'

`How come you're so involved?'

`I seem to have been caught up emotionally. For the last month, or more, I've been working every day until I almost dropped. My chief was responsible for the scheme and he's been involved in all the planning. I went with him when he visited the units that were taking part, and I met many of the officers who were going on the raid, either at conferences and briefings or in the various Messes afterwards. Some I met so often that I got to know them by their Christian names.

`The operation was something I've lived with so long I've become a part of it, and for the last two days it was as if I were being torn apart. Does that make sense to you?'

`Of course, I'm sorry. My appearance then can hardly have helped.'

Trina reached across the table.

`It wasn't your fault. Poor Alan, it must have been horrid for you, not knowing. I'm glad you're here though. It's helped. It really has.'

'Any time. Anything to oblige.'

It brought a grin from Trina, which quickly faded as she continued:

`Yesterday, we started getting all those dreadful reports. The chief 's face got grimmer and grimmer. We couldn't get any confirmed casualty figures, but it sounds as though they must be huge. I seemed to see their faces, those cheery, confident faces. It was terrible. I... I think I must have blacked out. I couldn't take it any more. There was nothing we could do. Our work was finished once the operation started.'

There were tears in her eyes again, and Alan went over to her.

`It's all right, Alan,' she said. I'll be all right. Finish your breakfast.'

After Alan had returned to his chair Trina continued.

'It was like a nightmare, when you can't wake up. In some way it kept reminding me of when I heard that Ian had been killed, and when I thought I'd lost you too. I knew, quite clearly, that I'd be seeing you in a few hours but it didn't make any difference.'

Trina suddenly stopped.

`My God, look at the time.'

She jumped to her feet and rushed into the bedroom to get her hat.

`Hang on,' Alan called as she raced back.

While Trina hovered nervously, Alan pulled trousers on over his pajamas and then followed her as she ran down the stairs. Mr Bumps had to get a move on too.

`I'm pretty sure I can get off by four this afternoon,' Trina said, as Alan concentrated on forcing Mr Bumps through the traffic.

`Would you like to go to a show?' Alan asked as he shot clear of a taxi that had slowed to make a U-turn.

Trina shook her head.

`No, not tonight. Let's have a quiet evening.' In Whitehall she jumped out of the car, then turned and leaned back over the door.

`Don't hang around here like that or I'll disown you.'

Before she disappeared into the grey stone building Trina turned, and seeing that Alan had not moved, made a shooing movement with her hands, which turned into a wave as she hurried through the door.

That afternoon Trina did not get away as early as she had hoped, and it was well after five when Alan heard her key in the door. She was breathless from running up the stairs.

`Sorry Alan,' she gasped.

Alan had been on the balcony. He had seen her coming, and was waiting just beside the door when Trina opened it.

He caught and kissed her before she had a chance to say any more, and in the process her hat became dislodged, slipping to the back of her head. When Alan released her, Trina looked thoroughly dissolute. The combination of bruised eyes and disheveled look was delightful. Alan grinned down at her.

`Why don't you go and get out of your armor?' he suggested.

They went into the bedroom and Trina saw herself in the mirror.

`I see why you were laughing.'

She smiled at her reflection and removed the offending hat. Alan relaxed on the bed while Trina changed into a cotton dress.

`How was it today?'

`It may not be as bad as we feared. From the latest news it seems as though more have been taken prisoner than first thought. I hope so anyway. At least they'll be alive.' She turned for Alan to fix the back of her dress, and in a softer tone added:

`There must still be an awful lot who've been killed.' Alan guessed that a sudden wave of misery had caught her and bent to kiss her neck, just above the fastening of her dress.

`Come on,' he said. `Let's have a drink. I let my head go today and bought a bottle of Scotch. I don't expect you'll make as much fuss over that as you did with the brandy.'

Trina made a face at him.

`Why didn't you get Scotch yesterday?'

`If I'd started you on Scotch last night I hate to think how you'd have finished up. I know what you're like.'

Trina was still down; as shown by the fact that she made no attempt to protest against this slur. Her need was for peace. That night she was happy to curl up on the settee resting against Alan as they listened to music.

They played many records but drank little of the Scotch. Trina refused to go out for dinner, and instead made up a scratch meal. By half past nine they were in bed.

They had one more day, a night and most of another day before Alan had to return to his ship.

When Trina arrived back from work next day she looked much better, or so it seemed to Alan. Though still shadowed by an air of fragility she looked less worn, and her smile was spontaneous. They kissed and he stood back to look at her.

`I've booked seats for a show... that's if you feel up to it,' and he watched carefully for her reaction. If Trina had shown any sign of hesitation he was ready to cancel the reservation.

`That's nice,' she agreed. `I haven't been to a show since the last time with you. Perhaps it's just what I need.'

The play was a situation farce; but neither Alan nor Trina seemed able to enjoy the humor and Alan was disappointed, feeling that he had made a poor choice.

When they left the theatre they walked through to Soho for a meal. Again it was not a success. Trina made a gallant effort to be bright but it was an act, and one impossible to maintain.

`You're still feeling wretched, aren't you?' Alan asked.

Trina nodded.

`Pity the show wasn't better,' he said. `It fell a bit flat I thought.'

`I doubt if any show would have been better tonight.'

Trina seemed to have read his thoughts and she continued: `We... well I... wasn't really in the mood. I'm sorry, I didn't mean to be a wet blanket. I keep remembering that this is your last night, and I've needed you so much these last few days.'

Trina was looking down at the table, her fingers nervously picking at the cloth.

`All right,' Alan said. `Eat up and we'll go and finish that Scotch.'

`I don't think I want any more to eat. I'm sorry Alan, it just doesn't seem right to waste food nowadays, but I'm simply not hungry.'

Again they collected Mr Bumps from the Piccadilly car park, but this time Trina looked on impassively as he performed his antics on the revolving floor. Strangely, when they got back to the flat, neither felt like drinking and the Scotch was untouched. Instead they made coffee and went to bed soon after.

When Alan woke in the morning he found that Trina was not in bed. It was only half past six, and when she did not reappear within a few minutes he got up. Entering the sitting room Alan saw that daylight was streaming in. The blackout screens had been taken down and the curtains drawn back. Beyond, he could see Trina on the balcony, her elbows resting on the safety railing.

Alan fetched his dressing gown and went out to join her. They stood, side by side, each with an arm around the other while they looked through the early morning mist that hung over the Thames.

`I often come here in the morning. A few quiet minutes seem to make a good start to the day.' There was a wistful smile on Trina's face as she spoke.

`Can't you have a few quiet minutes lying in bed?' Alan queried.

`Not when you're there,' she retorted.

`You're equivocating.'

`Ooh! I'm not that sort of girl.'

`You sound a bit better this morning.'

`Yes and no.'

`Lucid too.'

`Shut up Alan. That silly song, Old Father Thames, keeps running through my mind. I wish he'd stop for a while so you don't have to go away.'

` "I wish I loved the human race; I wish I loved its silly face." ' Alan quoted, then added: `Not very apt, but the only thing I can remember about wishes off hand.'

Trina looked at him suspiciously.

`Where does that come from?'

Alan grinned at her. `Yesterday's Telegraph. It was quoted in a letter to the editor about people's behavior in the Underground Railway stations during the blitz. It was written by Sir Walter Raleigh, the quote that is, not the letter. It wasn't Queen Elizabeth's Sir Walter, but another one who died about twenty years ago.'

`You've been waiting for an opportunity to quote it at me,'Trina accused.

`Of course, especially after that Shakespeare you threw at me last night.'

Trina was laughing as she remembered the circumstances `You mean – "Comparisons are odorous."'

It was very pleasant to see and hear Trina laugh again.

CHAPTER TWELVE

Yet what no chance could then reveal,
And neither would be first to own,
Let fate and courage now conceal,
When truth would bring remorse alone.
Richard Monckton Milnes, Lord Houghton

Miraculously all six were still alive, but there had been no more rain, and with an empty water drum the end could not be delayed for much longer. Let us eavesdrop on Alan's thoughts, while there is still time.

* * *

`Lights, lights everywhere, dancing lights... hold still and try to look, try to focus... Come back, come back from far away. Back to truth, thirst and pain.

`You flickering, shimmering lights of the sea, I know you for what you are. Your mockery is an empty, glittering array of flashing jewels; a scattering of diamond points that hurt my eyes; the elusive brilliance of fleeting reflections, mirrored darts of sunlight... I won't look at you. Your beauty is false...

`The sun is the life giver, but not for us. It has no life to give for our bodies.

`I see five figures, five still shapes. Are they alive? Am I alive?... No food for days... Does it matter how long? I don't want food.

`Water: that I can remember. Every hour, every painful hour since those last few sips yesterday... Con Mahoney's hands shaking as he tried to drink and spilling some precious drops, and Len Huskins, his vicious, hoarse, painful whisper.

`You clumsy little runt.'

`Their hatred of each other has grown. If they weren't so weak they'd be at each other's throats; instead they glare...

`Huskins always starts it. Why?... Every day he gets more unpleasant... more morose. It's finished now. Not even Len can make the effort to speak. I almost wish he could. Their abuse gave us something to listen to... I miss it now. Con never let an insult go unchallenged.

`Does their bickering do them any good? They drive us mad, with their quarrelling. Even when someone screams "Shut up!" they're only quiet for a little while. Then Len starts it again; the muttering, the needling until one or the other loses his temper.

'They never leave each other alone, never drift off into the distance of their inner selves. They're always here, in the boat. While they're alive I doubt if they'll be anywhere else. Probably not their fault. I guess they're creatures of the present, living instant by instant. Perhaps they're denied the safety valve of dreams like the rest of us.'

* * *

Con Mahoney looked at his legs and felt them through the thin material of his cotton check trousers.

'Christ, I've always been skinny, but now there's bugger all there except bone. Fat chance now of ever becoming Chef in a prestige hotel.'

The next wave passed beneath the boat, and as the crest approached Con looked out over the port bow...

`Fat chance of anything; might have known something would bloody happen to stuff up my plans... Was this all I've bloody slaved for?'

`Useless... Bloody useless, just sitting here, day after sodding day waiting to die. All that fucking effort to learn. Forcing the buggers to notice me; Chefs, Chief Stewards and Pursers, making the bastards wake up to how good I am, until they had to do something about it.

`I'd made it; and the Company sent me to Paris, to work under that shitty Froggy Chef... All bloody hands and whiskers. Still, the old bastard knew what he was about.

`That bloody prick Len Huskins...'

* * *

`Yes, Con is still alive. At least he's alive enough to glare again at Len.

`The others must be alive too. Len certainly is. He's glaring back at Con, and Jim moved about a minute ago. The other two don't really look dead, just comatose.' Alan wished that he could focus on them properly and make sure.

`It's not important, but I'd like to know... Things keep coming and going.

`Going... going down into darkness, sinking, deeper and deeper through the darkness into light, and I see again clearly.'

* * *

Trina had still looked worn when Alan left to return to Glasgow. His train did not leave until half past eight that night, and they had a few more hours together. Trina had been defiantly gay and flippant, and they had laughed, but it was laughter that was made, and not laughter that came.

Alan had rung for a taxi, and they waited for it at the end of the balcony where there was just enough space to stand side by side. From there they could see around the corner to the front of the building. Alan did not want to leave. Trina had been so close to complete breakdown; and he was sure it would not take much more pressure to undo the improvement of the last few days.

`I think you've had enough,' he told her. `Why not see if you can get a transfer.'

`I'm all right.'

`You're not you know. You need a rest. Much more of this and you'll really have had it.'

`I'd feel as though I was letting everyone down.'

`Not as badly as if you had a breakdown at some crucial moment.' Trina shook her head. `I wouldn't do that.' Alan could not help smiling at her determination as she said this.

`No you wouldn't,' he agreed. `But I hate to think what you'd be like when it was all over. Be sensible and see if you can get away, even if it's only for a few weeks. You've had a hell of a time these last six months or so.'

Trina shrugged, then pointed down to the street.

`Here's your taxi.'

They kissed, and Trina went downstairs with Alan. She leaned into the window of the cab.

`Don't start worrying about me,' she said. `It's bad enough me worrying about you.'

It was to be four months before they met again.

* * *

The American war effort had changed the whole outlook for the war in the west, and Ocean Monarch became caught up in the mass movement of men and materials that had begun to cross the Atlantic. She sailed empty to New York and returned to Glasgow carrying over seven thousand troops from the United States. Next she made a voyage to Iceland carrying troops to bolster the defenses there.

Returning to the Clyde, Ocean Monarch was kept at anchor off Gourock for nearly two weeks but no leave was granted. There was much secrecy and many rumors, but no one guessed the purpose of their next voyage. Other ships arrived and also lay at anchor, but this was normal when a convoy was assembling.

At last the order came to move upstream and into the King George V dock. In a matter of hours the ship was topped up with stores, fuel and water, and troops were embarking. A few more days at anchor and the convoy sailed.

The mood was unlike previous voyages, and there was fear and anticipation. Ocean Monarch passed through the Straits of Gibraltar at dusk, arriving off Algiers at dawn with the North African invasion convoy. During the night, one of the troopships was torpedoed and lost. Apart from this, and one noisy night of bombing in Algiers, the voyage was uneventful.

They returned to Liverpool, but again no leave. When the mail came on board, there was a letter from Trina. She could say very little, except for a hint that she might soon be on the move, and Alan feared that she might be sent overseas and that they would be separated until after the war.

The ship was in the Mersey for less than a day, and after fuelling she headed downstream in the early evening. Again their destination was New York. This was to begin a series of such voyages, and Glasgow became their regular port of disembarkation. Generally their stay in the Clyde was short, no more than a day or two before leaving on the next ferry run. American reinforcements were being rushed across the Atlantic to prepare for the landing in Europe, and there was no time to waste.

Trina's job in Whitehall had ended when the section she worked for was disbanded; and by sheer good fortune she was posted to Troon, not far from Glasgow. This suited Alan and Trina perfectly, and for once Uncle Harry had no hand in the move.

Her new job was much less demanding and Trina soon regained the weight she had lost. Even the first time they met in Glasgow, Alan found it hard to recall the tired, haggard face that had so worried him on his last leave. There were differences, but they were slight and not easily defined. What mattered to Alan was that Trina had regained her sparkle and vivacity.

Her work at Troon allowed Trina to keep track of Ocean Monarch from the time the ship entered the Western Approaches, and she always knew when Alan would be docking.

In her Wren officer's uniform, Trina had no difficulty in visiting the ship but they could not take too much advantage of this privilege. Some senior officers objected to Trina coming on board, but they knew she was Sir Harold Marsden's niece and were not game to make an issue of it.

Trina and Alan realized that it was a delicate situation, and she never stayed more than a few minutes while they arranged to meet ashore. Most times, Trina would have an overnight leave pass and booked into the Central Hotel before going down to the ship. Peter rarely wanted to leave the ship, and this was fortunate for Alan as it meant that he could usually get ashore whenever he wanted. Trina and Alan felt that their time together was always much too short; but knew how lucky they were to have even a few hours to share, and the brief meetings were important to them both. It was not only the immediate delight in each other's company, but it was something they could look forward to amid the grayness of war.

Trina found her job at Troon trivial and boring: there was hardly enough work to keep her occupied. For Alan, these meetings were snatched interludes of sanity away from the closed, predictable circle of people and topics on board ship. They could make that bland hotel room come to life with their laughter.

Laughter, that was how Alan would always hear Trina in his memory, even though it was impossible to remember all the things they had laughed at. Their talk was froth and inconsequence, that for most of the time was allowed to float over their deeper feelings. In March 1943 Ocean Monarch returned to Glasgow and the crew was told that a short leave would be granted. As usual it was to be divided into two periods. For those who lived in London, it meant two nights of traveling to have three days and two nights with their families. Alan knew that he must take this opportunity to go home. He had not seen his parents for seven months, and he opted to take the second leave period.

The day before his leave was due to start the Captain sent for him, and was gruffly apologetic. Captain Davies explained that the convoy sailing conference had been brought forward by twenty-four hours. This meant that Alan's leave would have to be cut short.

One of Alan's jobs was maintaining the ship's codebooks, which was why he had to attend these conferences with the Captain. While the Masters of the convoy ships met in the conference room, he would go to another section to be briefed on updates to schedules and procedures.

After leaving Captain Davies, Alan went ashore to meet Trina.

`I've lost half a day's leave,' he told her. `Now I'll have to be back on board by midday Tuesday.'

`Why? What's happened?'

`The convoy conference has been brought forward. Is there any chance of you getting leave Monday night?'

Trina bit her lip as she thought.

`I'm supposed to be on duty from midnight until eight all next week. I've already arranged to swap duty for Tuesday night, and I'd planned to come up early so I'd be here when you arrived Tuesday morning. I was going to book into the hotel for Tuesday night.'

`Do you think you can make the switch?'

Trina nodded. `I think so, but I'll have to be back to take duty Tuesday night if I have Monday off.'

`It's the best we can do,' Alan agreed. `If you can get off I'll come back Monday on the day train. That'll give us the night together.'

`D'you think you should? It's going to cut down your time at home.'

Alan shrugged. `I'll be going down on Saturday night. That'll give me all day Sunday, and it doesn't take more than a couple of hours to exchange news. After that there's always a strange awkwardness. The Damocles sword of imminent departure, or something. Anyway, I always feel we're just sitting, waiting until it's time for me to go. There's an unspoken emotion that at times is quite embarrassing.'

`Are you sure? I can't help feeling your mother thinks I'm taking up too much of your time. She never says anything when I see her, but I'm sure she feels that... well, that we should wait until we're married.'

`Bit late for that now,' Alan laughed. `I'm afraid as far as I'm concerned it's our business and nobody else's. If I don't come back on Monday we won't have any time together. If I get back Tuesday morning, we'll only have an hour or two before I leave for the conference.'

`Won't you have any free time after the conference?' Trina sounded surprised.

`Not much. I doubt if we'll get back to the ship before half past four. By the time everything's locked away it'll probably be five before I can get ashore. There's another change too. Because of the earlier sailing, all shore leave ends at nine on Tuesday. If you take out the time getting to and from the docks we'll only have an hour or two together that evening.'

`I see.' Then it doesn't matter if I don't have Tuesday night off. We'll still have the same time together before I catch the last train. That'll get me back to Troon before I'm due to go on duty.' The conversation took place in their room at the hotel, and in the background there was a constant, noisy rumble of traffic in the street below.

They had tumbled on to the bed as soon as the door was closed and Trina had taken off her jacket. She lay back and clasped her hands behind her head, smiling mischievously as she made her breasts strain at the tightened shirt. Slowly, and very deliberately, Alan undid the buttons while they talked. Trina waited until the last one was undone, then sat up and slipped her arms out of the sleeves.

`We haven't spent a whole night together for ages. Not since last year.'

As she said this Trina swung her legs off the bed and stood to remove her skirt, then turned back to face Alan. `Well, don't just lie there gawping. How about some action?'

Alan moved quickly, and she yelped, squirming, laughing and struggling as he manhandled her, removing the few remaining garments. He reached down to lift her up and Trina relaxed to lie quietly in his arms. She was turning her face to be kissed when Alan dumped her, unceremoniously, back on to the bed.

`You're a brutal, horrible pig,' she complained. Alan advanced menacingly, and Trina laughed throatily.

`I'm sorry, I didn't mean it... You're a nice pig and you're kind and... '

`And I'm going to get undressed too,' he interrupted.

`That's not what I was going to say.'

`What were you going to say?' Alan enquired.

`I'll tell you later... when you're undressed.'

The ship was not on standby so the usual shore leave expiry time of ten pm did not apply. All Alan had to do was set his alarm for early next morning, and to make sure he was back on board in time to go on duty.

Next day, Saturday, Alan rang Trina during the afternoon, and was told she had been able to exchange duty and would have the Monday night clear.

The journey to London was exhausting. With the train packed, Alan had to sit on his suitcase in the corridor for the whole way. However, the return trip on Monday was not as bad and there were even spare seats in the carriage. When the train pulled into the station at Glasgow, Trina was waiting for him. She had booked into the hotel, and they took Alan's bag up to the room before going out to eat. After their meal they sat for about three-quarters of an hour over coffee and liqueurs.

Relaxed and content, they drifted into talking about what life might be like when the war ended, taking it for granted that they would be together, and soon Trina brought the conversation around to a discussion of Alan's plans for after the war.

`The first thing will be to find another job,' Alan said thoughtfully.

`What do you mean?' Trina demanded. `Surely you'll be coming back to a shore job with the Company?'

Alan shook his head `I think not.'

`But...' Trina frowned as she hesitated. `Why not?'

`If I made any progress in the Company people would say it was because of you, and I'd be wondering about it myself. I guess you know that.'

`Yes, I see that,' Trina agreed. `But after a year or two in another job couldn't you return to Southern Oceanic?'

`I suppose so, but if I were making a success of another job there wouldn't be much point?' Trina was fidgeting, a sign that she had something important to say and was not sure how to say it.

`It could be worth while, as far as we're concerned,' she said at last.

`I'm sorry. I'm not with you.' Trina's eyes were focused on the glass in her hand, obviously considering some problem. Finally she made up her mind.

'It's like this,' she said. 'Now my brother's dead, it looks as though I'll inherit everything from mother. As you know, archaeology is her passion and she's not interested in shipping, but her shares could justify some representation on the Board.'

'You'll make the prettiest managing director the shipping world's ever seen,' Alan teased.

Trina was not amused.

'Stop it Alan. Please, I want to be serious about this.'

'OK, I'm listening.'

'If my brother had lived he'd have gone on to the Board when he retired from the Army. That was the way he looked at things, taking it for granted he'd be welcomed as a director when the army no longer wanted him. Ian was like that. He couldn't see he'd not be contributing anything worthwhile to running the firm.

'I remember Uncle Harry telling Ian; "You won't be of any use if you don't learn the business properly. The Army can't teach you to run a shipping line, and when I'm gone you'll be precious little help to John." But Ian had no ambition outside of the army, and it never seemed to worry him.'

She hesitated, and Alan wondered whether the memory of her brother was affecting Trina. He remained silent to give her the time she might need to recover.

In fact, Trina was just weighing up her next words, knowing that she would need to be very careful. Hesitating, she prevaricated by repeating what she had just said, but in slightly different words.

'It was no use telling that to Ian though. He had his heart set on the Army and he would never have been happy in an office.' She paused again and Alan felt it was time he said something.

'I can follow all that, but I can't see what it's got to do with me, or anything I decide to do.'

Trina laughed. 'Your prickles are showing,' she accused.

Alan's reaction had helped Trina, and she now knew that there was nothing for it but to state her thoughts plainly and as clearly as she could. She leaned across the table, propping her chin with her hands, and Alan was conscious of her eyes searching his face. 'I'm not interested for myself,' she told him. 'I don't want to go on working. I want to have children, and it's them I'm thinking about.

'As I was saying, once you've made a success of another job there's no reason why you shouldn't go back to Southern Oceanic. John's not all that bright. He's nice enough, but he'll need help; otherwise the business will soon end up being run by people outside the family. For the sake of our kids I don't think we should risk that happening.'

Trina caught her breath. Her words had come out in a rush and she was now feeling embarrassed. She had not only surprised Alan; she had surprised herself by what she had said.

It was one of the few times Alan had seen her so unsure. Never before had she risked suggesting that marriage might mean linking his future to the Marsdens.

Even more surprising to Alan was that, whenever they had talked about the future, there had been no thought of children. Trina's suggestion demolished their claim to have made no promises, no commitment. She had put into words what they had known for a long time.

If she had not been so confused Trina would never have made her next remark. As it was, she fumbled over the words.

'Uncle Harry asked... well not really asked... about a year ago... the last time I saw him. He wanted to know if I was still hearing from you. He...' She hesitated, then, as if for something to say added: 'It was just before your ship went missing...' Then paused and fiddled with her coffee cup, uncertain whether to continue.

'He what?' Alan prompted.

'Nothing... Oh, if you must know he asked me whether we were going to get married. Or, rather, whether we'd decided anything for the future. The fact that we're not engaged...'

Her voice trailed away as she looked at Alan trying to gauge his reaction.

'And what did you tell him?'

Trina looked at Alan defiantly.

'I told him we were, but not until after the war.'

'Did that meet with avuncular approval?'

Trina grinned, and seemed relieved by Alan's reaction and the tone of his question.

`I don't know. One never does with Uncle Harry, but he did say that John liked you.'

Trina appeared anxious now to change the subject, and without giving Alan a chance to comment on what she had just said, asked; `If you don't come back to the office d'you have any idea what you'll do?'

During their last voyage to Suez, Peter and Alan had become friendly with an army officer who was a director in a family-owned brewery in Reading, and whose father had reached the age where he wished to step down in favor of his son. Alan explained this to Trina. `Mark, that was his name, asked if I would be interested in a job with the brewery, supervising the catering side of the hotels they own. Their catering manager died recently, and under wartime conditions they decided not to replace him, but they'll need someone when the war ends.'

Alan could almost hear Trina's mind mesh into gear.

`That would be good,' she said enthusiastically. 'A couple of years experience with the brewery hotels, added to your shipboard knowledge, and you'd be set to step into Mr Carstairs' job. From there you could go on to the Board specializing in passenger and catering arrangements.'

`Hold it,' Alan protested. `You're jumping the gun a bit.' Then he laughed. `Don't get so worked up. Probably I'll be a complete flop at the brewery job.'

Trina realized she had let her wishes run ahead and that she was pushing Alan too hard. She began to laugh as well and relaxed back into her chair.

`You know me,' she said. `I always get carried away when I get an idea. Anyhow, who knows what it's going to be like when this rotten war ends.'

The course of the war was changing, and Trina and Alan were being forced to think seriously about the future. Yet there was an uncomfortable feeling at the back of Alan's mind, a sense of danger perhaps; the threat that he might find his life being organized by the Marsden money. This thought kept recurring, even next day when he was on his way to the conference with Captain Davies. He had no intention of breaking with Trina, he loved her far too much for that;

but neither would he surrender his independence any more than he would expect Trina to subordinate herself to him.

Later that afternoon, Alan was waiting for Captain Davies to come out of the conference room. He had finished his own job of updating procedures a quarter of an hour earlier. When Captain Davies did not emerge with the other ships' masters, Alan waited a couple of minutes then pushed the door open and peered inside. The room was empty except for Brian, the Senior Naval Officer's secretary.

`Any idea what's happened to Captain Davies, Brian?' he asked.

`He's with the SNO' was the reply. `They'll probably be a while. Come and wait in my office if you like.'

Alan had met Brian several times over drinks in the Officers' Mess. He now followed him into a small office at the far end of the conference room, separated from the SNO's office by a wooden partition. Brian and Alan exchanged a few remarks, but it was obvious that Brian had work to do and wanted to get started.

`Look,' Alan said, `If you've got work to do don't let me interrupt.'

Brian grinned back. `Well, I do have one or two things to do.' His fingers were already shuffling through some papers; and picking up his phone he was soon engrossed in a lengthy conversation. Alan had been conscious of voices in the next office and now, with nothing else to occupy his mind, found that he could follow the gist of what was being said. Both the SNO and Captain Davies possessed voices that could disregard the most hostile gale. Even if he had wanted to, Alan could hardly have failed to overhear much of their conversation. One of the first things he heard was the SNO saying;

`That's it then. The convoy will be timed to arrive off Bone just on dusk, and that's when you're to break away from the rest of the convoy and make for Malta at best possible speed.' The harsh voice of Captain Davies broke in.

`I don't like it, but must agree it gives us a reasonable chance of getting into Malta. We should be there soon after dawn. At night, and at full speed, the odds favor us. All the same, it's throwing away a good ship. They'll surely get us when we leave, even if they don't sink us in the harbor. They're bound to send planes from Sicily and they could even have a couple of U-boats waiting for us.'

There was a pause and some comment Alan couldn't catch. Then he heard the SNO again.

`Perhaps it won't be as bad as all that,' but his voice did not carry much conviction.

Again there were a few growled words from Captain Davies that Alan could not make out, but he heard the reply.

`I know, I know how you must feel, but it's an operation that must be carried out, even at some cost.'

`Some cost! I hope whoever dreamed this up knows what he's about.' Captain Davies sounded as if he thought this unlikely.

`I imagine so.'

From the tone of his voice Alan could imagine the SNO giving a shrug of his shoulders as he said this.

`They don't take me into their confidence,' he continued. `But I think they're scared of a German attack on Malta using parachutists. Same as they did in Crete.'

`Why the hell can't we fly in parachute troops of our own to stop them? It seems they're quite happy to sacrifice my ship.'

`Don't ask me. I don't know any more than I've got here, and it just says it's essential to get the troops into Malta. It must be, otherwise they wouldn't be taking such a risk. Look at it this way, if Jerry held Malta he'd be able to cover his shipments to Rommel. We'd be hamstrung in all our operations until we could get him out again.'

Captain Davies gave what could only be described as a snort of disgust.

`I suppose I have to do it, but I hope it really is for a good reason and not some back room boy's wild idea.'

They continued talking, and even though their voices were lower it was clear that they were studying a chart, working over speeds and timings. Meanwhile Alan had time to think over what he had just learned.

Bone? He searched his memory. Two hundred miles or so east of Algiers. It had been the most easterly point of assault in the African landings. The more Alan thought, the less he liked the prospect.

Recently a supply convoy had managed to get through to Malta, but only five ships out of fourteen reached their destination, and some of these were sunk in the harbor after arriving at Valetta.

Since then, to the best of Alan's knowledge, no surface ships had made the run. In the way whispers got around from ship to ship, they had heard that Malta was being supplied by air and submarine only. He would have been much happier if left in ignorance of what was in store and, ironically, he heard the SNO saying;

`Of course, no one, except you, is to know the plan until the last moment. It would be best if you didn't even mention it to your own officers until you're off Bone. The troops, except for their Commanding Officer, won't have been told their destination. It'll be up to him to decide when to tell them, after that you can use your own judgment about telling your crew. We don't want the troops to hear about it before their CO makes his announcement.' Alan looked across to Brian, but he had the phone jammed to his ear and had heard nothing. In front of him was the sheaf of papers, and he was checking details with whoever was on the other end of the line.

The information had been intended for the ears of Captain Davies alone, but he and the SNO did not allow for their windjammer voices being overheard, or for an eavesdropper in the Secretary's office. Neither was the type to speak in hushed tones.

In the taxi, on the way back to the ship, Captain Davies was no more taciturn than normal. That would have been impossible. He did grunt one enquiry, after looking at the bag that was fastened to Alan's wrist by a strap.

`Many changes?'

`Nothing much, Sir,' Alan answered.

There was no further conversation.

After the SNO's emphasis on secrecy, it never occurred to Alan that Trina might hear of their destination from her own sources. Alan's one thought was that she must not know. It was not secrecy or security that concerned him. Rather, he did not want her to go through another period of strain and worry. Much better that she did not know about it until it was all over.

If he had only known, but Alan did not know, not until it was too late.

CHAPTER THIRTEEN

The time is out of joint
Shakespeare - Hamlet

Captain Davies watched while Alan put the codebooks back into their weighted bag. He opened the safe and placed the bag inside before closing and locking the door. The codebooks would stay there while the ship was in port.

`That's all,' he said.

As Alan left the cabin and turned to close the door, he saw Captain Davies staring out through one of the for'ard portholes, hands clasped behind his back. Captain Davies commanded respect though he was not an easy person to like, but Alan felt a sudden sympathy for him. There was a sense of loneliness about the Captain, and Alan wondered what he was thinking as he contemplated the immediate future.

In his own cabin, Alan also faced a moment of truth. Alone, with nothing now to occupy his thoughts, he found that he was frightened. From the conversation he had overheard he knew that they would likely be attacked and almost certainly sunk by planes, U-boats or a combination of both. He had seen ships destroyed and it was never a pleasant sight.

Would he be killed in the attack? Would he be drowned? His terror of drowning struck at him. Would there be any hope of rescue for survivors? He knew so little about the Malta situation. Were there any Navy surface vessels still there, or vessels that might be used for search and rescue? He had no great confidence that the Germans would refrain from strafing any lifeboats or rafts. He did not know enough to guess at his chances of surviving the trip , but feared that they were not good.

Alan began to change out of uniform, and had taken off his shoes when the cabin steward entered and asked if he would like a cup of tea. Alan checked the time and found that it was already twenty to five.

`No, I don't think so, thanks Carter.'

The interruption had at least served to break into his morbid thoughts, and the glance at his watch made him aware that Trina would be arriving in less than half an hour. They had arranged to meet on board at five, and if Alan had not returned by then she would wait for him. This would give them a little extra time together.

Before coming down, Trina would have checked out of the hotel, as she would be returning to Troon that night. When Alan had left her that morning they had still not made up their minds what they would do in the few hours before she had to catch her train. A wave of dismay swept through Alan as he realized that this might be the last time he would ever see Trina. With that thought in mind, Alan knew he could not face the prospect of sitting in a restaurant watching the clock hands creeping closer to the moment when he must say goodbye.

He made a sudden decision, and called Carter back.

`Carter, I'll arrange with the Chef to have something to eat in my cabin tonight. I'd like you to pick it up from the galley just before you go off duty at six.'

`Very good, Sir. Would you like me to clear away later?'

`Thanks Carter, but there's no need. Leave the tray and I'll drop it into the pantry when I've finished.'

`Five to six be all right, Sir?'

`Fine. Oh, another thing. I have a guest coming so there'll be two of us.'

`Very good, Sir.'

Carter left, and Alan went down to Con Mahoney's cabin. The door was open, but Alan knocked and Mahoney looked up.

`Come in, Sir. Have a good leave?'

`Too short. How did yours go?'

Con Mahoney waved a hand in a deprecating gesture.

`Just as happy to be back on board,' he said. Then asked; `Is there something you want?'

`Yes, there is,' Alan replied. `Trina Grant is coming on board for a couple of hours tonight, and I wondered if you'd organize something cold and a pot of coffee. I've told Carter to come and see you shortly before he goes off duty.'

Mahoney's face broke into a smile.

`Leave it to me,' he said, then asked: `How is Miss Grant?'

Mahoney had known Trina from the days at Barringdale, and knew of Alan's association with her.

`She's fine,' Alan told him. `You may have heard she's stationed near here.'

Again Mahoney grinned.

`The word had filtered through.'

`She's coming down tonight, and I thought it would be nice if she stayed for a meal. By rights I should still be on leave, but had to return early to go to a conference with the Old Man, otherwise we'd have spent the day together.'

`That's all right, Sir. No trouble.' Then with his most suggestive leer added;

`Have fun, Sir.'

Alan made a rude sign at him and left. `Better let Peter know,' he thought, and made his way up a couple of decks to the Purser's office. Higgins was the only one there.

`Purser's in his cabin, I think,' he told Alan.

The Purser's cabin was on the same deck and, as the door was ajar, Alan pushed it open and looked in.

`Hi there, Peter.' Purser Redpath was leaning back in a chair, his feet on the desk and reading a book. He looked up.

`It's that time is it?' he stated, rather than asked. `Hell no, it's early yet, I just wanted to see you.'

`Conference go off okay?'

`Same as usual.'

`Are we're going back to New York?'

`Couldn't say.'

Alan was tempted to tell Peter what he had learned. It would have helped to have someone to talk with; someone to share the knowledge of what was in store for them.

`The Old Man didn't give any clue when he came out?' Peter asked.

Alan managed a laugh.

`You know what he's like. He only spoke two words the whole way back to the ship.'

`You all right?'

Evidently something in Alan's manner had seemed odd.

`Yes, fine.'

Alan hastened to change the conversation.

`Trina's coming on board tonight. She'll probably stay for an hour or two, and I've organized a meal in my cabin.' Peter looked at Alan but said nothing.

`I reckon it's fair enough,' Alan added hastily. Peter scratched his head but still offered no comment.

`Normally, she never stays more than a minute or two, but tonight's different.'

`Why do you say that?'

`Well, it's because that blasted conference mucked up our plans for the day.'

Peter shrugged. `It's your affair.'

As Alan left the cabin, Peter called out:

`Bring her along for a drink if you like.' It was nearly five o'clock by now and Alan decided not to meet Trina at the gangway. She knew her way about the ship and it would be less conspicuous if he stayed in his cabin. He took a few steps along the alleyway, then changed his mind and went up to "A" deck. From there he could see the length of the wharf, and he knew Trina would still have a hundred yards to walk after she came around the end of the shed. The dockyard area was not the safest place and Trina only came down to the ship during daylight hours, Even so, Alan was always worried when she was by herself. Until Trina turned the corner of the cargo shed she would be in full view of the police at the dock gates. On the wharf itself, there was a row of empty wagons on the railway line that ran the length of the wharf. This left an alleyway, about eight feet wide, between the wagons and the cargo shed. From the height of "A" deck Alan looked down over these wagons and would see her if she should walk between them and the shed. The boat deck was deserted and Alan walked its length until he reached the aft railing. He rested his hands on the solid teak, feeling the grain in the timber. Below him was the old first class swimming pool, partly sheltered by the changing rooms. Paper and other rubbish blown by the wind was lying in the bottom of the now empty pool. Further aft, a movement caught his attention on the stern deck as someone crossed between the three-inch anti-aircraft gun and the four-inch low trajectory gun. It was the Chief Petty Officer of the gun crew, and Alan guessed that he was checking the ready use ammunition lockers.

Immediately beside Alan was his own action station, the aft gunnery control tower. He looked up, and then turned away, trying to avoid all thought of what must lie ahead. He began to pace the deck impatiently. There was still no sign of Trina and he would have expected her to be early rather than late. Already it was ten past five.

In the dock, the still water was black, sullen and polluted. Alan let his gaze travel up the mast and beyond to the sky. It too was unclean, with patchy, ragged clouds, and there was little mercy in the cutting wind. The day was steel cold, unwelcoming and grey. He thought again of the voyage they were about to make, and shivered.

Trina was coming now; hurrying around the end of the shed she stepped through the gap between two wagons and walked down towards the ship, stepping boldly close to the edge of the wharf. Against the huge dockside cranes and the towering hull of the ship, she looked so small and Alan felt a stir of anticipation. When she reached the gangway he ran down to his cabin to meet her. In the event, she was barely a quarter of an hour late.

`I had trouble getting a taxi,' she explained. Trina started speaking the moment she opened the cabin door, and Alan reached out to her. She hesitated, fractionally, looking at him intently and then moved into his arms. With a fierceness that took Alan by surprise she responded to his greeting kiss.

`Hold on, give me a chance to get my shoes off,' he suggested. Trina had her hands clasped behind his neck and was arched backwards to look up at him. As usual her hat had been knocked askew, giving her a look of provocative wantonness, and she fluttered her eyelids at Alan.

`What's the matter? Last night too much for you?'

`I shall treat that remark with the ignorance it deserves.'

`Do we need to go ashore right away?'

The bunk in Alan's cabin had several drawers beneath it and was about four feet off the deck. Trina leaned back and rested her elbows on the mattress. She left no doubt what it was she had in mind.

`Ooh, you are awful,' Alan said, and laughed. `As a matter of fact I had the same idea.'

Trina interrupted, her eyes now wide and innocent. `What idea? I really don't know what you're talking about.'

`Why, staying on board of course. I've even organized some food for six o'clock.'

`Can I trust you?'

`No.'

`In that case I'll stay.'

They kissed again, and a few minutes passed before Alan said;

`Peter's invited us along for a drink. He's probably dying of thirst by now. Make yourself decent and we'll go.' Trina had often heard Alan talk about Peter, of how shy he was, and of his awkwardness when meeting people for the first time. She had seen him previously, but only in the distance, and had never spoken to him. Consequently, she was wondering what to expect when Alan made the introductions.

Typically, Peter chose that evening to play his charming act. He was suave and witty, apparently completely at ease, and a most congenial host. It was almost half past six when they left his cabin. `I thought you said he was shy.' Trina turned accusingly on Alan as they walked along the alleyway.

`He's a lot of other things too.'

`Such as?'

`Bloody unpredictable.'

Alan had no hope of convincing Trina that he really did understand Peter.

Con Mahoney had remembered Trina's fondness for asparagus, and when they reached Alan's cabin they discovered that Carter had found a table that would fit into the limited space. Instead of the tray Alan had expected, there was an immaculately served meal. They started with Crême d'Asparagus soup, which was followed by cold chicken and a salad with asparagus tips. To complete the meal, Carter served one of Joe Hayter's rich desserts that Mahoney had organized. In spite of Alan's instructions Carter came back with coffee, and stayed to clear away the table and dishes.

There was still nearly an hour and a half before Alan would have to take Trina to catch the train. When Carter left, Alan slid the catch on the door and turned around to find that Trina was already taking off her skirt. By the time he removed his jacket and was starting to unbutton his shirt, Trina was stepping out of her last garment. She stood with her back to him, but was watching Alan in the mirror over the dressing table and he moved to stand behind her. Using the mirror they looked into each other's eyes while he ran his hands over her body, kissing her neck and shoulders. Then, following the pressure of his touch, Trina allowed him to turn her around.

`Let's not take any precautions tonight,' she whispered. `It's so much nicer.'

`Bit risky isn't it?'

`I'll take a chance.'

`You didn't feel that way last night.' `Oh, last night was different.'

Alan moved back slightly so that he could see her face. `Why was it different?'

`I feel different tonight.'

`Feeling different may not stop you getting pregnant.'

`Who says I'll get pregnant?'

`I wouldn't like to gamble that either of us is sterile, according to your arithmetic...'

`Oh stop being stuffy about it.' Trina tried to pull Alan to her again, but he resisted.

`Be sensible, suppose you do get pregnant, what then?'

`Oh hell, I suppose you'd do the decent thing and marry me. Wouldn't you?'

Alan tried to be flippant to break the tension that was building.

`Put that question on the notice paper,' he said, leaning over to kiss the tip of her nose.

`Idiot,' she said, automatically, then insisted:

'Well, would you?'

`Do you really need to ask?'

Trina smiled.

`No, of course I don't.'

`Suppose I wasn't able to marry you. There is a war on, so I've heard.'

Trina buried her head against Alan's chest.

`Don't say that,' she whispered a little shakily.

Alan held her closer while he stroked her head. All sorts of emotions were running through him. A yearning for Trina was mixed with the fear that had lurked at the back of his mind ever since hearing that they were bound for Malta.

Finally Trina raised her head. There was a wild, staring look in her eyes, and also an element of calculation.

`Did you hear where you might be going this time?' Alan hesitated. He had no intention of telling Trina the truth but could not bring himself to a direct lie.

`I gather it's going to be short voyage, so perhaps it could be another trip to New York.'

Trina's eyes were searching his face, trying to see right into him.

`That's all right then. We'd have to be dead unlucky for something to happen to you and for me to get pregnant as well.'

Alan turned his head to escape her eyes. If they took no precautions Trina might well become pregnant. Would she be so keen to risk it if she knew where he was going? If he were killed she would get over it in time, but how would it be if she were stuck with a fatherless child?

`Dead unlucky might prove to be only too true,' he said without thinking.

Immediately he saw the hurt wash over Trina's face and would have recalled his words had he been able. Alan tried hard to modify what he had said.

`I mightn't get leave when we get back. We mightn't have time to get married, and the next voyage could take me away for six months or more. Suppose it wasn't possible for us to get married until after you'd had the baby? It might not worry us too much but I doubt that your mother would be very happy.'

There were tears in Trina's eyes now.

`You just don't love me,' she accused.

`That's not true and you know it.'

`Please Alan.'

`No Trina. Why tonight? I can't let you risk it. It'd be silly.'

Trina wrenched herself away from Alan and turned her back on him. Her shoulders were quivering, and her head bent forward so that he could not see her face in the mirror. Alan put out his hand and stroked her hair.

`Let's get married when I get back.'

`I hate you!'

That seemed a very definite answer to Alan's proposal, but he did not think that she really meant it.

`You can take all the chances you like then.'

Obviously he had said the wrong thing. Trina turned and glared at him.

`I think I've taken all the chances I'm going to take.'

Alan saw that she was furious with him, but could not understand why Trina was reacting so strangely.

She reached past him and picked up her bra.

`What are you doing?' he asked.

`I'm getting dressed. I want to go.'

Again she turned away from him. This time Alan caught hold of her, and although she resisted he made her turn to face him. To his surprise she burst into tears.

`Leave me alone Alan. Please, just leave me alone.'

`I don't understand. What's the matter?'

`You'd never understand,' she said bitterly.

Trina was determined to go, and there was no way Alan could reason with her. She was gripped by an emotion that would not even allow her to answer him. The tears had stopped but her features were hard and set. There was plenty of time before Trina had to catch her train, and Alan hated the thought of leaving with this lack of harmony between them. By the time they reached town she might be less intractable. There would be no hurry. With any luck it would be possible to talk it out over a cup of coffee, and to repair the damage before they said goodbye.

The day had been dull with heavy cloud, but even in the gathering darkness there was just enough light to see where they were going. To reach the dock gates they had two hundred yards to walk. Usually there would be a taxi or two waiting outside.

As soon as they stepped off the gangway they crossed the railway line, and passed behind the row of goods wagons. On their right was the solid bulk of the cargo shed, and in this alleyway between the shed and the wagons it was quite dark, and they had to pick their way carefully, avoiding scattered pieces of timber.

If the two men had remained still, Alan might not have noticed them until too late. As it was, a movement caught his attention and made him aware of possible danger. Beside one of the shed doors there was a stack of pallets about eight feet high, and in the angle between the stack and the door Alan could make out two dark shadows.

`Get ready to run,' he whispered to Trina. `I think we've got trouble. See if you can get to the end of the shed and yell for help to the police on the gates. I'll do my best to give you time.'

Over the previous months several crew members had been beaten and robbed in the wharf area. Usually it happened when they were returning from a run around the pubs. Alan was sure that the lurking figures were up to no good, and wondered what the approach would be. Would there be any preliminaries, or would they attack without any warning? Alan made up his mind. His only hope was to take them by surprise as soon as they moved.

`Excuse me Guv'nor...'

This was not a moment for doubts. They were moving closer and were only six feet away when Alan acted. He jumped forward and hit the one who had spoken with every ounce of strength he could muster, driving his fist deep into the man's solar plexus. Alan heard him gasp as the breath left his body. In the next instant there was an explosion against the side of Alan's head and he staggered a few steps before falling to the ground.

For nearly half a minute he lay there, completely dazed. Gradually his vision cleared and he realized that he was lying across the rail tracks, his cheek resting against cold metal. There was a moment of bewilderment before he heard a muffled cry and turned his head. Memory flooded back.

The man who had hit Alan now had hold of Trina. He was standing behind her, left arm under her chin and dragging her head back so that her body was arched away from him. His right hand was inside her uniform jacket and Trina was scrabbling, ineffectually, as she tried to pull his arm away from her throat. The man's attention was on what he was doing to Trina, and Alan was able to scramble to his feet unnoticed. Never before had Alan felt such cold rage, and he went berserk. Afterwards he was unable to recall anything he did, but when sanity returned he was standing over the man's prone figure. He could see a trickle of blood running across the attacker's cheek, coming either from his nose or the corner of his mouth. Alan did not bother to find out which it was; the man was unconscious and that was enough. `Alan! Alan!'

Trina was calling. Alan turned, and saw that the man he had hit first was trying to get to his feet, and at the same time protect himself with an upraised arm. Trina had taken off one of her heavy service shoes and was using it as a club to hit him over the head as hard as she could.

Alan strode over.

`Let me have him,' he said.

The man was still down on one knee. Alan reached for his collar and pulled him to his feet. He was shorter than Alan but thickset, and even in the gloom it was easy to see that he did not look very well. He was swaying slightly, clutching at his stomach as he tried to keep his balance, but Alan was in no mood to sympathize. Very deliberately he measured the distance, then moved in and hit the would-be mugger on the side of the chin.

As he watched the man fall, Alan was aware of an ice cold feeling in his mind and body. Even when he spoke to Trina his voice lacked any emotion.

`You can put your shoe back on now. I went to a lot of trouble to get those Nylons for you.'

He had meant the comment to be flippant but his voice was not under control. Much later, that same night after he had gone to bed, he realized that he had not even thanked Trina for her help, nor even asked her if she was all right.

Trina had suffered no physical harm, but it had been a nasty experience. Whenever he remembered that night he could not understand why he had behaved so badly, especially as Trina had fussed over him. The only excuse he could find was that the blow on the head had made him more stupid than usual.

After his comment, Trina put out her hand for support while she slipped the shoe back on to her foot. Alan's hand was warm and slightly sticky, and Trina bent for a closer view.

`Your hand, look at it.'

Alan held his hand above his head to catch what little light there was, and could see blood oozing from his knuckles. As he straightened his fingers he became conscious of pain.

`You'd better do something about that.'

`It'll be all right,' Alan muttered, and fumbled for a handkerchief to wrap around his right hand.

`We're going back on board where I can look at it in a decent light.'

`It's nothing,' he protested.

All the same he did not press the point. To tell the truth, reaction had set in and he was beginning to feel a little shaky. A good stiff drink was what he needed, and back in his cabin he insisted on pouring two strong Scotches before allowing Trina to look at his fingers.

When Alan finished his drink Trina took charge, fussing over his hands. He had no bandages in his cabin but did have some antiseptic lotion. Trina made a pad from one handkerchief and placed it over the split skin, then used another to hold the pad in place. Alan's left hand had only a small split and minor abrasions. Trina wrapped a third handkerchief around this after again using the antiseptic. Alan had already checked that he was able to move his fingers freely and was sure that there were no broken bones. Nevertheless he would have sore knuckles for a day or two.

Satisfied that she had done everything possible, Trina sat down and finished her own Scotch. An air of constraint had built between them since returning to Alan's cabin, with conversation restricted to essentials. Trina still seemed distracted and unwilling to help bridge the gap that had grown between them.

Alan checked his watch.

`We'll have to get moving or you'll miss your train,' he told her.

He stood beside Trina, intending to kiss and hold her when she stood up, but she was too quick for him. Even as she straightened Trina was turning away, reaching for her handbag on the dressing table.

`I wish I hadn't come down tonight. Then none of this would have happened.' There was impatience, even anger, in her voice.

`Oh I don't know.' Alan sought for a light-hearted comment; `It'll give us something to talk about in our old age.'

Trina turned to look at him with a gesture of exasperation. She hesitated as if about to say something, then changed her mind. With a quick, jerky movement Trina slung the strap of her handbag over her shoulder. Alan was standing by the door and as she approached he saw a glint of moisture in her eyes. He caught her and Trina tilted her head so that they could kiss. For a long moment she clung to him, then said;

`We'd better go.'

Before leaving, Alan went to the office and took a heavy round ruler from his desk, and held it up for Trina to see.

`I don't expect they'll still be there but... just in case. If they are, do as I tell you this time and run. Incidentally, why didn't you?'

`When he hit you I lost my temper and tried to scratch his eyes out.'

Theoretically Alan should not have left the ship to take Trina to the station. Before he could get back it would be well after nine when all leave was supposed to end. However nothing would have made him part from Trina that night until he had seen her safely on the train. It was most unlikely his absence would be noticed, and by half past nine he would be back on board.

In the taxi there was still a barrier, and neither was able to talk freely about what had happened between them earlier in the evening. Alan hesitated, puzzled by Trina's actions, and not willing to explain the reason for his own behavior. As a consequence, he was unsure what to say and fearful of making matters worse.

He put his arm around Trina and she did not protest, but neither did she relax against him. Holding her, he tried to sort out the meaning of the night's events, but found them unreal and inexplicable.

When Trina's train pulled out of the station these questions were still unanswered. As the last carriage disappeared into the night Alan felt a wave of nausea and just made it to the station lavatory before being sick.

Alan was suffering from a mild concussion.

* * *

The trauma of his memories jolted Alan back to reality, but it was only to a feeble awareness.

`So, I'm still alive... still remembering. Odd, it's the lifeboat that seems the dream, and the past alone is real.'

* * *

`It was ridiculous,' or so Alan thought later, that the part of the voyage he had been dreading was so uneventful. From the time they left the convoy off Bone until the time they rejoined it there was no interference from the Germans. All the excitement came while still with the convoy.

That they reached Malta as planned was not surprising. The whole gamble had been taken on the assumption that the enemy would not guess what was intended. What mattered was that the troops reach Malta. Too bad if Ocean Monarch failed to make it back.

The Germans must have seen Ocean Monarch soon after dawn when their first reconnaissance plane for the day flew over the island. A ship the size of Ocean Monarch could not have been overlooked.

To everyone's surprise, apart from one other reconnaissance plane there was no further activity from enemy aircraft.

During the day the weather deteriorated, and by the time they left had built up into half a gale with the promise of worse to come. Possibly the weather conditions discouraged the Germans from launching an air attack, and the rougher seas would have made conditions more difficult for any U-boat lurking in wait.

All the same, the crew of Ocean Monarch expected that aircraft would attack them soon after dawn. The early morning reconnaissance plane would report their departure from Malta, and the bombers should be able to find them within an hour or two. When daylight came they waited anxiously. From the aft gun control, where Alan was on standby, he had a good all-round view, except for'ard where the funnels were in the way. Hour after hour went by and nothing menacing appeared from the dark grey clouds. It was hard to believe, and tension did not ease until they saw the masts and hulls of ships appearing over the horizon. They were no longer on their own; the unbelievable had happened and they were about to regain the protection of the convoy.

Stand down was given, and Alan climbed from the tower. Peter Redpath, who had been on "A" deck for the previous half an hour, walked over to meet him.

`Am I glad that's over,' Peter said.

`Not half as glad as I am,' Alan replied.

`What makes you think you're so special?'

`Nothing, except that I've known where we were going since before we left Glasgow, and I've been shit scared the whole voyage.'

`You knew? You never said anything.'

`I wasn't supposed to know. I overheard the Old Man being sworn to secrecy. He was told he wasn't even to tell his own officers until after the troops had been briefed on where they were going. I could hardly spill the news, could I? The Old Man told everyone as soon as he thought it necessary.'

`You could have told me privately.'

`What good would it have done, Peter? Nothing except give you more time to worry about things.'

Peter did not seem to be convinced, and Alan tried to take his mind off what he appeared to consider a grievance.

`Wonder why we weren't attacked?'

`Weather's not the best,' Peter commented. `Could be that's what stopped them. Heavy cloud over Sicily or wherever.'

`Probably,' Alan agreed. `On the other hand they may have been busy elsewhere. Maybe we overestimate our own importance.'

`More likely their top brass got their wires crossed.' Peter had a superb lack of confidence in staff officers and the higher direction of the war, an opinion reinforced by the behavior of one or two high ranking officers who had traveled in the ship.

`The Cruiser's not there.' Peter had been checking the convoy numbers.

Alan had already noted this from the height of the tower, and pointed out something else.

`There aren't as many Destroyers either.'

`Now you mention it, there aren't.'

`You were down in the office when we broke away from the convoy weren't you?' Alan asked.

`That's right. I'd called up the leading hands to pass on the Old Man's message.'

`That's why you didn't see what happened. When we left the convoy the Cruiser pulled out as well, and a couple of Destroyers went with her. There was a deal of signaling, and I wouldn't be surprised if she were returning to Algiers or Gibraltar. She must have been fairly badly damaged anyway.'

It seemed much longer, but it had been only three days since the convoy had been attacked off Algiers by aircraft. Reconnaissance planes had found them early in the day, and several hours later the attack came. When the bombers arrived they had circled the convoy, frustratingly just out of range, and had launched radio-controlled bombs at the ships.

It had been a magnificent, truly Mediterranean day. Warm without being hot, the day sparkled with a clarity that made the ships stand out in minute detail against the blue of the sky and sea. When the attack came in, the contrast between this beauty and the ugliness of war was revolting. The Cruiser was hit early in the attack, but it was difficult to see whether she had suffered any major damage. When one of the troop ships was hit there was no doubt the wound was mortal. The bomb exploded in her engine room, and a cloud of steam and smoke spiraled high into the air to join the black smudges from bursting shells that marred the perfection of the sky.

That ship was packed with over two thousand troops and they died in hundreds.

When night came, and Ocean Monarch was making her run to Malta, Alan could not sleep. The horror of the day came back and added to the apprehension he had for their own immediate future. After several restless hours he switched on the light and tried to exorcise the memory by putting it down on paper. He wrote:

'Ten ships, all wrapped with sparkling sea:
ten planes to speck a cloudless sky:
ten thousand men who fear and wait
amid this beauty, and this hate.

A day of crystal sun washed blue:
a day when air is born anew:
a day of sudden fear and death
with tortured, pain filled, final breath.

Many men about to die
in the sea, and in the sky.
Each life an ebbing ripple flows
to distant hearts and anguish grows.

Cry out the hell of this despair:
the wanton pain which we must share.
Cry out the rage of futile shame
for lives whose promise never came.'

They were back in Glasgow in just over three weeks. There was no sign of Trina, so Alan assumed that she was on duty. As soon as he could get ashore he put in a phone call to Troon. After a short wait Trina came on the line.

`Hello, Trina Grant speaking.'

`Good morning, I'm carrying out a survey of Wren officers, and your name was mentioned as one who was worth surveying.'

`Alan, I wondered when you'd ring. How... how was the voyage?'

`Very pleasant. When am I going to see you? We'll only be here for the next two days.'

`I'm sorry Alan. We won't be able to meet this time.'

`How come?'

`There's a 'flu epidemic on the base, and we're short handed. I won't be able to get away.'

`Suppose I come down to Troon. Could we have a meal together?'

`I don't think I could even leave the base.'

`Pity, but if I come down you could at least invite me into the Mess for a drink.'

`Please Alan... I don't want you to come.'

`Why not?' There was no immediate answer, so Alan continued.

`Trina?'

`Yes?'

`That last night before I sailed was so... I don't know... unsatisfactory to put it mildly. I've been worried ever since. Isn't there any way we can get together if I come down?'

`No, please Alan.'

`Trina, something's wrong. What is it?'

`Don't make me tell you.'

Outside the phone box a heavy lorry ground slowly past. Alan looked through the scratched and dirty panes of glass, and all he could see was a high brick wall, barren and bland, except for a few crude scrawls. A drizzle of rain completed the desolation. All was ugly, harsh and cruel.

He heard himself speaking, as if listening to a stranger.

`There's someone else... Is that why you don't want me to come down?'

`Yes.'

There was a long silence, then Trina said; `I never thought it would be like this.'

Alan could think of nothing to say.

`Alan... Alan, are you still there?'

`Yes, I'm sorry too.'

`We... we did agree.'

`Yes we did. Yes... of course. You should have told me right away. Is this the end then?'

`Do you want it to be?'

`I don't know Trina. It's come as a shock. Do you want it to be the end?'

`I don't know either. Oh Alan, I just don't know what I want. I don't even understand myself. That last night together, coming back in the train... so much had happened and I felt so miserable. I felt that you'd humiliated me.'

`Oh God Trina! I'm sorry. I'd... That's the last thing I'd want to do.'

`I knew where you were going... and I couldn't tell you. I was afraid I'd never see you again.'

`You knew?'

`Yes.'

`Why didn't you tell me?... No, of course... I see. I didn't tell you either. I didn't want you worrying.'

Alan heard a hiss as Trina caught her breath.

`Alan, you knew all the time? You told me you were going to New York.'

`I didn't, you know, not in so many words. I just tried to give that impression.'

`Was that why you...? Of course! You didn't think you'd be coming back.'

There was a silence while they both digested their mutual discovery. Then Alan said;

`Perhaps this may teach us to keep nothing back in future. No matter what.'

`Alan, will you write to me while you're away?'

`Are you sure I can't come and see you, so we can talk it over quietly?'

`No Alan. I don't want you to meet... '

The operator's voice cut in.

`Three minutes. Are you extending?'

Before Alan had a chance to speak he heard Trina say:

`No thank you,' and then, quickly, `Goodbye Alan.' And the line went dead.

For a minute Alan hesitated, looking blankly at the phone still in his hand; and wondering whether to ring again.

`No!' He slammed the receiver down and went back to the ship.

That night he drank more than usual, but it did not help at all. Later, in bed, his imagination would not let him rest, and he seemed to hear an echo of Trina's voice saying:

`Yes! Yes!'

That `Yes' twice exclaimed, which always heralded her entrance into ecstasy.

CHAPTER FOURTEEN

I cried for madder music and for stronger wine,
But when the feast is finished and the lamps expire,
Then falls thy shadow, Cynara! the night is thine;
And I am desolate and sick of an old passion,
Yea, hungry for the lips of my desire:
I have been faithful to thee, Cynara! in my fashion.
Ernest Dowson

Ocean Monarch went back to the Atlantic run; and the voyage to New York with no passengers left Alan with time to think. To some degree he understood the trauma Trina had suffered, and blamed himself for his clumsy, tactless behavior that night, but could not accept that this justified Trina's behavior. He fluctuated between a bitter cynicism and sheer disbelief that Trina would behave the way she had. Although there had been times when they had talked lightly about the difference between love and sex, Alan could not accept that what Trina had done had been a meaningless physical act. It was not as if he had been away for months and months. It had been so short a voyage, and the added sting was that Trina had not wanted to see him.

The hurt festered, and by the time the ship reached New York Alan was convinced that he must forget Trina and free himself from the pain of longing. He discovered that it was easier to be calm and logical in theory than in practice, and he allowed bitterness into his mind.

At that time New York was a wonderful place to have fun. In addition to offers of hospitality sent to the ship, there were always attractive girls at the Allied Officers' Club and Alan decided that this was exactly what he needed. The club provided a meeting place. The furniture in its single room was limited to a Jukebox, a scattering of chairs and a drum of beer next to a table stacked with glasses. Otherwise the room was bare.

Visits to this club followed a ritual. First came a long walk from the entrance to the beer barrel and a few words of welcome might be exchanged. While pouring a beer, there was an opportunity to survey the unattached girls, conscious that they, in turn, were eyeing the newcomer. Then, it was simply a matter of walking over and joining the group that included the selected girl. For a while conversation would be general and all parties had time to complete an assessment before any commitment was made. Once an overture received a favorable response, the convention was that the visitor must remain with the chosen girl for the rest of the evening. If he tried to drop her he would be cold-shouldered by all the other girls.

For many of the girls it was a chance to break free from convention and offer temporary companionship to lonely servicemen, as a compassionate and patriotic duty. In this way their respectability was protected, and they could have discreet fun with a clear conscience. It was what most of them wanted, and what they called a "cute English accent" was a guarantee of success.

Ocean Monarch stayed in New York for ten days, and during that time Alan met four girls at the Officers' Club. He took them out and pretended that Trina no longer existed; but by the time the ship had returned to the Clyde Alan found it difficult to remember the girls individually and only fragments of memories remained. Not one had made a lasting impression. He had enjoyed the experience, saying and doing the correct things; acting the stage image of an Englishman for their entertainment and his own amusement.

It was as well to laugh. Alan found that the more he tried the less he could forget. He had taken what was offered and found it pleasant, but it did not replace what he had lost.

Alan was unable to write to Trina from New York. He did not know what to say, or whether he even wanted to write. Anyway, he would be back in Glasgow by the time she would get his letter. The mail came on board with the Pilot, and was sorted and distributed as they sailed up the Clyde. There was a letter from Trina, but it told Alan very little. Its tone was unnaturally stiff and restrained, as though she had found it difficult to write. The letter was dated two days earlier, and Alan guessed that she had put off writing it until the last possible moment. She started the letter abruptly, no `My dear' or `My darling', but simply;

`Alan... After you rang I put in an application for transfer. It seemed the easiest way to break the entanglement I had made. Uncle Harold pulled a few strings, and last week I received a posting to the Isle of Wight. I am leaving on the train tonight, and will not be sure of my new address until I report at Ventnor. I will write as soon as I know.'

Trina had signed the letter, apparently intending to say no more, but it looked as if there had been a last minute change of mind for she had added a scribbled note. She had written;

`I never stopped loving you.'

That was all.

As he read the few brief lines Alan felt a queer mixture of relief, rage and disappointment. Disappointment, because he would now have no opportunity to see her. Rage, with himself for not writing from New York. And relief? Yes, there was some consolation, mixed with pain, as he read that postscript.

When Ocean Monarch sailed two days later Alan was at cross-purposes with the world. He had not heard any more from Trina and had not expected to hear. He knew that by the time she learned her new address it would be too late for a letter to reach him before Ocean Monarch sailed. He felt guilty because he was procrastinating and had still not written. There had been no good reason for not writing immediately: he could have used the Troon address, and in due course it would have been forwarded. The truth was that he could not trust himself to write and the lack of address was an excuse. A letter was a once and forever black and white affair, with no chance to watch for a reaction. If he said the wrong things they would remain said. He would not be able to see Trina's face and know whether he was finding the right words.

At the last minute he dashed off a short note to go ashore with the pilot, and quoted Ralph Waldo Emerson; "Thou art to me a delicious torment". That was all, except to say that he hoped his letter would not take too long to reach her. He ended by saying; `I shall write, but I will not write those things that I would prefer to say.'

* * *

There was no movement in the boat. Lonely, abandoned, it drifted aimlessly; seeming to be the centre of a circle trapped within a blue shaded horizon. Yet there was life; there was thought; disjointed, incoherent; and it lingered in Alan.

* * *

'I'm hovering high in the air. From here, I look down and see passive bodies; still shapes sprawled in a boat. I see myself, slumped in the stern next to Jim Bristow... But the rest is wrong, like a puzzle with one piece missing. There should be four others and there are three. I'll count: Con Mahoney... Basil Allward... Queenie Pellew... Where's Len? He was there last time I looked.

'What's that....? Stop the noise. I don't like noise. It stops me thinking. Go away noise...Go away. I don't like you. I want peace. Peace! Do you hear?...It's not going. Noise you're getting noisier. Where are you, noise? Over my head you say…

'Here I go... It's easy. Float over on my back so I can look up to the sky. Yes, the sky's there. Pretty blue sky, someone's marked it with a cross.'

'It's the cross that makes the noise.

`Silly cross, you're pretending you're a Liberator, aren't you?

`Too late... I'm a liberator.

`No, no I'm not. I'm dead... I know I'm dead... See, that's my body down there. I must be dead.

`You are the liberator? But why pick on me? Why are you going around and around, over my head? I'm already free.

`Where are you Cross?...

`Here we go, in a slow circle, follow the Cross... Where have I heard that before?... The Cross has found a smudge of smoke.

`Contact! I'm a Liberator now... Over I go, see what the Cross is doing with the smudge.

`That's a joke! It's found a Destroyer. You're too late destroyer... we're all destroyed, so follow me destroyer. I'll show you. I'm the liberator now. I'll show you the way, the way...

`Follow the Cross... Follow the Cross and thou shalt find... a lifeboat... or a death boat.

`I'm back again. There's the boat, down below. The destroyer's coming... no need to hurry. It's quite comfortable... just floating up here.

`Poor bodies, you won't be left to rot. The destroyer will find you. They'll sew you up, then throw you back. No moldering bones, unknown... No skeletons left to wander, drifting, forever and ever... Amen?

`I'm going to sleep now, sleep... drifting... forever.'

* * *

Alan's letter and the Pilot had gone. It was May, and perversely the day was enchanting as Ocean Monarch moved out of the Clyde heading for the North Channel. In the distance, Barra and its surrounding isles floated in a calm sea, secret, mysterious. Alan leaned on the ship's rail and looked at the scene, yet scarcely saw it.

`Why can't I be calm too? Why this turmoil? She's done no more than I have, and now more often than she has, but she doesn't know... Those girls meant nothing to me. Why should I think "He" means anything to her? She says she's never stopped loving me. So? I've never stopped loving her.

`It didn't sound as though "He" meant nothing to her, when she told me about him.

`No! No! No! Don't think.'

Alan's thoughts kept turning and returning, rebuking and blaming himself for not acting more positively. Should he have been more humble; more direct? Should he have admitted, plainly, both his hurt and his love?

After clearing the Western Approaches, Ocean Monarch headed south for two days before swinging around to the west and zigzagging on a mean course for New York. It was then that the weather began to deteriorate. Within twenty-four hours the seas had risen, and Ocean Monarch was charging through long heavy rollers.

So much depends on stray chance. There were times when Peter Redpath could not sleep. He would get up before dawn and pace restlessly to and fro in his cabin, driven by some internal hyperactivity; and so it was that Alan was woken by Peter's hand shaking him as he lay in bed. Alan sat up.

`What's wrong?'

This was his first reaction.

The deadlight was fitted to the porthole, and Alan could not tell what time it was, whether day or night. He could feel the increased movement of the ship since he had gone to sleep, but there was nothing unusual about that.

`Get up,' Peter ordered. `You're out of condition. We'll get in an hour of quoit tennis before breakfast.' From bitter experience Alan knew it was useless to argue with Peter when he was in that mood. He climbed from his bunk reluctantly, pulled on shorts and sweatshirt and followed Peter to the top deck.

As Alan acknowledged later, it was Peter's sleeplessness that had saved his life, temporarily at least. After the torpedo hit, the ship sank with such incredible rapidity that only those who were on deck had any hope of getting clear. All those who made it to the boat had some lucky circumstance to thank. Lucky? Perhaps those who died quickly were better off.

Twelve made it. Now there were only five... five bodies? Five empty shells?

* * *

`Wake up! Wake up!

`Go away Peter.

`Peter's gone... Don't you remember him splashing?

`Wake up now. Watch the fun. See, things are happening. The destroyer is creeping up. It wants to take the bodies by surprise.

`Noise, noise, you're making too much noise.

`Some of the bodies are moving... Look! There's Queenie waving... Perhaps he's waving you away.

`Too late, you've caught him. Your marionettes have hooked the boat and they're climbing in. One is going to my body.

`Stop! you're hurting me.

`Pulling... pulling... and I can't see anymore. There's a shimmering in my mind and the vision has gone.

`I don't understand. There's something tight... wrapping me, gripping me and I'm in the water... They've sewn me up and thrown me in... I must be dead.

`I didn't think it would be like this. Thump, thump, thump... a heart beating, rapid, exploding beating, driving into my head. Pulling... and the water's gone. I'm floating again and it's not nice... It hurts this time. My leg... my chest.

`Stop it! Do you hear? I can't bear the pain. Is that my voice?... I'm falling... spinning... going...

`Still that noise, beating, dragging me back to pain, to voices.'

* * *

Hands, voices, pain, they all combined to bring Alan back from he knew not where.

`This is real.' The thought filtered into his conscious and he tried to understand.

`This is happening to me, a real me. I'm not dead. But where am I? I was in the boat, or was I? Where have I been? Where am I now? There's a hole in my memory. I was... I was...'

`He's coming round.'

`Right, see if you can get him to drink some water. Bathe his eyes too.'

`There's water on my lips... They wouldn't do that if I were dead... Someone's wiping my eyes with a wet cloth... My leg hurts... There's water in my mouth.'

`Lift him up a little.' Alan felt arms raising him. He could not see, could not understand the noise.

`That's better,' he thought. 'The water's not choking me now.' His eyes were still being bathed, water trickling down his face.

`There's light... a shadow of light. My right eye... The light hurts... Everything hurts. It's all too blurred.'

`Take it easy. You'll be all right.'

Alan began to see shapes; a shadow bending over his leg, and a wave of agony struck him. Now he could open both eyes, but was still confused; unsure of what was real, and what might be hallucination.

'Who are these people?' One black and rubbery, the other, in overalls, wore a Navy cap. With a flash of awareness came a glimpse of truth.

`The Navy... The noise? An aircraft... a helicopter. Why am I in a helicopter?' It was too hard to work out, and Alan closed his eyes. Let whatever would happen, happen.

He had been wrapped in blankets and someone was swabbing his arm, saying: `I'm giving you an injection. You'll find it'll help.' Alan could hear snatches of conversation, but could only catch a few words.

`...right then... we'll be... better... ' Hands were probing, feeling, adjusting. All was distant and blurred.

`It's cold in this plane,' he thought.

'Aeroplane?... Helicopter? Hold on to that thought; the plane crashing...

`No, that can't be right. I was in the boat. We were in the boat... Peter, Rapley, Mahoney, all of us. All there... It was a Destroyer, not a helicopter.

`There was an aeroplane, but it doesn't fit... Nothing makes sense.' The pain drifted away and Alan felt as if he were being wrapped in comfort. The faces became faceless, pale ovals hovering over him.

'The aircraft falling into the sea... so muddled .

'Trina, I wish we'd talked before I left. I hated leaving without seeing you... No, that's wrong. I can't remember... Trina, something strange.'

`I'm comfortable now Trina. A sensuous comfort, like lying with you in my arms... What happened to us?... It's too difficult to think. Much nicer to drift off to sleep... close beside you.'

* * *

Alan opened his eyes into a state of incomprehension. Gradually he became aware of hospital equipment, an unusual hospital with white painted metal walls... and the ship was rolling. Ship! It wasn't a hospital; it was a ship... a ship's Sick Bay. It must be the Destroyer... But no, everything was different. Had he dreamt the helicopter? Quietly now... think carefully.

He had no time to think, carefully or otherwise. A figure materialized beside the bed and Alan was now sufficiently awake to recognize the insignia of a Navy surgeon.

`I can't remember,' Alan thought. `Perhaps he knows.'

`What's happened?' That is what Alan wanted to say, but his lips, tongue and throat would not co-operate. The doctor checked his pulse and Alan tried to sit up, to make himself understood. He was too weak and the doctor placed a restraining hand on Alan's shoulder.

`Wha...' The doctor shook his head. `Don't try to talk. I'll tell you what's happening.'

Alan did not want to know what was happening. He wanted to know what had happened.

`We've done what we can for your leg,' the doctor said cheerfully. `But it needs specialist attention. We're heading for Plymouth, and when we're near enough you'll be taken straight to hospital in the helicopter. We should have you there inside twenty-four hours.' The doctor moved out of Alan's vision, but only for a few seconds. He paused at the foot of the bed. `I'll be back soon. I've got a few other patients to see.'

Then he was gone and Alan was left to wonder.

`What's happened? What's the matter with my leg? This didn't happen the last time.'

Alan clutched at the idea that had sprung into his mind.

`The last time?' and suddenly he realized.

`My God! This is different. There was a plane. Everything's so mixed up. The plane crash and Ocean Monarch, they're quite different... Ocean Monarch was before; but how long before? It feels as though it only just happened... Where have I been and what went on in between?... What happened after Ocean Monarch and this... this plane crash? I must think.

`Where to start? Go back to where I last remember clearly and work from there... Go back to being rescued the last time.'

* * *

They were picked up by a Destroyer, one of the escorts for a convoy of cargo ships, and it was a long, slow journey to Liverpool. After two days Alan was allowed to get up and exercise for short periods within the confines of the Sick Bay. It was nearly a week before he was able to move freely about the ship. Con Mahoney's progress followed the same pattern, but Basil Allward did not leave the Sick Bay until he went ashore in Liverpool on a stretcher. Jim Barlow must have died an hour or two before the Destroyer picked them up. Queenie was in the best condition, but they were only four, and they were all who survived from Ocean Monarch's crew. When allowed on deck, Queenie, Con Mahoney and Alan found a sheltered corner, and one of the Destroyer's crew brought some chairs for them. There were a few books and magazines on board, but for most of their time on board they formed a quiet, self-contained group. When Alan was first allowed on deck Queenie went with him, and they stood, silently, looking at all the ships. The convoy was wallowing through a moderate sea at a snail's pace, so slowly that Alan was amazed.

`Fancy having to travel at this speed,' he said.

`They're sitting targets,' Queenie agreed. `A U-boat has all the time in the world to get in position and attack.'

It was a subject neither cared to pursue. Later Mahoney joined them, and they wanted no other company: they had no desire to mingle with the Destroyer's crew. Their ordeal formed a bond that excluded those who had not been part of it. They would have to learn to live in the world again but were not yet ready. Sufficient that they were alive: this was as much as they could accept during those first days.

The Destroyer's crew seemed to know how they felt. They had seen survivors before, and knew the type of behavior to expect. They did what they could for the survivors, and left them alone with the memories they did not wish to talk about; not even among themselves.

There was one question Alan had to ask. How, and when, had Len Huskins gone. The last he could remember of Len was in the morning of the day they were rescued. Alan had been drifting in and out of consciousness during that last day when Huskins must have disappeared. Shortly before reaching Liverpool he got around to asking the question.

`Anyone know what happened to Len?'

There was silence for some seconds before Con Mahoney spoke. He was leaning on the rail looking into the distance, and did not turn his head.

`Bastard went mad.' Nothing else, simply the statement; and Alan did not ask any more questions.

They were not used to the sedate progress of cargo ships. To them, the convoy lumbered its way with painful slowness, and they were impatient to get ashore. Despite the bond that held them, each was anxious to get away alone and lose himself in a multitude so that, unrecognized, he could be an individual again. On board the Destroyer they were "the survivors", like a label hung around their necks. They wanted to forget, yet knew that this was impossible. Each day they would take it in turn to sit for a while with Basil Allward. For many days it had been doubtful whether he would pull through. They had all looked like scarecrows when rescued, but Basil also had blood poisoning from infected sores.

The other three found weakness their main problem. Each day showed an improvement, but they were still far from fit when they landed in Liverpool.

* * *

`So far so good,' Alan thought.

The details of his rescue from the lifeboat were now more or less clear. He suspected something similar had happened, and that his mind had confused the two incidents. But he had made some progress and should now be able to think more methodically; reconstructing the missing time. Was it weeks, months or years? He could not tell.

`If only I could keep my mind from wandering.' Alan's bunk was enclosed with a screen but he could just see one corner of the Sick Bay. Occasionally the Sick Bay attendant would look in to check, and sometimes Alan saw a figure passing through the unscreened area; but his vision kept blurring into a swirling mist, and most of the time he kept his eyes closed.

* * *

`...A hand on my wrist.' Alan opened his eyes. `Why won't everything stay still? Concentrate... that's better, I can see him... the doctor. Look at him. Try to make him understand.'

Alan tried to speak, to ask; `What happened?' But the words would not form, and the doctor took no notice.

`It's useless. He doesn't know what I want; and he's starting to spin again.'

`You're probably wondering about other survivors.'

`I'm not. Should I have been?' Alan thought; and now he discovered that his mouth, lips and tongue would not obey his will.

`We found six, a few hours before you were rescued. They were in an inflatable raft and all in pretty fair condition. Cuts, bruises and a few broken bones, but on the whole nothing serious.' Alan's eyes followed the doctor as he moved away, talking to someone who was out of sight; then he turned around and came back to Alan.

`I'll give you something to make you more comfortable in a minute.'

He continued talking, but Alan's mind was wandering and missed the first few words.

`...What did he say? I wasn't listening.' Alan tried desperately to concentrate.

`...You're the one who's lucky. The raft was miles from where you were found. After finding them, our navigator made a guess at the line of drift and we followed it up in the helicopter. That's how we found you. Even so it was a chance in a million that you were spotted. The helicopter continued the search but found no one else.' Alan had closed his eyes, but heard the attendant return and the doctor say; `Thanks.'

`He's swabbing my arm... another injection?'

`You'd better rest now. There'll be someone nearby if you need anything.'

The doctor walked away and Alan could hear his voice fade into the distance.

`Why am I so hot and dry? They've put tight bands around my leg. It's not hurting so much now though, and my head has stopped aching...'

Alan started to drift, then; `I remember!'

At first vague, then with a startling clarity it fell into place. Bermuda! That was it. He was on his way to see Trina. She had known that he was coming and would be meeting him. So much was still missing. Why was Trina in Bermuda? There it was, the same question. What had happened?

Alan struggled but could get no further. `Poor Trina, has she gone through it all again. What will she say when I see her?... I will see her... I know I will, now I know where she is. She'll say something like;

"Disappearing is getting to be a habit with you... and a bad habit at that."

`What else will she say? What are we to each other? I'm drifting again. I must remember though... What happened in between?'

* * *

In Liverpool they were taken straight from the Destroyer to hospital. There was no special treatment, just kept there a day or two for observation.

When Alan was allowed to leave, a clerk from the Company office came in a taxi to pick him up. He brought some suitable clothing, and for the first time Alan could believe that the nightmare of the sinking had really ended. The day was sunny and windy, with the sun's brightness throwing everything into bold relief. Alan felt unusually aware of his surroundings; the streets, the houses, the shops and offices no longer melted into a drab background. Now they were exposed by the unforgiving sun, naked and commonplace, mocked by the fleeting dust swirls. The brightness emphasised flaking paint and smoky grime, and Alan was left with the thought;

`Sunshine is meant for the open country and the wide sea. It's not comfortable with itself in the city.'

This feeling lingered, leaving Alan strangely detached: a foreigner in familiar streets; a spectator from within the taxi as it wound its way to the branch office.

Once in the office, all was business and efficiency. Alan was given an advance against his pay, and it was arranged that the Paymaster from head office would get in touch with him later. Alan was to have fourteen days Survivor's Leave. They did not know when there would be another ship for him; that was for Head Office to decide. He was to catch the train for London that afternoon; but must call at the Government Shipping Office first. He would need to get special clothing coupons to replace his uniforms; also ration cards to cover his leave.

There was so much to do that they nearly forgot to give him the telegram. It was from Trina and simply said:

`Welcome love, Trina.'

How like her to select two words only, two words that said all that could be said. Alan would be seeing her. That was sure; but he could be certain of nothing else. How would it be? Could they pretend that nothing had changed? It seemed unlikely; but would there be anything they could salvage?

Before leaving, Alan rang home. It was not an easy call to make, too many emotions were involved. Later, the first few hours at home were especially difficult. He could not answer his mother's questions but had to turn them aside with half-truths and evasions. It was impossible. How could he tell them all that had happened in the lifeboat? Each attempt to explain brought it all back and he could feel himself grow tense with every question. Concern and love was the reason for his mother's probing, Alan knew this, but it was still hard not to hurt her feelings by screaming; `Shut up!'

When he could, he rang Trina. She was expecting him to call, as his mother had rung earlier to say that Alan was on his way from Liverpool.

Trina's voice was carefully controlled when she spoke.

`Alan, you're back. How are you?'

`All the better for hearing your voice.'

`No, seriously, are you all right?'

`Of course, never better.'

`Liar!'

`How do you know? You haven't seen me.'

`I just assume you're running true to form. I don't need to see you.'

`I'm sorry about that. I need to see you.'

`Alan! At least you're still impossible. You know perfectly well I didn't mean it that way.'

`You mean you want to see me?'

`Of course. Shall I try to get leave? I'll work it somehow, even if I have to throw Uncle Harry at their heads.'

Alan laughed. `Heaven forbid, you would too. No, I wouldn't wish that on them. I'll come down next week.'

`You're sure?'

`Definitely, I'll have to stay here for a day or two. You can guess what it's like. I'm being smothered and you'll be a good excuse to get away.'

`Is that all I am, an excuse?' Alan hesitated; was this just the usual verbal battle or was there, perhaps, some deeper thought behind her question.

`Correction, substitute "reason" for "excuse". It sounds better than; "You 're the best excuse I could have."'

`I'll have to think about that. Will you give it to me in writing?'

`Not much fun in that. I plan to do better. I'll give it to you in person.'

For the first time he heard Trina give a soft laugh. `Typical!' she exclaimed, then added, `When?'

`I'll come down on Monday. Is there anywhere I can stay?'

`I'll make enquiries and book you in somewhere.'

Monday arrived, and the Isle of Wight turned on its charm. The sun shone and did its best for them; yet Trina and Alan were ill at ease. Looking back, Alan was sure that the fault lay in him. They would have been better able to find understanding if they had been open with each other; and if he had not been so tense and jumpy. Given the chance, Trina would surely have been prepared to talk frankly.

Trina could not get time off during the day, but they were able to spend every evening together. They stayed at a small hotel where Trina had booked them in as husband and wife, and each morning she had to leave at six.

`What do you do all day?' she asked one evening.

`Read a little, walk a little, eat a little and sleep a little.'

`Sounds exciting.'

`Excitement I can do without at present, thank you very much.'

`Sorry I asked.'

They did make a show of returning to their old carefree association. At times it seemed that they were succeeding and then, suddenly, Alan would get the feeling that they were merely acting out their parts. They were seeing each other differently, trying to adjust, and their words were careful rather than carefree.

The first night, when they went to bed, love did not come freely. There was none of their usual bawdiness. Desire was there but so were unspoken thoughts. If they had spoken those thoughts; if Alan had asked the 'Why? Why?' that tormented his thoughts. If...? But what use is if? Alan did not ask, and there was no going back.

When they did make love Alan discovered how weak he was. The act left him exhausted, and he felt that the last of his strength had drained from his body. Trina was frightened by his obvious distress, and when he had recovered she tried to make him stop talking. She was wasting her time. Neither was ready for sleep and instead they dropped into sporadic conversation.

`When did you hear we were missing?' Alan asked.

`About a week before you got back.'

`Only then?'

`The Company knew earlier, but there's always a delay before advising next of kin. They have to wait in case there's some news, survivors perhaps. Think of the fuss if they'd sent out missing notices straight away, that other time... that time when the Navy lost you.'

`Uncle Harry didn't let you know?'

`Not until next of kin were told. He tried to ring me but I wasn't here so he sent a telegram; but I'd already heard by the time I got it. Your mother told me.'

`I didn't know that. She didn't mention it.'

`Didn't she? I rang her from the flat. I'd been given twenty-four hours leave, and I'd gone to town to get some clothes I needed. It never occurred to me... I'd been thinking I might hear from you soon; you said you'd write. Anyway, I couldn't be sure you were still on the New York run. Being here isn't like Troon. There I could always check on where you'd gone.'

`I suppose my parents had only just heard when you rang?'

`Yes, I'd thought about ringing, as soon as I got to town but... but...'

`But what?'

`The way things were between us. I didn't know what to say. You might have said something to them. It's... it's just that I felt bad about us, and I kept putting it off.'

`I wouldn't have said anything. You should know that.'

`I suppose so. It was me really. I don't know why, but it wasn't until just before I left town that I screwed up my courage to phone. It was awful. They'd only just had the telegram. I wanted to go and see them, but I couldn't. There wasn't time.'

`It must have been quite a shock for you, too. What did you do?'

`Don't ask me. I don't really know. Somehow I got back here. The last thing I remember of that day was rereading your letter... and wondering.'

Trina was crying, and Alan held her. For some minutes the only sound was an occasional sniffle.

`Not to worry,' he told her. 'It's all over now.'

That was when he should have asked the "Why?", but for some reason he could not. His experience had left him empty, and a reaction had set in. He found it difficult to sit quietly and was easily irritated. It was this, this inner tension, that pinioned him and he dared not let himself go; dared not relax.

Trina suffered and soon learned not to ask how he was feeling.

During the days he was on his own, and had too much time to think. There was the affair Trina had told him about, the man she must have made love with at Troon; and he would recall every detail of that conversation.

Even on the day he arrived, when Trina came to Southampton to meet the train, he could see that she was nervous and embarrassed. He wanted to help her, but could not. His own hurt, his weakness, all the thoughts that had battered him over the last weeks and months combined to freeze his words. He did little to help her over that moment. The first chance to forgive... no, not forgiving; he had tried not to think of it like that. The first opportunity to heal the wound was lost.

Although it was uppermost in their minds, they never talked about what Trina had done, nor why she had done it. Every day, waiting for her to return to the hotel, it was this 'Why?' Which tormented him.

What rankled was knowing that his jealousy or indignation, call it what you will, was unjust. Each time he would remember the young widow in South Africa.

Trina was very patient and Alan was a poor companion, so often distracted by such thoughts as:

`Is it pride? A refusal to admit that our ideas were wrong? Or is it that I can't live up to them?... I don't know. I think it's plain jealousy on my part... I wonder if Trina enjoyed it?... Shall I ask her?... That wouldn't be according to the rules...'

Trina was speaking and Alan pulled himself together. 'What was that she just said?' He tried to recall the echo of her words, and answer;

`No, the Company hasn't given me any idea yet about what they have in mind for me. I've got to see them next week.'

Each evening when Trina arrived, Alan would be in a mental turmoil. No matter how he argued or tried to convince himself, he felt sure that Trina's affair had not been entirely casual. If it had not been important, why had she not wanted to see him? He had never said anything to her about South Africa. The girls in New York did not count. They were something that happened after...

He would try to imagine Trina's point of view, and tell himself to be fair. He had put Trina into a difficult situation by insisting on going to Troon. She had been forced to tell him. But why did she start it...? She had not thought he would come back. Did that make a difference?

He dared not pry. Afraid that if told the truth he would be unable to handle it. The ordeal he had been through made him insecure and introspective. If he had seen Trina when he returned from New York he would have wasted no time. Within minutes of meeting her he would have asked;

`What the hell's been going on?' They would soon have known exactly where they stood. Now Alan shrank away from the direct approach. He had lost the ability to handle his emotions and communicate effectively. Inevitably, they began to drift apart.

CHAPTER FIFTEEN

Since there's no help, come let us kiss and part.
Michael Drayton

Alan was stirring; the effect of the injection had worn off. His head was aching, and when he opened his eyes the deck head would not stay still nor would it come into focus, and there was a steady thud - thud - thud. For a moment he thought he was back in the helicopter, then realized it was his own blood throbbing with each heartbeat.

`It must be. Yes, I'm still in the Sick Bay.'

`Just relax and lie quietly.' Alan recognized the doctor's voice.

`I know that voice, it's the doctor... Temperature and pulse. Now he's gone. They're moving the screen... and voices, several voices... mumbling.'

`...change and... I need... Yes, that's right. Lift... not ready...'

`Hands, moving me, that hurts... They're tying me down. I'm trapped... I must fight, fight... It's no use. They're too strong. They're holding me. I can't fight any more. It's too hot and my head aches. I can't beat them.'

`Steady now, I want you to sleep again.'

`Coldness against my skin and the prick of a needle. I must relax, the pain will pass . . . so think about breathing... it's hard to breathe.'

* * *

Alan's long walks in the sun toned up muscles that had weakened with disuse. His body became stronger each day; and the gaunt look began to fade. He was sleeping better, but there were still nights when he would wake to hear his own voice calling to Peter. Those flailing arms splashing in the sea haunted him and he would hold Trina, knowing that she was real. He would hold her in silence, unwilling to risk a wrong word, unwilling to risk shattering the moment of fragile harmony.

Towards the end of the second week Alan returned to London to report to Southern Oceanic. There were regrets, but also an element of relief when they said goodbye. The days together had resolved nothing and they needed a space to be free from each other. A space in which Alan might discover his motives and desires; a time to pass before they again tested themselves together. They had found that their ties were still strong; they had been close for too long for it to be otherwise. Their bond had gone too deep to sit easily with the discord that hovered between them.

A few minutes before eleven on a Friday morning, Alan called at Southern Oceanic's London office. Mr Carstairs looked up as Alan entered his office, and came around from behind the desk holding out his hand.

'Anderson... Alan, it's good to see you. How are you after...?' He was looking for the correct word and Alan anticipated him.

'Just about fit again I'd say, Mr Carstairs.'

'Have you seen a doctor?'

'Not since I was discharged from hospital. The doctor there said there was no serious physical damage. I just needed rest and building up.'

'How long do you think it'll be before you're fit to go to sea again?'

Alan hesitated. He did not want to stay at home for any length of time. Also, if he stayed away from Trina his mother would wonder what was wrong and ask questions; questions he would not want to answer, or know how to answer. When he returned from another voyage, perhaps he and Trina would find it easier...

Mr Carstairs was waiting for a reply.

'I'm fit enough now. I'd like to get back to sea as soon as I can.'

Mr Carstairs returned to his desk and sat down. He picked up a pencil and fiddled with it.

`I'm not at all sure you're right about that. You don't look fully fit to me, and you've lost a lot of weight.'

`I'll get better food on board ship than on shore,' Alan laughed. `Seriously though Mr Carstairs, I'm sure it would be best for me to get back to sea as soon as possible. I don't want too much time with nothing to do except think about what happened.'

Mr Carstairs nodded. `I can understand that.'

He picked up a file from his desk, opened it and scanned the contents reflectively; then closed it before speaking.

`You may be aware that many Dutch ships, which were at sea when the Germans invaded Holland, are now operating under charter to the Ministry of War Transport.'

`I've seen a few in convoy Sir, but I'd no idea of how they were operating.'

This time Mr Carstairs tapped the file as though marshalling his thoughts.

`Most of their crews stayed aboard, and several of the ships have been passed over to us for operational administration. We've had quite a few problems, and have decided to put one of our own people on board each ship as Liaison Officer. Some Dutchmen chose to go home to Holland and this left the ships short handed, so we've made up the numbers by putting a small British crew into each vessel. That's part of the reason we want one of our own officers on board. There's been some trouble with British crew thinking that they're being treated unfairly. Probably just a few troublemakers, but you'd know the sort of thing I expect. Someone used to our seamen might handle them better and I'm sure they'll be happier under one of their own officers.'

`I see.'

`There'd be other duties too; such as working with the embarkation officers from the various Services, and with the ship's Permanent Army staff. We're suggesting to the Dutch that the job of Troop Officer, liaising between ship and service personnel, should be taken over by whomever we appoint.'

There was a pause while Mr Carstairs stretched back in his chair and studied Alan reflectively.

`I don't know that it would be an easy job.'

As Mr Carstairs said this, Alan had the impression a decision had just been made and was not surprised when Mr Carstairs leaned forward, again tapping the file.

`There's one here,' he said. `The Piet Bakker. She's in Liverpool at present. Probably be one or two weeks before she sails. Would you like the job as Liaison Officer?'

`I certainly would, Sir.'

`In that case you'd better see a doctor right away. Get a written opinion from him, then come back and see me on Monday.'

`What time Sir?'

`Say nine o'clock. I have to be in Barringdale by midday.' Alan saw his family doctor that same afternoon and persuaded him to write the required certificate. At nine on Monday morning he was knocking on the door to Mr Carstairs' office.

`Good morning Alan.' Mr Carstairs wasted no time. `Do you have the doctor's report?'

Alan handed it over and Mr Carstairs scanned the brief note.

`Right, you can join the ship as soon as you like. Anything you want to know?'

Alan smiled. `Anything I ought to know?' he suggested.

`I really couldn't say.' Mr Carstairs returned the smile. `Yours is the first appointment of this type, but I can tell you this; we've found the Dutch more than touchy if they think we're trying to interfere in the way they run their ship. I'd say you'll have to tread warily if you want to avoid corns. Just be as tactful as you can, and at the end of the voyage let me know how it's working out.'

That afternoon Trina rang.

`How are you?' she asked. `Are you feeling any better now?'

`Me, I'm fine. How're you?'

`Any news?'

`Yes, I'm leaving for Liverpool on Monday. I'm going to a Dutch ship.'

`A Dutch ship? Why aren't you staying with the Company?' Trina's voice had risen several tones higher than its normal level.

`I am. They're running half a dozen Dutch ships for the Government, and I've been given some vague sort of job as Liaison Officer.'

`They've a Dutch crew then?'

`According to Mr Carstairs, mostly Dutch, with some Javanese and a few Chinese. Also, there's a British crew who'll be my responsibility.'

`What's the name of it?'

`Fancy you asking that. Classified information: walls with ears etc.'

`And I've got ears too, so stop the piffle or I'll ring Uncle Harry.'

`I'm helpless before such a threat. Piet Bakker, if you must know. She's a bit smaller than Ocean Monarch, about eighteen thousand tons I think.'

`Alan, you're not well enough yet. They shouldn't send you back to sea. Do you really have to go?'

`No, I was given the choice.'

`You were what? And you said you'd go? You shouldn't. You're mad to say you will.'

`D'you think so? I don't. Listen, let's be honest. We're in a mess together, aren't we? No, don't say anything, let me finish. I think... I hope... it's only a temporary thing. I'm all in a tangle and you were marvelous the way you put up with me. I wanted to talk to you about... well about us, but I couldn't. I need time. Time to get back to normal after those weeks in the lifeboat. Meantime, I can't trust myself to be calm and rational.'

`All the more reason why you shouldn't go back to sea. Not yet, anyway.'

`Trina darling, I've got to go. I couldn't stay at home like this. Please don't think... I'm not running away from you. I'll be back... promise.'

`You've said that before.'

`Well? I kept it, didn't I?'

`Yes, I suppose you could say that... Alan, you've quite made up your mind about this?'

`I'm committed now, and I'm sure it's the right thing to do. Will you wait for me to get back?'

`D'you want me to? Really want me to?'

`Yes, really, and truly as well.'

`Alan?'

`Yes?'

`Try to look after yourself, and this time... don't be too long.'

* * *

The Piet Bakker had that desolate, lifeless feel which comes to a passenger ship in port. No matter how much movement there may be on deck, loading cargo and taking on stores, the accommodation decks are silent and deserted. When Alan walked up the gangway the ship was still many days away from sailing and there was no activity of any sort. With half the crew on leave, most of those remaining would go ashore each evening to pubs and dance halls, or to the cinema with girlfriends. After six o'clock only a handful of duty crew remained on board, and with little to do would be in their own quarters attending to personal chores or simply doing nothing. The atmosphere was strange because of the difference in the style of ship. The layout in Piet Bakker was nothing like Ocean Monarch, nor was the decor. The access companionways were not where Alan expected to find them, and the alleyways were narrower; but it was the furnishing that provided the greatest contrast.

In Ocean Monarch the emphasis had been on light colors, modern styles and soft easy chairs around low tables. In Piet Bakker the decor reflected solidity. Heavy, cumbersome chairs with dark timber frames, and tables in the same style stood at a dignified height. The main lounges echoed a past era; an era of Dutch colonial administrators, stolid in manner and gait. Men who traveled between Holland and their private empires: men who would look out of place with furniture which did not reflect their own conservative strength.

After some wandering, Alan discovered the Purser's office. The door was open and the lights on but there was no one there. He placed his suitcase behind a desk, where it would be out of sight, while he went in search of someone who could show him his cabin. There should certainly be an officer on duty in the Bridge flat. A light in one of the cabins led Alan to the Chief Officer. He was the only deck officer on board and had not been told that Alan was joining. He had no idea which cabin Alan was to use and obviously had no intention of disturbing himself to find out. He suggested that Alan find the Chief Steward or the Second Steward, saying that neither the Purser nor his assistant were likely to be on board. The Chief Officer's off-hand manner had hardly been welcoming, and when Alan finally located the Chief Steward's cabin it was locked and there was no answer to his knock. Alan went down a further two decks looking for someone who could direct him to the Second Steward's cabin. Seeing the dining saloon, he walked through to the galley where he found a night-watchman preparing himself an evening snack. The watchman's English was limited, but Alan gathered that the Second Steward had not been seen for several hours and was not in his cabin.

The Purser's office was still empty and Alan decided that he had had enough. Collecting his bag he headed for the gangway, intending to stay the night in an hotel and try again next morning. He had reached the main for'ard companionway when he met a leading hand who was on his way up from a lower deck. He looked at Alan enquiringly.

`Any idea where I might find the Chief Steward or the Second Steward?' Alan asked.

`They're both ashore. The Chief Steward won't be back until the morning, and you won't see the Second Steward on board before the pubs close.'

`That's that then. I'll come back in the morning. Perhaps by then there'll be someone on board who knows what's going on.'

`What are you looking for?'

`Well, for a start, my cabin. I'm joining the ship as Liaison Officer, but can't find anyone who knows about it. The Chief Officer certainly doesn't. He didn't even know there was to be a Liaison Officer.'

`Gottverdommer! I was in the office when Captain Meyboom told the Administrator to expect you.' He held out his hand.

`Van Rijk, Baggage Master,' he said. Van Rijk led the way back towards the Purser's office, talking as they went.

`You're to use the Administrator's, or Purser's cabin; close to the office. Mijnheer Roefstra, the Administrator, is moving to a "C" deck cabin.'

`Why's Mijnheer Roefstra moving out of his cabin?'

`He arranged it himself. The cabin he's moving to is slightly bigger, and with a bathroom suite. His old cabin just has a wash basin and the bathroom and toilet open off the alleyway.'

`I don't see much wrong with that,' Alan remarked. Van Rijk laughed. `When you get to know Mijnheer Roefstra you'll see why. His new cabin hasn't got a phone, and he'll think that an advantage. Captain Meyboom won't be able to contact the Administrator quite as easily.' Van Rijk, who was leading, turned and grinned.

'Mijnheer Roefstra probably hopes Captain Meyboom will get into the habit of 'phoning you instead. Also, for some reason the Administrator doesn't want you working in the Purser's office. Anyway, next to your cabin there's a small room. It's actually the safe deposit lock up, though the boxes aren't used nowadays, and he's decided you're to use it as an office.'

`Sounds very good.'

They had now reached the Purser's office and van Rijk went inside, emerging with two large keys. `These are for your cabin and the safe deposit room,' he explained.

Leading the way down a short alleyway that was immediately opposite the entrance to the Purser's office, he unlocked a door at the far end.

`Where are your bags?' he asked.

`At the station. I'll get them in the morning. I just brought an overnight bag with me.'

Van Rijk had now opened the door, and Alan entered a solidly appointed cabin. It was at least twice the size of any officer's cabin provided by Southern Oceanic. Next to the telephone, so disliked by the Dutch Purser, there were two more keys hanging on a hook and van Rijk drew Alan's attention to them.

`Those are for the toilet and bathroom.' He stepped back into the side alley, indicating to Alan two doors and then pointed to another door on the opposite side of the alleyway.

`That's the safe deposit room,' he said. Alan was astounded. He had been accustomed to living in one of four small cabins that shared a bathroom and toilet.

The Baggage Master was hesitating.

`Do you want something to eat? Or perhaps a drink?'

`I could certainly take a drink,' Alan assured him.

`I've just been down to get some cigarettes,' van Rijk explained. `Hendriks, the Purser's clerk, and me are having a few drinks if you'd like to come along...? He's gone to get sandwiches.' This was how Alan met the inseparable Hendriks and van Rijk. For the first six months, apart from these two and Klingen the Assistant Purser, hardly any of the Dutch crew ever spoke to him. They seemed to have an idea that he was a spy sent by the Ministry of War Transport and if Alan tried to join any group of officers he was pointedly ignored.

Alan finally discovered that part of the reason were the various concessions given to the ship's officers by the Dutch shipping company. The most important of these was an entertaining allowance that was deducted from their drinks bill each month. Southern Oceanic used a different system, and allowed their officers to buy drinks and cigarettes at a substantial discount. The Dutch had managed to combine these systems. First the discount was deducted, and after this was done, the fixed entertaining allowance was credited. There was one problem: they had to be careful not to end the month in credit.

Fortunately for Alan there were always plenty of people on board as well as the crew. The ostracism, though unpleasant, did not leave him completely isolated, and what was strange was the way it ended. It was as if he had served an apprenticeship. Six months after he joined the ship he was invited for drinks with a few of the deck officers. From then on he was accepted, but it was a few weeks before Alan found out why. It was due to a mistake by the barman who inadvertently deducted the entertaining allowance from Alan's bill. This led to his discovery of the system, and far from disapproving,

Alan had suggested that his earlier bills should also be adjusted. Soon after this sudden change Captain Meyboom sent for Alan. He waved him into a chair, then poured two tots of Bols Geneva.

`Prost!' he called and they drank.

Captain Meyboom placed his glass on the table with his usual deliberation, and Alan wondered what was coming.

`I think we're wasting a lot of time,' he said abruptly. He was silent for a moment, then picked up his glass and twirled it between his fingers, watching the viscous liquid swirl and cling to the glass before saying;.

`You know what co-operation we need from the Army staff. The things we can agree to, and what we can't allow. Generally you'd know as well as I do. In future, unless it's something you're not sure about, there's no need to refer to me. I'll tell the OC Troops that you speak with my authority.'

To say that Alan was surprised would be an understatement. Alan's job, as Troop Officer and Liaison Officer, was to interpret the ship's requirements to the OC Troops and his Adjutant. Alan was expected to anticipate, and try to eliminate, any friction that might arise between the ship's company and the troops. Previously Captain Meyboom had insisted on approving every small item himself, and Alan had felt that he was no more than an errand boy between the Orderly Room and the Bridge.

The change was most welcome, and Alan assured the Captain that he would not hesitate to ask if he had the slightest doubt on any matter. After pouring a second Bols, the Captain talked about Kent, where he always spent his leave. It was common knowledge that the Captain had found himself a middle-aged lady with whom he stayed. He had a wife in Holland who was, or so Alan had been told, large and domineering. The general opinion was that he would be looking for a divorce when the war was over.

Under the new arrangement Alan and the Adjutant worked well together and within half an hour, or an hour at most, would have organized fatigue parties and the rest of the day's business. After checking the British crew Alan would join the Captain's daily round of inspection. Once rounds were over, unless anything unusual occurred, the rest of the day was his to read, exercise, sunbathe or socialize. Alan's time on board Piet Bakker became a rest cure... as far as work was concerned.

The troopships were now mainly engaged in ferrying troops to Bombay or Colombo, and sometimes Italy. Nearly always they would have a contingent of girls on board, WAAF, WRNS, ATS and others. He no longer felt Trina to be a restraint, and he felt no shame, no disloyalty in making the most of any opportunity.

The two years Alan sailed in Piet Bakker became an interlude of ease that made him feel guilty. At a time when many were living and dying in primitive conditions, being slaughtered in Russian snow, Italian mud or Burmese jungle; his easy life often made him feel uncomfortable. True, there was still danger at sea; but as the months and years passed the risks lessened. U-boats and bombers were a diminishing threat. Three hours a day was not a heavy work load; his living quarters were comfortable and he had his own Javanese steward, Latip, to look after him.

Leave was frequent and generous. The Piet Bakker was powered by Swiss diesel engines and maintenance was a problem. Whenever they docked in the UK extensive repair work was always needed, and after each voyage they could count on at least a full week of leave. Usually Alan went to the Isle of Wight, but on two occasions Trina managed to get away and they spent the time together at her flat. They regained their companionship, but still shied away from any talk about what had happened at Troon. Perhaps they thought that, if ignored, the memory would fade. It never did, and Alan's behavior in Piet Bakker showed his acceptance of this.

They still enjoyed being together, particularly one golden day in the autumn of 1944. They were staying at the flat and knew that the next day would be the last of Alan's leave. They had gone to bed early and dim light filtered into the room. Alan looked at Trina as she lay in the bed, hands clasped behind her neck. He touched her, and she turned to him, smiling.

`Thanks...' she began.

`I haven't done anything yet,' Alan interrupted quickly, and was treated to one of her quelling looks.

`If you hadn't interrupted so rudely, I was going to say - thanks for a lovely day.'

`Well don't let me stop you.'

`No, I've changed my mind.'

`Why?'

`You've reminded me. The day's not over yet so my thanks might be premature.'

`Yes, I'm a bit tired. What say we go to sleep?' Trina uncoiled her arm, and let her fingers trickle over Alan's chest and stomach.

`I'm ready if you are.'

`What's so unusual about that?'

`For sleep I mean,' she protested.

`I know exactly what you mean.' Alan's hand was on her waist, and as it moved over her body he sensed her mounting excitement.

`Goodnight!'

He made as though to turn away. Trina hurled herself at him and they fought playfully. It was a good night; and the next day, also, was good. The morning was beautiful and Trina was drawn to the window to watch as the rising sun stroked the high flying clouds, bringing a blush of fleeting color to their purity.

`Do we have enough petrol to go out into the country?' she asked.

`A little over five gallons I think.'

`Let's go somewhere and picnic.' They made no plans; but three quarters of an hour later Alan was making his way out of London, taking the Epsom road without really thinking where he was going. After passing through Epsom, Alan knew that he and Trina were remembering the same things. This was the road they had taken to their first lovemaking. Alan hesitated, but did not take the turn off to Headley. Trina reached out and squeezed his hand.

`It wouldn't have been the same,' she said. The words were an echo of his own thoughts and Alan nodded. It was a memory that neither wished to tarnish.

There was no conscious decision; perhaps they let Mr Bumps decide, but they found themselves at Box Hill. Instead of driving to the top they parked the car and walked up, carrying the picnic basket. Near the top they found a sheltered spot where they could lie on the grass, and look out over the downs and the soft Surrey countryside. They talked little and were content in silence. Alan's thoughts went to the Spring of 1939 when their love was fresh; and he was torn by a hatred of war, and for what it had done to them.

Trina spoke, disturbing his memories, yet her remark was in harmony with his mood.

`No matter how we try, we've moved apart,' she stated.

`Perhaps it's just that we've grown up,' Alan answered. There was another long silence as they both relapsed into their reflections. Trina plucked a stalk of grass, then said; `I'm not the same as I was then.'

`You're five years older. Everybody changes.' Alan looked at her and smiled. Trina still had the habit of chewing grass, and he could not help adding; `You're just as beautiful.' Trina turned towards him and smiled her appreciation.

`Don't try to divert me. That's got nothing to do with what I was talking about, even if it were true.'

`You always divert me.'

`You were always easy to divert,' she retorted.

`Is that a complaint, an insult or a compliment?' Trina did not answer, and again conversation lapsed. Alan watched her chew grass for several minutes before saying, truthfully;

`I've never met anyone else I'd rather be with than you.' Trina looked at him oddly.

"That's exactly what I mean. Five years ago you'd have used the future tense.'

She was right and Alan could only be flippant.

'And I'd have been dead right. Here we are, five years later.' This was the only time the shadow passed over them that day. They picnicked, teased and taunted each other, rambled arm in arm and lay down in the warm sun and slept for nearly an hour. Later they drove to Guildford where they had afternoon tea and then, lazily, made their way back to London.

Until the moment when they said goodbye the next morning Alan held hope that they were finding their way back together, and that the trust they had shared might be regained. Trina still had two days of leave in hand when he left. She had made breakfast for Alan, and when the time came for him to go, put up her face to be kissed.

`Yesterday I meant what I said, about wanting to be with you more than with anyone else.'

Trina laughed. `So what? I believed you.'

`So what indeed; that's very much the question. We're going to have to face it.'

`Not now.'

Trina's voice was quick and tense, and Alan could not force the issue. It was not her words, but an odd, apprehensive look in her eyes that told him that their future together was uncertain. He felt suddenly weary and in no mood to pursue the matter.

`No, of course not. We don't have time to talk. The train's not going to wait for me.'

They kissed again. In the doorway he turned and waved to Trina. She was standing, very still, on the far side of the room where he had left her. She did not move, but called out;

`Take care of yourself.'

CHAPTER SIXTEEN

Better by far you should forget and smile
Than that you should remember and be sad.
Christina Georgina Rosetti

Alan did not see Trina during his next leave. He rang her when he arrived in London, expecting to arrange to go to the Isle of Wight. To Alan's surprise Trina told him that it would not be worth while.

`There's not much point, things have changed in the last week or two. We're now so busy it just isn't true. Lunch is no more than a sandwich and most nights we go back to work after dinner.'

`I see.' Alan's mind had gone back to that day in Glasgow, the telephone box and the call to Troon. He could not know that his fear was unjustified, and that Trina had been caught up in preparations for D-Day. His abrupt tone told Trina what he was thinking, but pride made her unable to say; `I know what you're thinking, and you're wrong.' Instead she said; `Alan, you can come down if you want to, but I may not be able to see you at all. Certainly not for more than a few minutes at a time.'

`As you say, not much point is there?'

`I'm sorry, Alan. I really am.'

'I'm sorry too, but if that's the way it is there's nothing we can do about it.'

Even as he spoke Alan knew that Trina was only telling him what was true. It would not be in character for her to do otherwise. He spent a miserable leave. All his friends were scattered by the war, and Alan was relieved to get back to the ship. He would find friends to talk to and drink with on board.

The next two times that Piet Bakker returned to England Trina was unable to get leave, and Alan went to the Isle of Wight. On the surface there was little difference, yet they were never completely as one together. At times they seemed to look at each other with the eyes of strangers.

They drank together; they laughed together and made love. In many ways they needed each other, having much to give and share. They fell into a tug of war between desire and stubborn pride, and pride won out. Neither was able to be the first to question and probe, to admit the need to invade the other's privacy. After the last visit they parted uneasily. Although nothing had been said they sensed that they had reached a watershed, and were looking at each other over a barrier they could not demolish.

Piet Bakker returned to Britain the day Germany capitulated, and sailed for Rotterdam a few days later. For the Dutch crew it would be their first opportunity to see families and friends since 1940. The ship stayed in Rotterdam for over a month, and Alan learned much more about the sorrows and cruelties of war. Some of the crew who rushed ashore so eagerly, returned before their leave was due to end. Many had found nothing to return to; others had found too much. Apart from unfaithful wives and sweethearts there were tales of horror and shame. Alan heard first hand descriptions of atrocities that turned his stomach.

The luckier crew members were able to take up their lives from where they had been interrupted by the war, and most of these left the ship intending to spend a long time ashore before deciding whether to go back to sea. After signing on replacements, Piet Bakker left Rotterdam.

In Southampton the ship took on stores and passengers, sailing within twenty-four hours. Alan tried to phone Trina, but she was not on duty and he was unable to try again later.

Their passengers were an assortment of Service replacements, civilian administrators and rehabilitation teams. The atomic bombs had been dropped and the Japanese were negotiating surrender. Piet Bakker's destination was Bombay, and it was an eerie experience to sail at night with full lights. They had become so used to sailing with a darkened ship, that it needed a conscious effort to step out on deck while smoking a cigarette.

On the second day out from Southampton Alan went on deck and saw a small, slim figure standing against the starb'd rail. She was looking out over the sea. He had noticed her previously, and had decided that she was easily the most interesting prospect on board. She was exceptionally attractive; and with so many men on board it was remarkable that she was alone on deck. Alan thought it probable that she had only just come up from her cabin. He joined her at the railing and she turned towards him. They smiled to each other.

`You're a member of the welfare team going to Bombay, aren't you?'

`Yes, how did you know?'

`It's part of my job to know who's on board.'

`You're not Dutch are you?'

`Not really, though I've sailed with the ship for so long I'm beginning to have my doubts.'

`What do you do on board?'

`I look for the prettiest girl in the ship and then go and talk to her.'

`If you're suggesting that's me; then thank you.'

She looked at Alan, amusement showing on her face.

`But I should say you've been kept busy,' she added.

`Perish the thought. I hope to be though.'

Her lips twitched and she said;

`You must have something else to do.'

Her voice was low pitched, soft and musical, and Alan was finding her to be even more interesting than he had hoped.

`Since you insist, I'll tell you. I'm Alan Anderson and my job is Liaison Officer, and at the moment I'm trying to liaise with you. You wouldn't want me to stop working; would you?'

`I don't believe a word of it.'

`I can prove it.'

`How?'

`Come down to my cabin and I'll show you the sign on the door. It says: "Liaison Officer".'

`I don't know that I'm ready for a liaison. I suspect it would be safer if I just believed you.'

`Never!' Alan protested, laughing. `Anyhow, now that you're going to believe me, you must tell me your name.'

`I don't see how that follows. However, it's Marcia, Marcia Easthope.'

And that was the way it started.

Alan could not help comparing Marcia with Trina. Marcia was better looking and petite, whereas Trina was slightly taller than average, but there was little to choose between them for shapeliness. Both Marcia and Trina were intelligent, and could talk well. Trina's mind worked more quickly, and with a sharp brilliance in conversation that Marcia lacked. Trina was champagne and Marcia was a smooth, still wine.

Whenever Alan came on deck to find Marcia, she would always be surrounded by Army or Air Force officers. With no more than fifty girls on board to four thousand men, of whom eight hundred were officers, this was hardly surprising. During the mornings while Alan was working, there would inevitably be a number of officers vying for her attention; and Alan had to find ways, fair or foul, to get her away from them.

Because of the shortage of fresh water, all baths and showers, except for those used by the crew, had been converted to salt water. Alan's fresh water shower was powerful bait, and very soon Marcia was coming twice a day to use his bathroom.

There was another privilege that Alan used. The ship's radio officers had cabins that opened on to a section of the boat deck. As watch-keepers, some of their sleeping was done during the day, and for this reason the space outside their cabins was screened and out of bounds to passengers. Alan would take Marcia into this private area where they could sit and talk, keeping their voices low so as not to disturb any sleeping watch-keeper. There was no other deck space where they could have been alone, and they spent many hours in this sheltered corner.

By the end of the first week they were together constantly and even Marcia's most persistent admirers became discouraged. The wartime custom in Piet Bakker was for ship's officers to eat in their own cabins, as the dining saloon was always overcrowded. Usually, two or three officers would arrange to eat together. There was nothing fixed or formal, just casual invitations.

Marcia now joined Alan each evening for dinner, and most nights there would be just the two of them, though sometimes Alan would invite one or two of the ship's officers for drinks before the meal. These private meals, while not exactly candle-lit suppers, did have an aura of intimacy that helped promote romance; and Alan's portable gramophone added music to the atmosphere.

Latip had never taken much notice of the girls who visited Alan's cabin, but Marcia won him over completely. The moment she arrived wearing a bathrobe, he would appear from nowhere with two tightly folded hot towels. These he would present with a beaming smile, especially when Marcia thanked him using the few Malayan words Alan had taught her.

In love-making Marcia was quite unlike Trina. There was no bawdiness or playfulness. She was quiet and deliberate in everything she did; but her abandonment, when it came, was complete. All the same, Alan could never picture Marcia hurling herself at him in violent assault, or throwing back her head and whooping with unrestrained laughter.

By the time the voyage ended they had convinced themselves that they were in love, and the night before arriving in Bombay they went on deck where it was cool. Here, they continued a conversation that had begun earlier in Alan's cabin.

`Well, do we get engaged?' Alan asked.

'We've only known each other three weeks. People will think we're mad.'

Even at that moment Trina intruded into Alan's thoughts. If he had been having this conversation with her, his next remark would have been;

`That's settled then.' He would have had an instant response - of some sort. Marcia's mind moved in more orderly steps, so instead he said; `They will, won't they?'

Marcia did not reply immediately, but in the dim light from the nearby cabins Alan could see that she was smiling.

`Of course they will,' she agreed, and Alan knew that he was committed.

Next day Marcia disembarked in Bombay after an early breakfast. Before going ashore she was told that she would be leaving by train for her posting later that day. However, after reporting to her organization's headquarters she would be free to go sightseeing, but would have to be back at their office by four that afternoon.

Half an hour after Marcia left, Alan also went ashore, going to the address she had given him, and waited impatiently for two hours. Formalities took longer than expected, and it was nearly midday before Marcia was free to leave.

They had lunch in the Taj Mahal hotel and afterwards Marcia shopped for a few small items. Time flew past, and it was already three-thirty when Alan led the way into a jeweler's shop. The previous evening he had suggested they buy an engagement ring, but Marcia insisted that she did not want one.

`I'm going to be here for at least a year, and probably it'll be two years before I get back to England. That's an awfully long time. Suppose we change our minds? You've only known me for about three weeks.'

`What's that got to do with it?' Alan asked. `I don't expect to change my mind, and even if we do I can't see that a ring would make any difference. You could just switch it to another finger.'

`I couldn't! I'd have to send it back to you, and somehow that would seem so melodramatic, and I'd hate it.'

`I expect I'd hate it too. Hey, why all this talk about breaking our engagement anyway?'

`I'm not, but... a ring seems so formal. I think I'm frightened that I'd be tempting fate. It won't make any difference. I'm sure it won't. It's just.. well, everything's happened so quickly that I can hardly believe it. Oh, why can't we have longer together and get used to being engaged?'

`Why indeed?' In the shop Alan said;

`I can't let you go without giving you something to keep as a reminder.' In spite of Marcia's protests he bought a silver bracelet, set with three small sapphires.

'That's for you because I want you to have something from me, and for no other reason.'

Although they rushed to get Marcia back to headquarters, she was still a minute or two late and there was no time for a long farewell. Alan was not sorry. A quick goodbye was the easiest way.

That night Alan looked at the photograph she had given him the previous evening after accepting his proposal. It was a studio portrait taken in her St John's Ambulance uniform. Alan opened the top drawer of his desk and took out a framed photograph of Trina in her Wren uniform, the latest in a series that had traveled with him for so long. He laid the photographs side by side on the desk. As he looked at the two girls Alan became acutely aware of the commitment he had made. All the time Marcia had been on board Trina had languished in the drawer; now, finally, she would have to go.

Alan undid the frame and removed the picture of Trina, then put Marcia in its place and turned the frame to centre the photo. It was a new picture in an old frame. It made him feel disloyal, though to which girl he was unsure, and he resolved to buy a new frame at the first opportunity. Perhaps Marcia's photo would not look so out of place in a new setting. Alan began to replace the back of the frame, then stopped. What was he to do with Trina? He could not throw her picture away, nor was he willing to leave it loose in the drawer where it would become scuffed or damaged. Picking it up he replaced it in the frame, behind the photograph of Marcia.

He never did get around to buying that new frame and Trina became an unseen presence in his cabin, always in the background when he looked at Marcia's photo. There was nothing he could do about it; Trina was a part of his life, and he could never discard that disturbing influence entirely.

Before leaving Bombay he wrote to Trina, even though he knew that the letter would not reach England before he did. It was only fair that she should know as soon as possible, and writing it eased his conscience.

Nearly two years had gone by since Trina and Alan had talked of marriage. They had avoided the subject, never entirely discarding the assumption of their years together that marriage was for after the war. Since the war had ended their only communication had been through letters, and there had been no urgency to decide; they had not had the incentive, nor the courage, nor perhaps the wish to kill this illusion.

It was a letter that Alan wrote with regret, and the half-formulated wish that he need not write it. He knew that it would be easier for him if he wrote, and hoped it would also be easier for Trina. He would phone her after he was sure that she would have read his letter. Twice he wrote and tore up what he had written. With time running out he completed a third version, and sealed it quickly before he could change his mind. After sending it ashore, Alan sat and worried over what he had said, wondering whether he could have found a better choice of words. He had written:

> `This is a letter I never expected to write. Now it must be written and it is best I tell you, at once, that I've become engaged.
>
> `I know that there was a time when you would have been hurt by such news. I hope that now you will not be hurt. Saddened, perhaps, as I am. I think we've both known, for a long time, that we have lost something we once had. There is a line, written by Robert Browning, that I think expresses our difficulty very closely: "One near one is too far."
>
> 'Having known the magic of complete unity and harmony, you and I could never settle for less. With different partners we may start afresh. For us, "one near one" is insufficient.

`Should I be telling you this instead of writing? Am I being a coward for not waiting until we are face to face? Probably I am, but also I fear for you. I fear that, even now, you may suffer some hurt. Hurt, that your pride would not allow you to show, to me or anyone else; nor, if you should shout for joy, is there any danger of hurt to mine.

> `I find it difficult to believe that I'm writing this to you whom, even as I write, I am conscious of loving.
>
> `If Richard Lovelace will pardon the parody; "I could not love thee, Dear, so much, had I not loved you more."' The fear that Trina might be hurt worried Alan even more as they neared England. On arrival there was a letter from her, but it had been

written before receiving the news of his engagement. They were in Liverpool for eight days before he went on leave, and when Alan arrived home there was another letter waiting for him. Alan took it to his bedroom where he would not be disturbed.

`Congratulations!

`I read your letter with mixed feelings; but on the whole, I think, with some relief. At least I know where I am now. I feel we had reached some sort of stalemate, where all we could do was unsettle each other.

`During the last few months I've been spending a lot of time with an Engineer Lt Cdr here. He's very nice, with a certain knack of off-beat humor.

`Did we become a habit with each other? We've shared so much Alan, meant so much to each other and perhaps unwittingly, certainly unwillingly, each has caused the other pain. In your letter you spoke about the harmony there has been between us. I agree that any pain has been far outweighed by the pleasure we've shared.

`When I've been with Keith, that's his name, I've sometimes been reminded of you and have felt, not guilt, but something like sad regret. I think you have the same feeling. My affair with Keith, if you can call it that, has never progressed beyond friendship, and there have been times when I have regretted this. It's my fault. Though I've become fond of him, I'm still unsure of myself.

`May we still write to each other? If you think it unwise I shall understand, but I would like to know what you are doing. If we could meet, as friends, it would make me very happy. Over seven years we've always had understanding - or nearly always - even when we've been out of sympathy. It doesn't seem right to throw that away.

`I've just read through what I've said, and it sounds as though I'm reluctant to let you escape. I don't think I am. I want to be happy for you. We've wasted so much that was good between us; but I have no regrets for the past, and intend to have none for the future.

`Defiantly I still send my love.
`Platonically, of course.'

Alan did not phone Trina. He thought of her taking the call in an office, surrounded by other people. She would not be able to speak freely, and they would both end up feeling frustrated and dissatisfied. He decided that it would be better to write his reply. `Your letter captured much of what I would have liked to say to you, but that I could not have said so well.

`Too often, I fear, we used words to cover our feelings. We mocked when we should have been sincere, and laughed when seriousness might have led to a better understanding of the rift between us. We were too careful of each other and never quarreled, except in fun. Instead we glossed over any frustration or anger. A screaming row would have been bad form. Misunderstandings might have been cleared if only we'd gone to battle over them.

`Here am I, analyzing uselessly, when I only intended to thank you for your letter and I am keeping my fingers crossed that, for us, parting will mean - in Swinburne's words;

"...winter's rains and ruins are over,
And all the seasons of snows and sins;
The days dividing lover and lover,
The light that loses, the night that wins."

`I don't suggest coming down this leave. If Keith, or anyone else can make you happy, I shall be glad. My presence, even as an ex-lover, might cause complications. Of course I will write, and of course I want to see you again, provided we can do so without hurting anyone, including ourselves.

`I too, send my love - in friendship.'

They did write and they did meet. Strangely, they found themselves in similar situations. At Christmas Trina became engaged to Keith, and in the New Year the Navy sent him to Denmark. When the Piet Bakker returned to England in February,

Alan left the ship. He had decided to take up the offer of a job with the brewery in Reading.

Trina had been demobilized - though how anyone could apply such a term to her was beyond Alan's imagination. She had gone back to work with Southern Oceanic and was living in her flat. She and Alan had kept in touch by phone and the occasional letter, and he knew that she was bored with spending evenings on her own. Alan had arranged to take a month's holiday before starting his new job, and he was lonely too. In the weeks before he left London, they spent their spare time together, and most nights he slept at the flat.

The tension had gone from between them. Trina and Alan remained as friends who enjoyed each other's company in the same way they had always done. Because they did not make physical love, a novelty was added to their association. They thought that they were individually happy, and that the years they had shared would no longer haunt them.

During the day while Trina was at work, Alan would often walk from the flat to Hyde Park. For some reason he was restless and could not be content with his own company. He put this down to the sudden change from shipboard life, and, at times, found it impossible to sit and read a book.

A few days before he was due to start his job; Alan walked along Constitution Hill to Hyde Park Corner, crossed the road and entered the park. Ahead of him a man was pushing a wheelchair, and Alan's attention was caught by something about him that was familiar. The man stopped before crossing the road, and when he turned his head to check for traffic Alan recognized him.

`Queenie!' he exclaimed. Queenie's eyes met Alan's in surprise, followed by recognition.

`Mr Anderson, fancy seeing you.' They shook hands, and the elderly man in the wheelchair twisted around trying to see who it was. Queenie noticed and swung the chair so that its occupant could see them both.

`This is Mr Edward Simbrazel,' he said. `You may remember I once mentioned that I was on the stage for a while. Edward was the one who helped me at that time.'

He bent down and spoke directly to Edward. `This is Mr Anderson. You've heard me talk about him. We were in the lifeboat together.'

Edward made an effort to speak, but only a few incoherent sounds came out. Queenie appeared to understand.

`That's right,' he said `Mr Anderson was the Assistant Purser.' Queenie turned back to Alan.

`What are you doing now, Sir?' Alan explained that he had just left the sea and was about to start a new job.

`I've often wondered how you were getting on,' Queenie said when Alan had finished. `You know that Con Mahoney's in America, I suppose?'

`No, I didn't. Sailing in the Dutch ship, I rather lost touch with what was going on in Southern Oceanic.'

Queenie nodded. `I don't know too much myself. It seems there was an American sergeant in charge of a fatigue party one voyage, one of the gangs sent to work in the galley. Con got friendly with him, and it turns out that this Yank was heir to an hotel chain, and he offered Con a job. I think he's Chef at some big hotel in San Francisco now.'

`And how about you?' Alan asked.

`Me? Oh I'm kept busy looking after Edward.' Queenie paused, then perhaps feeling his reply had been very brief, added an explanation.

`I won't go into the details of how, but I heard that Edward was ill; that he'd had a stroke and was in a nursing home. I went to see him and... well, as you see I'm now looking after him.'

Queenie looked as if he might be about to say something more. Instead he looked at Edward, and there was an awkward silence. To break it, Alan asked;

`That leaves Basil Allward. Did you ever hear anything of him?' Queenie seemed grateful for the diversion.

`Basil? Oh yes, while I was still at sea I went to his home a couple of times when the ship was in Tilbury. He was living in John's house then and boarding with Emily. He never really recovered, you know. There always seems to be something wrong with him and he's a bundle of nerves. If it wasn't for Emily I don't know how he'd manage.'

`It's a damn shame,' Alan said. `Is he still living with her?'

`They've moved, but she still looks after him.' Queenie looked down at Edward again and Alan saw him nod.

`I'll have to get Edward home, I'm afraid,' he told Alan.

`Of course. I shouldn't have kept you standing here. Perhaps I can walk with you a little way. I'm only out for a stroll and not going anywhere in particular.'

While they walked, Queenie told Alan more about Basil and Emily.

`Emily had quite a bit of money that John had put away, and early this year I heard she'd taken a pub at Purfleet. About two months ago I was down that way and thought I'd call in and see them. There's no doubt Emily's the one who runs the pub. Basil's just doing a barman's job...'

He broke off as though interrupting himself.

`Strange how wrong you can be about people,' he mused. `I never had much time for Emily while John was alive, but she's a different woman now. Perhaps it's having someone so dependent on her that's made the change. She mothers Basil, there's no getting away from it, and she tries to build him up in front of the customers. She's always giving him a boost, telling people she doesn't know how she'd manage without him. She tries to make it look like he's the one who makes the decisions.'

`Basil's lucky to have her,' Alan said.

`Perhaps,' Queenie replied, and there was a shrewd reflective tone in his voice as he spoke. `Perhaps,' he repeated. `But I think Emily may be the one who's lucky. I'm sure she's much happier, or at least more contented than she was. Perhaps now she's got some sort of purpose in her life and feels she's being useful. John was a hard man; difficult to know I'd say. Surprises me she hasn't married Basil.'

`Could be they're giving each other everything they need, just the way they are,' Alan suggested.

Meeting Queenie had taken Alan back in time. That night, as he sat with Trina over their meal, his mind went back to those years before Ocean Monarch was sunk. His life seemed to have been divided into a before and after. He found himself remembering, but took care not to analyze his feelings.

CHAPTER SEVENTEEN

Fare thee well! and if for ever,
Still for ever, fare thee well.
George Gordon, Lord Byron

Alan's work kept him busy during the next six months and he saw Trina only once, when they had lunch together. However, they kept in touch with an occasional phone call. Late in June a letter arrived from Marcia, who had been working in Kuala Lumpur for the previous two months. The program she was working with had been ended by a political decision, and she would be returning earlier than expected. She was due to leave for England in less than a fortnight from the date of her letter. As Alan read, he felt excitement mixed with a hint of nervousness. He picked up Marcia's photograph and looked at it thoughtfully. Would he and Marcia be able to take up from where they had left off? A year had passed since they said goodbye in Bombay, and Alan had not found it easy to keep up the intensity of emotion he and Marcia had felt during their brief time together.

Letters to Marcia had become hard to write. The "I love you" theme could not cover many pages. They had no shared background of memories, friends and acquaintances to bring variety to their writing. It had been easier for Marcia, as her work involved interesting people and places; but Alan's job had little day to day difference. Even under censorship, letters to Trina had never been a problem. Alan and Trina could write pages of tongue-in-cheek nonsense that seemed to say nothing, yet showed love and the warmth of a common bond. Even in the bad times, correspondence had kept their intimacy and companionship fresh and exciting. With Marcia, letters told only of doings and very little about the doer. After twelve months they knew each other no better than at the moment of saying goodbye.

Marcia was returning, and Trina must know. She and Alan had accepted that they would have to make a final break when Marcia or Keith returned. Neither wanted this, but it would not be fair to Marcia and Keith to do otherwise.

Alan checked his watch and saw it was just four o'clock. There would be a train from Reading to London in half an hour, and he made a quick decision. He had no appointments, and there was nothing that could not be left until after the weekend. His working hours were flexible, and no one would miss him if he were absent for the last hour of a Friday afternoon. He picked up the telephone. There was a delay while Trina was located, and then her voice was saying:

`Trina Grant speaking.' No need to tell Trina who was calling, she knew his voice better than she would have known her own.

`What are your plans for tonight?'

`Plans? Who makes plans? I... am just a leaf tossed by a passing breeze.'

`And when the breeze has passed, what do you intend to do?'

`I shall flutter to the ground and wait to see what happens.'

`If I catch the next train, could we flutter somewhere together?'

`I'd be fluttered.'

`That was unworthy. Hey! Would you have time to book tickets for a show? I'll phone when I reach town and you can tell me what you've booked. I'll pick up the tickets.'

`Any particular show in mind?'

`No, you choose.'

`Well there's... '

'You decide. I've got a train to catch.' Alan hung up leaving Trina still talking.

They went to the Palladium that evening, and after the show went back to the flat for supper. It was taken for granted that Alan would stay the night, in the same way that he had stayed there in the weeks before starting his new job. Then, he had slept on the settee in the sitting room and they had joked about their new-found morality. They appreciated the absurdity of the situation yet, in spite of their laughter, they clung to the remains of their old philosophy.

They had finished eating and were sitting side by side, drinking coffee, before Alan found the courage to tell Trina why he had come to town. He had waited until this moment before breaking the news, wanting her to enjoy this last evening together. He had not wished to spoil it by telling her earlier, but now it could be put off no longer. `I had a letter from Marcia today. She's on her way home.'

`Oh!... When's she due to arrive?'

`I don't know. She didn't give me the name of the ship, just said they were leaving in ten days time. The letter took twenty-five days to reach me, so she should be at least fifteen days on her way by now.'

`How long do you think?'

`Depends on the ship and her ports of call. Unless it's a cargo ship on a very roundabout route, I'd guess that she'll be here within the next ten days.'

`So, she may be here in less than a week?'

`Could be. That's why I had to come and see you.' Trina did not say anything. Instead she went across to the gramophone and looked through a pile of records. She made a choice, and as she came back to the settee the first notes of Eine Kleine Nachtmusik floated across the room. She sat down and took a sip of coffee.

`This will be our last little flutter then?'

`It seems like it,' Alan replied. He looked around the flat, thinking how often they had sat there together, moving only to change a record, completely content in each other's company. He found it almost impossible to believe that it would never happen again. Later they cleared away the supper dishes and Alan dried while Trina washed.

Alan could not tell how Trina was feeling while they worked; but to him there was an air of unreality, a distant dreamlike quality in every action they took. This unreality was emphasised by a heightened awareness. It was as if he were standing apart, a bystander, and yet a participant at the same time. The pattern of the dishes; the feel of the cutlery; the contents of cupboards and drawers, the tang of dish washing soap and the aroma of coffee grounds mingled, creating an image of past security in happiness. The image was painfully intensified by the faint scent of Trina's hair as he stood beside her. In that tiny kitchen there was scarcely room to move, and when they had finished Alan reached behind Trina to hang up the tea towel. At that moment she turned away from the sink and they were standing, face to face, their bodies almost touching.

As Alan withdrew his hand he hesitated, then stroked her cheek, and Trina moved her head slightly to press harder against his hand. Neither had anything to say. Instead they stood, looking into each other's eyes, surprised, uncertain. Absentmindedly Alan's thumb moved back and forth, gently caressing her face.

`Is there any law that says you must sleep on the settee?' Trina's voice was low and husky, and she raised her hand to Alan's shoulder. Even if he had wanted to, Alan would not have been able to reject that plea.

`I've never found the settee very comfortable,' he answered, and desire was immediate. Their lovemaking had always had a basic tenderness; but that night it was brutal, elemental and insatiate, as though they came together in anger. In the morning Alan and Trina were shattered and ashamed. Shattered by the violence of their passion, and ashamed of the pleasure each had given and received. Ashamed for Keith and Marcia, and guilty because they had been untrue to themselves. Breakfast was a silent affair, and afterwards Alan took Trina's hands.

`I'd better go.'

Trina nodded.

`Yes, this must be goodbye.'

She moved towards Alan for a final kiss. It was just a light brushing of lips.

`Goodbye.'

Alan left the flat quickly and did not look back. He no longer had the right to look back, and neither did Trina. Later that day, Alan was sitting in his flat thinking about Marcia and Trina. It was Saturday afternoon and he felt very much alone. "Fare thee well! and if forever, Still forever, fare thee well." Byron's words kept nagging in his mind until he took pencil and paper and paid a final tribute to Trina. After many attempts he wrote:

ADIEU MA BELLE, MA BELLE AMIE

'Fare thee well!
Let thy welfare
be thine to tell
and mine to care.
For, though I leave,
I pay my due:
I also grieve
at leaving you.

I gladly go,
yet sadly say;
My joy is woe,
my sadness gay.
My tattered heart
divides in two,
and one small part
remains with you.

I would I could
but know I can't.
Perhaps I should!
You know I shan't -
I'll not forget
how could that be?
Past love is yet
a part of me.

Spare no sad tears
for love that's done:
smile, for those years
when we were one.

Smile, for those years
beyond recall
and brave our fears;
remembering all.'

* * *

`...he's coming round again.' Distantly, Alan could hear voices. Nothing made sense. His eyes were open and light was hurting his new found consciousness. Blurred shapes crossed his vision and he could not move. Tight bands held him immobile.

`I must be dreaming... I must wake up.'

The distorted figures kept coming and going. Sometimes there was one, sometimes three or four swam into his uncertain gaze. For an age Alan struggled in what could only be a nightmare; then, gradually, his eyelids drooped. The strange sounds faded until, again, all was dark, and quiet, and still.

* * *

`Marcia! Where are you?'

Alan had picked up the phone in his office, and was startled to hear her voice. The thought flashed through his mind; `If she hadn't said "It's Marcia" would I have known who it was?'

For days he had been anxiously waiting to hear from her, but when it happened he was surprised and even a little apprehensive.

`At home – Bingley,' she explained. `I arrived here this afternoon.'

`When did you get back to England?'

`We docked yesterday at Southampton. I didn't have a chance to ring you then. The minute I got ashore it was a rush to catch the boat train to London. I could have rung you when we got there but it was too late. You'd have finished work and gone home.'

`If you'd known you could have rung the flat. I finally managed to get a phone about a fortnight ago. You said you'd only just got home to Bingley. How come it took you so long?'

`There was no train last night that made the connections, so I stayed in London and caught an early train this morning. Alan, I can hardly believe it's you I'm talking to.'

`I know, I'm feeling much the same.' They arranged that Alan would go to Bingley in three days time and spend the weekend there. He lived through the next few days with mixed feelings of excitement and concern. All the way to Bingley his nervousness mounted with each beat of the train's wheels; but when he arrived the tension melted immediately and Alan discovered that Marcia was as beautiful as he remembered, and as captivating. The delight of those days on board Piet Bakker came back. Marcia was loving, and in her calm way accepted the fact of an impending marriage. She had no doubts, and readily went with him to choose an engagement ring. Alan began to wonder how he could have had any uncertainty. To be with this tiny, lovely creature and not fall under her spell was quite impossible. They talked about setting a date for their wedding, but Marcia's mother was worried. Although it was now over a year since Alan and Marcia had met, her mother was concerned that they had spent so little time in each other's company. This was understandable, and they agreed to wait four months, intending to set a date in November.

During the next month Alan and Marcia saw each other on only two weekends, and after allowing traveling time they were left with little time together. Alan had been anxious for Marcia to come to London to see his parents who had still not met her; but it was well into August before she was able to leave Bingley. Her father had gone into hospital for an operation, and after being away for so long Marcia did not like to leave until he was well on the way to recovery.

When she did arrive in London Marcia stayed for a fortnight with Alan's parents, and during the first week Alan commuted daily from Reading. However, in the second week he was able to take a few days off from work.

Marcia did not know London at all and was keen to go sightseeing. Alan took her on a tourist round of Westminster Abbey, the National Art Gallery, St Paul's, the Monument and everywhere else she wished to see. Marcia was thrilled with London and Alan was happy to be her escort, enjoying her interest in all she saw. It was not until the day he took her to the Tower that Alan felt the first niggling doubt. Perhaps it was because, for him, the Tower would always have a strong association with Trina and the day they first met.

Marcia was as charming and as amiable as ever, but Alan became aware that he was weighing his words rather than saying the first thing that came into his mind. This surprised him, and he began to wonder why. There was no real reason; it was just that he was adapting his ways to suit a different girl.

When with Marcia, Alan tried to block Trina from his thoughts, but one day in Kensington he felt the same doubt; and again it was probably because of where they were, close to Trina's flat. Now, when he thought about it, Alan could see clearly what was happening. Even in the last few years there had only been the one subject that he and Trina had avoided, unwilling to risk reopening old wounds. This apart, they could talk in friendship, candidly, carelessly, without worrying what they said or how they said it, each confident of the other's acceptance.

Marcia's temperament was different. She was not demanding, but she did appreciate small courtesies, whereas Trina accepted them, yet still managed to look surprised when a door was held open for her. The difference, probably, between expecting and not caring. The same thing applied in conversation. In the heat of argument with Trina, half-serious derogatory comments would fly back and forth; but Marcia would have been hurt in such an exchange. Not that she and Alan ever had arguments. Conversation with Marcia did not have the explosive element that was present with Trina. Inevitably Alan found that he was making comparisons and finding that Marcia was not as much fun to be with as Trina. Where Marcia charmed, Trina amused; Marcia was beautiful but Trina was fascinating; Marcia smiled, Trina laughed; Marcia was loving and Trina was passionate. Alan could tease Trina about her almost imperceptibly bandy legs: Marcia, similarly teased, would have been surprised and hurt.

Alan recalled that eventful night with Trina, a night now distant in time, yet still painful in memory. Would Marcia have risked pregnancy without marriage? Would she allow her emotions to reach such a pitch that she must satisfy a sudden longing, come what may? No, that would not be her style. Marcia was sensible and calm. Marcia would not have stopped to fight any assailants either; she would have done as she was told and run for help.

Such thoughts left Alan with a whisper of dismay. Marcia would be an excellent wife; and she was certainly no dumb beauty. Her competence was almost frightening, and she managed to enclose herself within a circle of efficiency. Marcia would never be disorganized, and life with her would be smooth and well arranged.

Alan began to feel like a male spider before mating - in danger of being consumed. At best he would be trapped inside that circle of organized peace, part of Marcia's creation. Slowly he would be changed, molded with gentleness, until he fitted the pattern she visualized.

Perhaps this was nothing more than pre-wedding nerves, the fear of surrender and loss of individuality, and when he was with Marcia these doubts would fade. Marcia seemed to be happy, and there could be no pulling back now.

Towards the end of Marcia's second week in London, Alan took her out to dinner at a restaurant near Piccadilly. They parked the car, and walked up the Haymarket in drizzling rain. Marcia was still intrigued by the sights and sounds of London, and especially Piccadilly Circus at night. The rain had caused the streets and buildings to glisten, reflecting colored lights. At Marcia's insistence, they stood and watched for a few minutes before entering the restaurant. Inside, Alan checked in his raincoat and waited for Marcia, who had gone to remove her hat and coat. She was away five minutes, and when she came hurrying back to him Alan felt the thrill of satisfaction that so lovely a girl was happy to be going out with him. They entered the dining room, and stood while the Headwaiter checked his list of bookings. Satisfied, he led the way, followed by Marcia with Alan bringing up the rear. Idly, Alan scanned the tables, half looking to pick out the one to which they were being led.

Suddenly he saw her, and felt a tingle of shock. As if sensing Alan's presence Trina looked up and met his eyes. For an instant she seemed to freeze, and then her eyes swept to Marcia in an all-encompassing glance of appraisal. As Alan approached, Trina was facing him, and he could only see her companion's back. Level with Trina's table the waiter moved to the right and Marcia turned to follow him, then looked back for Alan.

He had stopped, uncertain, yet unwilling to walk past Trina as though ignoring a stranger. Trina made the first move.

`Hello Alan,' she said. `How are you? It's ages since I've seen you.'

`Yes, it is a long time. You're looking well. What are you doing nowadays?' Trina's lips twitched at the banality of the remarks.

`Alan, I'd like you to meet Keith, my fiancé.' Alan shook hands with Keith, conscious that Marcia was watching with interest.

`Marcia,' Alan turned to her and she stepped to his side.

`I'd like to introduce Trina Grant and her fiancé, Keith.' Alan turned back to Trina. `This is my fiancée, Marcia Easthope.'

There were murmurs of `How d'you do'. While making the introductions Alan was trying not to stare at Trina, and began to feel that it was time to make a move.

`The waiter waits and we mustn't keep him waiting,' he said hurriedly, then added; `It's been nice seeing you. Quite a surprise.' Trina had regained her composure, and there was a dangerous glint of amusement in her eyes. `Perhaps we could all meet up sometime?' she said, looking directly at Alan.

He could not resist the challenge.

`What a good idea, we'll have to see just what we can arrange.' Trina's eyes began to sparkle, and Alan was tempted to stay a little longer to find out how outrageous she would dare to be; but wisdom prevailed. He spoke quickly, before she had any opportunity for further comment.

`However, if you'll excuse us?' He released his eyes from Trina's, gave a nod to Keith and turned to Marcia, ushering her after the Headwaiter.

`She's bored,' he thought, and danger signals flashed. Trina, when bored, could be completely unpredictable.

`Who was that?' Marcia asked after they were seated.

`Trina? She and I used to work together.'

`When was that?'

'She was working for Southern Oceanic when I joined them in 1938.'

'You've known her a long time then?'

'Yes, 1938, before the war. Seems like another era, doesn't it?'

'Don't tell me you haven't seen her since then. You seemed much too friendly for me to believe that.' Alan looked at Marcia, and experienced a tiny flicker of irritation. She was smiling and was not, apparently, discomposed. He detected a faintly inquisitorial tone in the last question that made him disinclined to give a plain answer. He would have to tell Marcia about Trina, but in his own time, unhurriedly, and choosing the right words. Not like this, when it would appear that he was having the details extracted by question and answer; and certainly not in the restaurant with Trina sitting only a few feet away. Marcia's question was still hanging in the air, and almost automatically he replied. 'All right, I won't.'

The moment the words were out he realized that this was not the type of answer that Marcia could accept. Trina would not have asked the question in the first place; but if she had so phrased a similar question and received that answer, she would either have given Alan her long-suffering look or would have treated him to withering scorn. Finally she would have restated the question in direct terms. Not so Marcia. Before she had time to look hurt, Alan explained.

'Trina was stationed in London for part of the war. She was in the Wrens and when I was on leave we'd arrange to meet; but, as she said, it's ages since we've met.' Perhaps Alan should have told Marcia, then and there, that Trina had been more to him than just a past girlfriend. He only knew that he could not at that moment, and as in most personal decisions his reasons were mixed. Although Alan was so charmed by the dainty Marcia that he felt sure he loved her, he was still unable to predict her reaction to a detailed statement of his past love life. He felt guilt too, as though he had been caught doing something wrong. Guilt at the pleasure he had felt when talking with Trina. Whatever the reason, he had a reluctance to discuss Trina with Marcia that evening. The waiter arrived to take their order and provided a welcome diversion. Alan thought they were safely over what had threatened to become an embarrassing situation. When the waiter moved away, he reminded Marcia about their visit to Reading earlier in the day.

`You haven't had much to say about my flat. I get the feeling you weren't too impressed with it.'

`Oh no, it's not that. I can see, from your point of view, it's very good. Small, easy to clean and close to your work.'

`Come on, what don't you like about it?'

Marcia treated Alan to one of her warmest smiles. `If you must know, I thought it would drive me mad if I had to live there for any length of time. It's fine for you; you're only there in the evenings, so it doesn't matter. However, there's no garden, no view except uninteresting back yards, no park nor open country nearby. Just three tiny rooms, bedroom, sitting room and a minute kitchen.'

`And bathroom,' Alan added. Marcia smiled again. `I wasn't counting that.'

`Well, what d'you want to do?'

`If you agree, this is what I suggest. Let's go there after the honeymoon. We've got to live somewhere, in or near Reading, and your flat will be ideal while we look for somewhere else. There must be places, a cottage in a village close to Reading, that we can rent for a reasonable amount. That place, what was it called? The one you showed me on the way back, Sonning wasn't it? Somewhere like that they'd probably charge the earth, but there must be other villages not so worked over.'

`Cottages are all very well provided they're modernized; but don't think you're going to get me up at dawn to hoist water from a well, or make me find my way around at night with a candle.'

`Leave it to me.' Marcia had obviously been giving the matter some thought since the trip to Reading.

`Don't worry, I'll find something. When you go to work I won't have anything to do, and I'll spend the first few weeks searching until I find the place I'm after.'

Marcia's plans kept her safely talking, explaining what she would like in a house. She was in no way boring. Marcia had a knack for description, and could use words to paint a clear picture of what she had in mind. She had a flair for decorating, with a host of novel ideas. Also, she knew when to stop, not talking too long on any one subject.

Alan was surprised when she suddenly broke off in the middle of a sentence to say; `That girl, she keeps looking at you.'

`More likely to be looking at you. I've got my back to her.'

`Why should she look at me?'

`Probably envious of your good looks.' Alan was smiling at Marcia, but in truth it was more of an internal grin at the thought of what Trina might make of that diversionary tactic. She would be torn between applauding the technique and wrath at its substance.

If the answer did not satisfy Marcia, at least it distracted her sufficiently for Alan to lead the conversation back to safer paths. Another ten minutes passed, and then he saw that Marcia's gaze was fixed on a point over his shoulder.

`She's coming over here. I wonder what she wants?'

`You may well wonder,' Alan thought. `What the hell's Trina up to?'

He did not turn, but watched Marcia. Her eyes followed Trina as she approached, and Alan was able to study her expression unobserved. She was completely impassive; not even by the flicker of an eye did Marcia give the slightest indication of her thoughts. Trina walked past their table and Alan had difficulty in suppressing a sigh of relief. Obviously she was on her way to the powder room.

`She dresses well for an office girl.' Marcia made this comment after Trina passed out of earshot.

Alan shrugged. `I'm no expert, but now you mention it she does look well in that dress.'

Alan could see no future in mentioning that Trina's status was slightly higher than office girl, nor that he was well acquainted with that particular dress and its fastenings.

When Trina returned, Alan tried not to look at her as he continued a conversation with Marcia. It was a futile exercise. Before Trina had covered half the distance, he could feel himself losing track of whatever it was he was talking about. He would have to take a bolder line.

`Here's Trina on her way back,' he said to Marcia.

Trina saw Alan's head come up and that he was looking at her quite openly. She was wearing the unconscious smile she assumed when wistfully amused by the foibles of the world, or rather its inhabitants. The corners of her mouth were pulled down into an odd, inverted smile, while her right eyebrow was fractionally raised. Alan always referred to it as "Your kindly, tolerant smile." He could not help returning the smile.

`Having a good time?' he asked when she reached them.

`Of course, I always do when I'm with Keith.'

`When do you get married?' As Alan asked the question he felt a pang of jealousy, instantly suppressed as he realized it was no business of his.

`That's what we're trying to work out tonight. We'd planned to get married at Christmas, but now Keith's firm is sending him to South America. He's to take charge of a big construction job, and they want him to leave next week.'

`Not much notice then?'

`No, it's not. The man they had in charge died of a heart attack. He was only forty-two and it's upset the whole program.'

`How long will Keith be away?'

`That's the problem. He expects to be there for two and a half years. He might get a couple of months leave this time next year, but even that's not certain. He wants us to get married immediately, special license and all that sort of thing, so I can go with him.'

`What have you decided?'

`Get married I suppose. It seems the obvious thing to do. What are your plans?'

This last question Trina directed more to Marcia than Alan, and Alan also looked at Marcia, trying to draw her into the conversation. Trina was evidently on her best behavior, but for some reason Marcia did not accept the question. Trina glanced back to Alan, and he answered.

`We haven't finalized arrangements, but we'll probably get married during the third week in November.' Trina nodded, then again spoke directly to Marcia.

`I suppose I'd better be getting back to my fiancé and leave you to yours.'

Again Marcia failed to respond. Trina turned her attention back to Alan, and experience told him that her innate devilment was getting the better of her. He was sure some surprise remark would be made. Well, two could play at that game, and he would try to disconcert her first.

`Pity you'll be out of the country. I'd have liked to invite you and Keith to our wedding.'

`What a kind thought. Yes, if things had been different I'd have loved to be at your wedding.'

Trina smiled happily at Alan. She knew she had won that round. With difficulty Alan kept a straight face, and had to admire Trina's self control as she again turned to Marcia.

`Goodnight Marcia, it's been fun meeting you.' After Trina left Alan expected another bout of questioning, but Marcia appeared to have dismissed Trina from her mind.

CHAPTER EIGHTEEN

If two lives join, there is oft a scar,
They are one and one, with a shadowy third;
One near one is too far.
Robert Browning

The dream was peaceful and refreshing. Alan was in a cool, green room where curtains filtered the sun and a soft light showed him her face. His body felt weightless, non-existent; and Trina's face was calm, but sad. Alan tried to reach her with his mind, because his lips would not obey his will. 'You mustn't look sad my darling. It doesn't suit you.'

Trina's face came closer as if brushing a kiss on to his cheek. Then she was moving away, floating to the edge of his vision; and Alan strained to follow her movement.

'Alan, you're looking at me.'

'Silly girl, you know I always see you in my dreams.' The sadness had gone from Trina's face, and Alan was happy. The dream faded into darkness, but he did not mind. Trina was not sad any more.

* * *

It was the room of his dreams, and he was not dreaming. Alan could see that he was lying in bed and tried to sit up. There was movement from beyond the foot of the bed, and a figure came swiftly to his side. A face looked into his. A nice face, but not Trina's. When the nurse spoke it was with a cheerful, professional voice.

'Well hello, can you understand what I'm saying?'

'Yes.'

It was a whispered, croaking voice that surprised Alan, but he decided that it must have been his own. It was what he had tried to say, but it was so unlike... so unreal.

'Just you lie there quietly, I'll be back in a moment.' The nurse vanished, but was back within seconds, fussing about the bed smoothing and straightening sheets and pillows. 'The doctor will be here to see you soon,' she explained. Time was an irrelevance, something that did not exist. The doctor was there and then he was not there; nurses came and nurses went.

* * *

Pinpoints of light... The doctor looking into his eyes... dazzling with brightness. Alan tried to move and failed, which led to the interesting discovery that his right arm was strapped down. He managed to turn his head a little, and saw that the doctor was studying some apparatus on a trolley beside the bed. As if in slow motion Alan's mind began to work, and with it the knowledge that there must be something seriously wrong with him. Then came a surge of memory. The plane falling and hitting the water, and at once his mind was racing, filling in details. The helicopter, the Navy ship. This was no ship. He must be ashore. How long had he been unconscious?

The doctor was speaking.

'You had us worried, but you're going to be fine now. Just a matter of time and we'll have you back on your feet.' He talked quietly with the Sister who had come in with him, and appeared to be giving some instructions. He handed her a clipboard, which she placed on a table and he then left the room. Although Alan could not see him, he could hear the doctor talking to someone outside. He was no longer speaking in a hushed voice.

'Only two minutes,' he said. 'You may go in and see him, but I don't want him even trying to talk. Tomorrow perhaps, when he's had time to adjust, we may let you stay a little longer. He seems more aware of what's happening; but I'm not sure he's had time to get... ' Alan heard no more as the Sister had returned to his bedside. 'You have a visitor, but only for a minute or two and you're not to talk. Don't even try.' She placed her finger on her lips and shook her head to emphasize what she was saying. As the Sister left, Alan could again hear the doctor.

'...and we don't want to risk any relapse now that he's on the mend.' There were footsteps.

'Like hell!' Alan thought as Trina came into his range of vision. 'There's no way I'm going to have a relapse now.' Trina came near to the bed and she was smiling.

'At least not the way the doctor meant.' Alan amended his thought, and was sure that there must be a stupid grin on his face.

At first, Trina stood beside the bed and said nothing. Perhaps it was emotion, or embarrassment, or maybe she was having difficulty in deciding what to say. Alan could not tell, and then she was leaning down towards him.

'They say I'm not to stay. I'll come back tomorrow.' Trina bent to kiss Alan. Screened from the Sister by Trina's body, Alan could not resist the temptation. It was hard to move his lips, but he managed to whisper;

'They... are mad!'

'Unlike you, of course,' she retorted. Then quoted;' "He is mad in patches. Full of lucid intervals." '

That passage from Don Quixote was very familiar to Alan. She had tossed it at him many times. Trina turned and waved as she walked away, and Alan felt ridiculously smug and happy.

For the next two or three days, Trina's visits were limited to a few minutes. There was always a Sister or a nurse hovering nearby, and under instructions Trina did the talking. Alan would dearly have liked to point out that this instruction was entirely redundant; but speaking was difficult and painful, and not worth the effort.

Alan did manage the occasional question.

'When did you get here?'

'The same day you did.'

Alan tried to speak again but was shushed by Trina at once.

'I'll explain,' she stated imperiously. 'I knew, of course, that you had to be on board the plane that crashed. The pilot got off a message while it was going down. Because of the time difference I heard a news flash just as I was finishing breakfast.'

Trina paused, and Alan wondered what her thoughts had been.

'I checked with the airline office that you'd been booked on that flight, then used my contacts to confirm that you had, in fact, boarded the plane. There were no more details in later bulletins, and I made myself go to the office; but I can't remember what I did. Probably nothing. I do remember sitting there and thinking of you, of us, and the times we'd spent together. I'd been trying not to build too much on the fact that you were coming to Bermuda, but I'd been... excited I suppose.'

Whether it hurt or not, Alan could not resist saying; 'Too bad I didn't arrive with you in that condition.' He was treated to an aloof, down the nose, look.

'Mens sana obviously doesn't apply to you. What's the Latin for "a sick mind in a sick body…?" No, don't say anything. For once you're not allowed to answer me back….Doctor's orders.'

Alan had been about to say; 'Try putting an "in" in front of the "sana",' but it would have been too painful. Instead he relaxed, trying to look as though he had intended a witty comment and was indignant at being silenced. It was much too complicated a look to be successful.

Trina had begun to show some signs of emotion while she recalled that traumatic morning. The exchange brightened her, but only briefly.

'Now where was I?' She returned to her explanation.

'The next day was worse. Reports were coming in of unsuccessful searches. I kept remembering... '

Trina was silent. She looked at Alan, and her chin came up defiantly as she said; 'I remembered those other times when I didn't expect to see you again. Both times you came back, but this time it seemed there could be no doubt.'

Trina was quiet again. Alan watched her face, which was calm, but he guessed that she was doing battle with herself. He raised an eyebrow, and by the little twist to her answering smile knew that he was right. Soon, Trina regained control and continued.

'It was next morning... I heard on the radio that seven survivors had been found. I'd gone to bed early and had taken a sleeping pill, so hadn't heard the late news the night before. They didn't give any names, but said the seven people had been taken on board a British Destroyer. I couldn't wait. I had to find out immediately.'

The nurse, who had gone out of the room when Trina arrived, put her head around the door. 'Only another two minutes Miss Grant.'

'And so?' Alan prompted.

'I rang Uncle Harry. He was very kind. He didn't ask questions, though he must have wondered why I was in such a state. When he fixed me the job in Bermuda it was because I'd told him about my broken engagement. He already knew that you and I... that you were marrying someone else.'

'What...?'

Trina cut in quickly.

'Of course, you don't know about all that. Alan, there's such a lot we've got to talk about when you get better.'

Alan nodded his agreement.

'As I was saying, I rang Uncle Harry. He realized how upset I was and told me he'd ring back as soon as he could get anything definite. It can't have been more than twenty minutes before he was back on the line. He'd got on to someone he knows at the Admiralty, and had found out the names of the survivors within a few minutes. They had the details but weren't releasing them until they'd been in touch with next of kin. I'll never forget picking up the phone and hearing Uncle Harry's voice saying; "Trina, Alan's been found."'

Trina took a deep breath, and looked at Alan with large eyes before taking up her story again.

'I didn't even stop to think. I just acted. There was a flight out that morning, and within two hours I was on my way to England. Everything was such a rush I'd no time to wonder whether I was doing the right thing... not until I was seated on the plane.' Again Trina stopped speaking, but she smiled at Alan and he was conscious of how worn she was looking; and yes, she did have dark patches around her eyes.

'Was it bad?' he asked quietly, and she nodded. Alan studied her face as she sat, motionless and silent beside the bed, and knew that he loved her; but they could talk about that later, when the strain had passed. He could not let her go without saying something to help.

'I'm glad you wanted to come.'

'Thank you kind sir, she said.' Trina spoke flippantly to conceal her feelings before continuing.

'During the flight across the Atlantic I kept having the dismal thought that I would find Marcia by your side. I suppose I shouldn't say that, but it was the way I felt. Your telegram said "wifeless". I assumed you'd separated, but I didn't... don't know if that's true.'

'Didn't marry.' Each time Alan spoke it hurt more.

'Your mother only said you'd broken with Marcia: I phoned her after I got here, but didn't ask for details. I didn't like to, and anyway the "how" wasn't important. I've been ringing your mother every evening. That's why she hasn't come down here. It's a long way at her age, and there wasn't anything she could do while you were unconscious. Also, your father's in bed with bronchitis.'

The nurse re-entered the room. She had allowed more than the threatened two minutes.

'I was so afraid I was just being a sentimental idiot.' Trina stood, then bent to kiss Alan.

'I like idiots,' he whispered. Trina completed the kiss.

By the time Trina arrived the following afternoon, Alan was feeling much better; brighter and less lethargic. He had been taken off some of the drugs he had been given, and also had managed to get the doctor to tell him what had been going on.

'Let's see,' the doctor had said in brisk professional tones. 'Right leg badly broken in two places. We thought we might have trouble there, but we've managed to save it. I don't expect it'll ever be the leg it was before, but it shouldn't give you too much trouble. What else? A broken nose and cheekbone. That was one of the reasons you had difficulty with your eyes. Your face was so swollen you couldn't open them properly. The salt water didn't help either. You've a few cracked ribs, but there's nothing to worry about there; and then, of course, there were some internal injuries. On top of that you managed to get a fever with severe respiratory problems. That didn't help. Still, everything's under control, and you'll soon be up and about.' He removed the thermometer from Alan's mouth and glanced at it.

'All in all, you were pretty lucky.'

'Depends on the point of view,' Alan commented. Trina's visits were the high spots. At first, Alan could not speak without some pain and was willing to let her do most of the talking, but gradually the swelling went down, and it was only a few days before he felt able to sustain a conversation. It was time to start clearing up loose ends, and he asked Trina;

'What happened to Keith?'

Trina shrugged. 'I just couldn't go through with it. The evening you walked into that restaurant was the stone cold end. I thought I was fond enough of him for the marriage to work, and while everything was still some distance in the future it was all right. That night I was being faced with a wedding only a few days away.' Trina caught Alan's eye, and they grinned at each other as they recalled that evening.

'When you entered he'd just finished listing the advantages of an immediate marriage, and how it would help him in his work. I don't suppose he meant it, but it sounded quite cold blooded as though that was the whole point in marrying me. When I first met him he'd been fun to be with, and he's good looking too. However, when we'd been engaged for a while, I found myself wondering whether what had attracted me was no more than a carefully acquired veneer. In those early days we were still in the Navy and were rarely alone together for any length of time; mostly we'd be partying with a crowd of other officers and their wives and girlfriends. Keith fitted well in that company. As time went on I began to fear that all he had was a memory bank of witticisms and stock phrases; there was little that was creative in his humor.' Trina paused in her narrative, then added:

'And little that was rude and crude either.' She tried to give Alan a haughty look full of meaning, but could not prevent her face from reorganizing itself into a mischievous grin.

'When he came back from Denmark we went away on holiday together, and after a few weeks of being with him all the time some of his mannerisms began to irritate. I started to get the feeling that marriage to him would be no more than a sedate, unexciting, domestic life, and that basically... Oh, what's the word I want…? Stolid, I think. Yes, that would be it - stolid.'

Trina shook her head reflectively, while Alan felt a bubble of laughter at the thought of Trina being a sedate anything. She continued;

'I don't think he had enough for me to settle down with. When I saw you walking towards me, d'you know the first thing that struck me?'

It was Alan's turn to shake his head.

'I realized that the whole evening we'd been together, Keith and I that is, no one had said anything stupid or ridiculous.'

'Thank you very much,' Alan said. 'If that means what I think you mean, then I'm highly indignant.'

'Go ahead, be indignant then,' was Trina's airy reply.

'I'm maligned,' Alan complained to the ceiling.

'About time. You've needed straightening up for ages.'

'Ridiculous I may be, but I'd never inflict a pun like that on a bed-ridden sufferer.'

'Oh yes you have. I've suffered often enough, and I've been...'

'Silence woman. You have a low and disturbing mind, and anyway we're getting away from the subject.'

Trina laughed. It was a peculiarly Trina laugh, not full throated, but jerky, a cross between a laugh and a hearty chuckle. Most enticing, but definitely not ladylike.

'Where was I, before you started being indignant?' she asked.

'I was walking towards you, and you were being struck by a first thing.'

'So I was. Well, that's about it. I kept looking over and thinking I'd rather be with you than with Keith, and wondering, cattishly, what you were saying to Marcia. I could see why you wanted to marry her. She's lovely...' Alan nodded impatiently, and saw a smile flicker across Trina's face before she went on with her story.

'Poor Keith, I fear I was a little distracted, and not paying as much attention to him as he thought I should. When I did make myself concentrate on him, I knew I just couldn't rush into the marriage. Later, after leaving the restaurant, I did say I thought it best to wait until he'd settled into his new job.'

'How did he react?'

This time Trina's smile was a wry one.

'He'd been getting more and more frustrated all evening. I can't blame him; he hadn't been able to get any sort of a sensible answer from me. I was being evasive; but Alan, I wasn't being nasty. I don't know quite what it was I was trying to do; let him down lightly I think. Anyway, after we got into his car he became all dominant and laid it on the line. I was to marry him at once... or else.'

'Poor Keith indeed. I thought you said he didn't say anything stupid? He should've known you better. I take it that was the end? You followed with your ice block act, no doubt?' Trina laughed. On the many occasions when Alan had annoyed her and she tried to be distant, he would tease and torment her until her "block" had melted.

'It was no act that night,' Trina agreed.

'Why didn't you let me know?' Alan demanded.

'Now you are being stupid. As far as I knew, you and Marcia were cozily arranging which date in November would be the happy day.'

'She's right of course,' Alan thought. Neither had he contacted her. He, too, had thought he had no right to do so.

'You could've let me know you'd be able to come to my wedding,' Alan complained. He had just remembered the way Trina scored off him in the restaurant.

'I didn't think you'd want any impediment present,' Trina retorted.

'Don't you mean impedimenta - baggage?'

'Silentium facere - that ought to mean something like: "Shut your face." I'm not an impedimenta, if I may mix that indefinite article with a plural noun, and there was no need to add to the insult by translating.'

There was no further mileage in that digression and Alan returned to a less combative subject.

'I did call in to your work a couple of weeks later, after I'd had the brush off from Marcia. Just to make sure, in case you hadn't rushed off to South America. You didn't sound exactly certain of your plans that night. When I went into the office there was someone else sitting at your desk. I asked one of the girls where you were and she said you'd left, said you'd gone overseas.'

'Didn't she tell you where I'd gone?'

'I didn't ask. I was sure I knew. If you really want to know, I felt too miserable to ask, and if you say "poor Alan" I'll hit you when I'm fit enough to risk it.'

Trina resisted the temptation, then said;

'She probably didn't know anyway. I faded out of the office quietly, and only told one or two people where I was going. I wasn't too keen on talking about my affairs at that time... and I'll amend "affairs" to "concerns" before you nit pick at that.'

Alan ignored the jibe.

'Was that when you went to Bermuda?' he queried.

'Yes, I think I told you the other day. Next morning, after breaking with Keith, I confided in Uncle Harry, about the engagement that is. I didn't say anything about meeting you; there was no point, and anyhow I was a bit mixed up in my thoughts. I just wanted to get away somewhere. I... I didn't want any more accidental meetings.' 'They wouldn't have been accidental,' Alan commented. 'How was I to know? Uncle Harry thought for a while, and then suggested I go to Bermuda and take over the travel agency there. Our manager had been enticed away by another agency and had already left, which was convenient. Naturally, I jumped at the offer.'

'I suppose the agency there looks after the Bermuda end of the "Fly Bermuda/Cruise Caribbean" packages?'

'Yes, of course, you're in the travel business now, so you'd know all about Southern Oceanic's American cruises. Let's not talk about that though. Tell me, what happened to you and Marcia?'

'Do I have to tell?' Alan queried. 'I behaved very badly.'

'What's so unusual about that?'

'Do you want to hear the story or don't you?' Alan tried for an indignantly insulted look.

'It's probably not fit for my ears.'

'I'll have to think about that. What's the matter with your ears? How do you define what's not fit for them?' Trina was half laughing, half exasperated.

'Oh shut up Alan, get on with it.'

'You confuse me. Which do you want?' It was Trina's turn to look imploringly at the ceiling.

'Get - on - with - it!' Alan decided it was not safe to torment her any further.

'Very well. When Marcia and I sat down at our table that evening, she started grilling me about you, and how well I knew you.'

Trina laughed.

'I wish I could have heard. I hope you told the truth.'

'Let's say I didn't tell a lie. Still, she had sense enough to stop before I got annoyed.' Alan suddenly laughed.

'What's so funny?'

'I've just remembered how I distracted her.'

'How?'

'Not likely. I'll tell you someday, but I need to be mobile before I take the risk.'

Alan received a look of dark suspicion that he ignored, and continued talking.

'Later, I thought she was going to start again. That was after you stopped at our table, but she didn't. She waited until we were driving home; much the same as Keith must have done with you. I suppose some people don't like having their arguments in public. You know, I think she and Keith might have got on well. Pity we couldn't have swapped partners that night.'

'Don't diverge. What happened?'

'I suspect she suffered the same way as Keith had. Probably I hadn't been paying her as much attention as I usually did. Seeing you...'

Alan looked at Trina. She was leaning forward, elbows on the edge of the mattress; chin propped on her hands. There was no need for him to elaborate. Instead he studied her eyes, so close to his and looking larger than ever with their pupils dilated in the dim light. Alan's mind wandered, and it was an effort to pick up from where he had stopped talking.

'As I was saying, whatever it was, her suspicions were aroused that you were, shall we say, the other woman in my life.'

'What was the matter with her?' Trina asked, genuinely indignant.

'Did she think you'd been wrapped in cellophane until the time she met you?'

'Now, now, it's just that her mind doesn't work like yours. That might be why I wasn't paying her enough attention. I must admit to thinking more about you that evening than I should have done.'

Trina interrupted.

'I'm inclined to dispute that, but let it pass.'

'Well, if you must know I was comparing Marcia's sweetness with your....'

'Nastiness?'

'Pungency was the word I had in mind, but if you're happy, nastiness will do.'

'I resent that - bitterly!'

'That was Marcia's trouble. I discovered her sweetness was turning, shall we say, sour? She kept referring to you as "that girl" and she did succeed in annoying me.'

'You do surprise me. How did she manage that?'

Alan grinned at Trina.

'Poor Keith, poor Marcia, I don't think you and I are very nice people,' he said.

Trina sniffed haughtily.

'Just confine your thoughts to yourself.'

Alan relaxed, shifting his position in the bed slightly towards Trina. She was looking very much better and the dark patches were almost gone.

'Well?' she asked.

'All I did was to give Marcia truthful, but evasive, answers. I wanted her to stop prying and prodding. I'd have told her about us if she'd allowed me to do it in my own way. Eventually she made me really cross.'

'And you behaved badly?'

'I'm afraid so. You see, she quite deliberately asked me; "What is, or was, the relationship between you and That Girl?" Just like that.'

'How very difficult for you.' Trina seemed highly amused.

'Not really. As I said, I'd have told her anyway, but there was no need to be brutal about it. It was her direct question. So, I told her the truth.'

'Oh no! What on earth did you say?'

'I said "That Girl", as you call her, has been my mistress for the last seven years.' Alan watched Trina, waiting for her reaction, but she gave no sign and kept looking at him steadily.

'As soon as I'd said it, I was sorry and annoyed with myself.'

'I can believe that.'

'I wonder? Can you? I was annoyed because what I'd said was unfair to you.'

'Oh, I don't know. It seems a reasonably accurate statement.'

'It's not. Well not the way I ever thought about you, and I told Marcia so.'

'I don't follow. What did you say?'

'I told her it wasn't true, and that you were never my Mistress. By this stage Marcia was looking bewildered...'

Trina interrupted.

'I don't blame her. I don't know what you were getting at either.'

'Don't you? You should. Don't you remember what I often called you?'

Trina shook her head.

'You called me so many things.'

'Well, anyhow, what I told Marcia was this: I said; Trina is and always will be her own mistress. She was "ma belle amie", which not only sounds nicer but is technically more accurate.'

Trina pursed her lips and nodded fractionally.

'I'll accept that,' she agreed. 'I never reject flattery, as you well know.' She gave Alan one of her quirky smiles, then added, with a deliberate sigh;

'Oh dear, you went all lofty on her. You're right Alan, you're not nice when you behave like that, and I shouldn't be feeling pleased that you did. Does that make me not nice too?'

'Yes, in a very nice way.'

'What did Marcia do after you told her that?'

'What do you think? She gave me the cold, silent treatment.'

'Serves you right.'

'At least it was easier to handle than the interrogation. No! I must stop saying these things. I'm not being fair to Marcia now. The plain truth is that she's a very lovely girl, and it was entirely my fault. If I'd really wanted to I could have handled the situation and kept her happy. If I'd been so wrapped up in her, as I should have been, that seeing you meant nothing to me, she would have sensed that. Instead it worked the other way. She must have seen something in the way I looked at you. Yes, if I'd wanted to I could have kept her happy; I understand that now, but at the time I didn't fully realize why or what I was doing.'

'Did she break the engagement that night?'

'No, Marcia went back to Bingley, that's where she lived, and wrote breaking it off after she got home.'

'What did she say?' Before Alan could answer Trina stopped him.

'I'm sorry, now I'm prying. I'm worse than she was. Marcia was justified, and mine is idle curiosity.'

'You're right; about Marcia being justified, but it's not quite the same is it? The atmosphere's different. There's no mistrust between us.'

Trina had turned her head and was gazing, distantly, through the window. 'No,' she said softly. 'That's something which never came between us.'

Alan studied her profile and thought;

"There's no need to rush things.' They had been near before. They had been even closer than near. There had been a time when there had been no shadow. The hours together in the hospital allowed them to feel their way slowly, letting their confidence grow. There was more than Alan's body that needed to be healed. They had so much to talk about, and so much to learn. Trina had to know how Alan came to leave the brewery and start his own travel business.

He explained.

'I tried to boost the occupancy level of the rooms in the brewery's hotels. I came up with the idea of organizing cheap package tours by train and coach. Remember, there was still petrol rationing at that time. Individuals, or groups, could travel independently and each client would have an itinerary specially prepared. Tickets were prepaid; and each tour had a suggested list of things to do and places to see, with pamphlets and discount vouchers from places en route. I had the whole thing worked out; and without going into detail, my idea was based on the post-war currency restrictions that just about stopped overseas travel. People were more or less forced to holiday within the UK.'

'Were you trying to do this through the brewery?'

'Of course. Again I won't go into all the mechanics, but the idea was for hotel reception desks to handle it. I'd devised a simple kit showing about a dozen tours, also a map from which clients could select areas they wanted to visit. Everything would be confirmed by telex between the hotels and Reading. My idea was to use accommodation in brewery hotels as much as possible. Anyway, it came to nothing, as they wouldn't let me go ahead.'

'Why not?'

'Oh, they liked the basic plan, but didn't see themselves as tour operators. As far as they were concerned, the bar side was where their profit came from, and they only wanted me to maintain reasonable food and room standards. I realized that they didn't really care whether rooms were occupied or empty, provided bar sales were steady. I had done so much work on the scheme that, when the Board rejected it, I couldn't just shrug my shoulders and walk away. I decided to take a chance and go into the business myself.'

'I gather it worked. My curiosity got the better of me, and I checked with Oceanic Travel's London office while you were unconscious. They told me you were Travel Time Tours. I'd seen the name on our booking sheets, but of course I didn't know that you owned it.'

'How could you? I only dealt with your Cockspur Street office. Yes, when I started it was really hard, especially the basic organization and making the hundreds of contacts. Then, overnight almost, everything took off and the business was expanding so fast I could barely cope. When currency restrictions were eased, I went into the overseas side.'

'It must have been exciting. I wish I'd been with you.' Impulsively, Trina reached out for Alan's hand.

'I'd have liked that,' he said. 'I worked long hours because I had to. I needed to make a success of something. I had the feeling that everything I'd tried, or wanted, had failed. I used work as a drug. The fact that I wanted to think of nothing else made success certain.'

This conversation took place on the first day that Alan had been allowed out of bed for more than a few minutes, and he still could not use his legs. The broken ribs made crutches too painful, and he had been taken in a wheelchair to sit by the window. Trina sat beside him and their hands rested together on the arm of his chair.

There was one thing they still had to talk about. The time felt right, and Alan asked the question he should have asked years previously.

'What the hell happened while I was on that trip to Malta? Or, rather, why did it happen?' Trina's hand moved fractionally.

'Yes, we've got to talk about that. It just won't go away, will it?' It was easier not to look at each other, and they sat, side by side, looking straight ahead. Alan tried to find the right words.

'Until then, I believed there was nothing that we couldn't sort out together, but this was something we never tried to face.'

'No, perhaps we were afraid of losing what we had left,' Trina said.

'What we had left was nothing compared with what we'd lost,' he replied. Trina took up the theme.

'I'm not sure we ever did lose each other. Perhaps we only thought we had. We never had a chance to talk... That is, not until you came back after the sinking of Ocean Monarch.' Her hand tightened on Alan's.

'You keep doing it, don't you? Three times now I've thought that...'

Trina did not finish the sentence, but Alan kept quiet. He was sure she had more to say, and when Trina spoke again, she said;

'I think I'd have been happier if you'd got mad and told me to go to hell, at least I'd have known I really meant something to you. You didn't seem to care all that much.'

'God, did you honestly think that?'

'Of course I did. What else was I to think? I'd have sent you away if you hadn't looked so thin and haunted. When you stepped off that train I could hardly believe it was you.'

Trina's words brought back vivid memories. Trina standing there, her face white and tense, and the little confidence he still retained oozing out of him as he walked towards her. He had felt sick with apprehension and had forced himself to smile, to say hello and to kiss her.

He glanced sideways at Trina who was now silent beside him; and Alan knew that it must be his turn to talk again, to take them a step further on their journey through the past. He returned the pressure of her hand, and said;

'I'd had too much time to think. At first I wanted to lash out and hurt someone, even you.'

'Why didn't you?'

'It's funny how fresh and clear everything is. Do you know, when I was less than half conscious in the sea after the plane crash, I became all mixed up and thought, or dreamt, I was back adrift in the lifeboat. I experienced it all over again, almost day by day. I used to escape from the monotony by thinking of you, of us, everything we'd done together. There were times in that boat when I wasn't sure that I wanted to be rescued. There was so much time to think, and I discovered that all our talk about personal freedoms and recognizing each other's liberty meant little. Everything we'd talked about so glibly had become, for me, just so much rubbish. What you had done hurt, and hurt badly.'

Alan felt Trina shift slightly in her chair, but he did not look at her.

'I know,' she said. 'I was hurt too.'

Now that Alan had started, he had to finish what he must say.

'When I got back, after being rescued from the boat, I couldn't come to terms with myself. I was weak, mentally and physically. I had no confidence. In that lifeboat I came to realize that it's difficult for a man to tolerate free love for both sexes: that is when it touches himself, and the woman he loves is involved. Even if there's no immediate thought of children, he feels insecure. However unfair, he wishes to deny the woman the liberty he may take himself. It isn't just selfishness, or I don't think it is. It's more instinctive, more basic, more than a crude sex drive. He's at a disadvantage if he fears infidelity. A woman knows that a child is hers. A man is vulnerable, uncertain. I know, it's emotion blowing logic out of the door; but I had to be honest with myself and admit that, for me, emotion was going to win. Perhaps in a different social context, with other customs and conditioning, it might be possible to accept.'

'Why didn't you tell me all this at the time?'

Trina's voice was so soft Alan could only just make out the words.

'Tell you?... I was too stubborn to admit that I couldn't live up to the code we claimed to believe, and I'd no right to expect otherwise from you. I can tell you now, though I didn't at the time because it was also within our concept, but I'd taken advantage of the freedom we advocated. One time that meant nothing to me, nor to the girl, halted me if I ever thought of blaming you.'

'Where did it happen?'

'In Durban, far enough away from you, and at the time I never thought it could be a threat to us. It was almost innocent. Her husband had been killed in battle, and she was trying to get over it. That night she had a need and I happened to be there. I'm explaining, not excusing; but now that I'm exposing myself I must do it completely, so that you, too, can take everything into account.'

'I think I see what you're getting at Alan, and I don't think it's important, but thanks.'

'What was I saying before I digressed? That I was too stubborn to admit my jealousy. Well, that's what it was. I was afraid I'd lose you if I probed too deeply, and so did my best to act as if what had happened was of no importance. It seems I succeeded too well, and you thought I didn't care. Didn't care! All the time I wanted to scream at you - Why the hell did you do it?'

This time Alan did turn and look at Trina, but she did not respond and he repeated quietly;

'Why the hell did you do it?'

Still she did not answer, and Alan could see that Trina was thinking, wondering how to say whatever it was she had to say. He waited as patiently as he could.

'"The cruelest lies are often told in silence."' For an instant a wan smile came to Trina's lips as she added; 'Robert Louis Stevenson,' before relapsing into thought.

'You had rejected me,' she said at last. 'I felt inadequate and wanted reassurance. At least, I hope it was that. Perhaps I just wanted revenge. The whole evening seemed like a nightmare; and even the attack on the wharf was unreal, like something out of a horror story. *She paused briefly, then continued.*

'I got back to Troon; there was a man there, Peter. Sometimes I'd gone down to the pub with him for a few drinks. He'd been chasing me for months. The day after I got back from Glasgow I went out with him, and on the way back from the pub he stopped his car and tried again.'

Trina's voice was now so quiet that Alan had to strain to catch the words.

'I didn't stop him. It didn't seem to matter. Afterwards I knew that it did, but it was too late. I hated myself, but it seemed silly to refuse him after that. The only way I could end it was by getting myself posted from Troon.'

'Trina, I never rejected you.'

'I know that now, but at the time I was sure you had. It would have hurt less if you'd slapped me in the face. I knew you were going away, and I was sure you'd be killed. That night in the ship... I discovered that, deep down, I'm not civilized. I was being driven from inside. I was a wild, primitive thing with an uncontrollable urge to mate before I lost you: I can't explain my behavior any other way. I could have killed you when you refused me. You were so bloody righteous. I felt contempt for you. You wouldn't take what I was offering, and I couldn't tell you that it was possibly the last chance you'd ever have of making love to a woman.'

Trina's voice changed, dropping the harshness that had crept into it. 'Oh Alan, I wanted you so much that night. I wanted to give and give; and I didn't want anything to come between us, and I just couldn't make you understand.'

'Did I seem bloody righteous?'

Trina nodded.

'I didn't feel bloody righteous. Scared and sorry for myself more like. I wanted it to be a wonderful last evening together, and everything was going wrong. I couldn't carry it off. It was all I could do to keep calm, to act, as I thought, naturally. I kept thinking, "This may be the last time I see her," and I wanted to say something memorable, but there was nothing I could say. When you wanted to take a chance I couldn't let you. I had a vision of you, pregnant and trapped. It never crossed my mind that you might be prepared to accept exactly that.'

'I don't know that I was prepared for that.' The sun had set soon after Alan had been taken to the window, and now they were enclosed in a gathering twilight. Trina's voice was hushed.

'I hadn't thought it through. It was some instinct driving me on, and I didn't allow myself to think.'

'Is it too late now for me to thank you, or your instinct if you prefer, for the offer?' Trina did not answer. Instead she said; 'Can you forgive me for what happened afterwards?'

'Forgive? I don't like that word. When there's understanding there's nothing to forgive. I can't forget either. I won't pretend to that impossibility. I was hurt at the time, and it still hurts. The difference is that I don't resent it now.'

'I think I'm glad that it still hurts. Does that sound a nasty thing to say?'

'Not when you say it like that. It would only be nasty if you were saying it spitefully.' Something stirred in Alan's memory, and he quoted;

' "If two lives join, there is oft a scar, They are one and one with a shadowy third." ' Trina smiled.

'You quoted Robert Browning to me once before, remember? After I read your letter I turned up the quotation.' Alan was also smiling.

'I believe we've let in the light and dispersed our shadow.'

There was a long silence as Trina gazed through the window.

Finally she turned and studied him carefully. In the soft light of dusk it seemed to Alan that she was seventeen again, and there was a shyness in her eyes that he had not seen since the day when he first hinted that they become lovers.

'Do you really think we can be one and one again, without the shadow?' she whispered. Alan felt a sudden surge of emotion, and it needed an effort to control his voice as he replied;

'One could try.'

FARRAGO

Snatches by

Huw Evans

MISTRESS

Bring her from the cornfield
and bring her from the town:
Bring her, sparkling silver,
in strange translucent gown.
Her hair a wreath of roses:
her tongue a jewel rare,
and eyes twin topaz crystals
with wanton, wayward stare.
In torment see her wander,
her cruelty accuse:
yet hungering to touch her
and brush the hem of Muse.

Revised to August 1999

POEMS

FOR

ALISON

AUTUMN

For Alison my love is sure
past Seasons are at rest:
memories dimmed with no regrets
and all is found the best.

INSIGHT

I will love you all my days.
Your charm, your odd enchanting ways
will hold me in your bond.

There was a moment when I knew
my heart completely lost to you;
one instant swiftly sure.

Just you, a radiance, startling bright;
To me your smile was made of light
and nothing else remained.

I know that there were others there
because I grudged that they should share
your beauty, such my love.

Though we had never talked alone
I had to claim you for my own,
temptation sweetly met.

BODY LANGUAGE

A gentle touch, a warm caress
and searching fingers meet.
A look exchanged, a smile that's shared,
a message passed, complete.

No false coy act, no prudish shame
for flesh, is flesh, is flesh,
and light of love with ageless glow
is fresh, is fresh, is fresh.

"There is a certain kind of woman who, the first time that you see her, in some way bruises your heart"

(A fragment recalled from a book once read.)

TENDER BRUISE

You, who I love and always love,
may hold me free, yet so confined
I stay in willing ferment here,
seeking to test the touch which brings
my flesh and senses wide aware
that all must mingle, or depart.

Still is my secret dream, within
a restless shiver of delight,
the tender bruise of love recalled
with wonder for the coming days

Your loving gifts my life fulfill.
Apart, you make my ardor crave:
your presence complements my self
and future you defines my way.

LOVE-MAKING

Love - is love unconfined,
always new, always fresh
when in tune with your mind,
making melodies with your flesh.

SIMILE

To think of you is love
where all else fades, and all is one.

The power of love o'erwhelms
and vanquishes coherent thought
as waves, which flood the sand,
possess it first, then wipe it clean.

FEVER

. . . . . . .nor custom stale
Her infinite variety. . . . .

Anthony and Cleopatra,- Shakespeare

What say you Sir`? You ask have I the ague?
You'll find no ague and yet, in truth, it's fever.
A precious fever, nurtured in my heart,
clutched close to me and held in fond embrace.
You think me mad to cherish such an ill?
I care not. Call it madness if you will.
Yet `tis profane to say that love is mad
on all this earth it is the one thing sane.
How say you Sir? Bewitched by a wench?
Your pardon Sir, no wench nor yet bewitched.
Bewitched pertains to witch and which is which,
and so bemused, bewildered and befuddled.
Whilst I with clarity see beauty rare.
I'll damn your wench! Mine is a lady fair.
A creature finely wrought from precious jewels
with crystal soul and ruby for her heart.
A form divine and full of flowing grace,
stars for her eyes and honesty her face.
The sea is in her hair with all its waves.
Her lips with lurking smile are warmly soft,
and velvet tongue for murmuring words of love.
Her neck a beauteous chamber for her voice.
That liquid music, gentle to my ear
floats on her breath with purest fragrance clear.
Her breasts, exciting semi-spheres of joy,
perfect apart, and yet in twin perfection.
Each with its crown of glowing pink,
which I caress and make to stand erect.
With such strange beauty can there be a flaw?
Yet, see a scar that creeps toward her breast
reminding me of courage, pain endured.

And see! Another scar is here upon her back.
Is this a blemish? Does her beauty lack?
It is not so. That mark put there by fate
has special beauty. By its presence there
its contrast makes the rest more wondrous fair.
I kiss each stirring breast, then let my gaze
wander to that slim, enchanting waist
so tightly drawn against the curve of hips,
between which lies her stomach and her womb.
The first, a flowing line, surmounts the other,
the fruitful, sheltering chamber of a mother.
I feel the final, culminating mound
rise gently from her stomach, clad with hair,
soft to my touch, inviting more advance,
guide my hand between her parted thighs
searching the place where so much pleasure lies.
Her body makes a cushion for my joys.
Then captured, bliss alone remains;
and I lie there between those shapely legs
clutched lightly, gasping, sobbing for my breath.
You wonder that I love her 'till my death?
With pulse still pounding, kisses pour abandoned
until, relaxed, I steal away to sleep,
refreshed and glowing, soothed and sated.
No wonder that I worship every inch,
each fraction of her body and her self.
I tell you, Sir, that sickness is my life.
I'll keep it close, that fever, and my wife.

PHOENIX

Each act of love lives once,
alone and self fulfilled:
destroyed, in perfect bliss
a death, yet freely willed.
Within each passion's fire
a reborn love awakes
rekindling flames desire,
till death once more o'ertakes.

MISTRESS

Fair Mistress Alison,
beauteous Mistress mine,
my tender mistress
of sweet Venus' wine.
No bacchanalian cup,
though Bacchus self distilled,
could rend my senses lost
like cups that you have filled.
With Aphrodite's charms
to stir impassioned fire,
love's phoenix flame is burned
in each renewed desire.
No Siren's fateful song,
soft floating in the air,
can lure a heart long lost
to the fairest of the fair.

PLEA

When I forget
or fail to see
the moment where
a tender word,
packaged with love,
would give you ease;
remember then,
in love of you
I give my heart
gift wrapped in words
to plead my cause,
and tell my love.

INTERACTION

Dip your fingers in my pool
and see your likeness there
sent shimmering into fragments
as though beyond repair.

If you should stir those waters
and hidden depth distress,
a murk clad cloud, in anger,
may stain its gentleness.

So sit and wait in patience
until the waters still
and offer limpid languor,
convenient to your will.

I CAN NOT SPEAK

I can not speak for other men
Of how they love, or why or when.
I only know that in my life
My lasting love is for my wife.

In youth my loves were swift and strong
With many a maid who came along
To find herself, as if by chance
Encompassed by my amorous glance.

Sometimes, in passing, and with glee,
I'd find a soul completely free
who'd yield her body, sweetly kind,
a shapeliness for love designed.

At last there came the one whose charms
lingered when she left my arms.
The more she gave, the more my need
and from those charms I'll ne'er be freed.

REFLECTION

The way you look is far more dear to me
than was the way you looked when first we met.
For then your beauty blazed and stunned my mind,
which found its body seized in pounding joy.
Yet though your smile still holds me in its spell
and stirs my blood, my heart no longer faints.

But when you stand and look into your glass
and chide your face that it's no longer fair
I am amazed, for beauty's there to see.
The fleetest glance must tell you this is so.
Each tiny change in curve or line has been
soft sculpted by each year and passing scene.

For this I know, whatever else we'll share,
the radiance I have loved will still be there.

EVOCATION

If I should leave, my love,
And leaving, leave you lone,
know then a voice will echo
your name, in place unknown.
That secret void shall learn
the richness of your love,
and 'Alison' will be
an orison above;
a prayer of sweet delight
from my receding flame,

acknowledging the right

of love to know your name.

MOMENTS

(1) I hear your voice within your script
and feel your smile, your eager sparkled
eyes. In this brief span of penciled
lines I find you; posted stars
of distant past and see you then
not now. Imagination tries
and fails, projecting scenes of fancy.
The phone bell rings, and you are lost.

(2) My hand finds space and comes to know
through sleep drugged mind the place
that is not you. I wake with sense
of wrong to pillow punch the dregs
of sleep. Silence invades within
yet, outside, raindrops drown the day.
A finger's touch, the world intrudes:
the latest Pop and then the News.

(3) Persisting youth imprisoned here
in later days, hold back to seemly
pace lest discontentment rage;
for time is once, so small, so spare
and unrelenting. Universe
of speed, where slow hands feebly grasp
and I am gone before I knew.
Yet, wistful spark, hold dear my love.

(4) Cast off! The iron whale glides free
to freedom in the albatross
domain. Wheeling seagulls chase
with witches cry to tell the toll
of weed tombed bones. Their dread tales hush,
scurried on wind blown wings to banish
Friday's doom. Say; `First or Tourist?'
as bellied Jonahs find their caste.

(5) Walk you feet, walk the lively deck.
Let lubbers of the land sway wantonly
their hands beseeching urgent aid,
and clutch to hold the wayward way
which mocks their unsure stance, then heaves
to strike with upthrust stem. So creak
you Clyde side cow. Your ancient ribs
will bend and bow in wise assent.

(6) Windset spume hills swell the Bight
and salt tang blasts the desert decks,
while spew green wraiths release their guts
and feebly totter down below.
With golden hair unfettered, blown,
you stand alone, bewitched to watch
the albatross close belly hugged
glide, motionless, to skim the surge.

(7) Wind swept radiance turns in ploy
to find embrace as petals tempt
with nectar's sweet desire. Wild sense
scuds swiftly, oyster pearl displayed.
Sperm stirred want to Venus coiled
in baited beauty fairly trapped.
Seek each to each the quest to merge
and howl the winding tempest down.

(8) Chatter, clatter, bright lit bars,
glittered sweep of brazen gowns
reveled cups of shape alone;
as songstress sings unheeded songs
and boredom band plays on and on.
Tempted to the darkened deck
your stardust eyes outshine the night,
and pin fire heaven gives pale compare.

IMAGE

Your youthful beauty lives while I remain,
as every instant lives - in memory.
For what we see, ourselves alone create
and take into our private mystery.

Our bodies met and inward we explored
with careful touch, while searching mind sought mind
to seek the pictures we alone would paint;
each painting fixed, as by our thoughts defined.

The beauty I remember, you inspired:
a beauty no one else will ever see.
The memory I made is solely mine:
the you is you, and yet is part of me.

YEARNING

'Twas my belief
that grief
would ease,
and passing time
would heal
the weal
with balm to soothe,
and smooth,
the hurt.

But, evermore
encore
the sore.

THRENODY

Unsung my lines,
my fair designs
on brittle paper writ;
in yellow age
my love and rage
will crumble, bit by bit.

The songs I've sung,
the tears I've wrung
will soon be all forgot;
in darkling shade
to fade and fade
as though were ne'er begot.

I want that fame
should know your name,
bright words your charms to weave;
thus, beauty bring
in songs I sing
and make the world believe.

POEMS
FOR
OTHER
SEASONS

SPRING

Margot, newly minted, fresh and fair,
quietly composed with gentle ways,
shy smiling, brought me to her side.
Three weeks of finding, then to part.

We learned so much: so much unknown
and parting knew we needed more.
What we had learned was not enough
to take us into evermore.

SUMMER SEASON

My golden June, my summer girl
with sunny smile and heart,
so gaily honest and so fair,
you played an anguished part.

For, though we made no promises
and you did not complain,
I knew you wanted me to love;
and only brought you pain.

In freedom we made sweet embrace,
In words, we said: "No ties,"
but you had let me be your first
and love shone in your eyes.

So soon I met the one I love,
and was no longer free,
a love which took me far from you
and left you, loving me.

THE SEASON OF CONSTANCE 1938 - 1947

WINTER

Dear Constance of the wicked wit
when we were young, just seventeen,
we played the game of love and asked
of each no more. Expecting all
in all we shared, yet made no claims.

Nine years of tenderness we spent
while learning tolerance and love
in friendship, with no selfish thought.
We laughed a lot, and vainly laughed
in bitter times, sharing our fears
with understanding, words unsaid.
Such closeness thrust our ways apart,
we knew too much; and we became
just memories to both our pasts.

FADED LEAVES

We lay amid the tall grass
and heard its whispered song,
then slowly kissed, and slowly
made love to linger long.

Surrounded by the chatter
of woodland's ardent strife,
in soft concealing fastness
new love became our life.

We gave ourselves together
in Spring of urgent youth
and lay embraced to ponder
this new, ecstatic truth.

Though often joined in wonder
on flying wings of joy,
we lost that mad, mad rapture
which first held girl and boy.

Alas for tender wonder.
Alas for heavenly joy.
Alas for that mad rapture
and, alas for girl and boy.

NEW MOWN HAY

Fresh hay smell in the sweet of love
the senses compact truss to make,
and spread its aphrodisiac sap
scent sharpened at the time of age.
The knife edge sigh, the keening blade
takes fall to fall and cowherbs curl
all fragrant lived, as fragrance die;
a taste thread in a lilting breeze.
There breast to breast in swift spent flight
lie bound to earth. So instinct spreads,
with fluttered heart and fearful joy,
the pinioned wings now set to soar.

FREE LOVE

We fell in happy, untied love:
we loved each carefree day.
In pleasure let the time fly past
and laughed our love away.

The gaiety of that fresh love,
its tender, new found play
rejoiced our beating hearts, and yet
we laughed our love away.

We treated love so easily
and lightly trod our way
to greet, and part, with smiling words
that laughed our love away.

Two loves whose paths lie parallel
will never meet, they say;
though rueful minds across that gap
may laugh their love away.

We loved our freedom, fearing love
would fetter hearts so gay.
This humor left us free to roam
while laughing love away.

This languished love passed into shade.
With secret, sad dismay
we saw it slowly fade, and fade
yet, laughed that love away.

HUW EVANS

ADIEU MA BELLE, MA BELLE AMIE

Fare thee well.
Let thy welfare
be thine to tell
and mine to care.
For, though I leave
I pay my due.
I also grieve
at leaving you.

I gladly go,
yet sadly say
my joy is woe,
my sadness gay.
My tattered heart
divides in two,
and one small part
Remains with you.

I would I could,
but know I can't.
Perhaps I should.
You know I shan't.
I'll not forget
how could that be?
Past love is yet
a part of me.

Spare no sad tears
for love that's done.
Smile for those years
When we were one.
Smile for those years
beyond recall,
and brave our fears,
remembering all.

ECHO

Now your goodbye has been said. Shall I be glad
hearing an echo in time, whisper so sad?
Years have since drifted between. Long, long apart,
say that your days have been free, happy your heart.
Gone from my life through these years, why then return
sweet shrouded mist in my mind, faint to discern?
Left in the past, as a dream faded yet fair,
now that your spirit has fled why should I care?
Bitterness never despoiled: laughter we shared.
Smiling we made our farewell, knowing we cared.
Knowing we cared, yet we knew - care was our all;
love had long stolen away, heeding no call.

Tell me from out of the shade, tell me the truth.
Tell me, what was it we made, blindly, in youth?

FROM THE SHADE

Our love was made of passion's fire
illumined by desire:
joyful with the love of mind
Will o' the Wisp, undefined.
We added love of total care
allowed our souls to mingle, bare.
Then learnt to love within our grief
when love, itself, was made the thief.
We loved for days now long fled past;
those tender days that did not last
and, coming slowly, in the end
to find in love the love of friend.

We parted when our act was played,
Yet kissed and smiled!
That's what we made.

PICKING BLUE BELLS

For the blooms in the woods at Bushey
are a dim remembrance still,
where the snow in its cruel beauty
called our hearts with an icy chill.

For the old gallows hill where we frolicked
is now lost to the long dead past,
like some fabric of love worn and faded,
and left shrunken, and torn, and off cast.

For the summery days of your Maying
with the rich ripened lips to your womb,
rang the prelude which war left unfinished
and diminished its theme in the tomb.

For the world, as a world of undoing,
brings an echoing voice as it sighs.
So, so, soft is its whispering story
of a life it can never revise.

LOVE

SWEET COCOON

Vibrant warmth of sweet cocoon,
urgency in spate,
The fragile bond that dares to trust
and trusting needs to mate.

One self of two divided, shared,
Yet still apart made one.
A hot desire now jointly fused,
the life of love begun.

FACETS OF LOVE

Love that's flesh by touch and taste
exhilarating fond arm waist
caress by pain and stabbing dart
with osculating, tingling art.

Hard derisive cynic smile
feed lascivious lecher vile
eyeball bulging strip quite stark,
snidely sniggered coarse remark.

Coolly casual take and leave
airy-fairy words to weave
lightly taken lightly left,
love of love of love bereft.

Greenly grasping eyes aslant
hungry avaricious plant
grown within itself it feeds,
desire convinced of evil deeds.

Wearing tearing bearing sharing
tender storm tossed ever caring
fighting laughter smiling tear,
gladly given without fear.

BONDAGE

Love is a silken cord
which fetters heart and mind,
and bound in twisting coil
are pain and joy confined.

Each lover shapes his bonds
and love, to some, seems sure;
while others wayward flit
or tremble, insecure.

Faintness of heart may fear
and, fearful, turn within
lest naked self, exposed,
be punished for its sin.

Urgent where passions flow
and love is swift and strong,
all hell and hate may rage
yet be a heavenly song.

Bonded each lip may taste
and drink this nectar deep,
to live love's life alive
released from artless sleep.

DULCINEA BEREFT

The sparkle in those eyes
once more awakes his heart,
as Cupid's arrow flies
to tear his soul apart.

So let him now beware
of love's all sweet undoing,
that monstrous thieving care
demanding constant sueing.

His mind anaesthetizes
into ethereal pleading,
that never realizes
its hope of love succeeding.

So witless wander, careless
with thought and senses reeling,
a frozen waif, now fearless
emotions dead, unfeeling.

A PERFECT DREAM

(Chopin Etude Opus 10 No.3)

I once made a dream,
a perfect dream,
but now I see
my daydream was in vain;
and in my heart
songs I cared for, love I dared for
haunt me -----
and I feel all their pain.

* Such was my dream,
a perfect dream,
that left me here
with passion's lonely care,
to find my life
torn and tattered, worn and battered,
love has shattered all that mattered
so I do not, and I will not dare
to hope again,
for it was my dream.
Yes it was my dream

* Music restates the mood returning to opening melody at *. Repeat verse and end with:

a perfect dream,

    a perfect dream,

        a perfect dream.

SONGS SUNG

IN

FAERIELAND

I

WHEN THE QUEEN WALKS

'Tis magick self distilled
where love walks softly sighing,
its cobweb touch fulfilled.
So wildflower footfalls lead,
with murmured breeze soft crying
'Fair mistress come. Take heed.'

II

SEA QUEEN

You shall be the feet that float
and I shall be the sea.
There all the barks of heav'n shall sail
round you and over me.
For we shall brew a gentle storm
The barks will dance with glee
and all together make free form
in glorious ecstasy.

III

FEY QUEEN

Like thistledown her hair flies free
when standing on the crest
of smooth Brown Willy's sculptured scree,
and dreaming of the West.
There daylight ends and night is cool
gold sunlight bathes her head,
while shadowed down Dozmary pool
takes Arthur's sword to bed.

IV

DESERT QUEEN

Mysterious She among the dunes
with close wrapped head held low,
where shifting sands sing whistling tunes
and wavelike march is slow.
Her tread is light, her eyes are dark,
her slender hands are brown,
but instinct sees the hidden mark
Of beauty in that gown.

V

GODDESS QUEEN

Sweet fair of Aphrodite's foam
caressed within the waves,
esteemed in ancient Greece and Rome
where men were all her slaves.
Bikini clad now sunlit slim
on many, many a beach,
that slender nymph with anxious him
will tantalize and teach.
For though it seems all is displayed
fine contradictions weave
and he is left in doubt, dismayed,
to love or laugh or grieve.

VI

ELUSIVE QUEEN

I wander through the woodlands
And you are everywhere
Flitting, flirting, laughing;
a Faerie quean all fair.
I try in vain to catch you,
But when I stand quite still
You float into my aching arms
All fragrant to my will

VII

REMEMBERED QUEEN

This Faerie grows not old
she lives within my mind,
and youthful laughter echoes
a sound with joy defined.
In soft, sad, haunting vision
she turns and smiles to me,
for she, my sweet, fond shadow
lives on in memory.

WAR

RHONDDA

Sliding down a coal tip
on bent and battered tray:
fondling tunes of streamlets
in idle summer's day:
climbing to the hilltop
a kingdom far surveyed
there touch the brushing cloud drifts,
and truth of trembling maid.

Gathered with companions
we set the world to rights,
as winding lanes we wandered
in eve of starlit nights.

Where are those companions
and where that trembling maid?
Long lost those mystic summers
when we were unafraid.

Shot and shell have tolled them
the rest are turning grey,
a few just can't remember.
And I? I dream today.

MEDITERRANEAN CONVOY 1943

Ten ships, all wrapped with sparkling sea:
ten planes to speck a cloudless sky:
ten thousand men who fear and wait
amid this beauty, and this hate.

A day of crystal sun-washed blue:
a day when air is born anew:
a day of sudden fear and death
with tortured, pain filled, final breath.

Many men about to die
in the sea, and in the sky.
Each life, an ebbing ripple, flows
to distant hearts, and anguish grows.

Cry out the hell of this despair:
the wanton pain which we must share.
Cry out the rage of futile shame
for lives whose promise never came.

THE LIGHTS WENT OUT OVER EUROPE

Ours the youth that lost its name
Ours the youth that lived with shame
Ours the youth that flaunted fate
Ours the youth that dared not wait

Ours the day so short of time
Ours the day to mask and mime
Ours the day when fear was rife
Ours the day of frantic life

Ours the age of War's mad deed
Ours the age of life in need
Ours the age of wide-eyed grief
Ours the age of disbelief

Youth's day, youth's age, youth's essence fled
While Virtue slept in venal bed

HONOUR ROLL

(1)
Silence in the corridors where floorboards of the past
are worn, and hard wood knots stand proud to trip the feet.
Time, with careless student steps should change, and yet
they seem the same. Green baize, the boards are faded still
and team lists; 'All boys will . . .', the orders from a bygone
term remain; new names. Footsteps, echoing in vacant
cloisters, still recall the rush of slippered feet
to beat that breakfast deadline slam of doors.
Tradition bound, with time built laws, your ghostly rites
accuse that step beyond the bounds. My feet now crunch
the once forbidden path, and feel the guilt of wrong.
Across the Quad a lone slow gardener works at ease.

(2)
A wrought iron ring, metallic clunk of latch upraised
as soft hinge moan protests the parting swing of oak;
a dozen inches suffering entrance. Stained glass gloom
my eyes, sun dazzled, wait to see. There sat I,
there Fred, there Jim, with swell of voices broken, breaking
or still unbroken . . . Practicing toccata, fugue,
Freddie D. Mus. his fixed intent. And at the west
new boards beside the old: too many names, and names
with faces snap through memory, alpha and omega, ranged
in ordered care. Service awards and rank assembled:
such pride, such duty. Matched to the old their timber
still not dark with age; and Freddie - killed Italy - no D. Mus.

(3)
John de ffoulkes, with virgin thought you called 'Right Thing',
you white, you snow white knight of purposeful perfection
spurred to action. Oh yes, your drilled beliefs compelled
attainment; visioned in amour bright, blinkered to duty
and born to bear its burden. Empire's potent builder,
fair, impartial, ruling some far flung corner,
prideful to hold the legion's eagle, remote, remorseless

fixed intent. You and I, Freddie and James,
poles apart in thought, conditioned to conformity
and bonded by our circumstance. Your Biggles truth
a flaming fireball in the Dunkirk sky. Good show!

(4)
A shock of stiff and startled hair, your left arm stump
malformed at birth; handless yet vicious in the maul.
'Latbrush' Jim, we said; a latrine nickname hung
about your head. Then were the years when you and I
moved from team to team, Junior to First, the Rugby
field a special place where we could sense each other,
instinctive to react as fortune fared. Allied
in minor lawlessness. The summer's tall grown grass
hid nicotined indulgence; or boastful, furtive drinks
in back room bar. Carved in wood, sans serif,
I find your name. Far better if they cut: `Latbrush -
At sea - 1941 - The North Atlantic'.

HUW EVANS

CHRONICLE

You run in the light, where skyscraper blind
lie skeletal bones of all that is ruin,
and dust of the ages gathered by wind
is blowing as cloud heads, now smothered in dark
and scouring for secrets, but secrets are lost.
Cracked concrete decaying beneath its own weight
that atom by atom is loosened to change,
and building the tell of a far distant age.

So one foot and one foot with this you must run,
and ever, for ever within the same place
where background is moving but static the screen
and light speed is flash at the end of your days.

LIMITED WAR

The harsh cacophony of war's mad drum
discordant mutterings of maniac Mars:
crumbled and reproachful broken walls;
naked and defoliated trees
are ravaged, all around is waste. Creation
dead, sterility supreme, the grievous
heartbreak of a home in flames where each
charred ember of a piteous village tells
unnumbered tears.

HOLOCAUST

In land of silent sadness
hope for hope long gone
it is a quiet thing.
No drama tends its act.
Mere wanton agony
of emptied souls drained dry
commands no instant glamour
in worldly, strident ways.

The private cry of loss,
with inward hell and tears,
so tells of injured hearts
with individual pain,
and shows a still, stark self
of lonely, aching wounds
concealed within the terms
of brief communiqués.

Let instinct swift compassion
comprehend, and so,
with quickened understanding
ease these festering sores.
Although we fail, it helps
if we can show some care.

ARMAGEDDON

The night is dark
with darkness made of fear.
Why then stand I
who dread the call so near?
What is the mist,
the mist that shrouds my mind;
a fell deep mist
of cruelty refined?

Beyond is far
where all unknown does dwell.
Unknown, not known,
and so can not foretell.
The lost are lost,
and never shall regain
creation's pulse.
Their cry, their end, is vain.

THOUGHTS

HERAKLEITOS

The soaring sun has one recurring theme
yet every day must paint a different sky,
and what men lose they never can regain
nor step once more into the self same stream.

A petalled rose spreads fragrance in the air:
each blade of grass has individual sheen:
the static moment melts, to disappear,
and instant river fleets, no longer there.

This play of life is prompted every day:
each curtain rise is on a changing scene
and love, if hurt, can never be the same.
The stream, once touched, has fled too far away.

RAINFOREST

Arcing branches dapple black to sky,
leaf shine gleam: within a shade lit noon
unseen hustle of all death corrupts.
The past, a present food for future days
in turn to feed until the end is null.
The twist of life recycling its decay
as urgent sap tide flood spurts ever new.
The misted breath of rain no ebb foretold
to ancient dense of forest, tall, serene,
plucked screaming and destroyed. The log of time
to be unlogged, until the old ring breaks
and brings its breaker unexpected doom.

CHALLENGE

Leaves rustling brown lie underfoot
and softly kiss the springing heel,
as cushioned to the mould of age
upon the rim of nature's wheel.

Time paces through this pillared nave
where trees hang guardian over death,
and hush the day of reborn birth
which soughs its lay with stifled breath.

Beyond the cloistered woodland's bound
a myth of sentient, restless mind
creates, destroys, creates again.
Its means, its motives undefined.

So cry aloud to endless time;
'The next is last. The end be done.'
Yet seek the peak no man may climb
for one fight, still, remains unwon.

ENCORE

The sixth day it was mystery complete,
delivered wrapped. Unseen yet fragile thought
which curiously required that it enact
its part: an innocence unto the seeds
of malcontented quest, with thoughts misled
to fixed belief. See now how evil Cain,
progenitor incarnate of all force,
with greed of will unwraps the pack and tears
the foil of shining candor. Lustily
he grasps the powerful weapon of untruth,
that siren temptress of a despot's rule
the callous scepter of intolerance.
Contempt discards the age of gentleness
and rips the magic onion to its heart
as layer by layer, an ever shrinking orb,
it seeks within the genie's final strength
to loose at last the latent, mutant gene.
And so revolve to find that once first day,
the trickery of time to end all time;
here torn in rage, unveiled to show its empty
soul. Tell Ariel he's free to fly
the prison pine, and drift at careless will
inside that mystery from whence he came.

EGYPT - LA PLAGE DES ENFANTS

Crescent shaped to limpid sea,
edge to brothel bounded nest,
suntanned bronze oil supple curves
entice with wary eyes. Adonis
beds, but Mammon's wealth secures.
Enfants du soleil et rapacité,
plage des enfants sans enfants:
shrill of childish pipe decayed,
the sickened taste of crushed ice sweetness.
Service hastes as bare feet pad
and brush against the time worn sand:
the dying granules of a grander past.

VIVE LA DIFFERENCE

Intelligence! The human gift
that sets the race apart.
Precocious claim, precarious stance,
the head to rule the heart.

For what is reason to discern
when logic leads the way?
Its icy judgment coldly rules
to fix the price we pay.

The warm unreason of the heart,
with gentle kindness, shows
more claim to man's humanity
than logic ever knows.

A CASTALIAN PRAYER

In my hands and from my mind
Κασταλια
Give me words that I may find
a truth to tell to all mankind,
a little light to help the blind,
Κασταλια.

THE BREATHLESS HOUR

Hush now,
This haunting evening holds its breath.

Hold still,
the world unmoved in darkening shade.

No sound,
a waiting time here all suspended.

Soft air,
so liquid and with shadows hung.

All calm,
yet dreadly solemn, dimly grave.

An end,
ask 'where has all vibration gone?'

MICROCOSM

Life, the unbounded speck,
remote, forbidden thought,
heedless of itself,
unknown with understanding
claims its mortal tribute.

Relentless death dissolves
then seeks its empty place,
now filled with vacancy;
and takes its patterned coil
in store to secret day.

Then, of itself alone,
yet with that self made whole,
one strand of total care
may bind the cosmos down.

TOTALITOCRACY

Lost mortals suffer swift contempt
in bureaucrat decree
its rigid face, in paper wrapped,
scorns frail humanity.

The servant wields his master's power
subjected to his will,
for power makes master, and its strength
must dominance fulfill.

Computered to conformity
the jigsaw pieces bind
and system rules, while fearing still
the independent mind.

Then fear holds terror in its arms
and fear takes force to bed,
where fear and force breed slavery
with terror breeding dread.

Slow step by bureaucratic step
its python coils confine
and tendered options are but two;
to die, or be resigned.

UNREST

In springtime flood the youthful mind
flows free, forever questing;
searching, seeking, tearing down,
experimenting, testing.
White is white and black is black!
convincingly this truth
permits no motley shades of grey
to cloud the minds of youth.

In Shakespeare's day age counted less
and many, in their teens,
were known as men, and lived as men
in many daring scenes.
Reputation brought reward:
success produced a breed
of men, not qualified by age,
but qualified to lead.

Experience too, may play its role,
experience gained with age,
experience learned in part, perhaps
in youthful, ardent rage.
Yet age seems fated to forget
that ideas gained in youth
time has made rigid in its mind,
all else is false, uncouth.

In sadness then, youth's bright ideals
can tarnish as they age.
Best leave them to their heritance,
a world upon whose stage
the actors mime their own small parts
regardless of the play,
and even if they try, and fail,
the next may find a way.

ODDMENTS

JOY

I'll dance to the wind and say I am free
to cling to the clouds, and the sky, and the sea;
and laugh while I float there in fanciful style
with feelings enchanted and loves which beguile:
new music to hear and songs to be sung,
fresh words to be spoken and rhymes to be rung,
sweet lips to be savored with gentle caress;
the more to be taken, but never the less

SUBWAY

In cold snow day of winter's slushing feet
with side piled mounds dark stained and rotting wet,
make haste. Then deeply plunge to mole like train;
leave dusky dark and jostling light regain
where urgent shuffling shoes commuters fret.
Warm air, interred, is stale on buried street.

So swaying touch with vacant gaze to stare:
shell-self, recoiling, fears the antlike press.
The electric worm gives soft pneumatic hiss
and then bores on, to take and to dismiss.
Discarded, climb the concrete wilderness
to bright cold night, and diamonds in the air.

OPIATE?

(Quae sursum sunt quaerite)

No man seeks a sad sack cloud
wet weeping from a myriad pores.
No man joys a tear sprung ache
with empty heart and timeless hours.

No man calls for packaged pain
presented at his mortal door,
and no man cares to dream an end
of nothing, nothing, evermore.

BUTTERFLY

Gossamer chased to a verbal shape.

As a brush stroke seeks uncatchable color.
Thought, that is elephant in the street
laughable monster of words.
A green swathed
drama of sea spun light, where drowned men
find that their minds are dead.

In the distant
rumble and tumble and ringing of bells
where each false note is heard, and clattered
discord reigns, the stretch of voice is
lost, unknown, unclad: a king's new
clothes, and visible only to fancy.

There it is found. In its own sweet truth.

ALLOY

And from the ever distant sleep
those wild web echoes take a sound
within my head, and plant it fresh,
to tease and torment into life
a thread of thought.
So great intent
will make belief a fact and build,
swift brick by brick, some fancy's wall
into a house, or ivory tower,
where ego seeks a wisdom's due
and curious untried truth is told
which, tested, leaves a dish of dregs.

MANSION

There is a place, a public place
wherein I walk and show my face
that all may see, and, as they see,
say: 'Such a man as that is he'.

Another place, another life
shared with one who is my wife.
For that delightful, lovely she
the face I show is nearly me.

There is a chamber in my head
where falsehood fades and shams are shed,
and naked thoughts are almost free
to know myself with honesty.

Yet still there is a final room;
a room of doubt, a room of gloom
in which I shut with lock and key
the me I do not dare to be.

CHEATED MEMOIR

Touched by the poem's words,
in measured tread it grew;
a knowing in my mind,
swift, clear and true.
Yet full as knowledge built
I knew, I knew it not;
how and when and where,
or was it not forgot?
And so my mind grasped, fierce
this sudden truth to hold.
Yet, even as it caught,
thought slipped the fold.

WHILOM

When autumn holds with its golden glow
the fat full ripeness of summer days,
then I hear and I walk in another time
with a bygone love, playing bygone plays.

When thunder speaks like a distant war
with gun flash flickers in darkened sky,
then I hear and I walk in another time,
and I weep for the dead who have passed me by.

When organ notes from a nearby church
float, softly flattened, through sunlit dust
then I hear, and I walk, in another time
as a child untouched by a worldly lust.

When snatch of song, or a scented air
half heeded, wanders in mesh of mind
then I hear, and I walk, in another time
with a memory sprung as by chance defined.

A WISP OF TIME

Conscious I am me
chary of violation,
the individual self
lost and left to stray
in forests of proven facts.

Ex conscious I expand
a universal fragment,
in part the living whole
to search within and glimpse
creation's total love.

Pure love will bear no hates
nor seek and suffer pains,
for love the thought creates,
and love, at last, remains.

MIRROR, MIRROR

You do nothing but reflect
and there is nothing you reject,
but everything that passes by
you capture with your silver eye.

So much time, just to reflect,
it's only right we should expect
that both philosopher and fool
should gain great wisdom from your pool.

Never do you say a word;
our pleas with brittle deafness heard.
The only truth which lies in you
is what we see from our own view.

This your wisdom? This your truth
to tell the tale of passing youth,
to show the self ourselves have made
and watch us grow, and watch us fade?

HEDONIC MYSTERY

Penelope her web would weave,
her fingers wove the song.
but no test of her work took leave
to sift the right from wrong.

So who can sing the lilting air,
or who recall the rhyme
which speaks of pleasures, banished care
around the ring of time?

Within this weft and warp she hid
the ecstasy which cloys
bewildered minds, to make them bid
for sweet forbidden joys.

The Sirens loosed this magic spell,
and he who heard believed
but, true or false, we cannot tell.
The truth, her shroud received.

FORESHORE AT NIGHT

Indigo is sky backed inky hills
behind a viscous ebb, beyond a tamarind
fringe watered in bushy black. A spread
of rippled sheen towards a shining platter,
night's full compassed circle mote of man's
emotions quick to fear the unknown deep
of darkness, shows the shaded bright of night
and mocks the light of day. Poor loon of romance,
witchcraft's lamp to superstitious dread,
your cold reflected flame takes hard injustice
with disdain, and beauty's scornful eye
rejects the follies counted to your blame.

NOCTURNAL

Shadows beyond
a pool splash of light:
shadows that walk
through an endless night:
shadows of sex
with a sexless shape:
shadows all seeking
the shadowed escape.

The world of the old
and the world of the young:
the world of the dead
or the newly begun:
the world of the frightened
trapped by their fear:
the world which is far
but yet terribly near.

The shelter of shade
where the wounded can hide:
the shelter from truth
for tormented pride:
the shelter of dark
in the backyard of streets:
the shelter for hiding
away from defeats.

The city's side alleys
where care counts the cost:
the city's trains rumble
disturbing the lost:
the city's marred bodies
the wraiths of the night:
the city's unwanted
who vanish in light.

The shadows of menace;
the shadows of crime;
the shadows bewildered;
the shadows of grime;
the shadows forgetting
the shadows of name:
the shadows of those in
the shadows of shame.

TENEMENT

The concrete abstract stabs into the sky
to dominate with paralleled infinity,
impersonally punctuated
patterns suck the workers in
and out, neutered by that cold simplicity.

A girl stands crucified against a window,
the old man below waters a daffodil.

GIRL AT THE WINDOW

From my window
on the twenty-second floor
I see the birds fly by:
tousled wool strands, passing
swiftly overhead
upon the blue high sky,
hold my being
with imagination's wings.
'Now free my soul!' I cry.
Concrete canyons form
a prison of despair
to crush my hope. - Why try?

OLD MAN'S DAFFODIL

The parchment skin shows spot stained age;
Slow, wary move with fragile bones;
and watering eyes to see past shades
while memory lives for youth long gone.

The mirror's truth - Narcissus pain.
This top floor room an unloved tomb,
not here nor there in twist of time
but just a place where end must come.

A golden plant of Narcissus' kin
grows proudly, bearing beauty's fame,
its petals splayed to window sun;
and wasted hand of age brings rain.

WIND CHANGE

Sunlit trees were shimmering green,

brightness, whiteness through their sheen.

Lovelorn maiden in this setting

waited for her lover's petting:

breeze in branches softly sighing

whispered of his fickle lying.

Heedless, hoping, watching, waiting,

never once her faith abating:
waiting, waiting.

Forest trees in fury swaying,

knife sharp wind their foliage flaying,

all seems grey with dull disaster

riven heart no more beats faster.

Joyless, tearless dry with pain,

twisted, tortured near insane;

heart led mind once tuned to mating

now to vengeful thoughts relating,

hating, hating.

SILLINESS

ALTER EGO

Aloof I stand
not caring that my shade
makes gentle mock
to flaunt my seeming shape.
Distorted clown,
writhing to earth's rough face,
your melting kiss
is planted on the ground
with incorporeal touch
and dark caress.

My head held high
my shadow lowly lies.

FANTASY

I met my love at Pharaoh's court,
a virgin priestess whom I taught
to shun her vows and lay with me.
We both were strangled, publicly.

I met my love in ancient Greece
in time of plenty and of peace.
Though wisdom ruled the Golden Age
I killed my love in jealous rage

I met my love in distant Gaul.
She was my life, she was my all,
until the day farewells were said
when Romans came, and struck me dead.

I've jousted in the tourney's lists,
abducted her through Scottish mists,
I've won, and lost, her heart and hand
in every age and every land.

These fancies swirl around my head
like beads on an eternal thread.
Did they happen? Are there more
such beads of destiny in store?

A PRISONER LAMENTS

Let my wandering thoughts design
a paragon, in form divine
with fetching, tilting, small pert nose,
entrancing, tripping, dainty toes,
an eager swelling, perfect breast,
a haven where my head could rest.
The floating danger of her hair
a silken, golden misting snare.
Her tiny, tempting, wondrous waist
demands the right to be embraced.
See pools of joy within bright eyes,
the sensuous move of rounded thighs,
sweet quiver in those tender lips
and soft touch of her fingertips.

I would, I would all these were mine
to slake my thirst in beauty's wine!

TRUNDLER PARK

`WHAT'S IN A NAME ?

Customers please take a trundler from
storage before entering the Supermarket

(A notice in a New Zealand Supermarket)

`Trundler Park' she said.

Named for some stout
Victorian gent
no doubt.

`Trundler Park', inscribed
above the gate,
honors both man
and date.

`Trundler Park' a place
of skirts to rustle,
parasol and
bustle.
Pot bellied men with chains,
pure gold, of course,
to show their wealth
resource.
Seated in stiff enclave,
paunch parted thighs,
they sit and nod
most wise;
and sagely make their talk
of market bubbles
or the Irish
troubles.

`Trundler Park' Bandstand
of iron lace
where Sunday concerts
took place.

`Trundler Park' where boys
with hoops once played,
and youth would meet
his maid.

`Come on, wake up!' she cried.
`It's time to pay.'
What could I do
or say?
I paid the bill and then,
outside the door,
returned the trundler
to its store.

PODS AND PUSES

Learned men who use their nous
know one Greek foot is called a πουσ
But, fixed to one or lots of bodies
Grecian feet are known as ποδεσ

One would expect that several bods
of octopus were octopods,
and, likewise, although in reverse,
One cephalopod a cephalopus.

So why then beat around the bushes
with octopods as octopuses;
and, equally, if not as odd,
one cephalopus as cephalopod?

LUNACY?

So Moon, your mystery has gone
no longer pure but walked upon.
Will lovers linger in your gleam
when you reflect a laser beam?

Will cows still jump if you're defiled
or must new rhymes be taught the child,
of how your Man is now Mine Host
at space age Moon base staging post?

Men never have retracted yet,
and from now on you must forget
those peaceful days of wax and wane.
Perhaps you did make man insane!

GRAVITY

I went to have a dekko
at a silly little gecko
who was running on the ceiling and the wall.
He looked at me so sadly
as his feet were racing madly;
standing there, upon the floor, I looked so tall.
From his topsy-turvy eye view
he took a very wry view,
and wondered how it was I didn't fall.

ABOUT THE AUTHOR

Huw Evans's promising operatic career was interrupted by his call to duty as a ship's officer during World War II. His ship ferried literally thousands of troops from the USA to the European theatre of war.

Huw Evans has an extensive range of talent and an extraordinary life history. From creating several businesses to becoming President and CEO of Golden Era Mining Company, involving thousands of acres of land, he has managed to find the time to become a published poet and writer.

Most of his life has been spent along the east coast of Australia and the Great Barrier Reef, ranging from Melbourne to Cairns to Townsville. Since 1984 he has resided in Paluma where he is sometimes consulted on the history of the region.

His book title, "The Shadowy Third", was inspired by Robert Browning's poem "By the Fireside":

> "If two lives join, there is oft a scar,
> They are one and one, with a shadowy third;
> One near one is too far."

Printed in the United States
31906LVS00002B/10-30